DICK FRANCIS

Dick Francis, former National Hunt jockey, is the king of thriller writers, with thirty brilliant bestselling novels acclaimed across the world. In 1989 he received the Crime Writers' Association's prestigious award, the Cartier Diamond Dagger, in recognition of his outstanding contribution to the crime genre and in May 1991 Tufts University of Boston awarded him an honorary Doctorate of Humane Letters.

Also by Dick Francis in Pan Books

THE SPORT OF QUEENS
(autobiography)

LESTER: The Official Biography

DEAD CERT · NERVE · FOR KICKS
ODDS AGAINST · FLYING FINISH
BLOOD SPORT · FORFEIT · ENQUIRY
RAT RACE · BONECRACK
SMOKESCREEN · SLAY RIDE · KNOCK DOWN
HIGH STAKES · IN THE FRAME · RISK
TRIAL RUN · WHIP HAND · REFLEX
TWICE SHY · BANKER
THE DANGER · PROOF · BREAK IN
BOLT · HOT MONEY · THE EDGE
STRAIGHT · LONGSHOT · COMEBACK

Dick Francis

SLAY RIDE

AND

KNOCK DOWN

PAN BOOKS
LONDON, SYDNEY AND AUCKLAND

Slay Ride was first published in 1973 by
Michael Joseph Ltd

Knock Down was first published in 1974 by
Michael Joseph Ltd

This two-volume edition published 1993 by Pan Books Ltd
a division of Pan Macmillan Publishers Limited
Cavaye Place London SW10 9PG
and Basingstoke

Associated companies throughout the world

ISBN 0 330 33430 1

1 3 5 7 9 8 6 4 2

A CIP catalogue record for this book is available
from the British Library

Printed and bound in Great Britain by
Cox & Wyman Ltd, Reading, Berkshire

SLAY RIDE

CHAPTER ONE

Cold grey water lapped the flimsy-looking sides of the fibreglass dinghy, and I shivered and thought of the five hundred feet straight down to the sea-bed underneath.

An hour out of Oslo with the outboard motor stilled and my friend Arne Kristiansen taking all afternoon to answer some simple questions.

A grey day, damp, not far from rain. The air sang in my ears with stinging chill. My feet were congealing. The October temperature down the fjord was giving the land a twenty degree lead towards zero, and of the two of us only Arne was dressed for it.

Where I had a showerproof jacket over an ordinary suit and no hat, he had come equipped with the full bit: a red padded cap with ear flaps fastened with a strap under his chin, blue padded trousers tucked into short wide-legged gumboots, and a red padded jacket fastened up the front with silver coloured press studs. A glimpse of black and yellow at the neck spoke of other warm layers underneath.

He had arranged on the telephone to meet me at the statue in the Radhusplassen by the harbour, brushing aside my suggestion that he should come to the Grand Hotel, where I was staying. Even in those wide open spaces he had gone muttering on about being overheard by long range bugging machines (his words) and had finally insisted on taking to the dinghy. Knowing from past experience the quickest way in the end to deal with his perennial mild persecution complex was to go along with it, I had shrugged and followed him along the quay to where the small pale green craft bobbed beside a flight of steps.

I had forgotten that it is always very much colder out on open water. I flexed the stiffening fingers inside my pockets and repeated my last question.

'How would you smuggle sixteen thousand stolen kroner out of the country?'

For the second time, I got no answer. Arne produced answers as prodigally as tax collectors offer rebates.

He blinked slowly, the dropping of the eyelids marking some intermediary stage in the chess-like permutations going on in his head. He was no doubt, as always, considering every foreseeable consequence: if answer A might produce any one of five responses, and answer B lead on to six subsidiary questions, wouldn't it be wiser to answer C, in which case, though . . .

It made conversation with him a trifle slow.

I tried a little prompting. 'You said it was all in coins and used notes of small denominations. How bulky? Enough to fit in a small sized suitcase?'

He blinked.

'Do you think he just walked out with it through the customs?'

He blinked.

'Or do you think he is still somewhere in Norway?'

Arne opened his mouth and said grudgingly, 'No one knows.'

I tried some more. 'When a foreigner stays in one of your hotels, he has to fill in a form and show his passport. These forms are for the police. Have your police checked those forms?'

Pause.

'Yes,' he said.

'And?'

'Robert Sherman did not fill in any form.'

'None at all? What about when he arrived from England?'

'He did not stay in an hotel.'

Patience, I thought. Give me patience.

'Where, then?'

'With friends.'

'What friends?'

He considered. I knew he knew the answer. He knew he was eventually going to tell me. I suppose he couldn't help the way his mind worked, but this, God help us, was supposed to be an investigator.

What was more, I had taught him myself. 'Think before you answer any question,' I'd said. So now he did.

In the three months he had spent in England learning how the Jockey Club ran its investigation department we had grown to know each other well. Some of the time he had stayed in my flat, most of the time we had travelled together to the races, all of the time he had asked and listened and blinked as he thought. That had been three years ago. Two minutes had been enough to resuscitate the old warm feelings of tolerant regard. I liked him, I thought, more because of the mild eccentric kinks than despite.

'He stayed with Gunnar Holth,' he said.

I waited.

After ten seconds he added, 'He is a racehorse trainer.'

'Did Bob Sherman ride for him?'

This dead simple question threw him into a longer than ever session of mental chess, but finally he said, 'Bob Sherman rode the ones of his horses which ran in hurdle races while Bob Sherman was in Norway. *Ja.* He did not ride the horses of Gunnar Holth which ran in flat races while he was in Norway.'

God give me strength.

Arne hadn't actually finished. 'Robert Sherman rode horses for the racecourse.'

I was puzzled. 'How do you mean?'

He consulted his inner man again, who evidently said it was OK to explain.

'The racecourse pays appearance money to some foreign jockeys, to get them to come to Norway. It makes the racing more interesting for the racegoers. So the racecourse paid Robert Sherman to ride.'

'How much did they pay him?'

A rising breeze was stirring the fjord's surface into proper little wavelets. The fjord just below Oslo is not one of those narrow canyon jobs on the Come-To-Scenic-Norway posters, but a wide expanse of sea dotted with rocky islands and fringed by the sprawling suburbs of the city. A coastal steamer surged past half a mile away and tossed us lightly in its wake. The nearest land looked a lot further off.

'Let's go back,' I said abruptly.

'No, no . . .' He had no patience for such weak suggestions. 'They paid him fifteen hundred kroner.'

'I'm cold,' I said.

He looked surprised. 'It is not winter yet.'

I made a noise which was half laugh and half teeth beginning to chatter. 'It isn't summer either.'

He looked vaguely all around. 'Robert Sherman had made six visits to race in Norway,' he said. 'This was his seventh.'

'Look, Arne, tell me about it back at the hotel, huh?'

He attended to me seriously. 'What is the matter?'

'I don't like heights,' I said.

He looked blank. I took one frozen mitt out of its pocket, hung it over the side of the boat, and pointed straight down. Arne's face melted into comprehension and a huge grin took the place of the usual tight careful configuration of his mouth.

'David, I am sorry. The water to me, it is home. Like snow. I am sorry.'

He turned at once to start the outboard, and then paused to say, 'He could simply have driven over the border to Sweden. The customs, they would not search for kroner.'

'In what car?' I asked.

He thought it over. 'Ah yes.' He blinked a bit. 'Perhaps a friend drove him . . .'

'Start the engine,' I said encouragingly.

He shrugged and gave several small nods of the head, but turned to the outboard and pressed the necessary knobs. I had half expected it to prove as lifeless as my fingers, but the spark hit the gas in an orderly fashion and Arne pointed the sharp end back towards hot coffee and radiators.

The dinghy slapped busily through the little waves and the crosswind flicked spray on to my left cheek. I pulled my jacket collar up and made like a tortoise.

Arne's mouth moved as he said something, but against the

combined noises of the engine and the sea and the rustle of gaberdine against my ears, I couldn't hear any words.

'What?' I shouted.

He started to repeat whatever it was, but louder. I caught only snatches like 'ungrateful pig' and 'dirty thief', which I took to be his own private views of Robert Sherman, British steeplechase jockey. Arne had had a bad time since the said Bob Sherman disappeared with the day's take from the turnstiles of Øvrevoll, because Arne Kristiansen, besides being the Norwegian Jockey Club's official investigator, was also in charge of racecourse security.

The theft, he had told me on the outward chug, was an insult, first to himself, and secondly to Norway. Guests in a foreign country should not steal. Norwegians were not criminals, he said, and quoted jail statistics per million of population to prove it. When the British were in Norway, they should keep their hands to themselves.

Commiserating, I refrained from drawing his country's raids on Britain to his attention: they were, after all, a thousand or so years in the past, and the modern Vikings were less likely to burn, rape, pillage and plunder than to take peaceable photographs of Buckingham Palace. I felt moreover a twinge of national shame about Bob Sherman: I had found myself apologizing, of all things, for his behaviour.

Arne was still going on about it: on that subject unfortunately he needed no prompting. Phrases like 'put me in an intolerable position' slid off his tongue as if he had been practising them for weeks – which, on reflection, of course he had. It was three weeks and four days since the theft: and forty-eight hours since the Chairman of the racecourse had telephoned and asked me to send over a British Jockey Club investigator to see what he could do. I had sent (you will have guessed) myself.

I hadn't met the Chairman yet, nor seen the racecourse, nor ever before been to Norway. I was down the fjord with Arne because Arne was the devil I knew.

Three years earlier the hair now closely hidden under the

red padded hood had been a bright blond fading at the temples to grey. The eyes were as fierce a blue as ever, the wrinkles around them as deep, and the bags below a good deal heavier. The spray blew on to skin that was weather-beaten but not sunburned; thick-looking impervious yellowish-white skin lumped and pitted by forty-something winters.

He was still breaking out in bursts of aggrieved half-heard monologue, trudging along well-worn paths of resentment. I gave up trying to listen. It was too cold.

He stopped in mid-sentence and looked with raised eyebrows at some distant point over my left shoulder. I turned. A large speedboat, not very far away, was slicing down the fjord in our general direction with its bow waves leaping out like heavy silver wings.

I turned back to Arne. He shrugged and looked uninterested, and the outboard chose that moment to splutter and cough and choke to silence.

'*Fanden*,' said Arne loudly, which was nothing at all to what I was saying in my head.

'Those people will help us,' he announced, pointing at the approaching speedboat, and without hesitation he stood up, braced his legs, and waved his scarlet clad arms in wide sweeps above his head.

Twisting on my bench seat, I watched the speedboat draw near.

'They will take us on board,' Arne said.

The speedboat did not seem to be slowing down. I could see its shining black hull and its sharp cutting bow, and the silver wings of wave looked as high and full as ever.

If not higher and fuller.

I turned to Arne with the beginnings of apprehension.

'They haven't seen us,' I said.

'They must have.' Arne waved his arms with urgent acceleration, rocking the dinghy precariously.

'Hey!' Arne shouted to the speedboat. And after that he screamed at it, in Norwegian.

The wind blew his words away. The helmsman of the

speedboat didn't hear, didn't see. The sharp hard shining black prow raced straight towards us at forty knots.

'Jump!' yelled Arne; and he jumped. A flash of scarlet streaking into the sea.

I was slow. Thought perhaps that the unimaginable wouldn't happen, that the bow wave would toss the dinghy clear like it would a swan, that the frail craft would bob away as lightly as a bird.

I tumbled over the side into the water about one second before the bow split the fibre-glass open like an eggshell. Something hit me a colossal bang on the shoulder while I was still gasping from the shock of immersion and I went down under the surface into a roaring buffeting darkness.

People who fall off boats die as often from the propellers as from drowning, but I didn't remember that until the twin screws had churned past and left me unsliced. I came stuttering and gulping to the daylight in the jumbled frothing wake and saw the back of the speedboat tearing away unconcernedly down the fjord.

'Arne,' I shouted, which was about as useless as dredging for diamonds in the Thames. A wave slapped me in the open mouth and I swallowed a double salt water, neat.

The sea seemed much rougher at face level than it had done from above. I floundered in high choppy waves with ruffles of white frothing across their tops and blowing into my eyes, and I shouted again for Arne. Shouted with intensifying concern for him and with fear for myself: but the wind tore the words away and battered them to bits.

There was no sign of the dinghy. My last impression was that it had been cut clean into two pieces, which were now, no doubt, turning over and over in a slow sink down to the far away sea-bed.

I shuddered as much from imagination as from cold.

There was no sight anywhere of Arne. No red-padded head, no red waving arms above the waves, no cheerful smile coming to tell me that the sea was home to him and that safety and hot muffins were *this* way, just over here.

Land lay visible all around me in greyish misty heights. None of it was especially near. About two miles away, I guessed, whichever way I looked.

Treading water, I began to pull my clothes off, still looking desperately for Arne, still expecting to see him.

There was nothing but the rough slapping water. I thought about the speedboat's propellers and I thought about Arne's wide legged gumboots which would fill with water in the first few seconds. I thought finally that if I didn't accept that Arne was gone and get started shorewards I was very likely going to drown on that spot.

I kicked off my shoes and struggled with the zip of my raincoat. Ripped open the buttons of my suit jacket underneath and shrugged out of both coats together. I let go of them, then remembered my wallet, and although it seemed crazy I took it out of my jacket pocket and shoved it inside my shirt.

The two coats, waterlogged, floated briefly away and started to go down out of sight. I slid out of my trousers, and let them follow.

Pity, I thought. Nice suit, that had been.

The water was very cold indeed.

I began to swim. Up the fjord. Towards Oslo. Where else?

I was thirty-three and hardy and I knew more statistics than I cared to. I knew for instance that the average human can live less than an hour in water of one degree centigrade.

I tried to swim unhurriedly in long undemanding strokes, postponing the moment of exhaustion. The water in Oslo fjord was not one degree above freezing, but at least five. Probably not much colder than the stuff buffeting the English beach at Brighton at that very moment. In water five degrees above freezing, one could last . . . well, I didn't actually know *that* statistic. Had to take it on trust. Long enough anyway to swim something over two miles.

Bits of distant geography lessons made no sense. 'The

Gulf Stream warms the coast of Norway . . .' Good old Gulf Stream. Where had it gone?

Cold had never seemed a positive force to me before. I supposed I had never really been *cold*, just chilled. This cold dug deep into every muscle and ached in my gut. Feeling had gone from my hands and feet, and my arms and legs felt heavy. The best long-distance swimmers had a nice thick insulating layer of subcutaneous fat: I hadn't. They also covered themselves with water-repelling grease and swam alongside comfort boats which fed them hot cocoa through tubes on demand. The best long-distance swimmers were, of course, usually going twenty miles or so further than I was.

I swam.

The waves seemed frighteningly big: and I couldn't see where I was aiming unless I lifted my head right up and trod water, and that wasted time and energy.

The nearest-looking land seemed to my salt-stinging eyes to be as far away as ever. And surely Oslo fjord should be a Piccadilly Circus of boats? But I couldn't see a single one.

Dammit, I thought. I'm bloody well not going to drown. I'm bloody well *not*.

I swam.

Daylight was slowly fading. Sea, sky, and distant mountains were all a darker grey. It began to rain.

I travelled, it seemed, very slowly. The land I was aiming for never appeared to be nearer. I began to wonder if some current was cancelling out every yard I swam forward: but when I looked back, the land behind was definitely receding.

I swam mechanically, growing tired.

Time passed.

A long way off, straight ahead, pinpricks of light sprang out against the fading afternoon. Every time I looked, there were more. The city was switching on in the dusk.

Too far, I thought. They are too far for me. Land and life all around me, and I couldn't reach them.

An awful depth beneath. And I never did like heights.

A cold lonely death, drowning.

I swam. Nothing else to do.

When another light shone out higher up and to the left, it took at least a minute for the news to reach my sluggish brain. I trod water and wiped the rain and sea out of my eyes as best I could and tried to make out where it came from: and there, a great deal nearer than when I'd last looked, was the solid grey shape of land.

Houses, lights, and people. All there, somewhere, on that rocky hump.

Gratefully I veered fifteen degrees left and pressed on faster, pouring out the carefully hoarded reserves of stamina like a penitent miser. And that was stupid, because no shelving beach lay ahead. The precious land, when I reached it, proved to be a smooth sheer cliff dropping perpendicularly into the water. Not a ledge, not a cranny, to offer even respite from the effort of staying afloat.

The last quarter mile was the worst. I could *touch* the land if I wanted to, and it offered nothing to cling to. There had to be a break somewhere, if I went far enough, but I had practically nothing left. I struggled feebly forward through the slapping waves, wishing in a hazy way that I could surge through warm calm water like Mark Spitz and make a positive touchdown against a nice firm rail, with my feet on the bottom. What I actually did was a sort of belly-flop on to a small boat slipway bordered with large rock slabs.

I lay half in and half out of the water, trying to get back breath I didn't know I'd lost. My chest heaved. I coughed.

It wasn't dark; just the slow northern twilight. I wouldn't have minded if it had been three in the morning: the cold wet concrete beneath my cheek felt as warm and welcoming as goose feathers.

Footsteps crunched rhythmically along the quay at the head of the slipway and then suddenly stopped.

I did a bit towards lifting my head and flapping a numb hand.

'*Hvem er der?*' he said; or something like it.

I gave a sort of croak and he walked carefully, crabwise, down the slipway towards me, a half seen, well-wrapped figure in the rainy gloom.

He repeated his question, which I still didn't understand.

'I'm English,' I said. 'Can you help me?'

Nothing happened for a few seconds. Then he went away.

So what, I thought tiredly. At least from the waist up I was safe in Norway. Didn't seem to have the energy to drag myself uphill till my feet were out, not just for a minute or two. But I would, I thought, given time.

The man came back, and brought a friend. Ungrateful of me to have misjudged him.

The companion peered through the rain and said, 'You are English? Did you say you are English?' His tone seemed to suggest that being English automatically explained such follies as swimming in October in shirt and underpants and lying about on slipways.

'Yes,' I said.

'You fell off a ship?'

'Sort of.'

I felt his hand slide under my armpit.

'Come. Out of the water.'

I scraped myself on to the slipway and with their help more or less crawled to the top. The quay was edged with railings and posts. I sat on the ground with my back against one of the posts and wished for enough strength to stand up.

They consulted in Norwegian. Then the English speaking one said, 'We will take you to my house, to dry and get warm.'

'Thank you,' I said, and by God I meant it.

One of them went away again and came back with a battered old van. They gave me the front passenger seat though I offered to drip in the back, and whisked me about a quarter of a mile to a small wooden house, standing near two or three others. There was no village, no shops, no telephone.

'This is an island,' my rescuer explained. 'One kilometre long, three hundred metres across.' He told me its name, which seemed to me like 'gorse'.

His living-room was small and bright, and warmed by the huge stove which took up at least a sixth of the floorspace. Seen clearly in the light he himself was a short friendly man of middle age with hands that were used for work. He shook his head over me and produced first a blanket and then, after some rummaging, a thick woollen shirt and a pair of trousers.

'You are not a sailor,' he said matter of factly, watching me fumble off my shirt and pants.

'No,' I agreed.

My wallet fell on the floor. I was surprised it was still there; had forgotten it. The Norwegian-only rescuer politely picked it up and handed it to me, smiling broadly. He looked very like his friend.

Between hopeless bouts of shivering I told them what had happened and asked them how I could get back to the city. They talked to each other about it while I dressed, first with a lot of shaking of heads but finally with a few nods.

'When you are warmer we will take you by boat,' said the English-speaker. He looked at the wallet which lay now on a polished pine table. 'We ask only that you will pay for the fuel. If you can.'

Together we took out my sodden money and spread it on the table. I asked them to take whatever they liked, and after debate they chose a fifty kroner note. I urged them to double it. It wouldn't cost so much, they protested, but in the end they put two notes aside and dried the rest for me quickly on the stove so that the edges curled. After more consultation they dug in a cupboard and brought out a bottle of pale gold liquid. One small glass followed, and a moderate tot was poured into it. They handed it to me.

'*Skol!*' they said.

'*Skol!*' I repeated.

They watched interestedly while I drank. Smooth fire

down the throat, heat in the stomach, and soon a warm glow along all the frozen veins.

They smiled.

'Aquavit,' said my host, and stored the precious bottle away ready for the next needy stranger who swam to their doorstep.

They suggested I should sit for a while on the one comfortable-looking chair. Since various muscles were still trembling with weakness this seemed a good idea, so I rested while they busied themselves putting out businesslike sets of oilskins, and by the time they were kitted up my skin had returned from a nasty bluish purplish white to its more usual shade of sallow.

'D'you feel better?' my host observed, smiling.

'I do.'

They nodded, pleased, and held out a spare set of oilskins for me to put on. They took me in a big smelly fishing boat back up the twinkle-edged fjord to the city, and it rained all the way. I spent the journey calculating that I had been in the water for about two hours, which didn't prove anything in particular about the current in the fjord or the inefficiency of my swimming or the distance I had travelled, but did prove pretty conclusively that the temperature was more than one degree above freezing.

CHAPTER TWO

They waited while I changed at the Grand, so that they could take back the lent clothes. We parted with warm handshakes and great camaraderie, and it was only after they had gone that I realized that I didn't know their names.

I would have liked nothing better than to go to bed and sleep for half a century, but the thought of Arne's wife waiting for him to come home put a damper on that. So I spent the next couple of hours with various Norwegian authorities, reporting what had happened.

When the police finished taking notes and said they would send someone to tell Mrs Kristiansen, I suggested that I should go too. They agreed. We went in an official car and rang the bell of Flat C on the first floor of a large timber house in a prosperous road not far from the city centre.

The girl who opened the door looked inquiringly out at us from clear grey eyes in a firm, friendly, thirtyish face. Behind her the flat looked warm and colourful, and the air was thick with Beethoven.

'Is Mrs Kristiansen in?' I asked.

'Yes,' she said. 'I am Mrs Kristiansen.'

Not in the least what I would have expected. Oddballs like Arne shouldn't turn out to have slender young wives with thick pale blonde hair falling in loose curls on their shoulders. She looked away from my own less striking face to the policeman behind me, and the eyes widened.

'I'm David Cleveland,' I said. 'I was with Arne this afternoon ...'

'Oh were you?' she exclaimed. 'Oh, do come in ... I'm *so* glad ...'

She held the door wider and turned to call over her shoulder.

'Arne,' she said. 'Arne, see who's here.'

He stepped into the hall. Very much alive.

We stared at each other in consternation. My own face must have mirrored the surprise and shock I saw on his, and then he was striding forward with his hand outheld and his face creasing into the most gigantic smile of all time.

'David! I don't believe it. I have reported you drowned.' He clasped both my hands in both of his and shook them warmly. 'Come in, come in, my dear fellow, and tell me how you were saved. I have been so grieved ... I was telling Kari ...'

His wife nodded, as delighted as he was.

The policeman behind me said, 'It would seem Mr

Kristiansen wasn't drowned after all, then,' which seemed in our high state of relief to be extremely funny. We all laughed. Even the policeman smiled.

'I was picked up by some fisherman near Nesodden,' Arne told him. 'I reported the accident to the police there. They said they would send a boat to look for Mr Cleveland, but they weren't very hopeful of finding him. I'd better call them . . .'

'Thank you,' said the policeman. 'That would be helpful,' and he smiled once more at us all and went away.

Kari Kristiansen shut the front door and said 'Do come in, we must celebrate,' and led me through into the living-room. Beethoven was thundering away in there, and Kari switched him off. 'Arne always plays loud music when he's upset,' she said.

Out in the hall Arne busied himself with the telephone, and among his explanatory flow of Norwegian I caught my own name spoken with astonishment and relief.

'It is wonderful,' he said, coming into the room and rubbing his hands together. 'Wonderful.' He gestured to me to sit on a deep comfortable sofa near a cheerful wood-burning fire. 'The Nesodden police say they sent a boat out to search for you, but it was too dark and raining and they could see nothing.'

'I'm sorry they had the trouble,' I said.

'My dear fellow . . .' He spread his fingers. 'It was nothing. And now, a drink, eh? To celebrate.'

He filled glasses of red wine from a bottle standing already open on a side-table.

'Arne has been so depressed all evening,' Kari said. 'It is truly a miracle that you were both saved.'

We exchanged stories. Arne had torn off the red clothes and kicked his boots off instantly (I suppose I should have known that a man at home on the sea would wear *loose* gumboots), but although he had called my name and searched around for some minutes he had caught no sign of me.

'When I last saw you,' he said apologetically, 'You were

still in the dinghy, and I thought the speedboat must have hit you directly, so when I could not see you I thought that you must be already dead.'

He had started swimming, he said; and knowing a lot more than I did about tides and winds, had taken almost the opposite direction. He had been picked up near the coast by a small home-going fishing boat which was too low on fuel to go out into the fjord to look for me. It had however landed him in the small town where he reported my loss, and from there he had returned by hired boat to the city.

My story was so much the same that it could be told in two sentences: I swam to an island. Two men brought me back in a boat.

Arne searched among an untidy pile of papers and triumphantly produced a map. Spreading it out, he pointed to the widest part of the fjord and showed both Kari and me where we had sunk.

'The worst possible place,' Kari exclaimed. 'Why did you go so far?'

'You know me,' said Arne, folding the map up again. 'I like to be moving.'

She looked at him indulgently. 'You don't like to be followed, you mean.'

Arne looked a little startled, but that complex of his stood out like Gulliver in Lilliput.

I said, 'The police asked me if I saw the name of that speedboat.'

'Did you?' asked Arne.

I shook my head. 'No. Did you?'

He blinked through one of those maddening pauses into which the simplest question seemed to throw him, but in the end all he said was 'No, I didn't.'

'I don't think there was any name to see,' I said.

They both turned their faces to me in surprise.

'There must have been,' Kari said.

'Well . . . I've no impression of one . . . no name, no registration number, no port of origin. Perhaps you don't have things like that in Norway.'

'Yes we do,' Kari said, puzzled. 'Of course we do.'

Arne considered lengthily, then said, 'It was going too fast . . . and straight towards us. It must have had a name. We simply didn't see it.' He spoke with finality, as if the subject could hold no more interest. I nodded briefly and let it go, but I was certain that on that thundering black hull there had been nothing to see but black paint. How were they off for smugglers, I wondered, in this neck of the North Sea?

'It's a pity,' I said. 'Because you might have got compensation for your dinghy.'

'It was insured,' he said. 'Do not worry.'

Kari said, 'It's disgraceful he did not stop. He must have felt the bump . . . even a big heavy speedboat, like Arne says it was, could not crush a dinghy without feeling it.'

Hit and run, I thought flippantly. Happens on the roads, why not on the water?

'Arne was afraid you could not swim.'

'Up and down a pool or two,' I said. 'Never tried such long-distance stuff before.'

'You were lucky,' she said seriously.

'Arne too.' I looked at him thoughtfully, for I was younger by a good ten years and I had been near to exhaustion.

'Oh no. Arne's a great swimmer. A great sportsman, all round. Very fit and tough.' She smiled ironically, but the wifely pride was there. 'He used to win across-country ski races.'

There had been several sets of skis stacked casually in an alcove in the hall, along with squash rackets, fishing rods, mountain walking boots and half a dozen anoraks like the lost red one. For a man who liked to keep moving, he had all the gear.

'Have you eaten?' Kari asked suddenly. 'Since your swim, I mean? Did you think of eating?'

I shook my head.

'I suppose I was worried about Arne.'

She stood up, smiling. 'Arne had no appetite for his

supper.' She looked at the clock. Ten minutes before ten. 'I will bring something for you both,' she said.

Arne fondly watched her backview disappearing towards the kitchen.

'What do you think of her, eh? Isn't she beautiful?'

Normally I disliked men who invited admiration for their wives as if they were properties like cars, but I would have forgiven Arne a great deal that evening.

'Yes,' I said, more truthfully than on many similar occasions; and Arne positively smirked.

'More wine,' he said, getting up restlessly and filling both our glasses.

'Your house, too, is beautiful,' I said.

He looked over his shoulder in surprise. 'That is Kari as well. She . . . it is her job. Making rooms for people. Offices, hotels. Things like that.'

Their own sitting-room was a place of natural wood and white paint, with big parchment-shaded table lamps shedding a golden glow on string-coloured upholstery and bright scattered cushions. A mixture of the careful and haphazard, overlaid with the comfortable debris of a full life. Ultra-tidy rooms always oppressed me: the Kristiansens' was just right.

Arne brought back my filled glass and settled himself opposite, near the fire. His hair, no longer hidden, was now more grey than blond; longer than before, and definitely more distinguished.

'Tomorrow,' I said, 'I'd like to see the racecourse Chairman, if I could.'

He looked startled, as if he had forgotten the real purpose of my visit.

'Yes.' He blinked a bit. 'It is Saturday tomorrow. It is the Grand National meeting on Sunday. He will be at the racecourse on Sunday.'

Don't let a thieving jockey spoil the man's day off, Arne was meaning, so I shrugged and said Sunday would do.

'I'll maybe call on Gunnar Holth tomorrow, then.'

For some reason that didn't fill Arne with joy either, but I discovered, after a long pause on his part, that this was because he, Arne, wished to go fishing all day and was afraid I would want him with me, instead.

'Does Gunnar Holth speak English?' I asked.

'Oh yes.'

'I'll go on my own, then.'

He gave me the big smile and jumped up to help Kari, who was returning with a laden tray. She had brought coffee and open sandwiches of prawns and cheese and pineapple which we ate to the last crumb.

'You must come another evening,' Kari said. 'I will make you a proper dinner.'

Arne agreed with her warmly and opened some more wine.

'A great little cook,' he said proprietorially.

The great little cook shook back her heavy blonde hair and stretched her elegant neck. She had a jaw-line in the same class and three small brown moles like dusty freckles high on one cheekbone.

'Come any time,' she said.

I got back to the Grand by taxi at one in the morning, slept badly, and woke at seven feeling like Henry Cooper's punchbag.

Consultation with the bathroom looking-glass revealed a plate-sized bruise of speckled crimson over my left shoulder-blade, souvenir of colliding boats. In addition every muscle I possessed was groaning with the morning-after misery of too much strain. David Cleveland, it seemed, was no Matthew Webb.

Bath, clothes and breakfast didn't materially improve things, nor on the whole did a telephone call to Gunnar Holth.

'Come if you like,' he said. 'But I can tell you nothing. You will waste your time.'

As all investigators waste a lot of time listening to people with nothing to tell, I naturally went. He had a stable yard adjoining the racecourse and a belligerent manner.

'Questions, questions,' he said. 'There is nothing to tell.'

I paid off my taxi driver.

'You shouldn't have sent him away,' Gunnar Holth said. 'You will be going soon.'

I smiled. 'I can go back on a tram.'

He gave me a grudging stare. 'You don't look like a Jockey Club official.'

'I would appreciate it very much,' I said, 'if you would show me your horses. Arne Kristiansen says you have a good lot . . . that they've been winning big prizes this year.'

He loosened, of course. He gestured towards a large barn on the other side of an expanse of mud. We made our way there, him in his boots showing me I shouldn't have come in polished shoes. He was short, wiry, middle-aged and a typical stableman, more at home with his horses, I guessed, than with their owners; and he spoke English with an Irish accent.

The barn contained two rows of boxes fading into a wide central passage. Horses' heads showed over most of the half doors and three or four lads were carrying buckets of water and haynets.

'They've just come in from exercise,' Holth said. 'We train on the sand track on the racecourse.' He turned left and opened the door of the first box. 'This fellow runs tomorrow in the Grand National. Would you look at his shoulders now, isn't that a grand sort of horse?'

'Bob Sherman won a race on him the day he disappeared,' I said.

He gave me a sharp wordless glance and went in to pat a strong-looking character with more bone than breeding. He felt the legs, looked satisfied, and came back to join me.

'How do you know?' he said.

No harm in telling him. 'Arne Kristiansen gave me a list of Bob Sherman's last rides in Norway. He said that this horse of yours was likely to win the National, and if Sherman had had any sense he would have come back for that race and then stolen the National day takings, which would have been a better haul all round.'

Holth allowed himself a glint of amusement. 'That's true.'

We continued round the barn, admiring every inmate. There were about twenty altogether, three-quarters of them running on the Flat, and although they seemed reasonable animals, none of them looked likely to take Epsom by storm. From their coats, though, and general air of well-being, Holth knew his trade.

One end of the barn was sectioned off to form living quarters for the lads, and Holth took me through to see them. Dormitory, washroom, and kitchen.

'Bob stayed here, most times,' he said.

I glanced slowly round the big main room with its half dozen two-tiered bunk beds, its bare board floor, its wooden table, wooden chairs. A big brown-tiled stove and double-glazed windows with curtains like blankets promised comfort against future snow, and a couple of mild girlie calendars brightened the walls, but it was a far cry from the Grand.

'Always?' I asked.

Holth shrugged. 'He said it was good enough here, and he saved the expense of a hotel. Nothing wrong there now, is there?'

'Nothing at all,' I agreed.

He paused. 'Sometimes he stayed with an owner.'

'Which owner?'

'Oh . . . the man who owns Whitefire. Per Bjørn Sandvik.'

'How many times?'

Holth said with irritation, 'What does it matter? Twice, I suppose. Yes, twice. Not the last time. The two times before that.'

'How often did he come over altogether?'

'Six perhaps. Or seven . . . or eight.'

'All this summer?'

'He didn't come last year, if that's what you mean.'

'But he liked it?'

'Of course he liked it. All British jockeys who are invited, they like it. Good pay, you see.'

'How good?'

'Well,' he said, 'They get their fare over here, and a bit towards expenses. And the fees for riding. And the appearance money.'

'The racecourse pays the appearance money?'

'Not exactly. Well . . . the racecourse pays the money to the jockey but collects it from the owners who the jockey rode for.'

'So an owner, in the end, pays everything, the riding fees, the winning percentage, a share of the fares, and a share of the appearance money?'

'That is right.'

'What happens if after all that the jockey rides a stinking race?'

Holth answered with deadly seriousness. 'The owner does not ask the jockey to come again.'

We stepped out of the barn back into the mud. It hadn't actually rained that day, but the threat still hung in the cold misty air.

'Come into my house,' suggested Holth. 'Have some coffee before you catch the tram.'

'Great,' I said.

His house was a small wooden bungalow with lace curtains and geraniums in pots on every window sill. The stove in the living-room was already lit, with an orange metal coffee pot heating on top. Gunnar dug into a cupboard for two earthenware mugs and some sugar in a packet.

'Would the owners have asked Bob Sherman to come again?' I said.

He poured the coffee, stirring with a white plastic spoon.

'Per Bjørn Sandvik would. And Sven Wangen; that's the owner of that dappled mare on the far side.' He pondered. 'Rolf Torp, now. Bob lost a race the day he went. Rolf Torp thought he should have walked it.'

'And should he?'

Holth shrugged. 'Horses aren't machines,' he said. 'Mind you, I don't train Rolf Torp's horses, so I don't really know, do I?'

'Who trains them?'

'Paul Sundby.'

'Will Rolf Torp be at the races tomorrow?'

'Naturally,' Holth said. 'He has the favourite in the National.'

'And you,' I said. 'Would you have asked him to ride for you again?'

'Certainly,' he said without hesitation. 'Bob is a good jockey. He listens to what you say about a horse. He rides with his head. He would not have been asked so many times if he had not been good.'

The door from the yard opened without warning and one of the lads poked his head in: he was about twenty-five, cheerful, and wore a woollen cap with a pompom.

'Gunny,' he said, 'will ye be takin' a look at that bleedin' mare now? She's a right cow, that one.'

The trainer said he would look in a minute, and the head withdrew.

'He's Irish,' I said surprised.

'Sure. I've three Irish lads and one from Yorkshire. And three from here. There's a lot of British lads in Norwegian racing.'

'Why is that?'

'They get a chance of riding in races here, see? More than they do at home.'

We drank the coffee which was well boiled and all the stronger for it.

I said, 'What did Bob do for transport? Did he ever hire a car?'

'No. I don't think so. When he stayed here he used to go with me over to the course.'

'Did he ever borrow your car? Or anyone's?'

'He didn't borrow mine. I don't think he ever drove, when he came.'

'Did you take him anywhere except to the races, the day he disappeared?'

'No.'

I knew from a file of statements which had been awaiting my arrival at the hotel that Bob Sherman had been expected to leave the racecourse by taxi to catch the late flight to Heathrow. He had not caught it. The taxi driver who had been engaged for the trip had simply shrugged when his passenger didn't show, and had taken some ordinary race-goers back to the city instead.

That left public transport, all the taxi drivers who didn't know Bob by sight, and other people's cars. Plus, I supposed, his own two feet. It would have been all too easy to leave the racecourse without being seen by anyone who knew him, particularly if, as the collected notes implied, the last race had been run after dark.

I put down my empty coffee mug and Gunnar Holth abruptly said, 'Could you be doing something about Bob's wife, now?'

'His wife? I might see her when I go back, if I find out anything useful.'

'No,' he shook his head. 'She is here.'

'Here?'

He nodded. 'In Oslo. And she won't go home.'

'Arne didn't mention it.'

Holth laughed. 'She follows him round like a dog. She asks questions, like you. Who saw Bob go, who did he go with, why does no one find him? She comes to every race meeting and asks and asks. Everyone is very tired of it.'

'Do you know where she's staying?'

He nodded vigorously and picked up a piece of paper lying near on a shelf.

'The Norsland Hotel. Second class, away from the centre. This is her telephone number. She gave it to me in case I could think of anything to help.' He shrugged. 'Everyone is sorry for her. But I wish she would go away.'

'Will you telephone her?' I said. 'Say I would like to ask her some questions about Bob. Suggest this afternoon.'

'I've forgotten your name,' he said without apology.

I smiled and gave him one of the firm's official cards. He looked at it and me in disbelief, but got the Norsland Hotel on the line. Mrs Emma Sherman was fetched.

Holth said into the receiver, 'A Mr David Cleveland . . . come from England to try to find your husband.' He read from the card, 'Chief Investigator, Investigation Office, Jockey Club, Portman Square, London. He wants to see you this afternoon.'

He listened to the reaction, then looked at me and said 'Where?'

'At her hotel. Three o'clock.'

He relayed the news.

'She'll be waiting for you,' he said, putting the receiver down.

'Good.'

'Tell her to go home,' he said.

CHAPTER THREE

She was waiting in the small lobby of the Norsland, sitting on the edge of a chair and anxiously scanning the face of every passing male. I watched her for a while through the glass doors to the street, before going in. She looked small and pale and very very jumpy. Twice she half stood up, and twice, as the man she had focused on walked past without a sign, subsided more slowly back to her seat.

I pushed through the doors into air barely warmer than the street, which in a totally centrally heated city spoke poorly of the management. Emma Sherman looked at me briefly and switched her gaze back to the door. I was not what she expected: the next man through, sixtyish and military-looking, had her again halfway to her feet.

He passed her without a glance on his way to collect his room key at the desk. She sat slowly down, looking increasingly nervous.

I walked over to her.

'Mrs Sherman?'

'Oh.' She stood up slowly. 'Is there a message from Mr Cleveland?'

'I am,' I said, 'David Cleveland.'

'But,' she said, and stopped. The surprise lingered on her face among the strain and tiredness, but she seemed past feeling anything very clearly. At close quarters the nervousness resolved itself into a state not far from total breakdown.

Her skin looked almost transparent from fatigue, dark shadows round her eyes emphasizing the pebbly dullness of the eyes themselves. She was about twenty-two and should have been pretty: she had the bones and the hair for it, but they hadn't a chance. She was also, it seemed to me, pregnant.

'Where can we talk?' I asked.

She looked vaguely round the lobby which contained three chairs, no privacy, and a rubber plant.

'Your room?' I suggested.

'Oh no,' she said at once, and then more slowly, in explanation, 'It is small . . . not comfortable . . . nowhere to sit.'

'Come along, then,' I said. 'We'll find a coffee shop.'

She came with me out into the street and we walked in the general direction of the Grand.

'Will you find him?' she said. 'Please find him.'

'I'll do my best.'

'He never stole that money,' she said. 'He didn't.'

I glanced at her. She was trembling perceptibly and looking paler than ever. I stopped walking and put my hand under her elbow. She looked at me with glazing eyes, tried to say something else, and fell forward against me in a thorough-going swoon.

Even seven stone nothing of fainting girl is hard to support without letting her lie on a cold city pavement. Two passing strangers proved to have friendly faces but no English, and the third, who had the tongue, muttered something about the disgrace of being drunk at four in the afternoon and scurried away. I held her up against me with my arms under hers and asked the next woman along to call a taxi.

She too looked disapproving and backed away, but a boy of about sixteen gave her a withering glance and came to the rescue.

'Is she ill?' he asked. His English was punctilious stuff, learned in school.

'She is. Can you get a taxi?'

'*Ja*. I will return. You will . . .' he thought, then found the word . . . 'Wait?'

'I will wait,' I agreed.

He nodded seriously and darted away round the nearest corner, a slim figure in the ubiquitous uniform of the young, blue jeans and a padded jacket. He came back, as good as his word, with a taxi, and helped me get the girl into it.

'Thank you very much,' I said.

He beamed. 'I learn English,' he said.

'You speak it very well.'

He waved as the taxi drew away: a highly satisfactory encounter to both parties.

She began to wake up during the short journey, which seemed to reassure the taxi driver. He spoke no English except one word which he repeated at least ten times with emphasis, and which was 'doctor'.

'*Ja*,' I agreed. '*Ja*. At the Grand Hotel.'

He shrugged, but drove us there. He also helped me support her through the front doors and accepted his fare after she was safely sitting down.

'Doctor,' he said as he left, and I said, '*Ja*.'

'No,' said Bob Sherman's wife, in little more than a whisper. 'What . . . happened?'

'You fainted,' I said briefly. 'And doctor or no doctor, you need to lie down. So up you come . . .' I more or less lifted her to her feet, walked her to the lift, and took her up the one floor to my room. She flopped full length on the bed without question and lay there with her eyes closed.

'Do you mind if I feel your pulse?' I asked.

She gave no answer either way, so I put my fingers on

her wrist and found the slow heartbeat. Her arm was slippery with sweat though noticeably cold, and all in all she looked disturbingly frail.

'Are you hungry?' I said.

She rolled her head on the pillow in a slow negative, but I guessed that what was really wrong with her, besides strain, was simple starvation. She had been too worried to take care of herself, and besides, eating came expensive in Norway.

A consultation on the telephone with the hotel restaurant produced a promise of hot meat soup and some bread and cheese.

'And brandy,' I said.

'No brandy, sir, on Saturday. Or on Sunday. It is the rule.'

I had been warned, but had forgotten. Extraordinary to find a country with madder licensing laws than Britain's. There was a small refrigerator in my room, however, which stocked, among the orangeade and mineral waters, a quarter bottle of champagne. It had always seemed to me that bottling in quarters simply spoiled good fizz, but there's an occasion for everything. Emma said she couldn't, she shouldn't; but she did, and within five minutes was looking like a long-picked flower caught just in time.

'I'm sorry,' she said, leaning on one elbow on my bed and sipping the golden bubbles from my tooth mug.

'You're welcome.'

'You must think me a fool.'

'No.'

'It's just . . . No one seems to care any more. Where he's gone. They just say they can't find him. They aren't even looking.'

'They've looked,' I began, but she wasn't ready to listen.

'Then Gunnar Holth said . . . the Jockey Club had sent their chief investigator . . . so I've been hoping so hard all day that at last someone would find him, and then . . . and then . . . you . . .'

'I'm not the father-figure you were hoping for,' I said.

She shook her head. 'I didn't think you'd be so young.'

'Which do you want most,' I asked. 'A father-figure, or someone to find Bob?' But it was too soon to expect her to see that the two things didn't necessarily go together. She needed the comfort as much as the search.

'He didn't steal that money,' she said.

'How do you know?'

'He just wouldn't.' She spoke with conviction, but I wondered if the person she most wanted to convince was herself.

A waiter knocked on the door, bringing a tray, and Emma felt well enough to sit at the table and eat. She started slowly, still in a weak state, but by the end it was clear she was fiercely hungry.

As she finished the last of the bread I said, 'In about three hours we'll have dinner.'

'Oh no.'

'Oh yes. Why not? Then you'll have plenty of time to tell me about Bob. Hours and hours. No need to hurry.'

She looked at me with the first signs of connected thought and almost immediately glanced round the room. The awareness that she was in my bedroom flashed out like neon in the North Pole. I smiled. 'Would you prefer the local nick? One each side of a table in an interview room?'

'Oh! I . . . suppose not.' She shuddered slightly. 'I've had quite a lot of that, you see. In a way. Everyone's been quite kind, really, but they think Bob stole that money and they treat me as if my husband was a crook. It's . . . it's pretty dreadful.'

'I understand that,' I said.

'Do you?'

The meal had done nothing for her pallor. The eyes still looked as hollowed and black-smudged, and the strain still vibrated in her manner. It was going to take more than champagne and soup to undo the knots.

'Why don't you sleep for a while?' I suggested. 'You look very tired. You'll be quite all right here, and I've some reports which I ought to write. I'd be glad to get them out of the way.'

'I can't sleep,' she said automatically, but when I determinedly took papers out of my briefcase, spread them on the table and switched on a bright lamp to see them by, she stood up and hovered a bit and finally lay down again on the bed. After five minutes I walked over to look and she was soundly asleep with sunken cheeks and pale blue veins in her eyelids.

She wore a camel coloured coat, which she had relaxed as far as unbuttoning, and a brown and white checked dress underneath. With the coat falling open, the bulge in her stomach showed unmistakably. Five months, I thought, give or take a week or two.

I pushed the papers together again and returned them to the briefcase. They were the various statements and accounts relating to her husband's disappearance, and I had no report to write on them. I sat instead in one of the Grand's comfortable armchairs and thought about why men vanished.

In the main they either ran *to* something or *from* something: occasionally a combination of both. To a woman; from a woman. To the sunshine; from the police. To political preference; from political oppression. To anonymity; from blackmail.

Sometimes they took someone else's money with them to finance the future. Bob Sherman's sixteen thousand kroner didn't seem, at first sight, to be worth what he'd exchanged for it. He earned five times as much every year.

So what had he gone *to*?

Or what had he gone *from*?

And how was I to find him by Monday afternoon?

She slept soundly for more than two hours with periods of peaceful dreaming, but after that went into a session which was distressing her. She moved restlessly and sweat appeared on her forehead, so I touched her hand and called her out of it.

'Emma. Wake up. Wake up, now, Emma.'

She opened her eyes fast and wide with the nightmare pictures still in them. Her body began to tremble.

'Oh,' she said. 'Oh God ...'

'It's all right. You were dreaming. It was only a dream.'

Her mind finished the transition to consciousness, but she was neither reassured nor comforted.

'I dreamed he was in jail ... there were bars ... and he was trying to get out ... frantically ... and I asked him why he wanted to get out, and he said they were going to execute him in the morning ... and then I was talking to someone in charge and I said what had he done, why were they going to execute him, and this man said ... he'd stolen the racecourse ... and the law said that if people stole racecourses they had to be executed ...'

She rubbed a hand over her face.

'It's so silly,' she said. 'But it seemed so real.'

'Horrid,' I said.

She said with desolation, 'But where is he? Why doesn't he write to me? How can he be so cruel?'

'Perhaps there's a letter waiting at home.'

'No. I telephone ... every day.'

I said, 'Are you ... well ... are you happy together?'

'Yes,' she said firmly, but after five silent seconds the truer version came limping out. 'Sometimes we have rows. We had one the day he came here. All morning. And it was over such a little thing ... just that he'd spent a night away when he didn't have to ... I'd not been feeling well and I told him he was selfish and thoughtless ... and he lost his temper and said I was too damn demanding ... and I said I wouldn't go with him to Kempton then, and he went silent and sulky because he was going to ride the favourite in the big race and he always likes to have me there after something like that, it helps him unwind.' She stared into a past moment she would have given the world to change. 'So he went on his own. And from there to Heathrow for the six-thirty to Oslo, same as usual. Only usually I went with him, to see him off and take the car home.'

'And meet him again Sunday night?'

'Yes. On Sunday night when he didn't come back at the right time I was worried sick that he'd had a fall in Norway and hurt himself and I telephoned to Gunnar Holth . . . but he said Bob hadn't fallen, he'd ridden a winner and got round in the other two races, and as far as he knew he'd caught the plane as planned. So I rang the airport again . . . I'd rung them before, and they said the plane had landed on time . . . and I begged them to check and they said there was no Sherman on the passenger list . . .' She stopped and I waited, and she went on in a fresh onslaught of misery. 'Surely he knew I didn't really mean it? I love him . . . Surely he wouldn't just leave me, without saying a word?'

It appeared, however, that he had.

'How long have you been married?'

'Nearly two years.'

'Children?'

She glanced down at the brown and white checked mound and gestured towards it with a flutter of slender fingers. 'This is our first.'

'Finances?'

'Oh . . . all right, really.'

'How really?'

'He had a good season last year. We saved a bit then. Of course he does like good suits and a nice car . . . All jockeys do, don't they?'

I nodded. I knew also more about her husband's earnings than she seemed to, as I had access to the office which collected and distributed jockeys' fees; but it wasn't so much the reasonable income that was significant as the extent to which they lived within it.

'He does get keen on schemes for making money quickly, but we've never lost much. I usually talk him out of it. I'm not a gambler at all, you see.'

I let a pause go by. Then, 'Politics?'

'How do you mean?'

'Is he interested in communism?'

She stared. 'Good heavens, no.'

'Militant in any way?'

She almost laughed. 'Bob doesn't give a damn for politics or politicians. He says they're all the same, hot air and hypocrisy. Why do you ask such an extraordinary question?'

I shrugged. 'Norway has a common frontier with Russia.'

Her surprise was genuine on two counts: she didn't know her geography and she did know her husband. He was not the type to exchange good suits and a nice car and an exciting job for a dim existence in a totalitarian state.

'Did he mention any friends he had made here?'

'I've seen nearly everyone I can remember him talking about. I've asked them over and over ... Gunnar Holth, and his lads, and Mr Kristiansen, and the owners. The only one I haven't met is one of the owner's sons, a boy called Mikkel. Bob mentioned him once or twice ... he's away at school now, or something.'

'Was Bob in any trouble before this?'

She looked bewildered. 'What sort?'

'Bookmakers?'

She turned her head away and I gave her time to decide on her answer. Jockeys were not allowed to bet, and I worked for the Jockey Club.

'No,' she said indistinctly.

'You might as well tell me,' I said. 'I can find out. But you would be quicker.'

She looked back at me, perturbed. 'He only bets on himself, usually,' she said defensively. 'It's legal in a lot of countries.'

'I'm only interested in his betting if it's got anything to do with his disappearance. Was anyone threatening him for payment?'

'Oh.' She sounded forlorn, as if the one thing she did not want to be given was a good reason for Bob to steal a comparatively small sum and ruin his life for it.

'He never said ... I'm sure he would have told ...' She gulped. 'The police asked me if he was being blackmailed. I said no, of course not . . . but if it was to keep me from knowing something . . . how can I be sure? Oh, I do wish, I do wish he'd write to me . . .'

Tears came in a rush and spilled over. She didn't apologize, didn't brush them away, and in a few seconds they had stopped. She had wept a good deal, I guessed, during the past three weeks.

'You've done all you can here,' I said. 'Better come back with me on Monday afternoon.'

She was surprised and disappointed. 'You're going back so soon? But you won't have found him.'

'Probably not. But I've a meeting in London on Tuesday that I can't miss. If it looks like being useful I'll come back here afterwards, but for you, it's time now to go home.'

She didn't answer at once, but finally, in a tired, quiet, defeated voice, said 'All right.'

CHAPTER FOUR

Arne was having difficulty with his complex, constantly looking over his shoulder to the extent of making forward locomotion hazardous. Why he should find any threat in the cheerful frost-bitten looking crowd which had turned up at Øvrevoll for the Norsk Grand National was something between him and his psychiatrist, but as usual his friends were suffering from his affliction.

He had refused, for instance, to drink a glass of wine in a comfortable available room with a king-sized log fire. Instead we were marching back and forth outside, him, me, and Per Bjørn Sandvik, wearing out shoe leather and turning blue at the ears, for fear of bugging machines. I couldn't see how overhearing our present conversation could possibly benefit anyone, but then I wasn't Arne. And at least this time, I thought philosophically, we would not be mown down by a speedboat.

As before, he was ready for the outdoor life: a blue padded hood joined all in one to his anorak. Per Bjørn Sandvik had a trilby. I had my head. Maybe one day I would learn.

Sandvik, one of the Stewards, was telling me again at first hand what I'd already read in the statements: how Bob Sherman had had access to the money.

'It's collected into the officials' room, you see, where it is checked and recorded. And the officials' room is in the same building as the jockeys' changing-room. Right? And that Sunday, Bob Sherman went to the officials' room to ask some question or other, and the money was stacked there, just inside the door. Arne saw him there himself. He must have planned at once to take it.'

'What was the money contained in?' I asked.

'Canvas bags. Heavy double canvas.'

'What colour?'

He raised his eyebrows. 'Brown.'

'Just dumped on the floor?'

He grinned. 'There is less crime in Norway.'

'So I've heard,' I said. 'How many bags?'

'Five.'

'Heavy?'

He shrugged. 'Like money.'

'How were they fastened?'

'With leather straps and padlocks.'

Arne cannoned into a blonde who definitely had the right of way. She said something which I judged from his expression to be unladylike, but it still didn't persuade him to look where he was going. Some enemy lay behind, listening: he was sure of it.

Sandvik gave him an indulgent smile. He was a tall pleasant unhurried man of about fifty, upon whom authority sat as lightly as fluff. Arne had told me he was 'someone at the top in oil', but he had none of the usual aura of big business: almost the reverse, as if he derived pleasure from leaving an impression of no power, no aggression. If so, he would be a board-room opponent as wicked as a mantrap among the daisies. I looked at him speculatively. He met my eyes. Nothing in his that shouldn't be.

'What was it intended to do with the bags, if Sherman hadn't nicked them?' I asked.

'Lock them in the safe in the officials' room until Monday morning, when they would go to the bank.'

'Guarded,' Arne said, eyes front for once, 'By a night watchman.'

But by the time the night watchman had clocked in, the booty had vanished.

'How did the officials all happen to desert the room at once, leaving the money so handy?' I asked.

Sandvik spread his thickly-gloved hands. 'We have discussed this endlessly. It was accidental. The room can only have been empty for five minutes or less. There was no special reason for them all being out at one time. It just happened.'

He had a high-register voice with beautifully distinct enunciation, but his almost-perfect English sounded quite different from the home-grown variety. I worked it out after a while: it was his 'l's. The British pronounced 'l' with their tongue lolling back in the throat, the Norwegians said theirs with the tongue tight up behind the teeth. Retaining the Norwegian 'l' gave Sandvik's accent a light, dry, clear-vowelled quality which made everything he said sound logical and lucid.

'No one realized, that evening, that the money had been stolen. Each of the officials took it for granted that another had put the bags in the safe as they were no longer to be seen. It was the next day, when the safe was opened for the money to be banked, that it was found to be missing. And then, of course, we heard from Gunnar Holth that Sherman had disappeared as well.'

I thought. 'Didn't Gunnar Holth tell me that Bob Sherman stayed with you once or twice?'

'Yes, that's right.' Sandvik briefly pursed his well-shaped

mouth. 'Twice. But not the time he stole the money, I'm glad to say.'

'You liked him, though?'

'Oh yes, well enough, I suppose. I asked him out of politeness. He had ridden several winners for me, and I know what Gunnar's bunk room is like ...' He grinned slightly. 'Anyway, he came. But we had little of common interest except horses, and I think he really preferred Gunnar's after all.'

'Would you have expected him to steal?'

'It never crossed my mind. I mean, it doesn't does it? But I didn't know him well.'

Arne could not bear the close quarters of the crowd on the stands, so we watched the first race, a hurdle, from rising ground just past the winning post. The racecourse, forming the floor of a small valley, was overlooked on all sides by hillsides of spruce and birch, young trees growing skywards like the Perpendicular period come to life. The slim, dark evergreens stood in endless broken vertical stripes with the yellow-drying leaves and silver trunks of the birch, and the whole backdrop, that afternoon, was hung along the skyline with fuzzy drifts of misty low cloud.

The light was cold grey, the air cold damp. The spirits of the crowd, sunny Mediterranean. An English jockey won the race on the favourite and the crowd shouted approval.

It was time, Sandvik said, to go and see the Chairman, who had not been able to manage us sooner on account of lunching a visiting ambassador. We went into the Secretariat building adjoining the grandstand, up some sporting print-lined stairs, and into a large room containing not only the Chairman but five or six supporting Stewards. Per Bjørn Sandvik walked in first, then me, then Arne pushing his hood back, and the Chairman went on looking inquiringly at the door, still waiting for me, so to speak, to appear. I sometimes wondered if it would help if I were fat, bald and bespectacled: if premature ageing might produce more confidence and belief than the thin-six-feet-with-brown-hair job did. I'd done a fair amount of living, one way or another, but it perversely refused to show.

'This is David Cleveland,' Sandvik said, and several pairs of eyes mirrored the same disappointment.

'How do you do,' I murmured gently to the Chairman, and held out my hand.

'Er . . .' He cleared his throat and recovered manfully. 'So glad you have come.'

I made a few encouraging remarks about how pleasant I found it in Norway and wondered if any of them knew that Napoleon was promoted General at twenty-four.

The Chairman, Lars Baltzersen, was much like his letters to my office, brief, polite and effective. It took him approximately ten seconds to decide I wouldn't have been given my job if I couldn't do it, and I saw no need to tell him that my boss had died suddenly, eighteen months earlier, and left the manager-elect in charge a lot sooner than anyone intended.

'You sound older on the telephone,' he said simply, and I said I'd been told so before, and that was that.

'Go anywhere you like on the racecourse,' he said. 'Ask anything . . . Arne can interpret for those who do not speak English.'

'Thank you.'

'Do you need anything else?'

Second sight, I thought; but I said, 'Perhaps, if possible, to see you again before I go at the end of the afternoon.'

'Of course. Of course. We all want to hear of your progress. We'll all gather here after the last race.'

Heads nodded dubiously, and I fully expected to justify their lowly expectations. Either briefed or bored or merely busy, they drifted away through the door, leaving only Arne and the Chairman behind.

'Some beer?' suggested Baltzersen.

Arne said yes and I said no. Despite the glow from a huge stove it was a cold day for hops.

'How far is it to the Swedish border?' I asked.

'By road, about eighty kilometres,' Baltzersen said.
'Any formalities there?'
He shook his head. 'Not for Scandinavians in their own cars. There are few inspections or customs. But none of the frontier posts remember an Englishman crossing on that evening.'
'I know. Not even as a passenger in a Norwegian car. Would he have been spotted if he'd gone across crouching under a rug on the floor behind the driver's seat?'
They pondered. 'Very probably not,' Baltzersen said, and Arne agreed.
'Can you think of anyone who might have taken him? Anyone he was close to here, either in business or friendship?'
'I do not know him well enough,' the Chairman said regretfully, and Arne blinked a little and said Gunnar Holth, or maybe some of the lads who worked for him.
'Holth says he drove him only round to the races,' I said: but he would have had plenty of time to drive into Sweden and back before Emma Sherman had rung him up.
'Gunnar tells lies whenever it suits him,' Arne said.
Lars Baltzersen sighed. 'I'm afraid that is true.'
He had grey hair, neatly brushed, with a tidy face and unimaginative clothes. I was beginning to get the feel of Norwegian behaviour patterns, and he came into the very large category of sober, slightly serious people who were kind, efficient, and under little stress. Get-up-and-go was conspicuously absent, yet the job would clearly be done. The rat race taken at a walk. Very civilized.
There were other types, of course.
'The people I hate here,' Emma Sherman had said, 'are the drunks.'
I'd taken her to dinner in the hotel the evening before, and had listened for several hours, in the end, to details of her life with Bob, her anxieties, and her experiences in Norway.
'When I first came,' she said, 'I used to have dinner in the dining-room, and all these men used to come and ask if

they could share my table. They were quite polite, but very very persistent. They wouldn't go away. The head waiter used to get rid of them for me. He told me they were drunk. They didn't really look it. They weren't rolling or anything.'

I laughed. 'Considering the price of alcohol here, you wouldn't think they could.'

'No,' she said. 'Anyway I stopped having dinner. I needed to make my money go as far as possible and I hated eating on my own.'

Arne said, 'Where do you want to go first?'

Arne came into a third group: the kinks. You find them everywhere.

'Weighing room, I should think.'

They both nodded in agreement. Arne pulled his hood back over his head and we went down into the raw outdoors. The crowd had swelled to what Arne described as 'very big', but there was still plenty of room. One of the greatest advantages of life in Norway, I guessed, was the small population. I had not so far in its leisurely capital seen a queue or a crush or anyone fighting to get anywhere first. As there always seemed to be room for all, why bother?

The officials checking tickets at the gates between different enclosures were all keen young men of about twenty, most of them blond also, all with blue armbands on their anoraks. They knew Arne, of course, but they checked my pass even though I was with him, the serious faces hardly lightening as they nodded me through. Lars Baltzersen had given me a five-by-three-inch card stamped all over with *adgang paddock*, *adgang stallomradet*, *adgang indre bane* and one or two other *adgangs*, and it looked as if I wouldn't get far if I lost it.

The weighing room, black wood walls, white paint, red tiled roof, lay on the far side of the parade ring, where the jockeys were already out for the second race. Everything looked neat, organized and pleasing, and despite an eye trained to spot trouble at five hundred paces in a thick fog,

I couldn't see any. Even in racing, good nature prevailed. Several of the lads leading the horses round wore sweaters in the owner's colours, matching the jockey's; a good and useful bit of display I'd seen nowhere else. I commented on it to Arne.

'*Ja*,' he said. 'Many of the private stables do that now. It helps the crowd to know their colours.'

Between the paddock and the U-shaped weighing room buildings, and up into the U itself, there was a grassy area planted thickly with ornamental bushes. Everyone walking between weighing room and paddock had to detour either to one side or the other, along comparatively narrow paths: it made a change from the rolling acres of concrete at home but took up a lot of apology time.

Once inside the weighing room Arne forgot about bugging machines and introduced me rapidly to a stream of people, like the secretary, clerk of the course, clerk of the scales, without once looking over his shoulder. I shook hands and chatted a bit, but although they all knew I was looking for Bob Sherman, I couldn't see anyone feeling twitchy about my presence.

'Come this way, David,' Arne said, and took me down a side passage with an open door at the end leading out to the racecourse. A step or two before this door, Arne turned smartly right, and we found ourselves in the officials' room from which the money had been stolen. It was just an ordinary businesslike room, wooden walls, wooden floor, wooden tables acting as desks, wooden chairs. (With all those forests, what else?) There were pleasant, red checked curtains, first-class central heating, and in one corner, a no-nonsense safe.

Apart from us, there was no one there.

'That's all there is,' Arne said. 'The money bags were left on the floor . . .' he pointed, 'and the lists of totals from each collecting point were put on that desk, same as usual. We still have the lists.'

It had struck me several times that Arne felt no responsibility for the loss of the money, nor did anyone seem in the remotest way to blame him, but by even the most elementary requirements of a security officer, he'd earned rock bottom marks.

'Do you still have the same system.' I asked, 'with the bags?'

Arne gave me a look somewhere between amusement and hurt.

'No. Since that day, the bags are put immediately into the safe.'

'Who has the keys?'

'I have some, and the secretary, and the clerk of the course.'

'And each of you three thought one of the other two had stowed the money away safely?'

'That is right.'

We left the room and stepped out into the open air. Several jockeys, changed into colours for later races but with warm coats on at the moment, came along the passage and out through the same door, and they, Arne, and I climbed an outside staircase on to a small open stand attached to the side of the weighing room buildings. From there, a furlong or more from the winning post, we watched the second race.

Arne had begun looking apprehensively around again, though there were barely twenty on the stand. I found I had begun doing it myself: it was catching. It netted, however, the sight of an English jockey who knew me, and as everyone after the finish poured towards the stairs I arranged to fetch up beside him. Arne went on down the steps, but the jockey stopped when I touched his arm, and was easy to keep back.

'Hallo,' he said in surprise. 'Fancy seeing you here.'

'Came about Bob Sherman,' I explained.

I'd found that if I said straight out what I wanted to know, I got better results. No one wasted time wondering what I suspected them of, and if they weren't feeling on the defensive they talked more.

'Oh. I see. Found the poor bugger, then?'

'Not yet,' I said.
'Let him go, why don't you?'
Rinty Ranger knew Bob Sherman as well as anyone who'd been thrown together in the same small professional group for five years, but they were not especially close friends. I took this remark to be a general statement of sympathy for the fox and asked if he didn't think stealing the money had been a bloody silly thing to do.
'Too right,' he said. 'I'll bet he wished he hadn't done it, five minutes after. But that's Bob all over, smack into things without thinking.'
'Makes him a good jockey,' I said, remembering how he flung his heart over fences regardless.
Rinty grinned, his thin, sharp face looking cold above his sheepskin coat. 'Yeah. Done him no good this time, though.'
'What else has he done that was impulsive?'
'I don't know . . . Always full of get-rich-quick schemes like buying land in the Bahamas or backing crazy inventors, and I even heard him on about pyramid selling once, only we told him not to be such a bloody fool. I mean, it's hard enough to earn the stuff, you don't actually want to throw it down the drain.'
'Were you surprised when he stole the money?' I asked.
'Well of course I was, for Chrissakes. And even more by him doing a bunk. I mean, why didn't he just stash away the loot and carry on with business as usual?'
'Takes nerve,' I said, but of course that was just what Bob Sherman had. 'Also the money was in heavy canvas bags which would take a lot of getting into. He wouldn't have had time to do that and catch his flight home.'
Rinty thought a bit but came up with nothing useful.
'Stupid bugger,' he said. 'Nice wife, kid coming, good job. You'd think he'd have more sense.' And I'd got as far as that myself.
'Anyway, he's done me a favour,' Rinty said. 'I've got his ride in this here Grand National.' He opened his sheepskin a fraction to show me the colours underneath. 'The owner, fellow called Torp, isn't best pleased with Bob on any

account. Says he should've won at a canter that last day he was here. Says he threw it away, left it too late, came through too soon, should've taken the outside, didn't put him right at the water, you name it, Bob did it wrong.'

'He got another English jockey, though.'

'Oh sure. D'you know how many home-bred jump jocks there are here? About fifteen, that's all, and some of those are English or Irish. Lads they are mostly. You don't get many self-employed chaps, like us. There isn't enough racing here for that. You get them going to Sweden on Saturdays, they race there on Saturdays. Here Thursdays and Sundays. That's the lot. Mind you, they don't keep the jumpers to look at. They all run once a week at least, and as there are only four or five jump races a week – all the rest are Flat – it makes life interesting.'

'Were you and Bob often over here together?'

'This year, three or four trips, I suppose. But I came last year too, which he didn't.'

'How long is a trip?'

He looked surprised. 'Only a day usually. We race in England Saturday afternoon, catch the six-thirty, race here Sunday, catch the late plane back if we can, otherwise the eight-fifteen Monday morning. Sometimes we fly here Sunday morning, but it's cutting it a bit fine. No margin for hold-ups.'

'Do you get to know people here well, in that time?'

'I suppose it sort of accumulates. Why?'

'Has Bob Sherman made any friendships here, would you say?'

'Good God. Well, no, not that I know of, but then likely as not I wouldn't know if he did. He knows a lot of trainers and owners, of course. Do you mean girls?'

'Not particularly. Were there any?'

'Shouldn't think so. He likes his missus.'

'Do you mind thinking fairly hard about it?'

He looked surprised. 'If you like.'

I nodded. He lengthened the focus of his gaze in a most

satisfactory manner and really concentrated. I waited without pressure, watching the crowd. Young, it was, by British standards: at least half under thirty, half blond, all the youth dressed in anoraks of blue, red, orange and yellow in the sort of colourful haphazard uniformity that stage designers plan for the chorus.

Rinty Ranger stirred and brought his vision back to the present.

'I don't know . . . He stayed with Mr Sandvik a couple of times, and said he got on better with his son than the old man . . . I met him once, the son, that is, with Bob when they were chatting at the races . . . but I wouldn't say they were great friends or anything . . .'

'How old is he, roughly?'

'The son? Sixteen, seventeen. Eighteen maybe.'

'Anyone else?'

'Well . . . One of the lads at Gunnar Holth's. An Irish lad, Paddy O'Flaherty. Bob knows him well, because Paddy used to work for old Tasker Mason, where Bob was apprenticed. They were lads together, one time, you might say. Bob likes staying at Gunnar Holth's on account of Paddy, I think.'

'Do you know if Paddy has a car?'

'Haven't a clue. Why don't you ask him? He's bound to be here.'

'Were you here,' I asked, 'the day Bob disappeared?'

' 'Fraid not.'

'Well . . . Mm . . . anything you can think of which is not what you'd've expected?'

'What bloody questions! Let's see . . . can't think of anything . . . except that he left his saddle here.'

'Bob?'

'Yes. It's in the changing-room. And his helmet. He must have known, the silly sod, that he'd never be able to race anywhere in the world again, otherwise he'd never have left them.'

I moved towards the stairs. Rinty hadn't told me a great deal, but if there had been much to tell the police of one country or the other would have found Bob long ago. He followed me down, and I wished him good luck in the National.

'Thanks,' he said. 'Can't say I wish you the same, though. Let the poor bastard alone.'

At the bottom of the steps, Arne was talking to Per Bjørn Sandvik. They turned to include me with smiles, and I asked the offensive question with as much tact as possible.

'Your son Mikkel, Mr Sandvik. Do you think he could've driven Bob Sherman away from the races? Without knowing, of course, that he had the money with him?'

Per Bjørn reacted less violently than many a father would to the implication that his son, having entertained a thief even if unawares, had nonetheless kept quiet about it. Scarcely a ripple went through him.

He said smoothly, 'Mikkel cannot drive yet. He is still at school . . . his seventeenth birthday was six weeks ago.'

'That's good,' I said in apology; and I thought, that's that.

Per Bjørn said 'Excuse me,' without noticeable resentment and walked away. Arne, blinking furiously, asked where I wanted to go next. To see Paddy O'Flaherty, I said, so we went in search and found him in the stables getting Gunnar Holth's runner ready for the Grand National. He turned out to be the lad in the woolly cap with uncomplimentary opinions of a mare, and described himself as Gunny's head lad, so I am.

'What did I do after the races?' he repeated. 'Same as I always do. Took the runners home, squared 'em up and saw to their scoff.'

'And after that?'

'After that, same as always, down to the local hop. There's a good little bird there, d'you see?'

'Do you have a car?' I asked.

'Well, sure I have now, but the tyres are as thin as a stockpot on Thursday and I wouldn't be after driving on them any more at all. And there's the winter coming on, so there's my car up on bricks, d'you see?'

'When did you put it on bricks?'

'The police stopped me about those tyres, now . . . well, there's the canvas peeping through one or two, if you look close. Sure it's all of six weeks ago now.'

After that we drifted around while I took in a general view of what went on, and then walked across the track to watch a race from the tower. This looked slightly like a small airfield control tower, two storeys high with a glass-walled room at the top. In this eyrie during races sat two keen-eyed men with fierce raceglasses clamped to their eyes: they were non-automatic patrol cameras, and never missed a trick.

Arne introduced me. Feel free, they said, smiling, to come up into the tower at any time. I thanked them and stayed to watch the next race from there, looking straight down the narrow elongated oval of the track. Sixteen hundred metres for staying two-year-olds: they started almost level with the tower, scurried a long way away, rounded the fairly sharp bottom bend, and streamed up the long straight to finish at the winning post just below where we stood. There was a photo-finish. The all-seeing eyes unstuck themselves from their raceglasses, nodded happily, and said they would be back for the next race.

Before following them down the stairs I asked Arne which way the Grand National went, as there seemed to be fences pointing in every direction.

'Round in a figure of eight,' he said, sweeping a vague arm. 'Three times round. You will see when they go.' He seemed to want to be elsewhere fairly promptly, but when we had hurried back over to the paddock it appeared merely that he was hungry and had calculated enough eating time before the Norsk St Leger. He magicked some huge open sandwiches on about a foot of french loaf, starting at one end with prawns and proceeding through herring, cheese, pâté and egg to beef at the far end, adorned throughout by pickled cucumber, mayonnaise and scattered unidentified crispy bits. Arne stayed the course, but I blew up in the straight.

We drank wine: a bottle. We would come back later, Arne said, and finish it. We were in the big warm room he had shunned earlier, but the listeners weren't troubling him at that moment.

'If you're going home tomorrow, David,' he said, 'come to supper with us tonight.'

I hesitated. 'There's Emma Sherman,' I said.

'That girl,' he exclaimed. He peered around, though there were barely six others in the room. 'Where is she? She's usually on my heels.'

'I talked to her yesterday. Persuaded her not to come today and to go back to England tomorrow.'

'Great. Great, my friend.' He rubbed his hands together. 'She'll be all right, then. You come to supper with us. I will telephone to Kari.'

I thought of Kari's hair and Kari's shape. Everything stacked as I liked it best. I imagined her in bed. Very likely I should have allowed no such thoughts but you might as well forbid fish to swim. A pity she was Arne's I thought. To stay away would make it easier on oneself.

'Come,' Arne said.

Weak, that's what I am. I said, 'I'd love to.'

He bustled off instantly to do the telephoning and soon returned beaming.

'She is very pleased. She says we will give you cloud-berries, she bought some yesterday.'

We went out to the raw afternoon and watched the big flat race together, but then Arne was whisked off on official business and for a while I wandered around alone. Though its organization and upkeep were clearly first class, it was not on British terms a big racecourse. Plenty of room, but few buildings. Everyone could see: no one was pushed, rushed or crushed. Space was the ultimate luxury, I thought, as I strolled past a small oblong ornamental pond with a uniformed military band playing full blast beside it. Several children sat in bright little heaps around the players' feet and one or two were peering interestedly into the quivering business ends of trombones.

Øvrevoll, someone had told me, was a fairly new racecourse, the only one in Norway to hold ordinary flat and jump races. Most racing, as in Germany, was trotting, with sulkies.

For the Grand National itself I went back up the tower, which I found stood in the smaller top part of the figure of eight, with the larger part lying in the main part of the course, inside the flat track. Twenty runners set off at a spanking pace to go three and a half times round, which set the binocular men in the tower rotating like gyros. Soon after the start the horses circled the tower, cut closer across beside it and sped towards the water jump and the farther part of the course, took the bottom bend, and returned towards the start. In the top part of the course, near the tower, lay a large pond with a couple of swans swimming in stately unison across from two small devoted black-and-white ducks. Neither pair took the slightest notice of the throng of horses thundering past a few feet from home.

Rinty Ranger won the race, taking the lead at the beginning of the last circuit and holding off all challengers, and I saw the flash of his triumphant teeth as he went past the post.

The misty daylight had already faded to the limit for jumping fences safely, but the two races still to come, in a card of ten altogether, were both on the flat. The first was run in peering dusk and the second in total darkness, with floodlights from the tower illuminating just the winning line, bright enough to activate the photo-finish. Eleven horses sped up the dark track, clearly seen only for the seconds it took them to flash through the bright patch, but cheered nonetheless by a seemingly undiminished crowd.

So they literally did race in the dark. I walked thoughtfully back towards the officials' room to meet up with Arne. It really had been night-black when Bob Sherman left the racecourse.

There was bustle in the officials' room and a lot of grins

and assurances that the takings this day were safe in the safe. Arne reminded several of them that the Chairman had said they could come to the progress-report meeting if they liked: he said it in English in deference to me, and in English they answered. They would come, except for one or two who would wait for the night watchman. A right case of bolting stable doors.

The Chairman's room had too many people in it, as far as I was concerned. Fifteen besides myself. Every chair filled up, coffee and drinks circulated, and the eyes waited. Lars Baltzersen raised his eyebrows in my direction to tell me I was on, and shushed the low-key chatter with a single smooth wave of his hand.

'I think you've all met Mr Cleveland at some time today . . .' He turned directly to me and smiled forgivingly. 'I know we have asked the impossible. Sherman left no traces, no clues. But is there any course of action you think we might take which we have not so far done?'

He made it so easy.

'Look for his body,' I said.

CHAPTER FIVE

It seemed that that was not what they expected.

Per Bjørn Sandvik said explosively in his high, distilled English, 'We know he is a thief. Why should he be dead?' and someone else murmured, 'I still think he is in the south of France, living in the sun.'

Rolf Torp, owner of the Grand National winner, lit a cigar and said, 'I do not follow your reasoning.' Arne sat shaking his head and blinking as if he would never stop.

Lars Baltzersen gave me a slow stare and then invited me to explain.

'Well,' I said. 'Take first the mechanics of that theft.

Everyone agrees that the officials' room was empty for a very few minutes, and that no one could have predicted when it would be empty, or that it would be empty at all. Everyone agrees that Bob Sherman simply saw the money lying handy, was overcome with sudden temptation, and swiped it. Sorry . . .' I said as I saw their puzzlement, '. . . stole it.'

Heads nodded all round. This was well-worn ground.

'After that,' I said, 'we come to a few difficulties. That money was enclosed in five hefty . . . er, bulky . . . canvas bags fastened with straps and padlocks. Now a hundred-and-thirty-three-pound jockey couldn't stow five such bags out of sight under his coat. Anyone, however big, would have found it awkward to pick all of them up at once. To my mind, if Sherman's first impulse was to steal, his second would instantly be to leave well alone. He had no way of knowing how much the bags contained. No way of judging whether the theft would be worthwhile. But in fact there is no evidence at all to suggest that he even felt any impulse to steal, even if he saw the bags on the floor when he went in earlier to ask some question or other. There is no evidence whatsoever to prove that Bob Sherman stole the money.'

'Of course there is,' Rolf Torp said. 'He disappeared.'

'How?' I asked.

There were several puzzled frowns, one or two blank faces, and no suggestions.

'This must have been a spur-of-the-moment theft,' I said, 'so he could have made no preparations. Well, say for argument he had taken the bags, there he is staggering around with the swag . . . the stolen goods . . . in full view. What does he do? Even with a sharp knife it would have taken some time to slit open those bags and remove the money. But we can discount that he did this on the race-course, because the bags in fact have never been found.'

Some heads nodded. Some were shaken.

'Bob Sherman had a small overnight grip with him, which I understand from his wife was not big enough to contain five canvas bags, let alone his clothes as well. No one has found his clothes lying around, so he could not have packed the money in his grip.'

Lars Baltzersen looked thoughtful.

'Take transport,' I said. 'He had ordered a taxi to take him to Fornebu airport, but he didn't turn up. The police could find no taxi driver who took one single Englishman anywhere. Gunnar Holth says he drove him round to the racecourse at midday, but not away. Because the theft has to be unpremeditated, Sherman could not have hired himself a getaway car, and the police anyway could trace no such hiring. He did not steal a car to transport the money: no cars were stolen from here that day. Which leaves friends ...' I paused. 'Friends who could be asked to take him say to Sweden, and keep quiet afterwards.'

'They would be also guilty,' said Rolf Torp disbelievingly.

'Yes. Well ... he had been to Norway seven times but only for a day or two each time. The only friends I can find who might conceivably have known or liked him well enough to get themselves into trouble on his account are Gunnar Holth's head lad, Paddy O'Flaherty, and perhaps ... if you'll forgive me, sir ... Mikkel Sandvik.'

He was much more annoyed this time, but protested no further than a grim stare.

'But Paddy O'Flaherty's car has been up on bricks for six weeks,' I said. 'And Mikkel Sandvik cannot drive yet. Neither of them had wheels ... er, transport ... ready and waiting for Sherman's unexpected need.'

'What you are saying,' Baltzersen said, 'is that once he'd stolen the money, he couldn't have got it away. But suppose he hid it, and came back for it later?'

'He would still have much the same transport problem, and also the night watchmen to contend with. No ... I think if he had stolen and hidden the money, he would not have gone back for it, but just abandoned it. Sense would have prevailed. Because there are other things about that cash ... To you, it is familiar. It is *money*. To Bob Sherman, it was foreign currency. All British jockeys riding abroad have enough trouble changing currency as it is; they would not leap at stealing bagfuls of something they could not readily spend. And don't forget, a large proportion of it was in coins, which are both heavy and even more difficult to exchange in quantity than notes, once they are out of Norway.'

Per Bjørn Sandvik was studying the floor and looking mild again. Arne had blinked his eyes to a standstill and was now holding them shut. Rolf Torp puffed his cigar with agitation and Lars Baltzersen looked unhappy.

'But that still does not explain why you think Sherman is dead,' he said.

'There has been no trace of him from that day to this . . . No one even thinks they might have seen him. There have been no reports from anywhere. His pregnant wife has had no word of reassurance. All this is highly unusual in the case of a thief on the run, but entirely consistent with the man being dead.'

Baltzersen took his bottom lip between his teeth.

I said, 'It is usually fairly easy to account for a man's abrupt disappearance . . . during an investigation his motive emerges pretty strongly. But there seems to have been no factor in Bob Sherman's life likely to prompt him into impulsive and irreversible flight. No one would exchange a successful career for an unknown but not huge amount of foreign currency unless some secondary force made it imperative. Neither your police, nor the British police, nor his wife, nor Arne Kristiansen, nor I, have found any suggestion, however faint or unlikely, that there was such force at work.'

Arne opened his eyes and shook his head.

'Suppose,' I said, 'that someone else stole the money, and Bob Sherman saw him.'

The Stewards and officials looked startled and intensely gloomy. No one needed to have it spelled out that anyone caught red-handed might have had too much to lose, and from there it was a short step to imagine the thief desperate enough to kill Bob Sherman to keep him quiet.

'Murder?' Baltzersen spoke the word slowly as if it

were strange on his tongue. 'Is that what you mean?'

'It's possible,' I said.

'But not certain.'

'If there were any clear pointers to murder,' I said, 'your police would have already found them. There is no clarity anywhere. But if there are no answers at all to the questions where he went, why he went, and how he went, I think one should then ask *whether* he went.'

Baltzersen's strained voice mirrored their faces: they did not want me to be right. 'You surely don't think he is still *here*? On the racecourse?'

Rolf Torp shook his head impatiently. He was a man most unlike the Chairman, as quick tempered as Baltzersen was steady. 'Of course he doesn't. There are people here every day training their horses, and we have held eight race meetings since Sherman disappeared. If his body had been here, it would have been found at once.'

Heads nodded in unanimous agreement, and Baltzersen said regretfully, 'I suppose he could have been driven away from here unconscious or dead, and hidden . . . buried . . . later, somewhere else.'

'There's a lot of deep water in Norway,' I said.

My thoughts went back to our little junket in the fjord, and I missed some lightning reaction in someone in that room. I knew that a shift had been made, but because of that gap in concentration I couldn't tell who had made it. Fool, I thought, you got a tug on the line and you didn't see which fish, and even the certainty that a fish was there was no comfort.

The silence lengthened, until finally Per Bjørn Sandvik looked up from the floor with a thoughtful frown. 'It would seem, then, that no one can ever get to the truth of it. I think David's theory is very plausible. It fits all the facts . . . or rather, the lack of facts . . . better than any explanation we have discussed before.'

The heads nodded.

'We will tell our police here what you have suggested,' Baltzersen said in a winding-up-the-meeting voice, 'but I agree with Per . . . After so long a time, and after so much fruitless investigation, we will never really know what happened either to Sherman or to the money. We are all most grateful that you took the trouble to come over, and I know that for most of us, on reflection, your answer to the puzzle will seem the one most likely to be right.'

They gave me a lot of worried half-smiles and some more nods. Rolf Torp stubbed out his cigar vigorously and everyone shifted on their chairs and waited for Baltzersen to stand up.

I thought about the two graceful swans and the two little black and white ducks swimming around quietly out there on the dark side of the tower.

'You could try the pond,' I said.

The meeting broke up half an hour later, after it had been agreed with a certain amount of horror that the peaceful little water should be dragged the following morning.

Arne had some security jobs to see to, which he did with painstaking slowness. I wandered aimlessly around, listening to the Norwegian voices of the last of the crowd going home. A good hour after the last race, and still a few lights, still a few people. Not the most private place for committing murder.

I went back towards the weighing room and stood beside the clump of ornamental bushes on the grass outside. Well . . . they were thick enough and dark enough to have hidden a body temporarily, until everyone had gone. A jockey and his overnight grip, and five bags of stolen money. Plenty of room, in these bushes, for the lot. There were lights outside the weighing room, but the bushes threw heavy shadows and one could not see to their roots.

Arne found me there and exclaimed with passionate certainty, 'He can't be in those, you know. Someone would have seen him long ago.'

'And smelled him,' I said.

Arne made a choking noise and, 'Christ.'

I turned away. 'Have you finished now?'

He nodded, one side of his face brightly lit, the other in shadow. 'The night watchman is here and everything is as it should be. He will make sure all the gates are locked for the night. We can go home.'

He drove me in his sturdy Swedish Volvo back towards the city and round to his leafy urban street. Kari greeted us with roaring logs on the fire and tall glasses of frosty thirst-quenching white wine. Arne moved restlessly round the apartment like a bull and switched Beethoven on again, *fortissimo.*

'What's the matter?' Kari asked him, raising her voice. 'For God's sake turn it down.'

Arne obliged, but the sacrifice of his emotional safety valve clearly oppressed him.

'Let him rip,' I told her. 'We can stand it for five minutes.'

Kari gave me a gruesome look and vanished into the kitchen as Arne with great seriousness took me at my word. I sat resignedly on the sofa while the stereophonics shook the foundations, and admired the forebearance of his neighbours. The man who lived alone below my own flat in London had ears like stethoscopes and was up knocking on my door at every dropped pin.

The five minutes stretched to nearly twenty before Arne stopped pacing around and turned down the volume.

'Great stuff, great stuff,' he said.

'Sure,' I agreed because it was, in its place, which was somewhere the size of the Albert Hall.

Kari returned from exile with little wifely indulgent shakes of the head. She looked particularly disturbing in a copper-coloured, silky trouser suit which did fantastic things for the hair, the colouring and the eyes and nothing bad for the rest of her. She refilled our glasses and sat on some floor cushions near the fire.

'How did you enjoy the races?' she asked.

'Very much,' I said.

Arne blinked a bit, said he had some telephone calls to make, and removed himself to the hall. Kari said she had watched the Grand National on television but rarely went to the races herself.

'I'm an indoors person,' she said. 'Arne says the outdoor life is healthier, but I don't enjoy being cold or wet or cut up by the wind, so I let him go off doing all those rugged things like skiing and sailing and swimming, and me, I just make a warm room for him to come back to.'

She grinned, but I caught the faintest of impressions that wifely though she might thoroughly appear to be, she had feelings for Arne which were not wholehearted love. Somewhere deep lay an attitude towards the so-called manly pursuits which was far from admiration; and a basic antipathy to an activity nearly always extended, in my experience, to anyone who went in for it.

Arne's voice floated in from the hall, speaking Norwegian.

'He is talking about dragging a pond,' Kari said, looking puzzled. 'What pond?'

I told her what pond.

'Oh dear ... his poor little wife ... I hope he isn't in there ... how would she bear it?'

Better, I thought, on the whole, than believing he was a thief who had deserted her. I said, 'It's only a possibility. But it's as well to make sure.'

She smiled. 'Arne has a very high opinion of you. I expect you are right. Arne said when he came back from England that he would never want to be investigated by you, you seemed to know what people were thinking. When the Chairman asked for someone to find Bob Sherman and Arne heard that you were coming yourself, he was very pleased. I heard him telling someone on the telephone that you had the eyes of a hawk and a mind like a razor.' She grinned ironically, the soft light gleaming on her teeth. 'Are you flattered?'

'Yes,' I said. 'I wish it were true.'

'It must be true if you are in charge when you are so young.'

'I'm thirty-three,' I said. 'Alexander the Great had conquered the world from Greece to India by that time.'

'You look twenty-five,' she said.
'It's a great drawback.'
'A . . . what?'
'A disadvantage.'
'No woman would think so.'
Arne came back from the hall looking preoccupied.
'Everything all right?'
'Oh . . . er . . . *ja*.' He blinked several times. 'It is all arranged. Nine o'clock tomorrow morning, they drag the pond.' He paused. 'Will you be there, David?'
I nodded. 'And you?'
'*Ja*.' The prospect did not seem to please him; but then I was not wildly excited about it myself. If Bob Sherman were indeed there, he would be the sort of unforgettable object you wished you had never seen, and my private gallery of those was already too extensive.
Arne piled logs on the fire as if to ward off demons, and Kari said it was time to eat. She gave us reindeer steaks in a rich dark sauce and after that the promised cloudberries, which turned out to be yellowy-brown and tasted of caramel.
'They are very special,' Arne said, evidently pleased to be able to offer them. 'They grow in the mountains, and are only in season for about three weeks. There is a law about picking them. One can be prosecuted for picking them before the right date.'
'You can get them in tins,' Kari said. 'But they don't taste the same as these.'
We ate in reverent silence.
'No more until next year,' Arne said regretfully, putting down his spoon. 'Let's have some coffee.'
Kari brought the coffee and with amusement declined half-hearted offers from me to help with the dishes.
'You do not want to. Be honest.'
'I do not want to,' I said truthfully.
She laughed. A highly feminine lady with apparently no banners to wave about equality in the kitchen. Between her and Arne the proposition that everything indoors was her domain, and everything outside, his, seemed to lead only to

harmony. In my own sister it had led to resentment, rows, and a broken marriage. Kari, it seemed to me, expected less, settled for less, and achieved more.

I didn't stay late. I liked looking at Kari just a shade too much, and Arne, for all his oddnesses, was an investigator. I had taught him myself how to notice where people were looking, because where their eyes were, their thoughts were, as often as not. Some men felt profound gratification when others lusted after their wives, but some felt a revengeful anger. I didn't know what Arne's reaction would be, and I didn't aim to find out.

CHAPTER SIX

Monday morning. Drizzle. Daylight slowly intensifying over Øvrevoll racecourse, changing anthracite clouds to flannel grey. The dark green spruce and yellow birch stood around in their dripping thousands and the paper debris from the day before lay soggily scattered across the wet tarmac.

Round the lower end of the track, Gunnar Holth and one or two other trainers were exercising their strings of race-horses, but the top part, by and above the winning post, had been temporarily railed off.

Shivering from depression more than cold, I was sitting up in the observation tower with Lars Baltzersen, watching the dragging of the pond down below. Hands in pockets, shoulders hunched, rain dripping off hat brims, Arne and two policemen stood at the water's edge, peering morosely at the small boat going slowly, methodically, backwards and forwards from bank to bank.

The pond was more or less round, approximately thirty yards in diameter, and apparently about six feet deep. The boat contained two policemen with grappling hooks and a third, dressed in a black rubber scuba suit, who was doing the rowing. He wore flippers, gloves, hood and goggles, and had twice been over the side with an underwater torch to investigate when the grapples caught. Both times he had returned to the surface and shaken his head.

The swans and the black and white ducks swam around in agitated circles. The water grew muddier and muddier. The boat moved slowly on its tenth traverse, and Lars Baltzersen said gloomily. 'The police think this is a waste of time.'

'Still,' I said, 'they did come.'

'They would, of course.'

'Of course,' I said.

We watched in silence.

A grapple caught. The swimmer went over the side. submerged for a full minute, came up, shook his head, and was helped back into the boat. He took up the oars; rowed on. One each side of the boat, the two men swung the three-pronged grapples into the water again, dragging them slowly across the bottom.

'They considered emptying the pond,' Baltzersen said. 'But the technical difficulties are great. Water drains into it from all the top part of the racecourse. They decided on dragging.'

'They are being thorough enough,' I said.

He looked at me soberly. 'If they do not find Sherman, then, will you be satisfied that he is not there?'

'Yes,' I said.

He nodded. 'That is reasonable.'

We watched for another hour. The swimmer made two more trips into the water, and came up with nothing. The boat finished its journey, having missed not an inch. There was no body. Bob Sherman was not in the pond.

Beside me, Baltzersen stood up stiffly and stretched, his chair scraping loudly on the wooden boards.

'That is all, then,' he said.

'Yes.'

I stood and followed him down the outside staircase, to

be met at the bottom by Arne and the policeman in charge.

'No one is there,' he said to me in English, implying by his tone that he wasn't surprised.

'No. But thank you for finding out.'

He, Baltzersen and Arne spoke together for some time in Norwegian, and Baltzersen walked across to thank the boatmen personally. They nodded, smiled, shrugged, and began to load their boat on to a trailer.

'Never mind, David,' said Arne with sympathy. 'It was a good idea.'

'One more theory down the drain,' I agreed philosophically. 'Not the first, by a long way.'

'Will you go on looking?'

I shook my head. The fjords were too deep. Someone in the Chairman's room had reacted strongly to my mention of water, and if Bob Sherman wasn't in the pond he was somewhere just as wet.

Baltzersen, Arne, the senior policeman and I trudged back across the track and into the paddock enclosure, on our way to the cars parked beside the main entrance. Baltzersen frowned at the rubbish lying around in the shape of dropped race-cards and old tote tickets and said something to Arne. Arne replied in Norwegian and then repeated it in English.

'The manager thought it better that the refuse collectors should not be here to see the police drag the pond. Just in case, you see ... Anyway, they are coming tomorrow instead.'

Baltzersen nodded. He had taken the morning off from his timber business and looked as though he regretted it.

'I'm sorry,' I said, 'to have wasted your time.'

He made a little movement of his head to acknowledge that I was more or less forgiven. The persistent drizzle put a damper on anything warmer.

In silence we passed the stands, the ornamental pond (too shallow) and secretariat, and it was probably because the only noise was the crunch of our feet that we heard the child.

He was standing in a corner of the Tote building, sobbing. About six, soaked to the skin, with hair plastered to his forehead in forlorn-looking spikes. The policeman looked across to him and beckoned, and in a kind enough voice said what must have been, 'Come here.'

The boy didn't move, but he said something which halted my three companions in mid-step. They stood literally immobile, as if their reflexes had all stopped working. Their faces looked totally blank.

'What did he say?' I asked.

The boy repeated what he had said before, and if anything the shock of my companions deepened.

Baltzersen loosened his jaw with a visible effort, and translated.

'He said, "I have found a hand".'

The child was frightened when we approached, his big eyes looking frantically around for somewhere to run to, but whatever the policeman said reassured him, and when we reached him he was just standing there, wet, terrified, and shivering.

The policeman squatted beside him, and they went into a longish quiet conversation. Eventually the policeman put out his hand, and the child gripped it, and after that the policeman stood up and told us in English what he'd said.

'The boy came to look for money. The racing crowd often drop coins and notes, especially after dark. This boy says he always squeezes through a hole in the fence, before the rubbish collectors come, to see if he can find money. He says he always finds some. This morning he found twenty kroner before the men came. He means before the police came. But he is not supposed to be here, so he hid. He hid behind the stands up there.' The policeman nodded across the tarmac. 'He says that behind the stands he found a hand lying on the ground.'

He looked down at the child clutching his own hand like a lifeline, and asked Arne to go across to his men, who had packed up all their gear and were on the point of leaving, to ask them to come over at the double. Arne gave the child a sick look and did as he was asked, and Baltzersen himself slowly returned to businesslike efficiency.

The policeman had difficulty transferring the boy's trust to one of his men, but finally disengaged himself, and he, two of his men, Baltzersen, Arne and I walked up to and around the stands to see the hand which was lying on the ground.

The child was not mistaken. Waxy white and horrific, it lay back downwards on the tarmac, fingers laxly curled up to meet the rain.

What the child had not said, however, was that the hand was not alone.

In the angle between the wall and the ground lay a long mound covered by a black tarpaulin. Halfway along its length, visible to the wrist, the hand protruded.

Wordlessly the senior policeman took hold of a corner of the tarpaulin and pulled it back.

Arne took one look, bolted for the nearest bushes, and heaved up whatever Kari had given him for breakfast. Baltzersen turned grey and put a shaking hand over his mouth. The policemen themselves looked sick, and I added another to the unwanted memories.

He was unrecognizable really: it was going to be a teeth job for the inquest. But the height and clothes were right, and his overnight grip was lying there beside him, still with the initials R. T. S. stamped on in black.

A piece of nylon rope was securely knotted round the chest, and another halfway down the legs, and from each knot, one over the breastbone, one over the knees, led a loose piece of rope which finished in a frayed end.

One of the policemen said something to his chief, and Baltzersen obligingly translated for me.

'That is the policeman who was diving,' he said, 'and he says that in the pond the grapples caught on a cement block. He did not think anything of it at the time, but he says there were frayed ends of rope coming from the cement. He says it looked like the same rope as this.'

The policeman in charge pulled the tarpaulin back over the tragic bundle and started giving his men instructions. Arne stood several yards away, mopping his face and mouth with a large white handkerchief and looking anywhere but at the black tarpaulin. I walked over and asked if he was all right. He was trembling, and shook his head miserably.

'You need a drink,' I said. 'You'd better go home.'

'No.' He shuddered. 'I'll be all right. So stupid of me. Sorry, David.'

He came with me round to the front of the stands and we walked over to where Baltzersen and the top policeman had rejoined the little boy. Baltzersen adroitly drew me aside a pace or two, and said quietly, 'I don't want to upset Arne again . . . The child says the hand was not showing at first. He lifted the tarpaulin a little to see what was underneath . . . you know what children are like . . . and he saw something pale and tried to pull it out. It was the hand. When he saw what it was . . . he ran away.'

'Poor little boy,' I said.

'He shouldn't have been here,' he said, meaning by his tone, serve him right.

'If he hadn't been, we wouldn't have found Bob Sherman.'

Lars Baltzersen looked at me thoughtfully. 'I suppose whoever took him out of the pond meant to return with transport and get rid of him somewhere else.'

'No, I shouldn't think so,' I said.

'He must have done. If he didn't mind him being found, he would have left him in the pond.'

'Oh sure. I just meant . . . why take him anywhere else? Why not straight back into the pond . . . as soon as it was dark? That's the one place no one would ever look for Bob Sherman again.'

He gave me a long considering stare, and then unexpectedly, for the first time that morning, he smiled.

'Well . . . you've done what we asked,' he said.

I smiled faintly back and wondered if he yet understood the significance of that morning's work. But catching murderers was a matter for the police, not for me. I was only catching the two-five to Heathrow, with little enough margin for what I still had to do first.

I said, 'Any time I can help . . .' in the idle way that one does, and shook hands with him, and with Arne, and left them there with their problem, in the drizzle.

I picked up Emma Sherman at her hotel as I had arranged, and took her up to my room in the Grand. I had been going to give her lunch before we set off to the airport, but instead I asked the restaurant to bring hot soup upstairs. Still no brandy. Not until three o'clock, they said. Next time, I thought, I'd pack a gallon.

Champagne was emotionally all wrong for the news I had to give her, so I stirred it around with some orange juice and made her drink it first. Then I told her, as gently as I could that Bob had died at the time of his disappearance. I told her he was not a thief and had not deserted her. I told her he had been murdered.

The desperately frail look came back to her face, but she didn't faint.

'You did . . . find him, then.'

'Yes.'

'Where . . . is he?'

'At the racecourse.'

She stood up, swaying a bit. 'I must go and see him.'

'No,' I said firmly, holding her elbow. 'No, Emma, you must not. You must remember him alive. He doesn't look the same now, and he would hate you to see him. He would beg you not to see him.'

'I must see him . . . of course I must.'

I shook my head.

'Do you mean . . .' It began to dawn on her . . . 'That he looks . . . *horrible*?'

'I'm afraid so. He's been dead a month.'

'Oh God.'

She sat down with weak knees and began to cry. I told her about the pond, the ropes, the cement. She had to know some time, and it couldn't be much worse than the agony of spirit she had suffered through four long weeks.

'Oh my poor Bob,' she said. 'Oh darling . . . oh darling . . .'

The floodgates of all that misery were opened and she wept with a fearful outpouring intensity, but at least and at last it was a normal grief, without the self doubt and humiliating shame.

After a while, still shaking with sobs, she said, 'I'll have to get my room back, at the hotel.'

'No,' I said. 'You're coming home to England today, with me, as we planned.'

'But I can't . . .'

'Indeed you can, and indeed you will. The last place for you now is here. You need to go home, to rest, recover, and look after that baby. The police here will do everything necessary, and I'll see that the Jockey Club, and the Injured Jockeys' Fund perhaps, organizes things from the English end. In a little while we can have Bob brought home to England, if that's what you would like . . . But for today, it's you that matters. If you stay here, you will be ill.'

She listened, took in barely half, but in fact raised no more objections. Maybe the police would not be overjoyed at her leaving, I thought, but they'd had her around for a month, and there couldn't be much she hadn't already told them. We caught the flight on schedule, and she stared out of the window all the way home with exhausted tears running intermittently down her cheeks.

Her grandfather, alerted from Oslo, met her at Heathrow. Tall, thin, stooping and kind, he greeted her with a small kiss and many affectionate pats: her parents, she had told me, had died during her school days, leaving her and a brother to be shuttled between relays of other relations. She liked her mother's widowed father best, and wanted him most in her troubles.

He shook my hand.

'I'll see she's looked after,' he said.

He was a nice scholarly man. I gave him my private address and telephone number, in case she needed an inside edge on official help.

CHAPTER SEVEN

Tuesday morning from nine to ten I spent in the office finding out that everyone had been doing just great in my absence and would undoubtedly continue to do so if I disappeared altogether. On my desk lay neat reports of finished inquiries: the man we had suspected of running a retired high-class 'chaser under a hunter's name in a point-to-point had in fact done so and was now in line for a fraud prosecution, and an applicant for a trainer's licence in the Midlands had been found to have totally unsuitable training facilities.

Nothing to make the hair curl. Nothing like weighted bodies in Norwegian ponds.

The whole of the rest of the day was spent with two opposite numbers from the New York Racing Commission who had come to discuss the viability of a world-wide racing investigatory link-up, something along the lines of Interpol. It was one of a series of talks I'd had with officials of many countries and the idea seemed very slowly to be staggering towards achievement. As usual the chief stumbling block to any rapid progress seemed to be my own apparent youth: I supposed that by the time I was sixty, when I'd run out of steam, they would begin to nod while they listened.

I talked my throat dry, gave away sheaves of persuasive literature, took them to dinner at Inigo Jones, and hoped the seed hadn't fallen on stony ground. At farewell time the older of them asked a question I was by then well used to.

'If you succeed in setting this thing up, do you have it in mind to be head of it yourself?'

I smiled. I knew very well that if the baby was born it would very smartly be found to be not mine after all.

'Once it's set up,' I said, 'I'll move on.'

He looked at me curiously.

'Where to?'

'Don't know yet.'

They shook their heads and tut-tutted slightly, but gripped hands with cordiality as we separated into a couple of homeward taxis. It was after midnight when I reached the house where I lived behind the Brompton Road, but as usual the lights were still on in the rooms below my own small flat. The street door banged if you let it go, reverberating through the walls, and perhaps that, I thought, as I shut it gently, explained the ground floor tenant's hypersensitivity. He was a self-contained man, greyish, fiftyish, very neat and precise. Our acquaintanceship after six months of living stacked one over the other extended simply to his trips to my door urging an instant lessening of decibels on the television. Once I had asked him in for a drink, but he politely declined, preferring solitude downstairs. Hardly the *entente cordiale* of the century.

I went up, opened my own door, and shut that quietly also. The telephone bell, starting suddenly in all that noble silence, made me jump.

'Mr Cleveland?' The voice was hurried, practically incoherent. 'Thank goodness you're back at last . . . This is William Romney . . . Emma's grandfather . . . She didn't want me to ring you so late, but I must . . . Two men were searching her house when she went in and they hit her . . . Mr Cleveland . . . she needs your help . . .'

'Stop a minute,' I said. 'First thing you need is the police.'

He calmed down a fraction. 'They've been here. Just left. I called them.'

'And a doctor for Emma?'

'Yes, yes. He's gone, too.'

'What time did all this happen?'

'About seven this evening ... we drove over from my house just to fetch some things for her ... and there was a light on ... and she went in first and they jumped on her ... they hit us both ... I do wish ... well ... tell you the truth ... I think we're both still frightened.'

I stifled a sigh. 'Where exactly are you?'

'At Emma's house, still.'

'Yes, but ...'

'Oh, I see. Near Newbury. You go down the M4 ...' He gave me details of the journey, certain in his own mind that I would hurry to their aid. He made it impossible for me to say take a tranquillizer and I'll come in the morning, and anyway, by the sound of his voice, nothing short of a full anaesthetic was going to give him any rest.

At least at night it was a fast straightforward journey, so I took the MGB down there in fifty minutes flat. The Shermans' house proved to be a modernized pair of farm cottages down an uninhabited lane, a nerve-testing isolation at the best of times.

Lights were on in every window, and at the sound of my car William Romney's anxious figure appeared in the doorway.

'Thank goodness, thank goodness,' he said agitatedly, coming down the short path to meet me. 'I don't know what we would have done ... if you hadn't been coming ...'

I refrained from saying that I thought they should have gone back to his house or otherwise stayed in a hotel, and once through the door I was glad I hadn't, because it wouldn't have helped. Shock prevents people from leaving the scene of personal disaster of their own accord, and of the scope and depth of their shock there could be no doubt.

The house was a shambles. Pictures had been torn from the walls, curtains from the windows, carpets from the floor. Furniture was not merely turned inside out, but smashed. Lamps, vases, ornaments lay in pieces. Papers and books scattered the wreckage like autumn leaves.

'It's all like this,' Romney said. 'The whole house. All

except the spare bedroom. That's where they were when we interrupted them. The police say so ...'

Emma herself was in the spare bedroom, lying awake with eyes like soot smudges. Both of her cheeks were swollen and puffy, with red marks showing where blows had landed. Her lower lip had been split, and one eyebrow ended in a raw skinned patch.

'Hullo,' I said inadequately, and pulled up a chair so that I could sit beside her. Her grandfather hovered around making fussing noises, obviously freshly worried by the darkening bruises but tiring Emma beyond bearing. He looked more upset than ever when I asked him if I could speak to her alone, but in the end he reluctantly returned to the devastation below.

I held her hand.

'David ...'

'Wait a bit,' I said. 'Then tell me.'

She nodded slightly. She was lying on the blankets of the unmade bed, still wearing the brown and white checked dress, her head supported by two coverless pillows and with a flowered quilt over her from the waist down.

The room was hot with a pulsating gas fire, but Emma's hand was cold.

'I told the police,' she said, 'I think they were Norwegians.'

'The two men?'

She nodded. 'They were big ... They had thick sweaters and rubber gloves ... They talked with accents ...'

'Start at the beginning,' I said.

She loosened her mouth, obviously troubled by the split and swelling lip.

'We came over to get me some different clothes. I was beginning to feel better ... There was a light on upstairs but I thought Mrs Street who has been looking after the house had left it on ... but when I unlocked the front door and went into the hall they jumped on me ... they switched all the lights on ... I saw the mess ... One of them hit me in the face and I screamed for Grandad ... When he came in they knocked him over . . . so easily, it was awful . . . and they kicked him . . . One of them asked me where Bob would hide papers . . . and when I didn't answer at once he just went on . . . punching me in the face . . . with his fists . . . I didn't answer because I didn't know . . . Bob doesn't hide things . . . didn't . . . oh God . . .'

Her fingers curled tight round mine.

'All right, all right, Emma,' I said, meaning nothing except that I understood. 'Wait a bit.'

We waited until some of the tension left her body; then she swallowed and tried again.

'The telephone rang then, and it seemed to worry them. They talked to each other, and then suddenly they just threw me into a chair . . . and they went away . . . through the front door . . . Grandad got up off the floor but the telephone stopped before he reached it . . . but anyway he called the police . . .'

The tired voice stopped. I said, 'Did the men wear masks of any sort?'

'No.'

'Would you know them again?'

'The police asked . . . they want me to look at photographs . . . but I don't know . . . I was trying to avoid being hurt . . . I tried to put my hands in front of my face . . . and I shut my eyes . . .'

'How about your grandfather?'

'He says he might know them . . . but it was over so quickly, really.'

'I suppose they didn't tell you what papers they were looking for?'

She shook her head miserably. 'The police asked me that, over and over.'

'Never mind,' I said. 'How does your face feel now?'

'Awfully stiff. Dr West gave me some pills, though. He says he'll look in again tomorrow.'

'Here?'

'Yes . . . I didn't want to go back to Grandad's. This . . . this is . . . home.'

'Do you want the bed made properly?'

'No thank you. I'm comfortable like this . . . too tired to move.'

'I'll go down, then, and give your grandfather a hand.'

'All right . . .' Anxiety flooded her suddenly. 'But you won't go, will you?'

I promised her, and in fact I slept in trousers and shirt on the sofa in the sitting-room on a cleared oasis amid the rubble. William Romney, taxed almost too far, snored gently with a strong sedative on the double bed in the Shermans' own room, and from three o'clock to five the cottage was dark and quiet.

I awoke suddenly with a soft wail in my ears like the sound of a lamb in a snowstorm.

'David . . .'

It was Emma's voice from upstairs, urgent and quavery.

I tossed off the rug, stood up, and beat it up there fast. I'd left her door open and the fire on, and as I went in I could see the ultimate disaster looking out of her great dark eyes.

'David . . .' Her voice filled with inconsolable desolation. 'David . . . I'm bleeding.'

She lost the baby and very nearly her life. I went to see her three days after she'd been whisked away in a bell-ringing ambulance (three days because no one was allowed in sooner) and was surprised to discover that she could and did look even paler than she had in Oslo. The swellings had gone down in her face, though the bruises showed dark in patches. Her eyes were dulled, which seemed a mercy.

The five minutes visit passed on the surface.

'Nice of you to come,' she said.

'Brought you some grapes.'

'Very kind.'

'Sorry about the baby.'

She nodded vaguely, but some sort of drug was dealing with that pain also.

'Hope you'll soon be better.'

'Oh yes. Yes, I will.'

William Romney shook with fury, stamping up and down my office with outrage.

'Do you realize that it is a week tomorrow since we were attacked and no one has done *anything*? People can't just vanish into thin air . . . those men must be somewhere . . . why can't the police find them? It isn't right that thugs should just walk into a defenceless girl's house and tear things to pieces and hurt her so much that she nearly dies of it . . . It's *disgraceful* that the police haven't found those despicable *bastards* . . .'

The word was a strong one for him: he looked almost surprised that he'd used it, and nothing could have more clearly stated the fierceness of his feelings.

'I believe neither you nor Emma could identify the men from police photographs,' I said, having checked via a friendly police contact that this was so.

'They weren't there. There weren't any pictures of them. Can't say that's surprising . . . why don't the police get photographs of *Norwegian* crooks for us to look at?'

'It would probably mean your going to Norway,' I said. 'And Emma's in no state, physical or emotional, to do that.'

'I'll go then,' he said belligerently. 'I'll go, at my own expense. Anything . . . *anything* to see those men punished for what they've done to Emma.'

His thin face was flushed with the strength of his resentment. I wondered if part of his fury sprang from unnecessary guilt that he hadn't been young and strong enough to defend or rescue her from two aggressive toughs. Amends in the shape of effort and expense were what he was offering, and I saw no reason to dissuade him from a journey which would bring him mental ease even if no concretely helpful results.

'I'll fix it for you, if you like,' I said.

'What . . .?'

'To go to Norway and look at the mug-shots.'

His resolution took shape and hardened. He straightened

his stooping shoulders, calmed his voice, and stopped wearing out so much of the Jockey Club's carpet.

'Yes. Please do that. I'll go as soon as I can.'

I nodded. 'Sit down,' I said. 'Do you smoke? And how's Emma?'

He sat down, declined a desk-box of cigarettes, and said that last evening, when he'd seen her, Emma was very much stronger.

'She says she'll be out of hospital in two or three days.'

'Good.'

He didn't look as if it were good. He said in recurring worried anger, 'What on earth is that poor girl going to do? Her husband murdered . . . her home wrecked . . . I suppose she can live with me, but . . .'

'I'm sure she'll live in her own house,' I said. 'For a while, at least. Best if she does. Get her grieving done properly.'

'What an extraordinary thing to say.'

'When can you go?' I said, reaching for the telephone.

'At once.'

'Right.'

Øvrevoll racecourse answered in the shape of the manager who gave me the home and office telephone numbers of Lars Baltzersen. He answered from his office, and I explained the situation. Of course, he said in dismay, of course he could arrange it with the police. For tomorrow? Certainly. Poor Mrs Sherman, he said, please give her my condolences. I said I would, and asked if there had been any recent progress.

'None at all, I'm afraid,' he said. He hesitated for several seconds, and then went on, 'I have been thinking . . . I suppose . . . if the police don't solve this crime . . . that you wouldn't come back yourself, and see what you can do?'

I said, 'I'm not experienced in murder investigation.'

'It must in essence be the same as any other sort.'

'Mm . . . My masters here might not be willing for me to take the time.'

'If I asked them myself, as an international favour? After all, Bob Sherman was a British jockey.'

'Wouldn't Norway prefer to ship him home and forget about the whole nasty incident?'

'No, Mr Cleveland,' he said severely. 'A murder has been done, and justice should follow.'

'I agree.'

'Then . . . you'll come?'

I thought. 'Wait another week. Then if neither your police nor ours have found any new leads, and if you still want me to, well, maybe I can. But . . . don't expect too much, will you?'

'No more than before,' he said dryly, and disconnected.

William Romney had adjusted by then to the prospect of travelling the next day, and began to fuss mildly about tickets, currency and hotels. I shooed him out because he could do all that for himself, and I had a good deal of work on hand to start with, and more still if I had to clear time for another trip to Oslo. The police, I hoped, would quickly dig down to the roots themselves and save me from proving to the world that I couldn't.

William Romney went to Norway, spent two full days there and returned depressed. The Norwegian police did not have photographs of the intruders, or if they did, Romney did not recognize them.

Emma left hospital and went home to put her house straight. An offer from me to help her do that was declined; one to come down and take her out to lunch was accepted.

'Sunday?' I suggested.

'Fine.'

Sunday found the carpets flat on the floors, the pictures back on the walls, the broken mess cleared away, and the curtains bundled up for the cleaners. The house looked stark and unlived-in, but its mistress had come a long way back to life. For the first time since I had known her, she was wearing lipstick. Her hair was newly washed, her clothes neat, her manner composed. The pretty girl lurked not far away now, just below the still over-pale skin, just behind the still unhappy eyes.

'It's his funeral on Thursday,' she said.

'Here?'

She nodded. 'In the church in the village. Thank you for doing everything about bringing him home.'

I had delegated the whole job. 'I only got it done,' I said.

'Anyway . . . thanks.'

The October day was calm and sunny and crisp round the edges. I took her to a Thames-side pub where pointed yellow willow leaves floated slowly past on grey water and anglers flicked maggots on hooks to wily fish. We walked along the bank; slowly, because she was still weak from haemorrhage.

'Have you any plans?' I asked.

'I don't know . . . I've thought a lot, of course, while I've been in hospital. I'll go on living in the cottage for a while, I think. It feels right, somehow. In the end I suppose I'll sell it, but not yet.'

'How are the finances?'

She produced a flicker of smile. 'Everyone is being fantastic. Really marvellous. Did you know, the owners Bob rode for in Norway clubbed together and sent me a cheque? How kind people are.'

Conscience money, I thought sourly, but I didn't say so.

'Those two men who burst into your house, do you mind if we talk about them?'

She sighed. 'I don't mind.'

'Describe them.'

'But . . .'

'Yes, I've read what you told the police. You didn't look at them, you shut your eyes, you only saw their sweaters and their rubber gloves.'

'That's right.'

'No. What you told the police was all you could bear to remember, and you would have shut out even that if they hadn't pressed you for answers.'

'That's nonsense.'

'Try it another way. Which one hit you?'

She said instantly, 'The bigger one with the ...' Her voice stopped uncertainly.

'With the what?'

'I was going to say, with the reddish hair. How odd. I didn't remember until now that one of them had reddish hair.'

'What about the other?'

'Brown. Brown hair. He was kicking Grandad.'

'The one who was hitting you ... what was he saying?'

' "Where does your husband keep secret papers? Where does he hide things? Tell us where he hides things." '

'Good English?'

'Ye-es. Pretty good. He had an accent.'

'What were his eyes like, while he was hitting you?'

'Fierce ... frightful ... like an eagle ... sort of black and yellow ... very angry.'

There was a small silence, then she said, 'Yes, I do remember, like you said. I shut it out.'

After a few seconds, 'He was quite young, about the same as you. His mouth was very tight ... his lips were stiff ... his face looked hard ... very angry.'

'How tall?'

'Same as you, about. Broader, though. Much heavier. Big thick shoulders.'

'Big shoulders in a thick sweater. What sort of thick sweater? Did it have a pattern?'

'Well, yes, that was why ...' She stopped again.

'Why what?'

'Why I thought at once that he was Norwegian ... before he even spoke. Because of the patterns in his sweater. They were sort of white patterns ... two colours, though, I think ... all over a brown sweater. I'd seen dozens like it in the shops in Oslo.' She looked puzzled. 'Why didn't I think of that before?'

'Memories often work like that. Sort of delayed action.'

She smiled. 'I must say it's easier remembering things quietly here by the river than in all that mess with my face hurting and policemen asking me questions from all sides and bustling about . . .'

We went indoors for a drink and a good lunch, and over coffee I asked her other things.

'You said Bob never hid papers. Are you sure?'

'Oh yes. He wasn't secretive. Never. He was more careless, really, than anything else, when it came to papers and documents and things like that.'

'It seems quite extraordinary that two men should come all the way from Norway to search your house for papers.'

She frowned. 'Yes, it does.'

'And to search it so violently, so destructively, so thoroughly.'

'And they were so angry, too.'

'Angry, I expect, because they'd worked hard and hadn't found what they'd come for.'

'But what *did* they come for?'

'Well . . .' I said slowly. 'Something to do with Norway. What papers did Bob ever have that had anything to do with Norway?'

She shook her head. 'Nothing much. A few receipts, for the accounts. Race-cards, sometimes. A cutting from a Norwegian paper with a picture of him winning a race. Nothing, honestly, that anyone could want.'

I drank my coffee, considering. I said, 'Look at it the other way round . . . Did he ever take any papers *to* Norway?'

'No. Why should he?'

'I don't know. I just wondered. Because those men might have been looking for something he hadn't taken to Norway, not for something he had brought away.'

'You do think some weird things.'

'Mm . . .'

I paid the bill and drove her home. She was silent most of the way, but thoughtful, and the fruit of that was a plum.

'I suppose . . . well, it's stupid, really . . . but it couldn't have anything to do with blue pictures?'

'What sort of blue pictures?' I asked.

'I don't know. I didn't see them. Only Bob said that's what they were.'

I pulled up outside her gate but made no move to leave the car.

'Did he get them in Norway?'

She was surprised. 'Oh no. It was like you said. He was taking them over there with him. In a brown envelope. It came by hand the night before he went. He said they were blue pictures which a chap in Oslo wanted him to bring over.'

'Did he say what chap?'

She shook her head. 'No. I hardly listened. I'd forgotten all about it until you said . . .'

'Did you see the brown envelope? How big was it?'

'I must have seen it. I mean, I know it was brown.' She frowned, concentrating. 'Fairly big. Not an ordinary letter. About the size of a magazine.'

'Was it marked "photographs", or anything like that?'

'I don't think so. I can't remember. It's more than six weeks ago.' Her eyes filled suddenly with tears. 'He put it in his overnight grip at once, so as not to forget to take it.' She sniffed twice, and found a handkerchief. 'So he did take it to Norway. It wasn't in the house for those men to find. If that's what they were looking for . . . they did all that for nothing.' She put the handkerchief to her mouth and stifled a sob.

'Was Bob interested in blue pictures?' I asked.

'Like any other man, I suppose,' she said through the handkerchief. 'He'd look at them.'

'But he wouldn't collect them himself?'

She shook her head.

I got out of the car, opened the door her side, and went with her into the cottage. She looked at the racing pictures of Bob which hung in the hall.

'They tore all those photographs out of the frames,' she said. 'Some of them were ruined.'

Many of the prints were about ten inches by eight. A magazine-sized brown envelope would have held them easily.

I stayed another hour simply to keep her company, but for the evening ahead she insisted that she would be all right alone. She looked round the barenesses of the sitting-room and smiled to herself. She obviously found the place friendly, and maybe Bob was there too.

When I went she gave me a warm kiss on the cheek and said, 'I can't thank you enough . . .' and then broke off and opened her eyes wide.

'Golly,' she said. 'That was the second lot.'

'What of?'

'Blue pictures. He took some before. Oh . . . months ago. Back in the summer.' She shook her head in fresh frustration. 'I can't remember. I just remember him saying . . . blue pictures.'

I kissed her in return.

'Take care of yourself,' I said.

'You, too.'

CHAPTER EIGHT

A little matter of doping-to-win took me to Plumpton races in Sussex the following day but I saw no harm in some extra spadework on the side. Rinty Ranger, busy in second and fifth races, was comparatively easy to pin down between the third and the fourth.

'What did you say?' he repeated in exaggerated amazement. 'Take pornography to Scandinavia? Christ, that's like wasting pity on bookmakers. They don't need it, mate. They don't bloody need it.'

'Bob Sherman told his wife he was taking blue pictures to Norway.'

'And she believed it?'

'The point is, did he?'

'He never said a word about it to me.'

'Do me a favour,' I said. 'Find out in the changing-room here today if anyone ever asked any jockey to act as a messenger . . . a carrier . . . of any papers of any sort from Britain to Norway.'

'Are you serious?'

'Bob Sherman's dead.'

'Yes.' He thought. 'OK.'

He gave me a noncommittal wave as he walked out to the fifth, in which he rode a bright, tight, tactical race to be beaten half a length by a better horse, but came straight out of the weighing room after he had changed and put an end to my easy theory.

'None of them who have ridden in Norway has ever been asked to take over any papers or pictures or anything like that.'

'Would they say, if they had?'

He grinned. 'Depends how much they'd been paid to forget.'

'What do you think yourself?'

'Hard to tell. But they all seemed surprised. There weren't any knowing looks, sort of, if you see what I mean.'

'Carry on asking, would you? Tomorrow and so on. Say they can tell me hush hush, if they like. No kick backs if they've been fiddling currency.'

He grinned again. 'Some copper you are. Bend the rules like curling tongs.'

That evening I telephoned Baltzersen at his home. There was no news, he said. He had consulted his friends in the police, and they would raise no objections if I joined the hunt. On the contrary, they would, as before, let me see what they'd got, to save me reploughing their furrows.

'So, Mr Cleveland, will you come?'

'I guess so,' I said.

With flattering relief he said, 'Good, good,' explosively, and added, 'come tomorrow.'

' 'Fraid I can't. I have to give evidence in court tomorrow, and the case may last two days. Soonest would be Thursday morning.'

'Come straight to the racecourse then. We have a meeting on Thursday and another on Sunday, but I fear they may be the last this year. It's a little colder now, and we have had frost.'

I wrote 'warm clothes' in large letters on my memo pad and said I'd see him at the races.

'By the way,' I said. 'You know I told you the people who broke into the Shermans' house were looking for papers? Mrs Sherman now remembers that Bob took with him to Norway a packet which had been entrusted to him, which he believed contained blue pictures. Did anyone mention to you, or to the police, or to Arne in all those preliminary investigations into his disappearance, anything at all about his bringing such a packet with him, or delivering it?'

There was an unexpectedly long silence on the other end of the line, but in the end he only said uncertainly, 'Blue pictures . . . what are those?'

'Pornography.'

'I see.' Another pause. 'Please explain a little.'

I said, 'If the package reached its destination, then it cannot be that particular package that the men were searching for. So I could stop chasing after innocent blue pictures and start looking elsewhere.'

'*Ja*. I see.' He cleared his throat. 'I haven't heard of any such package, but perhaps Arne or the police have done. I will ask them. Of course you know it is unlikely that anyone would need to bring pornography secretly into this country?'

'It would have to be special,' I said, and left it at that.

All Tuesday and Wednesday morning I spent in court giving evidence for the prosecution in an insurance swindle involving grievous cruelty to horses, and Wednesday afternoon I sat in the office juggling six jobs at once like some multi-armed Siva. Looking for Bob Sherman's murderer had meant advancing myself a week's leave when I was too busy to take one, and by seven o'clock when I locked up and left, I was wishing he'd got himself bumped off at any other time.

I went home on tube and feet, thinking comforting thoughts about a large scotch indoors followed by a stroll round to a local grill for a steak. I shut the street door without letting it bang, put one foot in front of the other up the carpeted stairs, unlocked the door to my own flat and switched on the lights; and it was at that point that the day stopped operating according to schedule.

I heard, felt, maybe assimilated by instinct, a change in the air behind me. Nothing as definite as a noise. More a current. Undoubtedly a threat.

All those useful dormant jungle reactions came to my rescue before a thought process based on reason had time to get off the ground. So I was already whipping round to face the stairs and pushing further through my own doorway when the man with the knife did his best to send me early to the cemetery.

He did not have reddish hair, angry yellow eagle eyes or a Norwegian sweater. He did have rubber gloves, a stocky muscular body, a lot of determination and a very sharp blade.

The stab which had been supposed to stop my heart from the back ripped instead through some decent Irish tweed, through a blue cotton shirt below that, and down half a dozen inches of skin on my chest.

He was surprised and fed up that at first he hadn't succeeded, but he'd heard all about try try again. He crowded through my door after me with the knife already rising for another go. I backed through the tiny hall and into the sitting-room, unable to take my eyes off his intentions long enough to find any household object to fight him off with.

He came on with a feint and a slice at my middle regions and I got another rip in my jacket and a closer look at some narrowed and murderous eyes.

He tried next a sort of lunging jump, the point of the knife coming in fast and upward. I tried to leap away backwards, tripped on a rug, fell on my back and found my hand hitting the base of the standard lamp. One wild clutch and I'd pulled it over, knocking him off his aim just when he thought he finally had me. The lamp hit him with a crash and while he was off balance I got both my hands on his knife arm; but it was then that I discovered the rock-like muscles. And also, unfortunately, that he was more or less ambidexterous.

He shifted the knife like lightning from his right hand to his left and I avoided the resulting stab only by a sort of swinging jump over an armchair, using his arm as a lever. The blade hit a cushion and feathers floated up like snow-flakes.

I threw a cigarette box at him and missed, and after that a vase which hit but made no difference. As long as I kept the armchair between us he couldn't reach me, but neither did he give me much chance of getting past him to the still open door to the stairs.

Behind me on a wide shelf stood my portable television. I supposed it might stop him if I threw it at him, but on the other hand . . . I stretched out backwards without losing sight of his knife, found the on-off switch, and turned the volume up to maximum.

The din when it started took him totally by surprise and gave me a fractional chance. I pushed the armchair viciously forward at his knees and he overbalanced, twisting as he tried to get his feet under him. He went down as far as one knee, partially recovered, and toppled altogether when I shoved again with the chair. But it was nothing permanent. He was rolling back to his feet like a cat before I had time to get round the big chair and step on some of his tender bits.

Up until that point he had said not a word and now if he did I wouldn't hear: the television literally vibrated with the intense noise of some pop star or other's Special Spectacular; and if that didn't bring the US cavalry, nothing would.

He came. Looking cross. Ready to blow like a geyser. And stood there in consternation in my open door.

'Fetch the police,' I yelled, but he didn't hear. I slapped the off switch.

'Fetch the police,' I yelled again, and my voice bounced off the walls in the sudden silence.

The man with the knife turned to see, gave himself fresh instructions, and went for my friend from downstairs. I did a sort of sliding rugger tackle, throwing myself feet first at his legs. He stumbled over my shoes and ankles and went down on his side. I swept one leg in an arc and by sheer good luck kicked him on the wrist. The knife flew out of his hand at least ten feet, and fell nearer to me than him, and only at that point did he think of giving up.

He scrambled to his feet, looked at me with the first sign of uncertainty, then made up his mind, turned on his heel, crashed past my neighbour and jumped down the stairs in two giant strides. The front door slammed behind him with a force that shook the building, and from the window I saw him running like the Olympics under the street lamps.

I looked breathlessly at the mess in my sitting-room and at my man from downstairs.

'Thanks,' I said.

He took a tentative step into the sitting-room.

'You're bleeding,' he said.

'But not dying.'

I picked up the standard lamp.

'Was he a burglar?' he asked.

'A murderer,' I said. 'Enter a murderer.'

We looked at each other in what was no doubt professional curiosity on both sides, because all he said next was, 'Sit down, you're suffering from shock.'

It was advice I'd given pretty often to others, and it made me smile. All the same there was a perceptible tremble somewhere around my knees, so I did as he said.

He looked around the room, looked at the knife still lying where it had fallen, and took it all quietly.

'Shall I carry out your instructions, or were they principally a diversion?'

'Hm?'

'Fetch the police.'

'Oh . . . It can wait a bit.'

He nodded, considered a moment, and then said, 'If you'll excuse me asking, why was he trying to kill you?'

'He didn't say.'

My neighbour's name was Stirling. C. V. Stirling, according to the neat white card beside his bell push. He had grey patches neatly brushed back over his ears and nostrils pinched into an expression of distaste for bad smells. His hands looked excessively clean and well manicured, and even in these bizarre circumstances he wore a faint air of exasperated patience. A man used to being the brightest person around, I guessed, with the power to make it felt.

'Did he need to?'

'It would have been helpful,' I said.

He came a pace nearer.

'I could do something about that bleeding, if you like.'

I looked down at the front of my shirt, which had changed colour pretty thoroughly from blue to red.

'Could you?'

'I'm a surgeon,' he said. 'Ear, nose and throat, actually. Other areas by arrangement.'

I laughed. 'Stitch away, then.'

He nodded, departed downstairs, and returned with a neat flat case containing the tools of his trade. He used clips not needles. The slice through my skin was more gory than deep, bleeding away persistently like a shaving nick. When he'd finished, it was a thin red line under a sticking plaster.

'You were lucky,' he said.

'Yes, I was.'

'Do you do this sort of thing often? Fight for your life, I mean.'

'Very rarely.'

'My fee for professional services rendered is a little more chat.'

I smiled wryly.

'OK. I'm an investigator. I don't know why I was

attacked unless there's someone around who particularly does not want to be investigated.'

'Good God.' He stared at me curiously. 'A private eye? Philip Marlowe, and all that?'

'Nothing so fancy. I work in racing; for the Jockey Club. Looking into small frauds, most of the time.'

'This,' he waved at my chest and the knife and the scattered cushion feathers, 'doesn't look like a small fraud.'

It didn't. It didn't look, either, even like a severe warning off. It looked like a ruthless all-out push for a final solution.

I changed my clothes and took him round to the grill for the overdue steak. His name was Charles, he said, and we walked home as friends. When I let myself in upstairs and reviewed the general untidiness it occurred to me that in the end I had never called in the police. It seemed a little late to bother, so I didn't.

CHAPTER NINE

I caught the eleven twenty-five to Norway the next morning with the knife wrapped in polythene in my sponge-bag; or rather the black, zipped-leather case which did that duty. It was a hunter's knife, the sort of double-sided blade used for skinning and disjointing game. The cutting edges had been sharpened like razors and the point would have been good as a needle. A professional job: no amateur could have produced that result with a few passes over a carborundum.

The handle was of horn of some sort, but workmanlike, not tourist-trap stuff. Between handle and blade protruded a short silver bar for extra leverage with fingers. There were no fingerprints on it anywhere, and no blood. Punched into the blade near the hilt were the words *Norsk Stål.*

Its owner hadn't, of course, intended to leave it behind. Just one dead body neatly disposed inside its own front door, out of sight and undiscovered for a minimum of twenty-four hours.

He hadn't followed me into the house: he'd been there before I came, waiting higher up the stairs for me to come home.

At breakfast time I'd knocked on the doors of the other three tenants, the one in the basement, the one above me, and the one above that, and asked them if they'd seen my visitor on the stairs or let him in through the front door. I got negatives all round, but as one of them said, we were hardly a matey lot, and if the visitor entered boldly while one of the tenants was leaving, no one would have stopped him. None of them remembered him, but the basement man observed that as the laundry van had called that day, a stranger could easily have walked in with the man who collected and delivered the boxes from the hall.

There had been nothing suspicious or memorable about my visitor's appearance. His face was a face: hair brown, skin sallow, eyes dark. Age, about thirty. Clothes, dark grey trousers, navy close-fitting sweater, neat shirt and tie showing at the neck. Entirely the right rig for the neighbourhood. Even a little formal.

BEA landed on time at Fornebu and I took a taxi straight out to the racecourse. Nothing much had changed in the two and a half weeks I'd been away, not even the weather or the runners in the races, and within the first half hour I had spotted all the same faces, among them Gunnar Holth, Paddy O'Flaherty, Per Bjorn Sandvik, Rolf Torp and Lars Baltzersen. Arne greeted me with a beaming smile and an invitation to spend as much time with Kari and himself as I could.

I walked around with him for most of the afternoon, partly from choice, partly because Baltzersen was busy being Chairman. Arne said that whereas he personally was pleased to see me, many of the racecourse committee had opposed Baltzersen in the matter of bringing me back.

'Lars told us at the Tuesday committee meeting that you were definitely coming today, and that caused quite a row.

You should have heard it. Lars said that the racecourse would be paying your fare and expenses like last time, and half of them said it was unjustifiable to spend so much.'

He broke off rather suddenly as if he had decided not to repeat what had actually been said.

'I could easily have been persuaded to stay at home,' I said. But by words, I reflected. Not knives.

'Several of the committee said Lars had no right to act without taking a vote.'

'And Lars?'

Arne shrugged. 'He wants Bob Sherman's death explained. Most of them just want to forget.'

'And you?' I asked.

He blinked. 'Well,' he said, 'I would give up more easily than Lars or you. Which is no doubt why,' he grinned, 'Lars is Chairman and you are the chief investigator, and I am only a security officer who lets the racecourse takings be stolen from under his nose.'

I smiled. 'No one blames you.'

'Perhaps they should.'

I thought in my intolerant way that they definitely should, but I shook my head and changed the subject.

'Did Lars tell you all about the attack on Emma Sherman, and about her losing her baby?'

'Yes,' he said. 'Poor girl.' There was more lip-service in his voice than genuine regret. I supposed that no one who hadn't seen her as I had could properly understand all that she'd suffered; and I knew that it was in great part because of Emma that I was back in Norway. No one should be allowed to inflict such hurt on another human being, and get away with it. The fact that the same agency had murdered Bob and tried to see me off was in a curious way secondary: it was possible future victims who had to be saved. If you don't dig ground elder out of the flower beds it can strangle the garden.

Rolf Torp was striding about in a bad temper. His horse, he said, had knocked itself that morning and his trainer had omitted to tell him it couldn't run. He had taken the afternoon off from his mining office, which he wouldn't have done if he'd known, on account of being indispensable and nothing constructive ever being achieved in his absence.

After he had delivered himself of that little lot he adjusted his sights more specifically on me.

'I was against bringing you back. I'll tell you that myself. I told the committee. It is a waste of our money.'

His name was on the list Emma had given me of the contributors to the solidly worthwhile cheque the Norwegian owners had sent. If he thought that any available cash should only be spent on the living, perhaps it was a valid point of view; but he wasn't paying my expenses out of his own private pocket.

He was a man of less than average height and more than average aggressiveness: a little bull of a man with a large black moustache that was more a statement than an adornment. Difficult to please and difficult to like, I thought, but sharp of eye and brain as well as tongue.

His voice boomed as heavily as a bittern in the reed beds, and although his English was as comprehensive as most well-educated Norwegians', he spoke it unlovingly, as if he didn't care too much for the taste.

I said without heat, 'As a miner, you'll understand that surveys are a legitimate expense even when they don't strike ore.'

He gave me a hard look. 'As a miner I understand that I would not finance a survey to find slime.'

Klonk. One over the head for D. Cleveland. I grinned appreciatively, and slowly, unwillingly, the corners of his mouth twitched.

I made the most of it. 'May I come and see you in your office?' I asked. 'Just for a few questions. I might as well try my best to earn what you're paying me, now that I'm here.'

'Nothing I can tell you will be of any help,' he said, as if believing made it so.

'Still . . .'

The vestiges of smile disappeared, but finally, grudgingly, he nodded.

'Very well. Tomorrow afternoon. Four o'clock.' And he went so far as to tell me how to find him.

As he walked away Arne said, 'What are you going to ask him?'

'Don't know yet. I just want to see his background. You can't tell what people are really like if you only meet them at the races.'

'But,' he said, blinking furiously, 'why Rolf Torp?'

'Not especially Rolf Torp,' I said. 'Everyone who knew Bob Sherman.'

'David!' He looked staggered. 'It will take you months.'

I shook my head. 'Several days, that's all. Bob didn't know so many people here as all that.'

'But he could have been killed by a total stranger. I mean, if he saw someone stealing the money and didn't know him . . .'

'It's possible,' I said, and asked him if he had ever heard Bob talking about bringing any sort of package from England to Norway.

Arne wrinkled his forehead and darted a compulsive look over his shoulder. No one there, of course.

'Lars mentioned this mysterious package on Tuesday night. No one knew anything about it.'

'What did Lars actually ask?'

'Just said you wanted to know if anyone had received a package from Bob Sherman.'

'And no one had?'

'No one who was there, anyway.'

'Could you write me a list of those who were there?'

'Yes,' he said with surprise. 'If you want it. But I can't see what it could possibly have to do with Bob's death.'

'I'm a great one for collecting useless information,' I said, smiling, and Arne gave me a look which said, oh yeah, plain as plain.

The races proceeded the same as before, except that the watching crowd was a good deal thinner than on Grand National day. The birch trees had dropped most of their yellow leaves and looked silver, the daylight was colder and greyer than ever, and a sharp wind whipped round every corner. But this time I had come prepared with a skiing cap with ear flaps and only my nose, like everyone else's, was turning blue.

Gunnar Holth saddled two for the hurdle race, hurrying busily from one to the other and juggling both sets of owners with anxious dexterity. One of his runners was the dappled mare with the uncertain temper, whose owner, Sven Wangen, was on Emma's list. Arne confirmed that the big young man assiduously hopping out of the way every time the mare presented her heels was indeed Sven Wangen, and added that the brunette sneering at him from a safe distance was his wife.

The jockey mounted warily and the mare bucked and kicked every inch to the start. Arne said that like all mean, bad-tempered females she would get her own way in the end, and went off to invest a little something on the Tote.

Wise move. She won. Arne beamed and said what did I tell you, when she comes here bitching she always wins. Was she ever docile? I asked, and Arne said sure, but those were her off days. We watched her being unsaddled in the winner's enclosure, with Gunnar Holth and Sven Wangen both tangoing smartly out of her way.

I told Arne I would like to meet Sven Wangen because Bob had ridden a winner for him on that last day. Arne showed reservations, so I asked him why.

He pursed his mouth. 'I don't like him. That's why.'

'What's wrong with him?'

'Too much money,' Arne said reprovingly. 'He behaves as if everyone ought to go on their knees when they talk to him. He has done nothing himself. The money was his father's. His father was a rich man. Too rich.'

'In what way too rich?'

Arne raised his eyebrows at what evidently seemed to him a nonsensical question, because from the tone of his reply it seemed he held great wealth to be morally wrong.

'He was a millionaire.'

'Don't you have millionaires in Norway?'

'Very few. They are not popular.'

I persuaded him, however, to introduce me to the unpopular Sven Wangen, whose father had made a million out of ships: and I saw at once why Arne didn't like him.

Perhaps two inches taller than I, he looked down his nose as if from a great height: and it was clear that this was no accidental mannerism but the manifestation of deep self-importance. Still probably in his twenties, he was bulky to the point of fatness and used his weight for throwing about. I didn't take to his manner, his small mouth, or his unfriendly light-amber eyes: nor, in fact, to his wife, who looked as if she could beat the difficult mare's temper by a couple of lengths.

Arne introduced me, and Sven Wangen saw no reason at all why I should call upon him at any time to ask him questions. He had heavy, rust-brown hair growing long over his ears, and a small flat cap which made his big head look bigger.

I said I understood he was a member of the racecourse committee which had asked me to come.

'Lars Baltzersen asked you,' he said brusquely. 'I was against it. I said so on Tuesday.'

'The sooner I get the questions answered, the sooner I'll go home,' I said. 'But not until.'

He looked at me with intense disfavour. 'What do you want, then?'

'Half an hour in your house,' I said. 'Any time that would suit you except for tomorrow afternoon.'

He settled in irritation for Sunday morning. His elegantly thin wife manufactured a yawn and they turned away without any pretence of politeness.

'See what I mean?' Arne said.

'I do indeed. Very unusual, wouldn't you say?'

'Unusual?'

'The rich don't usually behave like that.'

'Do you know so many rich people?' Arne asked with a touch of sarcasm.

'Meet them every day of the week,' I said. 'They own racehorses.'

Arne conceded that the rich weren't necessarily all beastly and went off on some official tasks. I tracked down Paddy O'Flaherty and found him with five minutes to spare between races.

'Brown envelope of blue pictures?' he repeated. 'He never said a dicky bird to me, now, about any blue pictures.' He grinned, and then an uncertain memory floated back. 'Wait now, I tell a lie. Back in the summer, now, he told me he had a good little tickle going for him, do you see? Always one for a chance at easy money, so he was. And there was this day, he winked at me like, and showed me the corner of an envelope in his overnight bag, and he said it would make our hair curl, so it would. So then I asked him for a look, do you see, but he said it was sealed some way so he couldn't steam it. I remember that, sure now I do.'

'The last time he came, did he say anything about bringing an envelope?'

Paddy shook his head. 'Like I said. Not a word.'

I thought. 'Did he come straight to your stable from the airport? Did he arrive on time, for instance?'

'I'll tell you something now. No, he didn't.' He concentrated. 'He was that late I thought he'd missed the flight and would come in the morning. Then, sure, a taxi rolls up and out he hops, large as life. He'd bought a bottle of brandy on the plane and there wasn't much left of that, now, before we went to bed.'

'What did he talk about?'

'Bejasus, how do I know, after all this time?'

'You must have thought often about that night.'

'Well, so I have, then.' He sighed at my perseverance, but thought some more. 'Horses, of course. We talked about horses. I don't remember him saying why he was late, or anything like that. And sure now I'd have thought it was the flight that was late, that was all.'

'I'll check,' I said.

'Look now, there was only one thing he said . . . Late on,

when we'd maybe had a skinful, he said "Paddy, I think I've been conned." That's what he said now. "Paddy I think I've been conned." So I asked him what he meant, but he didn't tell me.'

'How insistently did you ask?'

'Insist . . . ? Bejasus, of course I didn't. Uh . . . there he was putting his finger over his mouth and nodding . . . he was a bit tight, do you see? So I just put my finger over my mouth like him and I nodded just the same. Well now, it seemed sensible enough at the time do you see?'

I did see. It was a miracle Paddy remembered that evening at all.

The afternoon ambled on. Gunnar Holth won the steeplechase with Per Bjørn Sandvik's Whitefire, which displeased Rolf Torp, who was second. Per Bjørn, it appeared, had not come to the meeting: he rarely did on Thursdays, because it showed a bad example to his staff.

It was Lars Baltzersen who told me this, with warm approval in his voice. He himself, he said, had to leave his work only because he was Chairman, and all his employees understood. As one who had played lifelong truant at the drop of a starter's flag I found such noble standards a bit stifling, but one had to admire them.

Lars and I crossed the track and climbed the tower and looked down at the pond below. With its surface ruffled by the breeze it was far less peaceful than when I'd first seen it and just as brownly muddy as the day it gave up its dead. The swans and the ducks had gone.

'It will freeze soon,' Lars said. 'And snow will cover the racecourse for three or four months.'

'Bob Sherman is being buried today,' I said. 'In England.'

He nodded. 'We have sent a letter of regret to Mrs Sherman.'

'And a cheque,' I said; because his name too was on the list. He made a disclaiming movement with his hands but seemed genuinely pleased when I told him how much Emma had appreciated their kindness.

'I'm afraid we were all a little annoyed with her while she was here. She was so persistent. But perhaps it was partly because of her that we asked you to come. Anyway, I am glad she is not bitter about the way we tried to avoid her continual questions. She would have a right to be.'

'She isn't that sort of person.'

He turned his head to look at me. 'Do you know her well?' he asked.

'Only since all this started.'

'I regret the way we treated her,' he said. 'I think of it often. Giving her money does not buy us off.'

I agreed with him and offered no comfort. He looked away down the racecourse and I wondered if it was his guilty conscience that had driven him to persuade me back.

After the next race, a long distance flat race, we walked across together to the weighing room.

I said, 'You were in the officials' room that day when Bob Sherman poked his head in and could have seen the money lying on the floor.'

'That's right,' Lars said.

'Well . . . what was the question?'

He was puzzled. 'What question?'

'Everyone's statement to the police was the same. You all said "Bob Sherman came to the door asking some question or other." So . . . what was the question?'

He looked deeply surprised. 'It can't have had anything to do with his disappearance.'

'What was it?'

'I can't remember. Nothing of the slightest importance, I assure you, or of course we would have told the police.'

We rejoined Arne, and Lars asked him if he by any chance remembered what Bob had wanted. Arne looked just as surprised and said he had no idea, he'd been busy anyway and probably hadn't even heard. The racecourse manager however knew that he had known once, because it was he who had answered.

'Let me think,' he said, frowning. 'He came in . . . not his feet, just his head and shoulders. He looked down at the money, which was lying in front of him. I remember that distinctly. I told the police. But the question . . . it was nothing.'

I shrugged. 'Tell me if you ever remember?'

He said he would as if he thought it unlikely, but an hour later he sought me out.

'Bob Sherman asked if Mikkel Sandvik had already gone home, and I said I didn't know.'

'Oh.'

He laughed. 'Well, we did tell you it was nothing important.'

'And you were right.' I sighed resignedly. 'It was just a chance.'

At the end of the afternoon Lars took me up to his Chairman's room to give me the copies the police had provided of their Bob Sherman file. He stood in front of the big stove, a neat, substantial figure in his heavy, dark blue overcoat and ear-flapped astrakhan hat, blowing on his fingers.

'Cold today,' he said.

I thought I probably knew him better than anyone I'd met in Norway, but all the same I said, 'May I call to see you in your office?'

He'd heard about my appointments and smiled wryly at being included. 'Saturday, if you like. I'll be there until noon.'

Declining a pressing invitation from Arne to dine with him and Kari, I ate early at the Grand and went upstairs to do my homework.

The police had been painstaking, but the net result, as Lars had said, was nil.

A long and immensely detailed autopsy report, filled with medical terms I only half understood, concluded that the deceased had died of three overlapping depressed fractures of the skull. Unconsciousness would have been immediate. Death followed a few minutes later: the exact interval could not be specified. Immersion was subsequent to death.

The nylon rope found on the deceased had been unravelled strand by strand, and an analysis had indicated it to be part of a batch manufactured the previous spring and distributed during the summer to countless shops and ships' chandlers throughout greater Oslo.

The nylon rope found embedded in a concrete block in the Øvrevoll pond was of identical composition.

The cement block itself was a sort of sandbag in wide-spread use for sea-walling. The type in the pond was very common, and none of the contractors currently using it could remember having one stolen. The writer of the report added his own personal opinion that no contractor would ever miss one single bag out of hundreds.

The properties of the bag were such that its ingredients were crumbly when dry, but solidified like rock under water. The nylon rope had been tied tightly round the cement bag while it had still been dry.

Extensive inquiries had dug up no one who had heard or seen any activity round the pond on either the night of the deceased's disappearance or the night he had been removed from the water. The night-watchman had proved a dead loss. There were lists of everything they had found in Bob Sherman's pockets and in his over-night bag. Clothes, watch, keys were all as they should be: it was papers I was interested in, and they, after a month submerged, were in a pretty pulpy state.

Passport and air ticket had been identified. Currency notes had been nearly all British: total value fifteen pounds sterling. There had been no Norwegian money to speak of, and certainly not five canvas bags of it.

The report made no mention of any papers or ruins of papers being found in the overnight bag. Nor of photographs: and photographic paper fared better than most under water.

I read everything through twice and drew no conclusions which the police hadn't. Bob Sherman had had his head bashed in, and later he'd been roped to a cement bag and dumped in the pond. By person or persons unknown.

By person or persons who were doing their damndest, also, to remain unknown.

I lifted the polythene-wrapped knife from my sponge case and propped it against the reading lamp; and immediately the slice down my chest took up throbbing where it had left off that morning. Why was it, I wondered irritably, that cuts only throbbed at night?

It was as well though to have that to remind me not to walk trustingly into hotel rooms or hail the first taxi that offered. Business had been meant in London, and I saw no safety in Oslo.

I smiled ruefully to myself. I was getting as bad as Arne at looking over my shoulder.

But there could be a lot more knives where that one came from.

CHAPTER TEN

In the morning I took the knife along to the police and told them how I'd come by it. The man in charge of the case, the same policeman who had been overseeing the dragging of the pond, looked at me in a sort of startled dismay.

'We will try to trace it, as you ask. But this knife is not rare. There are many knives of this kind. In English those words *Norsk Stål* on the blade merely mean Norwegian steel.'

His name was Lund. His air that of long-term policemen everywhere: cautious, watchful, friendly with reservations. It seemed to me that many policemen were only completely at ease with criminals; and certainly the ex-policemen who worked for the investigation branch of the Jockey Club always spoke of petty crooks more affectionately than of the general public.

Dedicated to catching them, policemen also admired criminals. They spoke the same language, used the same jargon. I knew from observation that if a crook and a detective who didn't know each other turned up at the same social gathering, they would unerringly seek each other out. Unless one of them happened to be chasing the other at that moment, they would get on well together; a fact which explained the apparently extraordinary shared holidays which occasionally scandalized the press.

Lund treated me with scrupulous fairness as a temporary colleague. I thanked him warmly for letting me use his files, and he offered help if I should need it.

I said at once that I needed a car with a driver I could trust, and could he recommend one.

He looked at the knife lying on his desk.

'I cannot lend you a police car.' He thought it over, then picked up a telephone, gave some Norwegian instructions, put down the receiver, and waited.

'I will ask my brother to drive you,' he said. 'He is an author. His books make little money. He will be pleased to earn some for driving, because he likes driving.'

The telephone buzzed and Lund evidently put forward his proposition. I gathered that it met with the author's approval because Lund asked when I would like him to start.

'Now,' I said. 'I'd like him to collect me here.'

Lund nodded, put down the receiver, and said, 'He will be here in half an hour. You will find him helpful. He speaks English very well. He worked once in England.'

I spent the half hour looking through mug-shots, but my London assailant was nowhere to be seen.

Lund's brother Erik was a bonus in every way.

He met me in the front hall with a vague distracted grin as if he had been waiting for someone else. A tallish man of about fifty-five, he had sparse, untidy blond hair, a shapeless old sports jacket, and an air of being totally disorganized: and he drove, I soon discovered, as if other cars were invisible.

He waved me from the police building to a small-sized cream Volvo waiting at the kerb. Dents and scratches of varying rust vintages bore witness to long and sturdy service, and the boot was held shut by string. Upon opening the passenger-side door I found that most of the interior was already occupied by a very large Great Dane.

'Lie down, Odin,' Erik said hopefully, but the huge dog understood no English, remained on his feet, and slobbered gently down my neck.

'Where first?' Erik asked. His English, as his brother had said, was splendid. He settled himself in the driver's seat and looked at me expectantly.

'What did your brother tell you?' I asked.

'To drive you around and if possible make sure no one bumps you off.' He said it as casually as if he'd been entrusted to see me on to the right train.

'What are you good at?' I said curiously.

'Driving, boxing and telling tales out of school.'

He had a long face, deeply lined round the eyes, smoother round mouth and chin: evidence of a nature more at home with a laugh than a scowl. In the course of the next few days I learnt that if it hadn't been for his highly-developed sense of the ludicrous, he would have been a dedicated communist. As it was he held good radical left wing views, but found himself in constant despair over the humourlessness of his fellow travellers. He had worked on the gossip pages of newspapers throughout his youth, and had spent two years in Fleet Street; and he told me more about the people he was driving me to visit than I would have dug out in six weeks.

'Per Bjørn Sandvik?' he repeated, when I told him our first destination. 'The upright man of the oil fields?'

'I guess so,' I said.

He took off into the traffic without waiting for a gap. I opened my mouth and shut it again: after all, if his brother was trusting him to keep me alive, the least I could do was let him get on with it. We swung round some hair-raising corners on two wheels but pulled up unscathed outside the main offices of Norsk Oil Imports Ltd. The Great Dane licked his great chops and looked totally unmoved.

'There you are,' Erik said, pointing to an imposing double-door entrance into a courtyard. 'Through there, turn left, big entrance with pillars.'

'You know it?'

He nodded. 'I know most places in Oslo. And most people.' And he told me about his years on the newspapers.

'Tell me about Per Bjørn, then.'

He smiled. 'He is stuffy, righteous, and has given himself to big business. During the war he wasn't like that at all. When we were all young, he was a great fighter against the Nazis, a great planner and saboteur. But the years go by and he has solidified into a dull lump, like the living core of a volcano pouring out and dying to dry, grey pumice.'

'He must have some fire left,' I objected. 'To be the head of an oil company.'

He blew down his nostrils in amusement. 'All the oil companies in Norway are tied hand and foot by government regulations, which is as it should be. There is no room for private speculation. Per Bjørn can only make decisions within a small area. For anything above ordering new ash-trays he has to have permission from the government.'

'You approve of that?'

'Naturally.'

'What do you know about his family?' I asked.

His eyes glimmered. 'He married a thoroughly boring plain girl called Ragnhild whose dad just happened at that time to be the head man in Norsk Oil Imports.'

I grinned and climbed out of the car, and told him I would be half an hour at least.

'I brought a book,' he said equably, and pulled a tattered paperback of *The Golden Notebook* out of his jacket pocket.

The courtyard, tidily paved, had a stone-edged bed of frostbitten flowers in the centre and distinguished pale yellow buildings all round the edge. The main entrance to the left was imposing, and opposite, to the right, stood a similar entrance on a much smaller scale. The wall facing the entrance from the street was pierced with tall windows and decorated with shutters, and the whole opulent little square looked more like a stately home than an oil company's office.

It was, I found, both.

Per Bjørn's secretary fielded me from the main entrance, shovelled me up one flight of carpeted stairs and into his office, told me Mr Sandvik was still at a meeting but would not be long, and went away.

Although the building was old the head man's room was modern, functional, and highly Scandinavian, with thickly double-glazed windows looking down into the courtyard. On the wall hung a simple chart of a rock formation with layers labelled impermeable, source, permeable and reservoir; a list saying things like spudded Oct 71, plugged and abandoned Jan 72; and three brightly-coloured maps of the North Sea, each of them showing a different aspect of the oil drilling operations going on there.

In each map the sea area was subdivided along lines of latitude and longitude into small squares which were labelled 'Shell', 'Esso', 'Conoco', and so on, but although I looked carefully I could see none marked Norsk Oil Imports.

The door opened behind me and Per Bjørn Sandvik came in, as pleasant and easy as ever and giving every impression of having got to the top without pushing.

'David,' he said in his high clear diction, 'sorry to keep you waiting.'

'Just looking at your maps,' I said.

He nodded, crossing to join me. 'We're drilling there . . . and there.' He pointed to two areas which bore an entirely different name. I commented on it, and he explained.

'We are part of a consortium. There are no private oil companies in Norway.'

'What did Norsk Oil Imports do before anyone discovered oil under the North Sea?'

'Imported oil, of course.'

'Of course.'

I smiled and sat down in the square armchair he indicated.

'Fire away,' he said, 'with the questions.'

'Did Bob Sherman bring you any papers or photographs from England?'

He shook his head. 'No. Lars asked us this on Tuesday. Sherman did not bring any papers for anyone.' He stretched out a hand towards his desk intercom. 'Would you like some coffee?'

'Very much.'

He nodded and asked his secretary to arrange it.

'All the same,' I said, 'he probably did bring a package of some sort with him, and he probably did pass it on. If anyone would admit to having received it we might be able to take it out of consideration altogether.'

He stared vaguely at his desk.

'For instance,' I said, 'if what he brought was straight pornography, it probably had nothing to do with his death.'

He looked up.

'I see,' he said. 'And because no one has said they received it, you think it did not contain pornography?'

'I don't know what it contained,' I said. 'I wish I did.'

The coffee arrived and he poured it carefully into dark brown crusty mugs.

'Have you discarded the idea that Bob Sherman was killed by whoever stole the money?'

'It's in abeyance,' I said, refusing the offered cream and sugar. 'Could you give me your impression of Bob Sherman as a man?'

He bunched his lips assessingly.

'Not over-intelligent,' he said. 'Honest, but easily influenced. A good rider, of course. He always rode well for me.'

'I gather Rolf Torp thought he rode a bad race for him that last day.'

Sandvik delicately shrugged. 'Rolf is sometimes hard to please.'

We drank the coffee and talked about Bob, and after a

while I said I would like very much to meet Per Bjørn's son, Mikkel.

He frowned. 'To ask him questions?'

'Well ... some. He knew Bob comparatively well, and he's the one good contact I've not yet met.'

He didn't like it. 'I can't stop you, of course. Or at least, I won't. But he has been very upset by the whole affair, first by thinking his friend was a thief, and now more since he knows he was murdered.'

'I'll try not to worry him too much. I've read his short statement to the police. I don't expect to do much more than cover the same ground.'

'Then why bother him at all?'

After a pause to consider it, I said, 'I think I need to see him, to get the picture of Bob's visits complete.'

He slowly sucked his lower lip but finally made no more objections.

'He's at boarding school now,' he said. 'But he'll be home here for the afternoon tomorrow. If you come at three, he'll be here.'

'Here ... in your office?'

He shook his head. 'In my house. The other side of the courtyard.'

I stood up to go and thanked him for his time.

'I haven't been of much use,' he said. 'We've given you a pretty hopeless job.'

'Oh well ...' I said, and told myself that things sometimes broke if one hammered on long enough. 'I'll do my best to earn your money.'

He saw me to the top of the stairs and shook hands.

'Let me know if there's anything I can do.'

'I will,' I said. 'And thank you.'

I walked down the quiet stairs to the large empty hall. The only sounds of life seemed to come from behind a door at the back of the hall, so I walked over and opened it.

It led, I found, straight into the next door building, one dedicated not to front offices but to getting the paper work done. Even there, however, things were going at a gentle pace without any feeling of pressure, and in the doorways of the row of small offices stretching away from me stood relaxed people in sweaters drinking coffee and smoking and generally giving no impression that commercial life was rushing by.

I retreated through the hall, through the courtyard, and back to Erik Lund. He withdrew his eyes from his Golden Notes as I climbed into his car and appeared to be wondering who I was.

Recognition of sorts awoke.

'Oh yes . . .' he said.

'Lunch, then?' I suggested.

He had few definite views on where to eat, but once we were installed in a decent restaurant he lost no time in ordering something he called *gravlaks*. The price made me wince on behalf of the racecourse, but I had some too, and it proved to be the most exquisite form of salmon, cured instead of smoked.

'Are you from Scotland Yard?' he asked after the last of the pink heaven had been dispatched.

'No. From the Jockey Club.'

It surprised him, so I explained briefly why I was there.

'What's all this about being bumped off, then?'

'To stop me finding out what happened.'

He gazed past me in thought.

'Makes my brother Knut a dumb cluck, doesn't it? No one's tried to get rid of *him*.'

'Knock down one policeman and six more pop up,' I said.

'And there aren't six more of you?' he asked dryly.

'The racing cupboard's pretty bare.'

He drank coffee thoughtfully. 'Why don't you give it up while you're still whole?'

'Natural bloody obstinacy,' I said. 'What do you know about Rolf Torp?'

'Rolf Torp the terror of the ski slopes or Rolf Torp who designs glass houses for pygmies?'

'Rolf Torp who owns racehorses and does something in mines.'

'Oh. Him.' He frowned, sniffed, and grimaced. 'Another goddam capitalist exploiting the country's natural resources for private gain.'

'Do you know anything about him personally?'

'Isn't that personal enough?'

'No.'

He laughed. 'You don't think money-grubbing says anything about a man's soul?'

'Everything any man does says something about his soul.'

'You wriggle out of things,' he said.

'And things out of people.'

'Well,' he said smiling, 'I can't actually tell you much about that Rolf Torp. For one thing I've never met him, and for another, capitalists make dull copy for gossip columns unless they're caught in bed with their secretaries and no pyjamas.'

Blue pictures for blackmail, I thought irrelevantly. Or black and white pictures for blackmail. Why not?

'Do you know anyone called Lars Baltzersen?' I asked.

'Sure. The Chairman of Øvrevoll? Every man's idea of a respectable pillar of society. Entertains ambassadors and presents prizes. Often a picture on the sports pages, always beside the man of the moment. Mind you, our Lars was a live wire once himself. Did a lot of motor racing, mostly in Sweden. That was before banking finally smothered him, of course.'

'Family?'

'Dutch wife, lots of solid children.'

I paid the bill and we strolled back to the car. Odin stared out of the front window with his huge head close to the glass and his eyes unblinking. Some people who stopped to try 'isn't-he-a-nice-boy' noises got a big yawn and a view down a cavernous throat.

Erik opened his door, gave the dog a shove and said '*Fanden ta dig*.' The Dane shifted his bulk towards the back seat without taking offence, and the journey continued.

'What did Lars do in the war?'

'He wasn't here,' he said promptly. 'He was in London,

reading the news in Norwegian on the radio.'

'He didn't tell me he'd lived in London.'

'He's quiet now. Another dead volcano. More pumice.'

Erik crossed some traffic lights three seconds after they turned red and genuinely didn't seem to hear six other motorists grinding their brake drums to screaming point. Odin gave him an affectionate nudge in the neck and Erik put out the hand he needed on the gear lever and fondled the huge wet nose.

He pulled up in front of a modern square-built glass and slab affair a mile out of the city centre, a far cry from Sandvik's architectural elegance.

'This is the address you gave me,' Erik said dubiously.

'Fine,' I said. 'Would you like to wait inside?'

He shook his head, though the afternoon was cold and rapidly growing dark. 'Odin gives off heat like a nuclear reactor and I don't like sitting in plastic lobbies being stared at.'

'OK.'

I left them to their companionship and rode a lift up to Rolf Torp's office, where again as I was early I was asked to wait. This time not in Torp's own office, but a small purpose-decorated room overflowing with useful handouts about 'Torp-Nord Associates'.

The walls here also were hung with diagrams of rock formations, charts of progress and maps showing areas being worked. These maps were not of the North Sea but of the mainland, with the thickest cluster of work-tags to the west of Oslo, in the mountains.

Someone had told me Rolf Torp's business was silver, but it wasn't or no longer chiefly. His associates had switched to titanium.

Before he finally turned up (at four twenty) for his four o'clock appointment I had learnt a good deal I didn't especially want to know about titanium. For example that it weighed only 0·163 lb per cubic inch and in alloy form could reach a tensile strength of 200,000 lb per square inch. Bully for titanium, I thought.

Rolf Torp was much like his product in tensile strength but couldn't match it for lightness. He made no effort to conceal that my visit was a nuisance, bursting into the waiting room saying, 'Come on, come on then. I can give you ten minutes, that's all,' and stomping off to his own office without waiting to see if I followed.

I did, of course. His office was much like Sandvik's: same type of furniture, fabrics and carpet, a reflection of prevailing style but no clue to the occupant. The walls here were dotted with framed photographs of various stages of metal production, and another large map with thumb tacks took pride of place.

'How do you mine titanium?' I asked, and sat in the visitors' chair without being invited. Irritably he took his own place behind half an acre of tidy desk and lit a cigarette.

'Like one?' he said belatedly, pushing a box towards me.

'No, thank you.'

He flicked a lighter and deeply inhaled the smoke.

'You don't find titanium lying around like coal,' he said. 'Are you sure you want to use your ten minutes on this?'

'Might as well.'

He gave me a puzzled look over the heavy black moustache, but seemed to find his own subject a lot less temper-disturbing than mine.

'Titanium is the ninth most common element on earth. It is found in ninety-eight per cent of rocks and also in oil, coal, water, plants, animals, and stars.'

'You can hardly dig it out of people.'

'No. It is mostly mined as a mineral called ilmenite . . . which is one third titanium.'

'Does your firm do the actual mining?'

He shook his head. 'We survey, do first drillings, advise and establish.'

I looked vaguely at the photographs on the walls.

'Apart from high speed aircraft, what's the stuff used for?'

He reeled off technical uses as if he'd been asked that one once or twice before. Towards the end, slowing down, he included paint, lipstick and smokescreens. There was little you couldn't do, it seemed, with the strength of the Titans.

'Did Bob Sherman bring you any photographs?'

I asked him casually without looking at him directly, but if it jerked him at all I couldn't tell, as he swept any involuntary movement into a quick gesture to flick off ash.

'No, he didn't.'

'Did he ask your advice about anything?'

'Why should he?'

'People do need advice sometimes,' I said.

He gave a laugh that was half a scowl. 'I gave him some. He didn't ask. I told him to ride races better or stay in England.'

'He didn't please you?'

'He should have won on my good horse. He went to sleep. He stopped trying to win, and he was beaten. Also he did not ride as I told him, all the way round.'

'Do you think someone bribed him to lose?'

He looked startled. For all his bad-tempered criticism it hadn't occurred to him, and to be fair, he didn't pounce on the idea.

'No,' he said heavily. 'He wanted to ride that horse in the Grand National. It started favourite and it won.'

I nodded. 'I saw the race.'

'That's right. Bob Sherman wanted to ride it, but I would have got someone else anyway. He rode it very badly.'

I imagined that any time Rolf Torp's jockey didn't win, he had automatically ridden badly. I stood up to go, which puzzled him again, and shook his hand.

'Coming here has been a waste of your time,' he said.

'Of course not . . . I'll let myself out.'

He didn't stop me. I closed his door and did a brief exploration. More offices. More bustle than at Sandvik's. More impression of work being done, but nothing so earthy as a lump of ore.

Erik was not parked out front where I had left him. I went through the big glass entrance doors, peered briefly into the darkness, and ignominiously retreated. One thing I did not plan to do was walk around at night alone, making everything easy for assassins.

After ten minutes I began to wonder if he'd simply forgotten about me and gone home, but he hadn't. The small cream Volvo returned at high speed and stopped outside in its own length. Its owner extricated himself from the quivering metal and strolled towards the building.

'Hullo,' he said, as I met him. 'Hope you haven't been waiting. I had to get Odin's dinner. Forgot all about it.'

In the car, Odin loomed hungrily over my head, dribbling. Just as well, I thought, that he was about to be fed.

Erik returned us to the Grand at tar-melting speed and seemed disappointed that I hadn't wanted any longer journeys.

CHAPTER ELEVEN

The receptionists of the Grand considered me totally mad because I was insisting on changing my room every day, but they would have thought me even madder if I'd told them the reason. I asked them just to allocate me the last empty room, or if there were several, to give me a random choice at bed time. They did it with politely glazed eyes while I thankfully put my trust in unpredictability.

When Erik dropped me at the door and took his big friend home I telephoned to Arne and Kari and asked them to dinner.

'Come here,' Kari demanded warmly, but I said it was time I repaid their kindness, and after much demur they agreed to the Grand. I sat in the bar and read a newspaper until they arrived, and thought about growing old.

It was strange, but away from her chosen setting, Kari looked a different person. Not so young, not so domesticated, not so tranquil. This Kari, walking with assurance into the bar in a long black skirt and white ruffled shirt was the woman who designed interiors as a business. This Kari, wearing perfect make-up, diamonds in her ears and hair smoothly pinned up, looked at once cooler and more mature than the casual home-girl. When she put a smooth sweet-smelling cheek forward for a kiss and gave me a pretty look from under her lashes I found I both liked her less and wanted her more; both of which reactions were disconcerting and no good.

Arne was Arne, the antithesis of a chameleon, his personality so concretely formed that it retained its own shape whatever the environment. He swept four-square into the bar and gave it a quick suspicious survey to make sure no one could listen at his shoulder.

'Hallo David,' he said, shaking my hand vigorously. 'What have you been doing all day?'

'Wasting time,' I said smiling, 'And wondering what to do next.'

We sat in a comfortable corner and drank (as for once it was the right hour on the right day) whisky.

Arne wanted to know what progress I had made.

'Not much,' I said. 'You might practically say none.'

'It must be very difficult,' Kari said sympathetically, with Arne nodding in agreement. 'How do you know what to look for?'

'I don't often look for things. I look at what's there.'

'All detectives look for things. Look for clues and follow trails. Of course they do.'

'And trudge up dead ends and find red herrings,' I said.

'Herrings are not red,' Kari said in puzzlement.

Fifty-seven varieties of herring in Norway, and not one of them red.

'A red herring is something that doesn't exist,' Arne said, but had to explain it again to her in Norwegian.

She laughed, but returned to her questions. 'How do you solve a crime?'

'Um . . . you think what you might have done if you'd been the crook, and then you look to see if that's what he did. And sometimes it is.'

'No one else solves crimes like David,' Arne said.

'Believe me,' I said. 'They do.'

'What do you think the crook did this time?' Kari asked.

I looked at her clear grey eyes, asking the question I couldn't answer without freezing the evening in its tracks.

'There's more than one,' I said neutrally. 'Emma Sherman saw two.'

We talked about Emma for a while. Arne had met her grandfather during his brief visit, and knew he had not been able to identify either of the intruders.

'And nobody knows what they were looking for,' Kari said thoughtfully.

'The men knew,' I said.

Arne's eyes stretched suddenly wide, which made a change from blinking. 'So they did,' he said.

'Of course they did,' she said. 'I don't see the point.'

'It isn't really a point. Only that someone somewhere does know what is missing. Or what was missing, because it may have been found now.'

Kari thought it over. 'Why do you think they didn't search the Shermans' house at once, as soon as they'd killed Bob Sherman? Why wait a month?'

Arne went back to blinking fit to bust, but he left it to me to answer.

'I think,' I said, 'it was because Bob Sherman was found, and whatever it was that was missing wasn't found with him.' I paused. 'Say Mr X kills Bob and dumps him in the pond, for a reason as yet unknown. Suppose this was after Bob delivered a package he had been bringing with him. Suppose also that Bob had opened the package and taken out some of the contents, but that Mr X did not discover this until after he'd killed Bob and put him in the pond. OK so far? So then he has to guess whether Bob had the missing contents in his pockets or his overnight bag, in which case they too are safely in the pond, or whether he passed them on to someone else, or even posted them home to himself in England, before he was killed. Short of getting Bob out of the pond, Mr X can't find out for certain, but the longer the missing contents don't turn up, the surer Mr X becomes that they are with Bob. Right. But then Bob is found, and the missing contents are still missing. So a search party is sent out to find out if Bob took them out of the package at home before he even left England, and Emma was unfortunate enough to choose just that moment to go back for some fresh clothes.'

Kari's mouth had slowly opened. 'Wow,' she said. 'And it seemed such a simple little question.'

'I told you,' Arne said. 'Give him one fact and he guesses the rest.'

'And a guess is all it is.' I smiled. 'I don't know why they took a month to start searching. Do you?'

Kari said 'But you must be right. It sounds so reasonable.'

'Like the earth is flat.'

'What?'

'Sounds reasonable until you know different.'

We went in to dinner. There was an orchestra playing, and dancing, and later, with the coffee, a singer. It was all too much in the end for Arne who stood up abruptly, said he needed some air, and made a compulsive dash for the door.

We watched his retreating back.

'Has he always been like that?' I asked.

'Always since I've known him. Though lately, perhaps, it has been worse. He used not to worry about bugging machines.'

'He used not to know they existed.'

'Well . . . that's true.'

'How did it start? His persecution complex, I mean.'

'Oh . . . the war, I suppose. When he was a child. I wasn't born until after, but Arne was a child then. His grandfather was shot as a hostage, and his father was in the resistance. Arne says he was always frightened when he was a child, but he wasn't always sure what he was frightened of. Sometimes his father sent him to run with messages and told him to be sure not to be followed. Arne says he was always terrified those times that he would turn round and find a big man behind him.'

'Poor Arne,' I said.

'He has been to psychiatrists,' Kari said. 'He knows . . . but he still can't help it.' She looked away from me, at the couples slowly circling on the square of polished floor. 'He can't bear dancing.'

After a few seconds I said, 'Would you like to?'

'I don't suppose he'd mind.'

She stood up without hesitation and danced with natural rhythm. She also knew quite well that I liked having her close: I could see it in her eyes. I wondered if she'd ever been unfaithful to Arne, or ever would be. I wondered about the age-old things. One can't help it, I find.

She smiled and moved forward until our bodies were touching at more points than not, and no woman ever did that unless she meant to. What we were engaged in from that moment on was an act of sex: upright, dancing, public and fully clothed, but an act of sex none the less. I knew theoretically that a woman could reach a vivid orgasm without actual intercourse, that in fact some could do it when all alone simply by thinking erotic thoughts, but I had never before seen it happen.

It happened to Kari because she wanted it to. Because she rubbed closely against me with every turn of the dance. Because I didn't expect it. Because I didn't push her off.

Her breathing grew slower and deeper and her eyes lost their brightness. Her mouth was closed, half smiling. Head up, neck straight, she looked more withdrawn and absent-minded than passionately aroused. Then quite suddenly her whole body flushed with heat, and behind her eyes and right through her very deep I was for almost twenty seconds aware of a gentle intense throbbing.

After that she took a great deep gulping breath as if her lungs had been cramped. Her mouth opened, the smile broadened, and she unplastered herself from my front.

Her eyes grew bright as stars, and she laughed into mine.

'Thank you,' she said.

She had finished with dancing. She broke away and walked back to the table, sitting down sociably as if nothing had happened. Oh thanks very much, I thought, and where does that leave me? Dealing with an unscratchable itch and without the later comfort of doing it on my own like she had, because I'd never found that much fun.

'More coffee?' I said. One had to say something, I supposed. How about 'Damn your eyes you selfish little pig'?

'Thank you,' she said.

The waiter brought more coffee. Civilization won the day.

Arne returned looking windblown and a little happier. Kari put her hand on his with wifely warmth and understanding, and I remembered ironically that I had wondered if she were ever unfaithful to him. She was and she wasn't: the perfect recipe for having it both ways.

They left shortly afterwards, pressing me to spend another evening at their flat before I went home.

'See you on Sunday at Øvrevoll,' Arne said. 'If not before.'

When they had gone I collected my suitcase from the hall porter and took myself to the reception desk. There were five empty rooms to choose from, so I took a key at random and got myself a spacious double room with a balcony looking out towards the parliament building. I opened the well-closed double doors and let a blast from the Arctic play havoc with the central heating. Then I shut them again and went coldly to bed, and lay awake for a long time thinking about a lot of things but hardly at all about Kari.

Erik came to breakfast the next morning. He joined me with a grin, helped himself to half a ton of assorted pickled fish from the buffet, and ate as if there were no tomorrow.

'Where to?' he asked after two further bread rolls, four slices of cheese and several cups of coffee.

'Øvrevoll,' I said.

'But there's no racing today.'

'I know.'

'Well, if that's what you want, let's go.'

Odin, in a friendly mood, sat centrally with his rump wedged against the rear seat and his front paws and huge head burying the handbrake. When Erik gave him a nudge with his elbow the dog lifted his chin long enough for his master to release the wheels. A double act of long standing, it seemed.

The journey was a matter of staring death in the face, but we got there. The main gates of the racecourse stood open with various trade vans standing inside on the tarmac, so we simply drove in and stopped near the weighing room. Erik and Odin unfolded themselves and stretched their legs while I went on my short and abortive mission.

There were cleaners, a man and two women, in the weighing room building, and none of them spoke English. I went outside and cajoled Erik, the easiest task on earth, to do my talking.

He asked, listened, and passed on the bad news.

'They say Bob Sherman's saddle was here for a long time. In the changing room, on the peg nearest the corner.'

I had just looked all round the changing room. No saddles on any pegs and no trace of Bob Sherman's.

'They say it went at about the time the body was found in the pond. They don't know who took it.'

'That's that, then.'

We left the weighing room building and strolled the few yards to the racecourse rails. The morning was icy, the wind fresh, the trees sighing. Winter on the doorstep, snow on the way.

Down the sand track Gunnar Holth's string was starting a canter, and as we watched they came up fast towards us and swept past along to the winning post and round the top of the course where the pond lay. Paddy O'Flaherty in his brilliant woollen cap rode in front, giving a lead and setting the pace. With racing the next day, it was little more than a pipe-opener, and the string presently slowed to walk home.

'Next stop,' I said, 'is Gunnar Holth's stable.'

We drew up in the yard as the horses came back from the track, steaming like kettles under their rugs. Gunnar Holth himself jumped down from Sandvik's Whitefire, patted him vigorously, and waited for me to open the game.

'Morning,' I said.

'Morning.'

'Can we talk?'

He nodded resignedly, led Whitefire off into the barn, returned, jerked his head towards his bungalow and opened his door. Erik this time chose to stay in the car for which Gunnar Holth, having spotted Odin, looked thankful.

'Coffee?'

Same orange pot on the stove. Same coffee, I dared say.

'I am looking for Bob Sherman's saddle,' I said.

'His saddle? Didn't he leave it behind? I heard he did...'

'I wondered if you knew who had it. I want to find it... It belongs to his wife now.'

'And saddles are worth money,' he said, nodding. 'I haven't seen it. I don't know who has it.'

I asked him obliquely twice more in different ways but in the end was satisfied that he knew nothing helpful.

'I'll ask Paddy,' I said. But Paddy too had few ideas.

'It was there, so it was, until they pulled the poor devil out of the water. Sure I saw it there myself on Grand National day. Then the next meeting, on the Thursday, it was gone.'

'Are you sure of that?'

'As sure as I'm standing here.'

I said mildly, 'Why? Why are you so sure?'

His eyes flickered. 'Well... as to that, now...'

'Paddy,' I said. 'Come clean.'

'Uh...'

'Did you take it?'

'No,' he said positively. 'That I did not.' The idea apparently outraged him.

'What, then?'

'Well now then, do you see, he was after being a real mate of mine, Bob was... Well I was sure now, in my own mind, that he would want me to do it...' He ran down and stopped.

'To do what?'

'Look now, it wasn't stealing or anything like that.'

'Paddy, what did you do?'

'Well . . . there was my helmet, see, and there was his helmet, hanging there with his saddle. Well now, my helmet had a strap broken, so it had, and Bob's was there, good as new, so I just swapped them over, do you see . . .'

'And that was on Grand National day?'

'That's right. And the next race day, after Bob was found, his saddle was gone. And my helmet was gone with it, do you see.'

'So Bob's helmet is . . . here?'

'It is so. In my box, now, under my bunk.'

'Will you lend it to me for a while?'

'Lend it?' He was surprised. 'I thought you'd be taking it away altogether, now, as by rights it belongs to his missus.'

'I expect she'd be glad for you to keep it.'

'It's a good helmet, so it is.'

He went and fetched it and handed it over, an ordinary regulation jockey helmet with a chin strap. I thanked him, told him I'd let him have it back, waved goodbye to Gunnar Holth, and set off on the perilous passage back to central Oslo.

In between bounces I pulled out the padded lining of the helmet and looked underneath. No photographs, papers or other missing objects. Nothing but black regulation padding. I put it back into place.

'No good?' Erik said sympathetically, peering round Odin.

'All stones have to be turned.'

'Which stone next, then?'

'Lars Baltzersen.'

The route to his bank lay past the front door of the Grand, so I stopped off there and left Bob Sherman's helmet with the hall porter, who was already sheltering my newly re-packed suitcase. He told me he would take good care of anything I left with him. I left three ten-kroner notes with him, and with a smile he took good care of those.

Lars had almost given up.

'Thought you'd changed your mind,' he said, showing me into his office.

'Had to make a detour,' I said, apologizing.

'Well, now that you are here . . .' He produced a bottle of red wine and two small glasses from a discreet cupboard, and poured for us both.

His room, like Sandvik's and Torp's, was standard Scandinavian, modern vintage. Commerce, I supposed, must be seen to be up to date, but as a source of personal information these interiors were a dead loss.

No maps on his walls. Pictures of houses, factories, office blocks, distant ports. When I asked him, he told me that his banking firm was chiefly concerned with the financing of industrial projects.

'Merchant banking,' he said. 'Also we run a building scheme very like an English building society. Except that here, of course, we lend at a much lower interest rate, so that mortgages are cheaper.'

'Don't the investors complain?'

'They get almost the same return as British investors. It is just that Norwegian societies don't have to pay big taxes. It is the tax which puts up the British mortgage rate.'

He told me that there were many small private banks in Norway running building schemes, but that his own was one of the largest.

'There is a terrible shortage of building land round Oslo,' he said. 'Young couples find it very difficult to find a house. Yet far out in the country there are whole farms standing empty and derelict. The old people have died or are too weak to work the fields, and the young people have left the hard life and gone to the towns.'

'Same everywhere,' I said.

He liked wooden houses best, he said. 'They breathe.'

'How about fire?' I asked.

'It always used to be a fearful risk. Cities were burnt sometimes. But now our fire services are so fast, so expert, that I am told if you want to burn your house for the insurance, you have to hose it down with petrol. Otherwise the fire will be put out at the first puff of smoke.'

We drank the wine and Lars smoked a cigarette. I asked him about his years in London and about his motor racing in Sweden, but he seemed to have no interest left in them.

'The past is over,' he said. 'It is banking and Øvrevoll which I think about now.'

He asked me if I yet knew who killed Bob Sherman. Such faith in the way he put it.

'Not yet,' I said. 'What's my limit on expenses?'

I couldn't pin him to an amount. It seemed that if I succeeded there was no limit. If I failed, I had already overspent.

'Have you any ideas?' he asked.

'Ideas aren't enough.'

'You need proof as well, I suppose.'

'Mm . . . have to make like a poacher.'

'What do you mean?'

'Set traps,' I said. 'And keep my feet out of other poachers' snares.'

I stood up to go. He too said my visit had been a waste of time because he had told me nothing useful.

'You never know,' I said.

Erik and I had lunch in a café not far from his brother's headquarters because I wanted to call in afterwards to see him. He would be off duty at two o'clock, he said on the telephone; if that would do, he could see me before he went home.

Erik spent most of lunch explaining with chapter and verse why all revolutions ended in gloom because all revolutionaries were incapable of humour.

'If the activists knew how to be funny,' he said, 'the workers would have ruled the world long ago.'

'Jokes should be taught in school,' I suggested.

He looked at me suspiciously. 'Are you taking the micky?'

'I thought that was the point.'

'Oh God, yes.' He laughed. 'So it is. What makes you spend your life detecting?'

'Curiosity.'

'Killed the cat.'

'Shut up.'

'Sorry,' he said, grinning. 'Anyway, you're still alive. How did you train for it? Is there a school for detectives?'

'Don't think so. I went to university. Tried industry, didn't like it. Didn't want to teach. Liked going racing . . . so got a job going racing.'

'That's as smart a canter over the course as I've ever heard, and as a gossip columnist I've heard a lot. What did you read at which university?'

'Psychology at Cambridge.'

'Ah-hah,' he said. 'Ah absolutely *Hah.*'

He came with me up to Knut's office, leaving Odin in charge of the car. Knut was tired after an apparently frustrating spell of duty, yawning and rubbing his eyes when we walked in.

'I am sorry,' he said. 'But I have been awake since two o'clock this morning.' He shook his head to clear it. 'Never mind. How can I help you?'

'Not in detail today. Tell me if your terms of reference would let you catch a rabbit if I enticed one out of a hole.' I turned to Erik. 'Explain to him. If I set a trap, can he help me to spring it? Is he allowed to, and would he personally want to?'

The brothers consulted in their own language, Knut neat, restrained, over-tired, and Erik with undisciplined gestures, bohemian clothes and wild, wispy hair. Erik was older, but in him the life force still flowed with generous vigour.

In the end they both nodded. Knut said, 'As long as it is not against the regulations, I will help.'

'I'm very grateful.'

He smiled faintly. 'You are doing my work.'

He collected his coat and cap and came down to the street with us. His car, it appeared, was along with Erik's in the side road running down beside a small railed public garden.

Erik's car was a centre of attention.

About ten feet away from it, ranged round in a semicircle, stood about a dozen children and one uncertain looking policeman. His face changed thankfully at the sight of Knut, and he saluted and began to shift his anxiety on to someone else.

Erik translated for me, looking puzzled.

'One of the children says a man told her not on any account to go near my car. He told her to run home as fast as she could.'

I looked at the car. Odin was not facing out of the front window as usual, but out of the back and he was looking down, not interestedly at the crowd. Something in the great dog's world seemed wrong to him. He was standing rigidly. Much too tense. And the boot was no longer tied up with string.

'Oh Christ,' I said. 'Get those children out of here. Make them run.'

They simply stared at me and didn't move. But they hadn't been near the Old Bailey in London on 8 March 1973.

'It could be a bomb,' I said.

CHAPTER TWELVE

The children recognized the word but of course they didn't believe it. The people in London hadn't believed it until the flying glass ripped their faces.

'Tell them to run,' I said to Knut.

He decided to take it seriously, even if it were a false alarm. He said something unequivocal to the policeman, and he grabbed hold of Erik's arm.

He knew his brother. He must have loved him more than

most. He grabbed him tight just as Erik took his first step towards the car, saying 'Odin,' half under his breath.

They more or less fought. Knut wouldn't let go and Erik grew frantic. Knut put a lock on Erik's arm which would have arrested a twenty stone boxer with a skinful, and Erik's face crumpled into despair. The two of them, step by contested step, retreated from the car.

The policeman had chased the children away to a safe distance and was yelling to approaching pedestrians to get behind cover. No one paid any attention to me, so I nipped smartly along the pavement, put my hand on the handle, wrenched the door open, and sprinted.

Even then the wretched dog didn't come out at once. It took a screeching whistle from Erik to get results, and Odin came bounding after me down the pavement as if it were playtime.

The bomb went off just as he drew level, twenty feet from the car. The blast slammed us both down in a heap, hitting like a fierce blow in the back, knocking all breath out, leaving one limp, weak, and shaken.

Not a big bomb by Irish standards. But this one had presumably not been meant to destroy the neighbourhood. Just the occupants of a car. Two men and a dog.

Knut helped me to my feet and Erik took hold of Odin's collar, kneeling down and patting him solicitously. Odin slobbered all over him, as good as new.

'That was stupid,' Knut said.

'Yes,' I said.

'Are you hurt?'

'No.'

'You deserve to be.'

'It might not have gone off for hours.'

'It might have gone off while you were beside it.'

Erik's car was gutted. Windows blown out, interior torn to shreds, boot burst wide open. I picked splinters of glass out of the hair on the back of my head and asked him if it was insured.

'I don't know,' he said vaguely. He rubbed his arm where

Knut had locked it. 'Knut wanted me to wait for an expert to come to see if it was a bomb, and if it was, to dismantle it.'

'Knut was quite right.'

'He didn't stop you.'

'I'm not his brother. He had his hands full with you, and the bomb probably had my name on it in the first place.'

'What a bloody awful way to die.' He stood up and grinned suddenly, his whole face lighting up. 'Thanks anyway,' he said. Which was pretty generous, considering the state of his Volvo.

Once the fireworks were over the children came back, staring at the wreck with wide eyes. I asked Knut to find the little girl who'd been told to run home, and he said he'd already sent his policeman to bring her.

Apart from the car, there was little damage. The windows had been broken in a severe-looking building on the far side of the road, but neither the railings nor the shivering bushes in the little public garden nearest the Volvo seemed to have suffered. Cars parked several yards away fore and aft were slightly scratched with glass splinters but otherwise undamaged. If the bomb had gone off while we had been driving along a busy street, there would have been a lot more mess.

The little girl was blonde, solemn, hooded and zipped into a red anorak, and accompanied now by a scolding older child of about thirteen who had fallen down on the job of looking after her and was busy justifying herself. Knut, as with the boy on the racecourse, won the smaller girl's confidence by squatting down to her level and chatting along quietly.

I leant against the railings and felt cold, and watched Erik smoothing Odin's sand-coloured skin over and over, seeing him dissipate an overwhelming build-up of tension in small, self-controlled gestures. Odin himself seemed to be enjoying it.

Knut stood up, holding the little girl's hand.

'Her name is Liv. She is four. She lives about half a mile away and she was playing in the park with her big sister. She came out of the gate down there and walked up the road here. Her sister had told her not to, but Liv says she doesn't do what her sister says.'

'The sister's too damn bossy,' Erik said unexpectedly. 'Little Fascist.'

'Liv says there was a man cutting some string at the back of the car and the big dog looking at him out of the window. She stopped to watch. She was behind the man. He didn't see her or hear her. She says he took something out of his coat and put it inside the boot, but she didn't see what shape it was. She says the man tried to shut the back of the car, but it wouldn't shut. Then he tried to tie the string where it had been before, but it was too short because he had cut it. He put the string in his pocket, and that was when he saw Liv. He told her to go away, but she seems to be a child who does the opposite of what she's told. She says she went up to the car and looked through the side window at the dog, but the dog went on looking out of the back. Then the man shook her and told her to run home at once and not to play near the car. Then he went away.'

Knut looked at the small crowd of children beginning to cluster again round Liv.

'She is one of those children who draws others to her. Like now. They came out of the park to join her, and she told them about the man cutting the string and trying to tie the boot shut again. It was that which interested her most, it seemed. Then my policeman came along, on his way to start his afternoon duty, and he asked the children why they were standing there.'

'Then we came?'

'Right.'

'Has Liv said what the man looked like?'

'Big, she said. But all men are big to little girls.'

'Could she see his hair?'

Knut asked her. She answered. Knut said, 'He was wearing a woollen cap, like a sailor.'

'What did his eyes look like?'

Knut asked. Her little voice rose clear, high, definite, and all the children looked interested.

'He had yellow eyes. Sharp, like a bird.'

'Did he have gloves?'

Knut asked. 'Yes,' he reported.

'What sort of shoes?'

Back came the answer: big, soft, squashy shoes, like on a boat.

Children were the best witnesses on earth. Their eyes saw clearly, their memories were accurate, and their impressions weren't interpreted by probability or prejudice. So when Liv added something which made Knut and Erik and the older children laugh, I asked what she'd said.

'She must have been mistaken,' Knut said.

'What did she say?'

'She said he had a butterfly on his neck.'

'Ask her what sort of butterfly,' I said.

'It's too late for butterflies,' Knut said patiently. 'Too cold.'

'Ask her what it was like,' I urged.

He shrugged, but he asked. The reply surprised him, because Liv described it with sharp positive little nods. She knew she'd seen a butterfly.

Knut said, 'She says it was on the back of his neck. She saw it because his head was bent forward. It was between his woolly cap and his collar and it didn't move.'

'What colour?'

He consulted. 'Dark red.'

'Birth mark?'

'Could be,' he agreed. He asked her one or two more questions and nodded to me. 'I should think so,' he said. 'She says it had two wings lying open flat, but one was bigger than the other.'

'So all we need now is a big man with yellow eyes and a butterfly birthmark.'

'Or a small man,' Erik said, 'With the sun in his eyes and a dirty neck.'

'No sun,' I said. The iron grey sky pressed down like an army blanket, without warmth. The shivers in my gut, however, had little to do with the cold.

Knut sent his policeman to fetch experts in fingerprints and explosives and took the names and addresses of half the children. The crowd of watchers grew a bit, and Erik restively asked Knut when he could go home.

'What in?' said Knut pointedly, so we stamped around on the pavement for nearly another hour.

With darkness we returned to Knut's office. He took his coat and cap off and looked wearier than ever.

I borrowed his telephone and rang the Sandviks to apologize for my non-arrival. I spoke, in the event, to Mrs Per Bjørn, who explained that her husband was out.

'Mikkel did wait for you, Mr Cleveland,' she said in heavily accented English. 'But after one hour he went away with some friends.'

'Please tell him I'm very sorry.'

'I will tell him.'

'What school does he go to?'

'College of Gol,' she said, and then thought better of it. 'But I do not think that my husband would like . . .'

I interrupted, 'I just wondered if I could see him this evening before he goes back.'

'Oh . . . He is going straight back with the friends. They will have started by now.'

'Never mind, then.'

I put down the receiver. Knut was organizing coffee.

'Where is the College of Gol?' I asked.

'Gol is in the mountains, on the way to Bergen. It is a holiday ski town, in the winter. The college is a boarding school for rich boys. Are you going all the way out there to see Mikkel Sandvik? He knows nothing about Bob Sherman's death. When I saw him he was very upset about his friend dying like that. He would have helped me if he could.'

'How upset? Crying?'

'No, not crying. Pale. Very shocked. Trembling. *Upset.*'

'Angry?'

'No. Why should he be angry?'

'People are usually furious when their friends are murdered. They feel like strangling the murderer, don't they?'

'Oh, that,' he said, nodding. 'No, I don't remember that Mikkel was especially angry.'

'What is he like?' I asked.

'Just a boy. Sixteen. No, seventeen. Intelligent, but not outstanding. Average height, slim build, light brown hair, good manners. Nothing unusual about him. A nice boy. A little nervous, perhaps.'

We sat around and drank the coffee. Odin had some too, in a bowl, with a lot of sugar. Erik had recovered from the nearness of losing his companion and was beginning to think about his car.

'I'll need to hire one, I suppose,' he said. 'For driving David around.'

'You're not driving David any more,' Knut said positively.

'Of course I am.'

'No,' said Knut. 'It's too dangerous.'

There was a small meaningful silence. Anyone in future who drove me must be presumed to be at risk. Which put me high in the unpopularity stakes as a passenger.

'I'll manage,' I said.

Erik said, 'Where do you plan to go?'

'Tomorrow, to call on Sven Wangen, then to Øvrevoll. On Monday . . . I don't know yet.'

'I could do with another of those Grand breakfasts,' he said.

'No,' said Knut. They argued heatedly in private, and Knut lost. He turned a grim face and a compressed mouth to me. 'Erik says he never leaves a job unfinished.'

Erik grinned and rubbed a hand over his straggly blond hair. 'Only dull ones.'

Knut said crossly, 'I suppose you realize that one of these attempts will be successful? Two have failed, but . . .'

'Three,' I said. 'Someone tried to drown me in the fjord the first day I came to Norway.'

I told them about the black speedboat. Knut frowned and said, 'But that could have been an accident.'

I nodded. 'At the time, I thought it was. I don't think so

any longer.' I got up to pour myself some more hot strong black coffee. 'I do rather agree with you that they will succeed in the end, but I don't know what to do about it.'

'Give up and go back to England,' Knut said.

'Would you?'

He didn't answer. Nor did Erik. There wasn't an answer to give.

Knut sent me back in a police car to the Grand, where as the bar was again shut (Saturday) I ate an early dinner, collected my suitcases and Bob Sherman's helmet from the porter, picked a room at random from those available, and spent the evening upstairs alone, sitting in an armchair and contemplating several unpalatable facts.

Such as, there was a limit to luck and little girls.

Such as, next time they could use a rifle, because sniping was the surest way of killing.

Such as, tomorrow if I went to the races I would be scared to death the whole bloody day.

Not much comfort in the hope that old yellow eyes with the birthmark might be a lousy shot.

There were various other thoughts, chiefly that somewhere there existed a particular way of discovering who had killed Bob Sherman, and why. There had to be such a way, for if there wasn't, no one would need to kill me. Knut hadn't found it. Maybe he had looked the solution in the face and not recognized it, which was easy enough to do. Maybe I had, also, but could be expected to understand later what I had heard or seen.

Yellow eyes must have followed Erik's car, I thought. Erik's breakneck driving and red light jumping made it exceedingly unlikely that anything bar a fire engine could have tailed us to Øvrevoll: but then I'd considerately returned to the Grand to dump the helmet, and made it easy for a watcher to pick us up again.

I hadn't spotted a follower, nor had Erik. But our trip to Baltzersen's and from there to where we parked for lunch had been comparatively short and, in retrospect, almost legal. Anyone risking a couple of head-on crashes could have kept us in sight.

Yellow eyes was the man who had attacked Emma; and it seemed likely that the man who kicked her grandfather was the man who'd tried to knife me. Both, it seemed to me, were mercenaries, paid to do a violent job but not the instigators. They hadn't the aura of principals.

To my mind there were at least two others, one of whom I knew, one or more I didn't. To bring out the unknown, I had to bamboozle the known. The big snag was that when it came to setting traps, the only bait at present available was myself, and this cheese could find itself eaten if it wasn't extremely careful.

It was easy to see that to bring out the big boys, yellow eyes and brown eyes would have to be decoyed away while at the same time a situation needing instant action was temptingly arranged elsewhere. How to do it was another matter. I stared at the carpet for ages and came up with nothing foolproof.

I wished there was a way of knowing what Bob Sherman had been bringing to Norway. Unlikely to be straight pornography, because Bob had told Paddy O'Flaherty that he, Bob, had been conned. If he had opened the packet and found that it did not contain ordinary pornography, he might well have thought that.

Suppose . . . he had opened the packet and reckoned he was not being paid enough for what he was carrying.

Suppose . . . he had removed something from the packet, meaning to use it to up the stakes.

But . . . he couldn't have used it, because, if he had, the enemy would have known he had taken it, and would not have killed him without getting it back.

So suppose . . . simply opening the packet and seeing the contents was in itself a death warrant.

Suppose . . . the enemy killed him for knowing the contents, and only discovered afterwards that he had removed some of them.

It came back to that every time.

So . . . what the *hell* was in that packet?

Start another way.

When had he opened the packet?

Probably not at home. Emma had seen him put it in his overnight bag so as not to risk forgetting it. Yellow eyes and friend had subsequently smashed the place up looking for things from it, and hadn't found any. So it seemed reasonable to suppose that he had set off from home with the envelope intact.

He had had all day at Kempton races. Time enough if he'd urgently wanted to open it: but if he'd felt like that, he'd already had it available all night.

Not much time at Heathrow between arriving from Kempton and boarding the aeroplane. Hardly the opportunity for an impulsive bit of snooping.

He had turned up at Gunnar Holth's an hour or so later than expected. So he could have done his lethal bit of noseyparkering either on the flight or in the first hour after he'd landed.

On the flight, I thought, was most likely of all.

A couple of drinks under his belt, an hour or so to while away, and a packet of blue pictures temptingly to hand.

Open the packet and see . . . what?

Suppose he had had perhaps half an hour before landing to come up with the idea of demanding a larger freight fee. Suppose he took something out of the envelope and hid it . . . where had he hidden it?

Not in his pockets or his overnight bag. Perhaps in his saddle, but doubtful, because for one thing his racing saddle was tiny, and for another he'd ridden three races on it the following day.

Not in his helmet: no papers or photographs lurked inside the padded headband.

Which left one unaccounted-for hour, during which he could have left any object at the reception desk of any hotel in Oslo, with a request to keep it for him until he returned.

In one hour he could have hidden something anywhere.

I sighed. It was hopeless.

I stood up, stretched, unpacked a few things, undressed, brushed my teeth.

Bob's helmet lay on my bed. I picked it up and dangled it by the chin strap as I pulled back the quilt and pushed up the pillows as a back-rest for reading before sleep. Sitting between the sheets I turned the helmet idly over in my hands, scarcely looking at it, thinking about Bob and the last day he'd worn it.

I thought seriously about wearing it myself to Øvrevoll to protect my head, and buying a bullet-proof vest besides. I thought ungenerous thoughts about Emma's husband because I too could still die for what he'd done.

No papers. No photographs. I pulled the soft black padding out again. Nothing, still nothing tucked behind it.

In the crown there was just the small round centrepiece of black-covered padding suspended by straps fixed into the shell itself. A marvellous piece of engineering, designed to prevent a man falling on his nut at thirty miles an hour off a galloping horse from bashing his skull in. The central suspended piece of padding shielded the top of the head and stopped it crashing into the shell itself at concussion speed.

Underneath the central piece of padding there was no room at all for any papers or photographs or anything out of magazine-sized packets. I put my hand below it, just to make sure.

And there, in the roof of his helmet, Bob had left the key.

Literally, the key.

I felt it there with complete disbelief.

Fixed to the hard outer casing by two crossed strips of sellotape, unseen until one deliberately pushed the central piece of padding sideways out of position, was a key.

I unstuck it from the helmet and pulled off the sticky tape. It was a yale-type key, but with a small black tag bonded on instead of the usual round metal thumb plate. A small white number, C14, was stamped on the black plastic on the side which had been against the helmet's wall. The key itself, at first, second, third glance, had been unnoticeable: and Bob certainly could have ridden his races with it firmly and invisibly in place.

C14.

It looked like a locker key. Very like those from the left-luggage lockers of any big airport or railway station in the world. Nothing at all to show to which city, country or continent it belonged.

I thought.

If the key had been in the package, one would have expected it to be of extreme importance. Vital enough to be worth dragging the pond for, when it was found to be missing. Or searching for at once in the house in England.

The men searching the house in England had specifically mentioned papers. They had been looking for papers, not a key.

So, suppose Bob had left the papers somewhere in a locker, and this was the key to it.

Much easier. It cut out New York, Nairobi and outer Mongolia and narrowed the search to most of southern England or anywhere in Oslo.

The harmless-looking little key promised to be everything I needed. I closed my hand over it, with an illogical instinct to hide it, to keep it safe.

Bob too must have felt like that. The care with which he'd hidden it revealed the strength of his instinct. And he hadn't known at the time how true that instinct had been.

Smiling at myself I nevertheless followed his example.

There was in my suitcase a fresh unopened dressing for the cut on my chest, thoughtfully provided by Charles Stirling in case I needed it: but since the intermittent throbbing had faded to an intermittent itch, I'd left his original handiwork undisturbed.

Laying the key on the bedside table I pulled off the old dressing to take a look: and dark, dry and healthy, the slit was healing fast.

I fetched the new plaster and stuck it on, with Bob Sherman's precious key snug inside it against my skin.

CHAPTER THIRTEEN

Erik came to breakfast looking almost as depressed as the freezing wet day outside. He brought two plates heaped like the Matterhorn over from the buffet, sat opposite me, and toyed with the foothills.

'Did you sleep well?' he asked.

'No.'

'Nor did I. Kept hearing the bang of that bloody bomb.' He looked at the smoked fish I had acquired before his arrival. 'Aren't you eating?'

'Not madly hungry.'

He raised a grin. 'The condemned man syndrome?'

'Thanks.'

He sighed, adjusted his mind to the task and began proving his stomach was as big as his eyes. When both plates were empty of all but a trace of oil and six dorsal fins he patted his mouth with a napkin and resurfaced to the dangerous Sunday.

'Are you seriously going to the races?' he said.

'Don't know yet.'

'I didn't bring Odin today. Left him with a neighbour.' He drank his coffee. 'I hired a bigger Volvo. A fast one. Here's the bill.' He dug in his pocket and produced a receipt.

I took out my wallet and paid him. He didn't say leave it until later.

A party of English racing people came into the restaurant in ones and twos and sat together at a table near the window. I knew most of them: a top amateur jump rider, a pro from the flat, an assistant trainer, an owner and his wife. When they'd chosen their food and begun to eat I drifted over to them and pulled up a chair.

'Hi,' they said. 'How's things?'

Things, meaning mostly their chances that afternoon,

were relaxedly discussed, and after a while I asked the question I had joined them for.

'Remember the weekend Bob Sherman disappeared? Did any of you happen to come over with him on the same flight?'

The top amateur rider had. Glory be.

'Did you sit next to each other?'

He explained delicately that he had travelled first class, Bob tourist.

'But,' he said, 'I gave him a lift into Oslo in my taxi.'

'Where did you drop him?'

'Oh . . . here. I was staying here, but he was going on to that trainer feller he rode for. He thanked me for the ride . . . and I think he said he would catch the Lijordet tram if there was one. Anyway, I remember him standing on the pavement with his bag and saddle and stuff. But does it matter? After all, he rode next day, all right.'

'Was the flight on time?'

'Don't remember that it wasn't.'

I asked a few more questions, but the amateur remembered nothing else of much significance.

'Thanks anyway,' I said.

'Hope you get whoever did it,' he said. He smiled. 'I expect you will.'

If he didn't get me, I thought with a twinge, and went back to collect Erik.

'Where first?'

'All the railway stations.'

'All the *what*?'

'The nearest railway station,' I amended.

'Whatever for?'

'I want a time-table.'

'They have them here at the hotel desk.'

I grinned at him. 'Which is the nearest station?'

He said doubtfully, 'The Østbanen, I suppose.'

'Off we go, then.'

He shook his head in exasperation, but off we went.

From the Østbanen, I discovered, trains ran through Gol on the line to Bergen. Trains ran also to Lillehammer, Trondheim, and the Arctic circle. Østbanen was the main long-distance terminus in Oslo.

It had left-luggage lockers and it even had a C14. But the locker was empty, the key was in the open door, and the tag was different.

I took time-tables which included Gol, where Mikkel Sandvik's school was.

One never knew.

'What now?' Erik said.

'The other railway stations,' I said, and we went there, but without finding any matching black tags.

'Where else would you find lockers like those?'

'Besides railway stations? At the airport. In factories, offices, schools. Lots of places.'

'Available to a foreign traveller at eight-thirty on a Saturday evening.'

'Ah . . . Fornebu. Where else?' Where else indeed. 'Shall we go there?'

'Later,' I said. 'After Sven Wangen.'

Erik objected. 'He lives in the opposite direction, further out than the racecourse.'

'All the same,' I said. 'Sven Wangen first.'

'You're the boss.'

He looked carefully several times in the driving mirror as we set off, but said he was sure we were not being followed. I believed him. Nothing could have stayed with Erik when he was really trying.

'Tell me about Sven Wangen,' I said.

He pursed his mouth in much the same disapproving way that Arne had.

'His father was a collaborator,' he said.

'And no one forgets it?'

He sniffed. 'Officially, the past is past. But after the war, the collaborators didn't thrive. If some town wanted a bridge built or a school, for instance, it would happen that an architect or a builder who had worked well with the

Nazis would just not be the one to get the contract.'

'But Sven Wangen's father was already rich ... from shipping.'

He looked at me sideways while taking a sharp turn to the left and missed a lamp post by millimetres.

'Arne Kristiansen told me,' I said.

'Inherited wealth is immoral,' Erik said. 'All estates should be distributed among the masses.'

'Especially the estates of collaborators?'

He grinned. 'I suppose so.'

'Was the father like the son?' I asked.

Erik shook his head. 'A hard-headed greedy businessman. He made a lot of money out of the Nazis.'

'Surely that was patriotic of him?'

Erik wouldn't have it. 'He did nothing for his fellow-countrymen. He made money only for himself.'

'The father destroyed the son,' I said.

'Destroyed him?' He shook his head. 'Sven Wangen is an overpowering boor who always gets his way. He's nowhere near destroyed.'

'He's an empty person. Because of his father, I shouldn't think he ever had a chance to be normally liked, and people who are spurned for no fault of their own can become terribly aggressive.'

He thought it over. 'Guess you may be right. But I still don't like him.'

Sven Wangen lived in the style to which he had been born in a huge country house built mostly of wood, partly of stone. Even on a cold wet early winter morning it looked neat, clean and prosperous. Everything growing was sharply clipped into geometric precision, a regimentation totally uncongenial to Erik's casual, generous and untidy mind. He stared around in distaste, his give-everything-to-the-masses expression much in evidence.

'All this for two people,' he said. 'It's wrong.'

The place oppressed me as well, but for a different reason. There were too many windows all looking with black eyes towards the car. If I got out and stood away from its protection I would be a sitting target for anyone in that house with a gun.

Erik got out of the car. I had to force myself to follow him.

And of course, no one shot. If I'd really thought they would I wouldn't have gone. But it was one thing telling myself that Sven Wangen wasn't going to kill me on his own doorstep and another getting my nerves to believe it. Something, I thought grimly, was going to have to be done about those stupid nerves, or I'd never complete the course.

A middle-aged woman came to open the front door and show me down the hall to a small sitting-room with windows facing the drive. Through them I could see Erik pacing up and down in the rain radiating Marxist disapproval and stamping the undeserving bourgeoisie into the gravel with each crunch of his heel.

Sven Wangen strolled into the room eating a sugary pastry and staring with cold eyes down from a great height.

'I'd forgotten you were coming,' he said. 'Have you solved everything yet?' A slight sneer. No friendliness.

'Not everything.'

A small bad-tempered flash in the supercilious eyes.

'I've nothing to tell you. You are wasting your time.'

They'd all told me that, and they were all mistaken.

Without a hat, Sven Wangen was revealed as going prematurely bald, the russet hair as thick as ever round the back and sides, but almost as thin as Erik's on top. He took a large sticky bite, chewed, swallowed: added another fraction to his overweight.

'The last day Bob Sherman rode for you, did he say anything unexpected?'

'No, he did not.' He hadn't bothered to think about it.

'Did you take him for a drink to celebrate the winner he rode for you?'

'Certainly not.' He started another mouthful.

'Did you talk to him at all . . . either before or after the race?'

He chewed. Swallowed. Looked closely at the pastry, prospecting the next area.

'In the parade ring, I gave him his orders. I told him I expected better than he'd just done for Rolf Torp. He said he understood.'

Bite. Munch. Swallow.

'After the race, he unsaddled the horse and went to weigh in. I didn't see him again.'

'While he was unsaddling, did he tell you how the mare had run?'

'No. I was telling Holth she needed a good thrashing to quieten her down. Holth disagreed. I didn't speak to Sherman.'

'Didn't you congratulate him?' I asked curiously.

'No.'

'Do you wish you had?'

'Why should I?'

You might need to eat less, I thought, but refrained from saying so. His psychological hang-ups weren't in this instance my affair.

'Did he mention delivering a package which he had brought from England?'

'No.' He stuffed the rest of the gooey goody into his mouth and had difficulty closing his lips.

'Did you ask him to ride the mare next time he came?'

He stared, then spoke round the dough and currants. 'He didn't come again.'

'I mean, that last day, did you ask him to ride for you again?'

'Oh. No.' He shrugged. 'Holth always engages the jockeys. I just say who I want.'

'You never telephoned to Sherman in England personally to discuss his rides for you?'

'Certainly not.'

'Some owners do talk to their jockeys,' I said.

'I pay Holth to do that sort of thing.'

What a lot you miss, I thought. Poor fat unloved deprived rich young man. I thanked him for his time and went back to Erik. Sven Wangen watched us through the window, licking the sugar off his fingers.

'Well?' Erik said.

'He might have issued the orders, but he never killed anyone himself.'

Erik grunted as he started the hired Volvo towards the gate. 'Where now?'

'You're wet,' I said. 'Why did you stay out in the rain?'

He was almost embarrassed. 'Oh . . . I thought I'd hear you better if you yelled.'

We went in silence for five miles down the road and then he pulled up at a fork.

'You'll have to decide here,' he said. 'That way to Øvrevoll, and that way to the airport. The racecourse is much nearer.'

'The airport.'

'Right.'

He blasted off down the road to Fornebu as if trying to fly there.

'Mind we aren't followed,' I said.

'You're joking.'

The thirty mile journey, from one side of Oslo to the other, took just over half an hour.

No one followed.

C14 was locked and C13 next to it had a key in its door with a black tag, just the same. Both were large lockers in the bottom row of a three-high tier.

Erik, who had allotted himself full bodyguard status, stood at my elbow and peered at the ranks of metal doors.

'Are these the lot you're looking for?'

I nodded. 'I think so.'

'What do we do now, then?'

'We walk around for a bit to make sure there's no one here we know.'

'A sensible idea.'

We walked around and stood in corners to watch, but as far as I could see every person in the airport was a complete stranger. Drifting gently back to the lockers, Erik stood stalwartly with his back to C13 and looked ready to repel boarders while I inconspicuously fished out the hidden key and tried it in the lock next door.

The right key, no mistake. The locker door swung open revealing a space big enough for two large suitcases: and on the scratched metal floor, looking lost and inappropriate, lay a folded piece of paper.

I bent down, picked it up, and tucked it into my inside jacket pocket.

'See anyone?' I asked Erik, straightening again.

'Not a soul we know.'

'Let's grab some coffee.'

'What about the locker?'

I looked down at C14 with its key in the lock and its door open.

'We don't need it any more.'

Erik steered us to the airport buffet and bought coffee for both of us and a couple of open sandwiches for himself. We sat at a plastic-topped table amid travellers with untidy hand luggage and children running about doing what they were told not to, and with an almost fluttery feeling of expectation I took out the paper Bob Sherman had left.

I had supposed it would prove to be a base for blackmail: incriminating letters or photographs no one dared show his wife. But it proved to be neither of those things. It proved to be something I didn't recognize at all.

For one thing, the paper was thinner than I had at first supposed, and only seemed to be thick because it was folded several times. Unfolded, it turned out to be a strip six inches across but nearly three feet long, and it was divided into three columns which were intended to be read downwards. One could not, however, actually read them, as each inch and a half wide column seemed to be composed of variously shaded blocks and squares, not letters or figures. Down the long left-hand edge of the paper were numbers at regular intervals, starting with 3 at the top and ending with 14 at the bottom. Across the top in hand-written capitals was a single heading: Data Summary.

I refolded the strip and put it back in my pocket.

'What is it?' Erik asked.

I shook my head. 'Don't know.'

He stirred his coffee. 'Knut will find out.'

I considered that and didn't especially like it.

'No,' I said. 'This paper came from England. I think I'll take it back there to find out what it is.'

'It's Knut's case,' he said with a certain amount of quiet obstinacy.

'Mine as well.' I hesitated. 'Tell Knut I found the paper if you must, but I'd rather you didn't mention it to anyone at all. I don't want it leaking out round Oslo, and if you tell Knut he will have to record it, and if he records it, you never know who will see it. I'd much rather tell him myself when I get back. We can't anyway make a useful plan of campaign until we know what we're dealing with, so nothing can really be gained by telling him now.'

He looked unconvinced, but after a while all he said was, 'Where did you find the key to the locker?'

'In Bob Sherman's helmet.'

His obstinacy slowly melted to resignation.

'All right,' he said. 'I won't tell Knut. He could have found the key first.'

As logic it hardly stood up, but I was grateful. I looked at my watch and said, 'I can catch the two five to Heathrow.'

'Right now?' He sounded surprised.

I nodded. 'Don't tell anyone I've gone. I don't want any friend of yellow eyes waiting at the other end.'

He grinned. 'David Cleveland? Who's he?' He stood up and turned to go. 'I'll give your regards to Odin.'

I watched his untidy back depart forthwith through the scattered crowd towards the distant exit and felt unexpectedly vulnerable without him. But nothing dire happened. I caught the flight and landed safely at Heathrow, and, after thought, left my car where it was in the car park and took myself by train to Cambridge.

Sunday evening in mid-term was as good a time as any to beard professors in their dens, but the first one I backed was a loser. He lectured in Computer Science: but my Data

Summary, he said, had nothing to do with computers. Why didn't I try Economics? I tried Economics who said why didn't I try Geology.

Although it was by then getting on for ten o'clock I tried Geology, who took one brief glance at the paper and said, 'Christ, where did you get this, they guard these things like gold dust.'

'What is it?' I asked.

'A core. A chart of a core. From a drilling. See those numbers down the left-hand side? I'd say they refer to the depth of each section. Might be in hundreds of feet. Might be in thousands.'

'Can you tell where the drilling was done?'

He shook his head, a youngish earnest man with a mass of reddish hair merging into an undisciplined beard.

'Could be anywhere in the world. You'd need the key to the shadings even to guess what they were looking for.'

I said in depression, 'Isn't there any way of finding out where it came from?'

'Oh Lord, yes,' he said cheerfully. 'Depends how important it is.'

'It's a long story,' I said doubtfully, with a look at his clock.

'Sleep is a waste of time,' he said like a true scholar, so I told him more or less exactly why I wanted to know.

'Have a beer?' he suggested, when I'd finished.

'Thanks.'

He found two cans under a heap of uncorrected essays and ripped off the rings.

'Cheers!' he said, dispensing with a glass. 'All right. You convinced me. I'll pass you on to the people who drew that chart.'

I was astonished. 'How do you know who drew it?'

He laughed. 'It's like knowing a colleague's handwriting. Any research geologist could probably tell you where that chart came from. It's a research lab job. I'll give the managing director a ring in the morning and explain, and see if he'll help you. They're awfully touchy about these charts.' He eyed it thoughtfully. 'I shouldn't be surprised if there'll be an unholy row, because from what you've said I should think it was stolen.'

The seeds of the unholy row were plain to see, next day, on the face of Dr William Leeds, managing director of the Wessex-Wells Research Laboratory. An impressive man, small, calm and decisive, he looked deeply disturbed at what I'd brought him.

'Sit down, Mr Cleveland,' he said.

We sat one each side of his managerial desk.

'Tell me where you got this.'

I told him. He listened intently, without interrupting. At the end he said, 'What do you want to know?'

'What this chart is about. Who could benefit from getting hold of it, and how.'

He smiled. 'Fairly comprehensive.' He looked out of his big first floor office window for a while at a row of leaf-dropping willows across a stretch of lawn. Deep in the heart of Dorset, the laboratory stood in ancient parkland, a Victorian country residence sitting easily beside new low flat-topped workaday workshops. Dr Leeds's window overlooked the main artery of pathways linking the complex, a neat finger on the pulse if ever I saw one.

'Almost anyone could benefit from getting hold of it,' he said. 'If they were unscrupulous. This chart cost perhaps half a million pounds.'

My mouth fell open. He laughed.

'Well . . . you have to remember that drill rigs are enormously sophisticated and expensive. You don't get a core by digging a hole with a spade. This one . . .' he tapped the paper, 'is only five inches in diameter but about fourteen thousand feet in depth. A fourteen thousand foot drilling costs a lot of money.'

'I can see,' I said, 'that it does.'

'Of course you couldn't sell it for that, but I should think this particular chart might be worth a hundred thousand, if you had a market.'

I asked if he would explain in more detail.

'A chart like this is information. You can always sell information illegally if you know someone ready to buy. Well . . . suppose this core showed a deposit of nickel, which it doesn't, incidentally, and you knew exactly from which particular drilling it came, you would know whether it was worth investing money in the drilling company, or not. For instance, during the Poseidon nickel boom in Australia, you'd have been able to make literally millions on the stock market through knowing infallibly in advance which of the dozens of prospecting companies had made the drilling that was richest in ore.'

'Good grief,' I said.

'It can work the other way too,' he said. 'If you know that a concession which has been expected to give a high yield is in fact not going to be good, you can sell out while the share price is still high.'

'So it wouldn't only be people engaged in mining who would be ready to buy such a chart.'

'Certainly not. The people who make most out of the earth probably don't know what a drill looks like.'

I said, 'Why sell the chart to someone else? Why not make millions on the stock market yourself?'

He smiled. 'It's much safer to be paid a lump sum into a nice anonymous Swiss bank account than to start dealing in shares. Any geologist dealing much in significant shares would be detected at once.'

'Do people approach geologists, asking them to sell information?'

'They do. We try to protect our geologists here by not letting them know exactly where the material they're working on has come from. But obviously we have not been entirely successful.' He looked bleak. 'We know from past experience that a working geologist is usually approached by a middle man, an entrepreneur who buys information from the research source and then sells it to a bigger fish who operates in the world markets.'

'Am I dealing with the middle man or the big fish?'

He smiled and shook his head. 'Can't tell. But the middle man, I suspect, as you found the chart so close to source.'

'What exactly do these columns mean?' I asked.

He picked up the chart and showed me. 'The first column is lithology . . . the composition of the rock layers. The second is the original particle type . . . that means micro- and macrofossils and micrite. The third . . .' He compressed his lips, clearly most upset by this one. 'The third is a fairly new and highly secret process, scanning electron microscopy. Our clients will be particularly furious that this finding has been leaked. They paid a mint for it. We can stay in business here only as long as every client remains convinced that the analysis he is paying for will never be seen by anyone except himself.'

I said, 'This chart wouldn't be much use, though, without the key to the various shadings.'

'No.' He thought. 'If I had to guess, I'd say that this might be used as a sort of appetizer, or a proof that the middle man had the real goods to sell. We don't normally make up charts in this form. This is an abbreviation. A condensed, composite edition. Specially made.'

'But would the rest of Bob Sherman's package be worth anything without this chart?'

'Oh, sure. It depends what else was in it. A written analysis would be just as good as a chart. If they had a written analysis it wouldn't matter all that much if they lost the chart.'

I thanked him for his help. 'Could you tell me where that drilling was made . . . and what for?'

He glanced at it. 'I can tell you in general just by looking at it. But do you want to know precisely, to the half mile?'

'Please,' I said.

'Then come with me.'

He led me along a wide passage, through some swing doors, and into a modern wing tacked on to the back of the original house. We were bound, it seemed, for the records department, but to get in there even the managing director had to announce himself to the inmates and get the door unlocked electronically from inside.

He smiled wryly at my surprise.

'We usually pride ourselves on our security. We're going to have a great upheaval sorting out which of our people sold the information on this chart.' A thought struck him. 'I suppose you wouldn't like to come back and work on it yourself?'

I wouldn't have minded, but explained about the Jockey Club.

'Pity,' he said.

He unerringly sorted out one particular folder from the thousands in the filing cupboards which lined the walls. He knew exactly which company had commissioned the analysis, and he knew roughly from where the core had been taken.

He turned a few pages, comparing the chart with the notes.

'There,' he said finally, pointing with his finger. 'Those are the coordinates you want.'

I looked over his arm. Read the coordinates.

Read the name of the company.

I'd never heard of it.

'Thank you very much,' I said.

CHAPTER FOURTEEN

I called to see Emma.

The cottage was warm and welcoming in the cold afternoon, alive with a glowing log fire and a huge vase of bronze chrysanthemums. None of the furniture had been replaced and the curtains were still at the cleaners, but Emma herself during the past week had made strides. There was at last a shade of colour in her cheeks and the faintest of sparkles in the eyes. The pretty girl had come back to life.

'David! How great to see you. Have a hot scone. They're just out of the oven.'

We sat in front of the fire eating the scones with butter and jam and concentration.

'Golly, you must have been hungry,' she said later, eyeing the almost-empty dish. 'I really made them to take over to Grandfather.' She laughed. 'Guess I'd better make some more.'

'They were lovely.' What with bombs and general chasing around I had missed a lot of meals and picked at others. With Emma, for the first time in days, my stomach nerves felt safe enough to encourage intake.

'I don't know whether to ask,' she said, 'but have you found out anything about Bob?'

'Not enough.' I looked at my watch. 'May I use your telephone?'

'Of course.'

I called a stockbroker I knew who owned racehorses and asked him about the share movements of the company which had commissioned the analysis of the core.

'That's easy,' he said. 'About two months ago the share price started to soar. Someone had a hot tip, bought at the bottom and made a real packet.'

'Who?' I said.

'Impossible to tell, but probably a syndicate, considering the huge sums involved. All done through nominees, mostly on overseas markets.'

I thanked him and rang off; and after that I called SAS, who made warm noises and said sure there was a free seat on the six-thirty. A lot of my mind persisted in telling me that there was another flight in the morning and widows were meant for consoling: well, maybe, but not this one, not yet.

I kissed her goodbye.

'Come again,' she said, and I said, 'I will.'

I handed in at Heathrow the car I'd hired that morning in Cambridge, and squeezed into the six-thirty at the last call.

I didn't seem able to help the tension screwing up again as we began the descent into Oslo, but a harmless taxi took me uneventfully to the hotel, where the reception desk resignedly let me choose my own room.

I telephoned to Erik.

'Where are you?' he demanded.

'At the Grand.'

'For God's sake . . . didn't you go?'

'There and back.'

'Did you find out . . . ?'

'Up to a point. I know what it is, but not who it belongs to. Look . . . could you give me Knut's home number?'

He told me. 'Do you want any more driving done?'

'I'm afraid so, if you can face it.'

'Count,' he said, 'on me.'

I rang Knut who yawned and said he'd just come off duty and wouldn't be back until two o'clock the following afternoon.

'Do you know a place called Lillehammer?' I asked.

'*Ja.* Of course.'

'What's it like?'

'How do you mean? It is a big town. A tourist town in the summer, and a ski place in the winter. No visitors go there in October and November.'

'If you wanted to meet someone secretly in Lillehammer, within fairly easy walking distance of the railway station, where would you suggest?'

'Not in a public place?'

'No. Somewhere quiet.'

There was a pause. Then he said, 'It might be better to walk away from the town itself. Down towards the lake. There is a road going down to the bridge over the lake. It is the main road to Gjøvik, but there is not much traffic, and there are some small side roads down to the houses round the lakeside. Is that what you want?'

'Sounds perfect.'

'Who are you going to meet?'

I told him at considerable length. Somewhere along the

way he shed his fatigue, because when he next spoke his voice was alert and even eager.

'*Ja*. I understand. I will arrange everything.'

'I'll see you in the morning, then.'

'*Ja*. Agreed. And . . . er . . . take good care, David.'

'You bet,' I said.

I rang Erik again, who said certainly he would come to breakfast, drive me to Knut's office, and get me to the station in time to catch the ten o'clock to Lillehammer.

'Is that all?'

'No . . . Would you meet me again when I get back? Four thirty, I think.'

'All right.' He sounded almost disappointed.

'Bring knuckledusters,' I said, which cheered him.

Next, Lars Baltzersen.

'Of course I've heard of that company,' he said. 'Their shares are booming. I bought some myself a few weeks ago and already they show a good profit.'

'Do you know anyone else who bought any while the price was still low?'

A pause, then he said, 'Rolf Torp did. I believe it was Rolf who told me about them, but I can't be sure.' He cleared his throat. 'I have heard worrying rumours, though, that the really big buyers were in the Middle East. One cannot be sure. There is much secrecy. But it seems likely.'

'Why would that be worrying?' I asked, and he told me.

Last of all I telephoned Arne. Kari answered, her voice warm, amused, and full of memory from our last meeting.

'Haven't seen you since Friday,' she said. 'Why don't you come to dinner here tomorrow?'

'Love to,' I said, 'but I don't think I can.'

'Oh. Well . . . how's the case going?'

'That's really what I wanted to talk about with Arne.'

She said she would fetch him, and he came on the line. He sounded glad that I'd called.

'David . . . haven't seen you for days,' he said. 'What have you been doing?'

'Ferreting,' I said. 'Look, Arne, I've had a piece of luck.

Some man in a place called Lillehammer telephoned and said he could tell me something about Bob Sherman being killed. He said he almost saw it happen. He wouldn't say any more on the phone, but I'm going to meet him tomorrow. The thing is . . . I wondered if you'd like to come with me. I'd be glad of your company, if you could spare the time. And he didn't speak very good English . . . so you could interpret for me, if you would.'

'Tomorrow?'

'Yes. I'm catching the ten o'clock train in the morning.'

'Where in Lillehammer are you meeting this man?'

'On the road to Gjøvik, down near the bridge over the lake. He's going to be there at midday.'

He said doubtfully, 'I suppose I could . . .'

'Please do come, Arne,' I said.

He made up his mind. '*Ja.* I'll come. Are you still staying at the Grand?'

'Yes,' I said. 'But you are nearer the station. I'll meet you there.'

'Right.' He hesitated again. 'I hope he isn't some lunatic, making up stories.'

'So do I,' I said.

I slept with my bed pushed right across the door, but nobody tried to get in.

Erik had brought Odin again to assist with the guard duty, although I now knew from longer acquaintance that the Dane's fierce appearance was only a front. A right great softy lived inside the sandy skin.

Together nonetheless they conveyed me safely to the police station where Knut met us, keenly awake a good five hours before he was due on duty. Up in his office I gave him the geological chart, which he inspected curiously.

'Don't lose it,' I said.

He smiled. 'Better to lose my life, I suspect.'

'You'll get it photo-copied?'

He nodded. 'Straight away.'

'See you this evening, then.'

We shook hands.

'Be careful,' he said.

Erik and Odin stuck beside me while I bought my ticket and walked to the barrier. It was the worst morning yet for jumpy nerves, with me far outstripping Arne in the matter of looking over my shoulder. By this evening, I thought grimly, I'd either be safe or dead. It seemed an awful long time to the evening.

Arne, already waiting on the platform, greeted me with a big smile.

'What number is your ticket?' he asked.

I hadn't realized that each ticket bore a seat number on the train, but it was so.

'I'll see if I can change mine to be next to you,' he said, and vanished on his errand at high speed. While he was gone I found my allotted number, a window seat facing forward, halfway up one of the large, airy coaches. With only a few minutes to go to departure time about half the seats were filled with respectable-looking citizens, and I managed to look over my shoulder only twice.

Arne returned with an air of satisfaction and the ticket for the seat beside mine.

'That's better,' he said, and gave all the worthy fellow travellers a severe inspection before sitting down. 'I should have waited for you at the ticket office . . . didn't think of it in time.'

Erik, with Odin still beside him, suddenly appeared on the platform outside the window, rapping to attract my attention and vigorously beckoning me to talk to him. I pointed to the rear of the carriage, excused myself past Arne, and went to the door to hear what Erik wanted to tell.

'I saw him,' he said, almost stuttering with urgency. 'Get off the train and come with me.'

'Who?'

'It'll go if you don't get off quickly. The man who planted the bomb. Big, with a butterfly birthmark. I saw it. He was buying a ticket . . . he dropped some change and bent to pick it up. I saw his neck . . . and I saw his eyes. They really are a sort of yellow. Very light and bright and odd. Do hurry, David. There was another man with him. They got on this train, in the rear carriage. Three carriages back from here.'

A whistle blew. He practically danced with frustration.

'Get off. Get off . . .'

I shook my head. 'I'll find a way of avoiding them.' The train began to move. 'Thanks a lot. See you this afternoon. Mind you come.'

'Of course I'll come.'

The train gathered speed, diminishing my protectors second by second until I could no longer see the bewilderment on Erik's face or the patient lack of comprehension on Odin's.

'Who was that?' Arne asked as I returned to my place.

'Someone I hired to drive me around.'

'Extraordinary looking chauffeur, isn't he?'

I smiled. 'His driving is pretty hair-raising as well.'

'Tell me about this man we're going to see.'

'I don't know much, really. He said his name was Johan Petersen . . .'

Arne grunted. 'There are dozens of Johan Petersens.'

'He said he was at the races the day Bob Sherman disappeared. He said he would like to tell me something about that. He said he lived at Lillehammer and worked there in the timber yard. I asked him to come to Oslo, but he said he couldn't take the day off. He said he'd meet me during his lunch break today. It was very difficult to understand him clearly, as he spoke so little English. It'll be fine with you there.'

Arne nodded, blinking away as usual. The train took things easily, sliding quietly through the outer suburbs in a typically unhurried Norwegian fashion.

'How will you know him?'

'He said he would know me. All I have to do is walk down towards the bridge carrying an English newspaper.'

'Did you bring one?'

I nodded. 'In my coat pocket.'

The train was well heated. Coats were expected to be shed, and there was a rail at the rear equipped with hangers, where Arne's coat and mine hung side by side.

The line ran north through farmland and woods and alongside an extensive lake. On any other day I would have enjoyed the journey but it was extraordinary how a little fear could keep the mind focused close at hand. Old yellow eyes and his pal were a sight too near for comfort, and I'd developed an even worse over-the-shoulder compulsion through passengers walking up the centre aisle through the train. Every bang of the door from one carriage to the next had me looking to make sure.

A woman in a blue overall pushed a trolley into the carriage, selling from it hot drinks, biscuits and sweets. Arne bought me coffee. The trolley trundled away, and bang went the door behind her.

We stopped lengthily at a largish town, Hamar, a junction with masses of open windswept platforms and no air of shunting or bustle. Then on again, moving faster, on towards Lillehammer. Two and a half hours, altogether, on the train.

'I missed you at the races on Sunday,' Arne said.

'Yes. I meant to go, but it was so cold.'

He gave me a look of friendly contempt.

'I might be going home soon,' I said.

'Are you?' He was surprised. 'I thought... you'd never leave us without finding out...'

'Well, after this trip today we should know a lot more. With a bit of luck. And then there's the key...'

'What key?'

'I found a luggage-locker key stuck in Bob Sherman's riding helmet.'

'You didn't!'

I nodded and told him about the trail to Paddy O'Flaherty's. 'So you see, although I'll go home soon, we should have most of the answers.'

Arne was enthusiastic. 'That's great,' he said. 'All we have to do now is find what's in the locker which the key fits.' A thought struck him. 'Perhaps it's that money. In the canvas bags . . . you know, the money that was stolen.'

'It's a thought,' I said. I didn't launch into explaining what actually had been in the locker; time enough for that later, as from the way the other passengers were standing up and putting on their coats it was clear we had nearly arrived. The train ran beside Lake Mjøsa and in the distance I could see the timber yard, with acres of pine tree logs floating in the water.

Arne held my coat for me, and I his for him. He smiled a little sadly.

'Kari and I will miss you.'

'I'll be back one day. I like Norway very much.'

He nodded. The train passed the end of the bridge to Gjøvik, climbed a hill slowly, inched into Lillehammer station, and sighed to a stop. We stepped out into a stinging wind under a grey cloud-filled sky. So much, I thought, for all those happy holiday posters of sun and snow and people on skis showing their suntans and teeth. It was odd, too, how none of the far frozen north railway stations had sheltering roofs over the platforms. Perhaps no one ever stood waiting in the open air, so that roofs were redundant and there was some point in them all still looking like the last scene in *Anna Karenina*.

'Are you coming, David?' Arne said.

'Yeah.' I stopped looking around vaguely and followed him through the main doors into the booking hall. At the far end of the platform two men, by-passing the station buildings, had set off quickly in the general direction of the road to the bridge. One was big. The other, of the same build as my attacker in the flat. They were too far away for me to swear to it in court.

But I was sure, just the same.

The small booking hall was scattered with prospective travellers wearing limbo expressions, waiting for time to pass. There were seats round the walls, doors to washrooms, a window for buying tickets: all the amenities in one central area. Arne said he wanted to make a telephone call before we set off to the meeting with our informer down the road.

'Carry on,' I said amiably.

I watched him through the glass wall of the booth feeding money into the slot and talking earnestly into the mouthpiece. He talked for a good long time, and came out smiling.

'All done. Let's go,' he said.

'Arne . . . ' I hesitated. 'I know this is going to sound silly, but I don't want to go.'

He looked dumbstruck. 'But why not? This man might have seen who killed Bob Sherman.'

'I know. But . . . I can't explain it. I have . . . the weirdest feeling of premonition. I've had it before . . . I can't . . . I can't ignore it. Something tells me not to go. So I'm not going.'

'But David,' he said. 'That's crazy.'

'I can't help it. I'm not going.'

'But what about the man?'

I said helplessly, 'I don't know.'

Arne grew impatient. He tried insults. He tried persuasion. I wouldn't budge.

In the end he said, 'Give me the newspaper. I'll go and meet him myself.'

'But,' I objected, 'if my premonition means there is some danger down that road, it must be dangerous for you as well. I had a premonition about a street once before . . . I wouldn't go down it, and a few seconds later several tons of scaffolding collapsed on to where I would have been. Ever since then, when I've a strong feeling against doing something, I don't do it.'

He blinked at me earnestly. 'If I see any scaffolding, I'll keep away from it. But we must see this Johan Petersen and hear his story. Give me the newspaper.'

Reluctantly I handed him the previous day's *Express*.

'I'll wait for you here,' I said.

He nodded, still not pleased, and set off on his own. I chose a place to sit at one end of one of the bench seats, with solid wall at my back and on one side. On my other side sat a plump teenage girl in a shaggy sheepskin coat eating herring sandwiches noisily.

A few people came. A train arrived and took most of them away, including my neighbour. Time passed very slowly.

An hour and a half between our arrival and the train back to Oslo. An hour and a half to kill. Correction, I thought wryly. To stay alive. I wished I smoked or bit my nails or went in for yoga. I wished my heart wouldn't jump every time people walked past the window in pairs. I wished I knew what views yellow eyes and brown eyes held on murdering in public, because if only I was sure they wouldn't risk it I could save myself a lot of fretting. As it was I sat and waited and slowly sweated, hoping I'd judged their limit right.

When passengers for the Oslo train started arriving and buying tickets I bought two myself for Arne and me. I asked particularly for the most public pair of seats in the carriage, as observed on the way up, and although I had difficulty explaining what I wanted as the ticket seller spoke little English, I got them.

Back in my careful corner I found myself flanked by an elderly man with an ear-flapped cap topping cream-coloured skin over an elongated skull. He had heard me speak English at the ticket window and was eager to tell me that he'd been in England the year before on holiday with his son and daughter-in-law. I encouraged him a bit, and got in return a minute by minute conducted tour from Tower Hill via Westminster Abbey to the National Gallery. By the time Arne came back, a quarter of an hour before train time, we were chatting away like old friends.

Arne was looking anxious. I stood up to meet him, gesturing to the elderly man and saying, 'We've been talking about London . . .'

Arne glanced at the man without really seeing him and abruptly interrupted. 'He didn't come.'

'Oh no,' I said.

Arne shook his head. 'I waited. I walked down to the

bridge twice. I showed the newspaper. No one spoke to me. No one even walked past looking as if they were looking for anyone.'

I made frustrated noises. 'What a bloody nuisance. I'm so sorry, Arne, to have wasted a whole day for you . . . but he sounded so definite. Perhaps he was delayed and couldn't help it. Perhaps we could telephone the timber yard . . .'

'I did,' he said. 'They haven't any Johan Petersen working there.'

We stared at each other.

I said depressedly, 'I banked so much on his giving us some really vital information.'

He looked at me uncertainly.

'My premonition was all wrong then,' I said.

'I told you.'

'Yes, you did.'

He began to fish out his wallet.

'I've got the tickets,' I said, producing them. 'Two seats together.'

'Oh . . . good.'

The train arrived, dark red and silver, and we climbed aboard. The seats were all I'd hoped, right down at one end, with their backs to the wardrobe end but facing every other seat in the coach. By a stroke of luck my elderly friend of the London holiday took his place on the aisle three seats down. He had a clear view of Arne and me, and waved and smiled. I told Arne how friendly he had been. Like all Norwegians, I said.

Arne jerked a look over his shoulder. Only a row of hangers with coats; but he didn't look happy.

Two bright-eyed young girls came and sat in the two seats directly facing us. I moved my feet out of the way of theirs, and smiled at them. They smiled back and said something in their own language.

'I'm English,' I said, and they repeated 'English' and nodded and smiled again. 'And this is my friend Arne Kristiansen.' They put the introduction down to the eccentricity of foreigners, saying hello to him with giggles. Arne said hello back, but he was old enough to be their father and not interested in their girlish chat.

The train started back towards Oslo. We talked for a while about the non-appearance of Johan Petersen and I said we would just have to hope that he would telephone again.

'You'll let me know if he does?'

'Of course,' I said.

The lady in blue overalls arrived, pushing her comforts trolley down the aisle. I said it was my turn to buy the coffee, and despite Arne's protestations I did so. I also offered drinks to the two girls who thought it a great lark and went pink. They asked Arne to see if it was all right for them to have orangeade, as they didn't like coffee. The lady in blue overalls patiently attended to all Arne's translations and finally with a smile gave him my change.

Arne began to wear the hunted look he often did in crowds.

'Let's go somewhere quieter,' he said.

'You go,' I said. 'But I rather like it here.'

He shook his head, but he stayed.

To his relief and my regret the two young girls got off at Hamar, giggling goodbye with backward glances. No one embarked to take their empty places, but after the train had started again my elderly friend got to his feet and came inquiringly towards us.

'May I sit here with you?' he said. 'It is so interesting to talk about England.'

Too much for Arne. He rose abruptly to his feet and dived through to the next carriage. The door banged behind him.

'Have I upset your friend?' asked the elderly man anxiously. 'I am sorry.'

'He has problems,' I said. 'But not of your making.'

Relieved, he launched into more reminiscences which bored me to death but quite likely kept me alive. He was still there, tal'-ing inexhaustibly, as we drew into Oslo. And on the platform, flanked by Odin, stood Erik anxiously looking out for me, just as promised.

There wasn't much time left. If they were going to make an attempt now they were going to have to do it in the open.

I stepped off the train and turned towards Erik. And there between us, looking sickeningly businesslike, stood the two men I least wanted to see.

CHAPTER FIFTEEN

Battle never commenced.

Erik saw them at the same moment I did, and yelled 'Police' at the top of his lungs.

Every person within earshot stopped to look.

'Police,' he yelled again, pointing at yellow eyes and brown eyes. 'These are thieves. Fetch the police.' And he repeated it in Norwegian, very loudly.

It broke their nerve. They looked round at the growing circle staring at them wide-eyed, and suddenly made a bolt for the exit. No one made much effort to stop them, and the chief expression on every beholder's face was astonishment.

Erik strode up to me and pumped my hand.

'Just putting your theory into practice,' he said.

I looked blank.

He explained. 'Knut told me you didn't think they'd kill you while people were looking. So I just got a few people to look.'

'Thanks.'

'Call it quits,' he said with a grin, and patted Odin.

I discovered that the palms of my hands were wet and a lot of me was quietly shaking.

'I need a telephone,' I said.

'You need a good stiff drink.'

'That too.'

I rang Knut. 'I'm back at the terminus,' I said.

'Thank God for that.'

'Did it work?'

I asked with some intensity, because I'd risked my skin for nearly seven shivery hours and no one could be entirely objective after that.

'Yes,' he said, but there was an odd note of reservation in his voice. 'At least . . . *ja*.'

'What's the matter?'

'You had better come here, to the police station. It will be easier to explain.'

'All right.'

I stepped outside the box and almost fell over Odin who was lying across the door like a medieval page. He gave me a reproachful look, stood nonchalantly up, and yawned.

I asked Erik, 'Did you see Arne Kristiansen anywhere?'

'Who?'

I scanned the crowd without success. 'Never mind. I expect he's gone home.'

In gathering dusk Erik drove sedately (only one near-miss) to the police building, where I went upstairs and found Knut sitting alone and chewing a pencil. He gestured me to the visitors' chair and produced only the vestige of a smile.

'Well . . . we did everything you suggested,' he said. 'We planted the chart in a locker at Fornebu and put the key loose in the helmet in your room at the Grand. We sprinkled anthracene dust over every surface an intruder would touch and we waited at Fornebu to see if anyone would come.'

He rattled the pencil along his teeth.

'Someone did come,' he said.

'Who?'

He sighed. 'You'd better come and see.'

He led the way out of his meagre office and down an uncarpeted corridor, and stopped outside a cream painted door. Bright light from inside shone through a small glass panel let into the wood at viewing height.

'Look,' Knut said.

I looked.

The room was small and bare, containing only a simple

table and three chairs. One chair was occupied by a young uniformed policeman looking stolid. On another, smoking quietly and as calm as if he were back in his own board-room, sat Per Bjørn Sandvik.

I pulled my head away from the glass and stared at Knut.

'Come back to my office,' he said.

We went back and sat down as before.

'He came to Fornebu and opened the locker,' Knut said. 'That was at . . .' he consulted a note-pad, '. . . fourteen thirty-five hours precisely. He removed the chart from the locker and put it in an inside pocket. I myself and two other officers went up to him as he was walking away from the lockers and asked him to accompany us to this police station. He seemed surprised but not . . . not deeply disturbed. I have arrested so many people . . . Per Bjørn Sandvik did not behave like a guilty man.'

He rubbed thumb and finger down his nose.

'I don't know what to make of him, David. He shrugged and said he would come with us if we liked, but he said almost nothing else until we got back here. He was completely calm. No sign of stress. None at all. He has been here now for about an hour and a half, and he has been calm and courteous the whole time.'

'What explanation did he give?'

'We went into that interview room and sat on the chairs, with a constable to take notes. Mr Sandvik offered me a cigarette. He said he had only been trying to help the investigation into Bob Sherman's death. He said Arne Kristiansen had telephoned to say that you had found a key which might lead to useful information, so he went to the Grand Hotel to fetch the key, which he recognized as having come from Fornebu, as he has often used those lockers in the past. So he went to the airport . . . to see what Bob Sherman had left there. He said he thought it might have been the missing money, but it was only a paper. He hadn't done more than glance at it when we stopped him.'

'Did he give any reason for doing all this himself and not

waiting for Arne or me to get back or enlisting the help of the police?'

'*Ja.*' He smiled a small tight smile to mock me. 'He said Arne asked him to do it. Arne wanted to prove to the racecourse committee that he was worth his salary as an investigator, so he telephoned to Sandvik as a member of the racecourse committee to tell him about the key. Arne apparently said that if he and Mr Sandvik helped with the case, the committee would not be able to give all the praise to you.'

'What do you think?'

He looked depressed. 'Per Bjørn Sandvik is a leader of industry. He is much respected. He is being very reasonable, but if we keep him here much longer he will be angry.'

'And your superiors will lean on you?'

'Er . . . *ja.*'

I thought.

'Don't worry, Knut,' I said. 'We've got the right man.'

'But he is so confident.'

I nodded. 'He's working on a false assumption.'

'What's that?'

'He thinks I'm dead.'

Per Bjørn Sandvik got a very nasty shock indeed when I walked into the interview room.

Muscles round his eyes and mouth contracted sharply, and his pale skin went perceptibly paler. But his resilience was extraordinary. Within three seconds he was smiling pleasantly with the deceptive lack of agitation which was so confusing Knut.

'David!' he said as if in welcome, yet I could almost hear and certainly sense the alarm bells going at panic strength.

'I'm afraid this isn't the happiest of meetings,' I said.

He was making such an urgent reappraisal that the muscles round his eyes were moving in tiny rhythmical spasms: which booted out of me any hint of complacency, because people who could think as quickly and intently as that in such adverse circumstances had brains to beware of.

Knut followed me into the room and told the young policeman to fetch another chair. While he went to get it I watched Per Bjørn finish reorganizing his thoughts. Infinitesimally, he relaxed. Too soon, I reckoned; and I couldn't afford to be wrong.

The extra chair came, and we all sat down round the bare table as if to a simple business discussion.

I said, 'It must have occurred to you by now that there was no Johan Petersen at Lillehammer.'

'I don't understand,' he said pleasantly in his high, distinct diction. 'I thought we were talking about the locker key and Fornebu airport.'

'We're talking about Arne Kristiansen,' I said.

A pause. I waited. But he was too cautious now to take any step without prospecting for quicksand, and after some time, when he said nothing, I invited him a little further along the path.

'You shouldn't rely on Arne,' I said. 'Arne is deep in, up to the neck.'

No response.

'Come to think of it,' I said. 'Up to his neck and over his head, considering the amount of swimming he's done.'

No reaction.

'All that messing around in the fjord,' I said. 'There was me thinking Arne had drowned, while all the time he had a scuba suit on under his red anorak. Nice snug black rubber with yellow seams, fitting right up over his head to keep him warm.' I'd seen the black-and-yellow under his anorak. It had taken me days to realize it had been rubber. But then that chug down the fjord happened before I'd begun to be sure that Arne was on the other side.

'A strong swimmer, Arne,' I said. 'A tough all-round sportsman. So there he is standing up in the dinghy waving his arms about as if to warn the speedboat not to run us down while all the time signalling to it that yes, this was the dinghy it was supposed to be sinking. This dinghy, not some other poor innocent slob out on a fishing trip. Arne swam ashore, reported an accident, reported me drowned.'

A pause.

'I don't know what you're talking about,' Per Bjørn said, and patiently sighed.

'I'm talking about Arne putting on his scuba suit and diving into the pond at Øvrevoll to get Bob Sherman out of it.'

Silence.

Arne had been sick when he saw the month-dead body. At night, when he'd fished Bob out and wrapped him in tarpaulin it couldn't have seemed so bad: but in the light of a drizzly day it had hit him a bull's-eye in the stomach.

'I'm talking about Arne being the one person who could be sure no one saw him putting bodies into ponds, taking them out again, and later putting them back again. Arne was security officer. He could come and go on that racecourse as he pleased. No one would think it odd if he were on the racecourse first, last, and during the night. But he could also make sure that the night-watchman saw nothing he shouldn't, because the night-watchman would carry out any attention-distracting task Arne gave him.'

Nothing.

'This is speculation,' he said.

Knut sat still and quiet, keeping his promise that he would make no comment, whatever I said. The young policeman's pencil had made scarcely a mark on the page.

'Arne stole the money himself,' I said. 'To provide a reason for Bob Sherman's disappearance.'

'Nonsense.'

'The impression of most people in the officials' room was that the money had been put in the safe. And so it had. Arne himself had put it there, as he usually does. He has keys to every gate, every building, every door on the place. He didn't take the money during the five minutes that the room happened to be empty. He had all night to do it in.'

'I don't believe it. Arne Kristiansen is a respected servant of the racecourse.'

He sat there listening to me with long-suffering courtesy as if I were a rather boring guest he was stuck with.

'Bob Sherman brought a packet of papers with him from England,' I said.

'Yes, you've already asked about that. I told you I couldn't help you.'

'Unfortunately for him, he was curious. He opened the package and saw what he had no business to see. He must have done this on the flight over, as he left some of the contents in a locker at Fornebu.'

Per Bjørn slowly turned his good-looking head until he was facing Knut, not me, and he spoke to him in Norwegian. Knut made gestures of regret and helplessness, and said nothing at all.

'Bob Sherman was too fond of schemes for getting rich quickly,' I said. 'He was being paid for bringing the envelope, but it seemed to him that he could push the price up a bit. Very much his mistake, of course. He got bonked on the head for his pains. And no one discovered until long after he was dead and in the pond that when he'd opened the envelope he'd taken something out.'

Per Bjørn sat impassively, waiting for the annoying gnat to stop buzzing around him.

I buzzed a bit more.

'Because what he took out was in a way a duplication of what he left in.'

That one hit home. His eye muscles jumped. He knew that I'd noticed. He smiled.

I said, 'Bob Sherman took the precaution of hiding the key to the Fornebu locker in his racing helmet. By the time he was brought out of the pond it had been discovered that he had removed a paper from the envelope, but a search of his waterlogged clothes and overnight bag failed to produce any sign of it. So did a search of his house in England. By the time I realized what must be going on, and came to wonder if Bob had somehow hidden the missing object in his racing saddle or helmet, others had had the same idea. His saddle, which had stayed on its peg in the changing room for a month after he disappeared, was suddenly nowhere to be found.'

He sat. Quiet.

'However, the helmet with the saddle was no longer Bob's but Paddy O'Flaherty's. I told Arne about the exchange. I told him I'd found the key.'

Per Bjørn crossed one leg over the other and took out his cigarettes. He offered them round, then when no one accepted, returned his case to his pocket and lit his own with a practised flick on a gas lighter. The hand which held the lighter was rock steady.

'I didn't tell him that we had already opened the locker and seen what it contained,' I said. 'We wanted to find out who else besides Arne was looking for the missing paper, so we gave that person an opportunity of finding it.'

'Ingenious,' he said. 'What a pity you had made the fundamental mistake of believing Arne Kristiansen to be connected with Bob Sherman's death. If he had been guilty of all you say, of course it would have been an excellent trap. As it is, of course . . .'

He delicately shrugged. Knut looked worried.

'There was the problem of the two men who searched Bob Sherman's house,' I said. 'If we didn't decoy them away they would be available to fetch the key and open the locker. So we provided an urgent reason for them to leave Oslo. We invented, in fact, a possible eye-witness to the killing of Bob Sherman. I told only Arne Kristiansen that I was going to Lillehammer to meet this man, and I asked Arne to come with me. On the train I told him about the key and said that as soon as I got back I was going to give it to the police. I told him that the police were expecting me to report to them at once on my return, to tell them what the man in Lillehammer had said. This meant to Arne that if I didn't return the hunt would be on immediately and there might be no later opportunity to get into my room for the key. It had to be done quickly. A risk had to be taken.'

I paused.

'You took it,' I said.

'No.'

'You believed no one knew of the existence of the key

except Arne and myself. You were wrong. You believed there was a possible eye-witness to Bob's murder and you sent your two assassins to deal with him. You expected them also to kill me as well. They aren't very successful at that. You should sack them.'

'This is ridiculous,' he said.

I said, 'I asked the reception desk at the Grand not to worry if anyone asked for my room number or my door key.' And extremely odd they'd thought it, after all the hide and seek of the previous days. 'We made it as easy as we could.'

He said nothing.

Knut had sprinkled the room with anthracene dust, which clung invisibly to any clothes or flesh which touched it and showed up with fluorescence under a strong ultra-violet light. Anyone denying he'd been in my room would have been proved to be lying. But Per Bjørn had out-thought that one and hadn't denied it. He must have done a great deal of fast figuring during his non-speaking ride from Fornebu to the police station. He couldn't have known about the anthracene, but he must have guessed that a trap so complicated in some respects wasn't likely to be naïve in others.

I said, 'The paper you were looking for is a chart of a core taken from area twenty-five/six of the North Sea.'

He absorbed that shock as if he were made throughout of expanded polystyrene.

I gave him some more. 'It was stolen from the Wessex-Wells Research Laboratory in Dorset, England, and the information it contains was the property of the Interpetro Oil Company. It is a chart showing exceptionally rich oil-bearing rock of high porosity and good permeability at a depth of thirteen thousand feet.'

It seemed to me that he had almost stopped breathing. He sat totally without movement, smoke from the cigarette between his fingers rising in a column as straight as honesty.

I said, 'The Interpetro Oil Company isn't part of the consortium to which your own company belongs, but it is or was mainly Norwegian owned, and the well in question is in the Norwegian area of the North Sea. Immediately after Bob Sherman brought his package to Norway, the Interpetro shares started an upward movement on the world stock markets. Although a great deal of secrecy surrounds the buying, I'm told that the most active purchasers were in the Middle East. You would know far better than I do whether it is to Norway's advantage to have one of her most promising oil fields largely bought up by oil-producing rivals.'

Not a flicker.

I said, 'Norway has never really forgiven the citizens who collaborated with the Nazis. How would they regard one of their most respected businessmen who sold advance news of their best oil field to the Middle East for his own personal gain?'

He uncrossed his legs and recrossed them the other way. He tapped the ash off his cigarette on to the floor, and inhaled a deep lungful of smoke.

'I wish,' he said, 'to telephone to my lawyer. And to my wife.'

CHAPTER SIXTEEN

Knut and I went back to his office and sat one each side of his desk.

'Can you prove it?' he said.

'We can prove he went to the Grand, fetched the key and opened the locker.'

'Anything else?'

I said gloomily, 'It's circumstantial. A good defence lawyer could turn everything inside out.'

Knut chewed his pencil.

'The scandal will ruin him,' he said.

I nodded. 'I'll bet he's got a fortune tucked away somewhere safe, though.'

'But,' Knut said, 'he must care more for his reputation than for just money, otherwise he would simply have left the country instead of having Bob Sherman killed.'

'Yes.'

We sat in silence.

'You are tired,' Knut said.

'Yeah. So are you.'

He grinned and looked suddenly very like Erik.

I said, 'Your brother told me Per Bjørn Sandvik was in the Resistance during the war.'

'*Ja*. He was.'

'Nothing wrong with his nerve,' I said. 'Nothing then, nothing now.'

'And we are not the Gestapo,' Knut said. 'He knows we will not torture him. We must seem feeble to him, after what he risked when he was young. He is not going to give in and confess. Not ever.'

I agreed.

'These two men,' I said. 'Yellow eyes and brown eyes. They're too young to have been in the Resistance themselves. But . . . is there a chance their fathers were? Arne's father was. Could you run a check on the group Per Bjørn belonged to, and see if any of them fathered yellow eyes?'

'You ask such impossible things.'

'And it's a very long shot indeed,' I sighed.

'I'll start tomorrow,' he said.

Some coffee arrived, very milky. I could have done with a treble scotch and a batch of Emma's scones.

'You know,' I said after another silence, 'there's something else. Some other way . . . There has to be.'

'What do you mean?'

'I mean . . . It was just luck finding that key. If Paddy hadn't swapped the helmets we would never have found the paper at Fornebu.' I drank the coffee. It wasn't strong enough to deal with anything but thirst. 'But . . . they tried to kill me before they knew the chart wasn't in the pond with Bob Sherman. So there must be something else which they couldn't afford for me to find.'

I put down the cup with a grimace.

'But what?' Knut asked.

'God knows.'

'Something I missed,' he said with gloom.

'Why would they think I would see it if you didn't?'

'Because you do,' he said. 'And Arne knows it.'

Arne . . . My friend Arne.

'Why didn't he kill you himself, out on the fjord?' Knut asked. 'Why didn't he just bang you on the head and push you overboard?'

'It isn't that easy to bang someone on the head when you're sitting at opposite ends of a small dinghy. And besides . . . leading a beast to the abattoir and slitting its neck are two different things.'

'I don't understand.'

'Arne was keen for me to die but wouldn't do it himself.'

'How do you know?'

'Because he didn't. Over the last few weeks he's had more chance than anybody, but he didn't do it.'

'You couldn't be sure he wouldn't.'

'He's a complex person but his attitudes are all fixed . . . if he didn't do it the first time he wouldn't do it afterwards.'

A few more minutes dawdled by while I tried to concentrate on what I hadn't discovered.

Useless, I thought.

Yesterday, I thought, I didn't know who had manipulated Interpetro Oil. Today I did. Did that make any difference?

'Oh my Christ,' I said, and nearly fell out of my chair.

'What is it?' Knut said.

'I'm bloody mad.'

'What do you mean?'

'You remember that bomb . . .'

'Well, of course I do.'

'It was such a sloppy way to kill someone,' I said. 'It might have gone off before we got back to the car . . . It didn't kill us, so we thought of it as a failure. But it didn't fail. Not a bit. It was a roaring success. It did just what it was meant to.'

'David ...'

'Do you remember where I was going that afternoon? I didn't go, because the bomb stopped me. I'm so damned stupid ... it isn't *what* I haven't seen, it's *who*.'

He just stared.

'*It's Mikkel Sandvik*.'

I telephoned to the college of Gol and spoke to the headmaster.

'Oh, but Mikkel isn't here,' he said. 'His father telephoned on Sunday morning to say that Mikkel must go and visit his aunt, who was dying and asking for him.'

'Where does the aunt live?'

'I don't know. Mr Sandvik talked to Mikkel himself.'

There was some speaking in the background, and then he said, 'My wife says Mikkel told her his Aunt Berit was dying. He went to catch the Bergen train. We don't know where he went after that ... Why don't you ask his father?'

'Good idea,' I said.

'What now?' Knut said, when I told him.

'I think ... I'll go and see Mrs Sandvik, and see if she'll tell me where Mikkel is.'

'All right. And I will do what I must about keeping Mr Sandvik here all night.' He sighed. 'A man like that ... it doesn't seem right to put him in a cell.'

'Don't let him go,' I said.

'Oh no.'

Erik had gone home long ago but Knut reckoned I was on police business and sent me to the Sandvik house in a police car. I walked through the arch into the courtyard, turned right, and rang the bell outside the well-lit imposing front door.

A heavy middle-aged woman opened it. She wore frumpy clothes and no make-up, and had a positive, slightly forbidding manner.

'*Ja?*' she said inquiringly.

I explained who I was and asked to see Mrs Sandvik.

'I am Mrs Sandvik. I spoke to you on the telephone a few days ago.'

'That's right.' I swallowed my surprise. I had thought she would already have known about her husband being at the police station, but apparently he hadn't yet made his two calls. When we had left him, Knut had said he would arrange for a telephone to be taken to the interview room and plugged into the socket there, which I supposed took time. No one was positively rushing to provide facilities for a suspect, not even for Per Bjørn Sandvik.

It made it easier, however, for me to ask questions.

'Come inside,' she said. 'It is cold with the door open.'

I stepped into the hall. She invited me no farther.

'Mikkel?' she said in surprise. 'He is at school. I told you.'

I explained about his Aunt Berit.

'He has no Aunt Berit.'

Wow.

'Er . . .' I said. 'Does he know anyone at all called Berit?'

She raised her eyebrows. 'Is this important?'

'I cannot go home until I have seen Mikkel. I am sorry.'

She shrugged. After a longish pause for thought she said, 'Berit is the name of an old nurse of my husband. I do not know if Mikkel knows any other person called Berit. I expect so.'

'Where does your husband's old nurse live?'

'I don't know.'

She couldn't remember the old nurse's surname, and she wasn't sure if she was still alive. She said her husband would be able to tell me, when he came home. She opened the door with finality for me to leave, and with a distinct feeling of cowardice, I left. Per Bjørn had smashed up her secure world and he would have to tell her about it himself.

'He might be with his father's old nurse,' I told Knut. 'And he might not.'

He reflected. 'If he caught the Bergen train, perhaps the Gol ticket office would remember him.'

'Worth a try. But he could be anywhere by now. Anywhere in the world.'

'He's barely seventeen,' Knut said.

'That's old, these days.'

'How did Mrs Sandvik take the news of her husband's arrest?'

'I didn't tell her. I thought Per Bjørn should do that.'

'But he has!'

'She didn't know,' I said blankly.

'But,' Knut said, 'I am sure he made his two calls almost half an hour ago.'

'Bloody hell,' I said.

He steamed out of the office at twenty knots and yelled at several unfortunate subordinates. When he returned he was carrying a piece of paper and looking grim, worried and apologetic all at once.

'They find it difficult not to obey a man with such prestige,' he said. 'He told them to wait outside the door while he spoke to his wife and his lawyer, as both calls were of a private nature. They did what he said.' He looked at the paper in his hand. 'At least they had the sense to dial the numbers for him, and to write them down. They are both Oslo numbers.'

He handed the paper over for me to see. One of the numbers meant nothing. The other meant too much.

'He talked to Arne,' I said.

I pressed the bell outside Arne's flat and after a long interval Kari opened the door.

'David.' She seemed neither surprised nor pleased to see me. She seemed drained.

'Come in,' she said.

The flat seemed somehow colder, less colourful, much quieter than before.

'Where's Arne?' I said.

'He's gone.'

'Where to?'

'I don't know.'

'Tell me everything he did since he came home.'

She gave me an empty stare, then turned away and walked through to the sitting-room. I followed her. She sat on the cream-coloured sofa and shivered. The stove no longer glowed with warmth and welcome and the stereo record player was switched off.

'He came home upset. Well . . . he's been upset ever since this Bob Sherman thing started. But today he was very worried and puzzled and disturbed. He played two long records and marched about . . . he couldn't keep still.'

Her voice had the calmness of shock. The reality of whatever had happened had not yet tipped her into anger or fear or despair: but tomorrow, I thought, she might suffer all three.

'He rang Per Bjørn Sandvik's house twice, but they said he wasn't in. It seemed to worry him very much.'

There was a tray on the coffee table in front of her laden with an untouched dish of open sandwiches. They made me feel frantically hungry as I hadn't eaten since a pin-sized breakfast, but she gave them an indifferent glance and said, 'He left them. He said he couldn't . . .'

Try me, I thought: but hostessing was far out of her mind.

'Then Per Bjørn Sandvik rang here. Only a little while ago . . . but it seems hours and hours . . . Arne was relieved at first, but then . . . he went so quiet . . . I knew something was wrong.'

'What did he say to Per Bjørn? Can you remember?'

'He said *Ja*, and No. He listened a long time. He said . . . I think he said . . . don't worry, I'll find him.'

'That was all?'

She nodded. 'Then he went into the bedroom and he was so quiet . . . I went to see what was the matter. He was sitting on the bed, looking at the floor. He looked up at me when I came. His eyes were . . . I don't know . . . dead.'

'And then?'

'He got up and began packing a suitcase. I asked him . . . he said don't worry me . . . so I just stood there. He packed

... he threw things into the case ... and he was muttering away, mostly about you.'

She looked at me intently but still with the numb lack of emotion.

'He said ... "I told him, I told him David would beat him ... I told him at the beginning ... he still says David hasn't beaten him but he has, he has ..." I asked Arne what he was talking about but I don't think he even heard me.' She pressed her fingers against her forehead, rubbing the smooth skin. 'Arne said ... "David ... David knew all day ... he made the trap and put himself into it as bait ... he knew all day." Then he said something about you using some girls and an old man, and something about orangeade ... and a premonition you invented. He said he knew you would be the end of everything; he said so before you came.'

She looked at me with the sudden awakening of awareness and the beginnings of hostility.

'What did you do?' she asked.

'I'm sorry, Kari. I gave Arne and Per Bjørn Sandvik a chance to show they knew more than they ought about Bob Sherman's death, and they took it.'

'More than they ought ... ?' she repeated vaguely: then overwhelmingly understood. 'Oh no. Oh no. Not Arne.' She stood up abruptly. 'I don't believe it.' But she already did.

'I still don't know who killed Bob Sherman,' I said. 'I think Arne does know. I want to talk to him.'

'He's not coming back. He said ... he would write, and send for me. In a few weeks.' She looked forlorn. 'He took the car.' She paused. 'He kissed me.'

'I wish ...' I said uselessly, and she caught the meaning in my voice though the words weren't spoken.

'Yes,' she said. 'In spite of everything ... he likes you too.'

It was still not yet eight o'clock and Per Bjørn was still in the interview room when I got back to the police station.

'His lawyer is with him,' Knut said morosely. 'We won't get a word out of him now.'

'We haven't had so many already.'

'No.' He flicked the paper with the telephone numbers which was lying on his desk. 'This other number . . . it isn't the lawyer's.'

'Whose, then?'

'It's a big second class hotel near the docks. Dozens of incoming calls; they couldn't remember one more than any other. I have sent a policeman down there with a description of the man with yellow eyes.'

'Mm. Whoever he spoke to at the hotel then telephoned the lawyer.'

'*Ja*,' he said. 'It must be so. Unless Arne did.'

'I don't think so, from what his wife said.'

'He had gone?'

I nodded. 'In his car.'

He put his hand again on the telephone. 'We will find the number and put out an alert: and also check with the airport and the frontier posts with Sweden.'

'I know the number.' I told it to him. He looked surprised, but I said, 'I've been in his car . . . and I've a memory for numbers. Don't know why.'

He put out his alerts and sat tapping his pencil against his teeth.

'And now we wait,' he said.

We waited precisely five seconds before the first call came through. He scooped up the receiver with a speed which betrayed his inner pressure, and listened intently.

'*Ja*,' he said eventually. '*Ja . . . takk*. Thank you.'

He put down the receiver and relayed the news.

'That was the policeman I sent to the hotel. He says the man with yellow eyes has been staying there for a week, but this evening he paid his bill and left. He gave no address. He was known to the hotel as L. Horgen. My policeman says that unfortunately the room has already been cleaned because the hotel is busy, but he has directed them to leave it empty until we've searched it and tried for fingerprints. Excuse me while I send a team to do that.'

He went out of the office and was gone a fair time, but when he came back he had more to tell.

'We've found Arne's car. It is parked not far from the quay of the Nansen shipping line, and one of their ships left for Copenhagen an hour ago. We are radioing to the ship and to Copenhagen to pick him up.'

'Don't let them relax at Fornebu,' I said.

He looked at me.

I grinned faintly. 'Well . . . If I wanted to slip out by air I'd leave my car beside a shipping line and take a taxi to the airport. And Arne and I once discussed quite a lot of things like that.'

'He'd know you'd guess, then.'

'I'd pin more hope on the ship if he'd left his car at the airport.'

He shook his head and sighed. 'A good thing you're not a crook,' he said.

A young policeman knocked, came in, and spoke to Knut.

He translated for me. 'Mr Sandvik's lawyer wants to see me, with his client. I'll go along to the interview room . . . Do you want to come?'

'Please,' I said.

With Per Bjørn, his lawyer, Knut, me, and a note-taking policeman all inside with the door shut, the small interview room looked overcrowded with dark suits and solemnity. The other four sat on the hard chairs round the plain table and I stood leaning against the door, listening to a long conversation of which I understood not a word.

Per Bjørn pushed back his chair, crossed his legs and set fire to a cigarette, much as before. His lawyer, a heavy self-possessed man of obvious worldly power, was speaking in an authoritative voice and making Knut perceptibly more nervous minute by minute. But Knut survived uncracked and although when he answered he sounded friendly and apologetic, the message he got across was 'No.'

It angered the lawyer more than the client. He stood up, towering over Knut, and delivered a severe caution. Knut looked worried, stood up in his turn, and shook his head. After that the young policeman was sent on an errand, presently returning with a sergeant and an escort.

Knut said 'Mr Sandvik . . .', and waited.

Per Bjørn stood up slowly and stubbed out his filter tip. He looked impassively at the escort and walked calmly towards them. When he drew level with me at the doorway he stopped, turned his head, and stared very deliberately at my face.

But whatever he was thinking, nothing at all showed in his eyes, and he spoke not a word.

Knut went home, but I spent the night in his office sleeping on the floor on blankets and pillows borrowed from the cells; and I daresay I was less comfortable than the official guest downstairs.

'What's wrong with the Grand?' Knut said, when I asked him to let me stay.

'Yellow eyes is on the loose,' I said. 'And who knows what instructions Per Bjørn gave him?'

Knut looked at me thoughtfully. 'You think there's more to come?'

'Per Bjørn is still fighting.'

'*Ja*,' he sighed. 'I think so too.'

He sent a policeman out to bring me a hot meal from a nearby restaurant, and in the morning at eight o'clock he came back with a razor. He himself, trim in his uniform, seemed to have shed yesterday like a skin and arrived bright eyed and awake to the new day. I shivered blearily in my crumpled clothes and felt like a reject from a doss house.

At eight forty-five the telephone rang. Knut picked up the receiver, listened, and seemed pleased with what he heard.

'*Ja. Ja. Takk*,' he said.

'What is it?'

He put the receiver back. 'We've had a message from Gol. The man who was on duty in the ticket office on Sunday remembers that a boy from the College bought a ticket to Finse.'

'Finse . . .' I thought back to my timetables. 'On the Bergen line?'

'*Ja*. Finse is the highest town on the line. Up in the

mountains. I will find out if he is remembered at the station there. I will find out if anyone has seen him in the streets or knows if he is staying.'

'How long will that take?'

'One can't tell.'

'No.' I thought it over. 'Look ... the train for Bergen leaves at ten, if I remember right. I'll catch it. Then if you hear that Mikkel is or isn't at Finse, perhaps you could get a message to me at one of the stops up the line.'

'Have you forgotten yellow eyes?'

'Unfortunately not,' I said.

He smiled. 'All right. I will send you to the station in a police car. Do you want a policeman to go with you?'

I thought. 'I might get further with Mikkel if I go alone.'

On the train I sat next to a total stranger, a cheerful young man with little English, and spent an uneventful journey looking out at peaceful fields and bright little dolls' houses scattered haphazardly on hillsides.

At Gol there was a written message.

'Young man disembarkation to Finse the Sunday. One knows not until where he gone. The questions is continue.'

'Thank you very much,' I said.

The train climbed slowly above the tree line into a landscape of blue-grey rock and green-grey water. Snow scattered the ground, at first in patches, then in profusion, and finally as a thin white rug over every sloping surface, with sharp rock edges like hatchets showing through.

'Is small snow,' said my companion. 'In winter in Finse is two metres.'

'Two metres deep?' I asked.

He nodded. '*Ja.* Is good for ski.'

The railway ran for a time alongside a fiercely cold-looking wind-ruffled grey-green lake and slowed with a sigh of relief into Finse.

'Is hot summer,' my friend said, looking around in surprise. 'Is snow gone.'

He might think so, but I didn't. Snow still covered everything worth mentioning, hot summer gone by or not; and icicles dangled from every roof like stiff, glittering fringes. Once out of the warmth of the train the cold bit sharply and even in my ear-covering cap and padded jacket I wrapped my arms round my chest in a futile attempt to hold on to my body heat.

I was met by the bulk of the Finse police force in the shape of a broadly smiling officer of turnstile-blocking size.

'Mr Cleveland.' He shook my hand. 'We do not know where is this boy Mikkel Sandvik. We have not seen him in the village. There are not many strangers here now. In the summer, and in the winter, we have very many strangers. We have the big hotel, for the ski. But now, not many. We have look for an old woman who is called Berit. There are two. It is not one, because she is in bed in the house of her son and she is . . . er . . . she is . . . old.'

'Senile?' I suggested.

He didn't know the word. 'Very old,' he repeated.

'And the other Berit?'

'She lives in a house beside the lake. One and a half kilometres out of Finse. She goes away in the winter. Soon, now. She is a strong old woman. In the summer, she takes people who come to fish, but they have all gone now. Usually on Wednesdays she comes for food, so we have not gone to see her. But she is late today. She comes in the mornings.'

'I'll go there,' I said, and listened to directions.

The way to the house of Berit-by-the-lake turned out to be merely a path which ran between the railway line and the shore, more a matter of small stones and pebbles through an area of boulders than any recognizable beaten track. With its roughnesses still half-covered with crusty ice, it was easy to imagine that once the new snows fell it would be entirely obliterated.

CHAPTER SEVENTEEN

I looked back.

A bend had taken Finse out of sight.

I looked forward. Nothing but the sketchy path picking its uncertain way through the snow-strewn boulders. Only on my right could be seen any evidence of humanity, and that was the railway. And then that too ran straight ahead behind a hill while the shore curved to the left, so that in the end there was just me and the stark unforgiving landscape, just me trudging through an energetic wind on a cold, wild and lonely afternoon.

The path snaked its way round two small bays and two small headlands, with the hillside on my right rising ever more steeply the farther I went, and then all of a sudden the house lay before me, standing alone on a flat stony area spread out like an apron into the lake.

The house was red. A strong crimson. Roof, walls, door, the lot. The colour stood out sharply against the grey and white of the shore and the darker grey-green of the water; and rising beyond it at the head of the lake stood dark towering cliffs, thrown up like a sudden mountain against the Northern sky.

Maybe it was a grand, extraordinary, awe-inspiring sight. Maybe it should have swelled my spirit, uplifted my soul. Actually it inspired in me nothing more noble than a strong desire to retreat.

I stopped.

Surely Sandvik wouldn't have sent his son to this threatening place, even if he did urgently want to hide him. Surely Mikkel was half the world away by now, with Arne cantering post haste in his wake to look after him.

Damned bloody silly place to build a house, I thought.

Enough to give anyone the creeps, living with a mountain on the doorstep.

I went on. The house had a landing stage with a motor boat tied to a post like a hitched horse in a Western. It also had looped up lace curtains and geraniums on the window sills. Red geraniums. Naturally.

I looked in vain for smoke from the chimney, and no one stared out at me as I approached.

I banged the knocker. The door was opened straight away by a ramrod-backed old woman, five feet tall, sharp eyed, entirely self possessed. Far, very far, from dying.

'*Ja?*' she said inquiringly.

'I'd like to talk to Mikkel,' I said.

She took a very brief pause to change languages, and then in a pure near-Scots accent said, 'Who are you?'

'I am looking for Mikkel.'

'Everyone is looking for Mikkel.' She inspected me from head to foot. 'Come in. It is cold.'

She showed me into the living-room, where everything was in process of being packed away in crates. She gestured round with a fine-boned hand. 'I am leaving now for the winter. It is beautiful here in the summer, but not in winter.'

'I have a message from his father,' I said.

'Another one?'

'What do you mean?'

'Already one man came this morning. Then another. Both of them said they had a message from his father. And now you.' She looked at me straightly. 'That is very many messages.'

'Yes . . . I have to find him.'

She put her head on one side. 'I told the others. I cannot judge which of you I should not tell. So I will tell you. He is on the mountain.'

I looked through the window to the wall of rock and the end of the lake.

'Up there?'

'*Ja.* There is a cabin up there. I rent it to visitors in the summer, but in the winter the snow covers it. Mikkel went up there this morning to bring down the things I do not want to leave there. He is a kind boy.'

'Who were the other men who came?'

'I don't know. The first one said his name was Kristiansen. They both said they would go up and help Mikkel bring down the things, although I said it was not necessary, there are not many things and he took the sleigh.'

'The sleigh?'

'*Ja*. Very light. You can pull it.'

'Perhaps I had better go up there as well.'

'You have bad shoes.'

I looked down. City casuals, not built for snowy mountains, and already darkly wet round the edges.

'Can't be helped,' I said.

She shrugged. 'I will show you the path. It is better than the one round the lake.' She smiled faintly. 'I do not walk to Finse. I go in the boat.'

'The second man,' I said. 'Did he have extraordinary yellow eyes?'

'No.' She shook her head decisively. 'He was ordinary. Very polite. Like you.' She smiled and pointed through the window. 'The path starts over there behind that big rock. It is not steep. It winds away from the lake and then comes back. You will see it easily.'

I thanked her and set off, and found almost at once that she was right about the shoes. One might be able to see the path easily, but that was because it was a well-worn track through the snow, patterned widely on either side by the marks of skis, like a sort of mini highway.

I slithered along in the brisk wind, working round the hillside in a wide, ever upward-sloping U. But it proved to be not as far as I'd feared, because, long before I expected it, I came to the top of a small rise and found below me, suddenly only a few yards away, a sturdy little log hut, built to the traditional Norwegian pattern like a roofed box standing on a slightly smaller plinth.

It was already too late to make a careful inconspicuous

approach. I stood there in full view of a small window: so I simply walked straight up and looked through it.

The cabin was dark inside and at first I thought it was empty. Then I saw him. Huddled in a corner, with his head bent over his knees, slowly rocking as if in pain.

There was only one small room. Only one door. I put my hand on its latch and opened it.

The movement galvanized the figure inside into action, and it was only something half seen, half instinctive, which had me leaping sideways away from the entrance with adrenalin scorching down to my toes. Blast from a shotgun roared through the doorway, and I pressed myself against the heavy log wall alongside and hoped to God it was impervious to pellets.

A voice shouted something hysterically from inside.

Not Arne's voice. Young. Stretched to breaking.

'Mikkel,' I said. 'I will not harm you. I am David Cleveland.'

Silence.

'Mikkel . . .'

'If you come in, I will shoot you.' His voice was naturally high pitched like his father's, and the tension in it had strung it up another octave.

'I only want to talk to you.'

'No. No. No.'

'Mikkel . . . You can't stay here for ever.'

'If you come in, I'll shoot.'

'All right . . . I'll talk from here.' I shivered with cold and wholeheartedly cursed him.

'I will not talk to you. Go away. Go away.'

I didn't answer. Five minutes passed with no sound except the blustering wind. Then his voice from inside, tight and frightened. 'Are you still there?'

'Yes,' I said.

'Go away.'

'We have to talk sometime. Might as well be now.'

'No.'

'Where is Arne Kristiansen?' I asked.

His reply was a high keening wail which raised goose-bumps up my spine. What followed it was a thoroughly normal sob.

I crouched down low and risked a quick look through the door. The gun lay in one hand on the floor and with the other he was trying to wipe away tears. He looked up and saw me, and again immediately began to aim.

I retreated smartly and stood up outside against the wall, as before.

'Why don't you tell me?' I said.

A long pause of several minutes.

'You can come in.'

I took another quick look. He was sitting straight legged on the floor with the gun pointing at the door.

'Come in,' he said. 'I won't shoot.'

'Put the gun on the floor and slide it away.'

'No.'

More time passed.

'The only way I'll talk,' he said, 'is if you come in. But I will keep the gun.'

I swallowed. 'All right.'

I stepped into the doorway. Looked down the double barrels. He sat with his back against the wall, holding the gun steady. A box of cartridges lay open beside him, with one or two scattered around.

'Shut the door,' he said. 'Sit down opposite me, against the wall. On the floor.'

I did as he said.

He was slight and not full grown. Brown hair, dark frightened eyes. Cheeks still round from childhood; the jaw line of an adult. Half boy, half man, with tear stains on his face and his finger on the trigger.

Everything movable in the bare little cabin had been stacked in a neat pile to one side. A heavy table and two solid chairs were the total to be left. No curtains at the single small window. No rugs on the bare wood floor. Two collapsible camp beds, folded and strapped together for transport, leaned against a wall. A pair of skis stood beside them.

No logs by the cold stove, and no visible food.

'It'll be dark soon,' I said. 'Within an hour.'

'I don't care.' He stared at me with burning eyes and unnerving intensity.

'We should go down to Berit's house while we can still see the way.'

'No.'

'We'll freeze up here.'

'I don't care.'

I believed him. Anyone as distracted as he was tended to blot even extreme discomforts out of his mind: and although he had allowed me into the hut he was far from coming down off the high wire. Little tremors of tension ran in his body and twitched his feet. Occasionally the gun shook in his hands. I tried not to think gloomy thoughts.

'We must go,' I said.

'Sit still,' he said fiercely, and the right forefinger curled convulsively. I looked at it. And I sat.

Daylight slowly faded and the cold crept in inexorably. The wind outside whined like a spoilt child, never giving up. I thought I might as well face it: the prospect of the night ahead made the fjord water seem in retrospect as cosy as a heated pool. I put my padded mitts inside my padded pockets and tried to kid myself that my fingers were warm. And it was a minor disaster that the jacket wasn't really long enough for sitting on.

'Mikkel,' I said. 'Just tell me. You'll explode if you don't talk to someone. And I'm here. So just . . . tell me. Whatever you like.'

He stared fixedly through the gathering dusk. I waited a long time.

'I killed him,' he said.

Oh God.

A long pause. Then on a rising note he said it again, 'I killed him.'

'Who?' I said.

Silence.

'How?' I said.

The question surprised him. He took his gaze for one moment off my face and glanced down at the gun.

'I ... shot ...'

With an effort I said, 'Did you shoot ... Arne?'

'Arne ...' The hysteria rose again. 'No. No. No. Not Arne. I didn't kill Arne. I didn't. I didn't.'

'All right,' I said. 'All right, Mikkel. Let's wait a bit ... until you can tell me. Until you feel it is the right time to tell me.' I paused. 'Is that OK?'

After a while he said, '*Ja.* OK.'

We waited.

It got darker until it seemed that the only light left was the reflection from the window in his eyes. I could see them long after the rest of him dissolved into one amorphous shadow, two live agonized signals of a mind desperately afraid of the help it desperately needed.

It must have occurred to him as to me that after total darkness I would be able to jump his gun, because he stirred restlessly on the floor and muttered something in Norwegian, and finally in a much more normal voice said, 'There is a lamp in a box. On top of the things.'

'Shall I find it and light it?'

'*Ja.*'

I stood up stiffly, glad of the chance to move, but sensing him lift the gun to keep me where it mattered.

'I won't try to take the gun away,' I said.

No answer.

The heap of gear was to my right, near the window. I moved carefully, but with many small noises so that he should know where I was and not be alarmed, and felt around for the box on top. Nothing wrong with his memory: the box was there, and the lamp in it, and also a box of matches.

'I've found the lamp,' I said. 'Shall I strike a match?'

A pause.

'*Ja.*'

It proved to be a small gas lamp. I lit it and put it on the table from where it cast a weak white light into every corner. He blinked twice as his irises adjusted, but his concentration never wavered.

'Is there any food?' I asked.

'I'm not hungry.'

'I am.'

'Sit down,' he said. 'Where you were.'

I sat. The gun barrels followed. In the new light I could see down them a lot too well.

Time passed. I lit the lamp at four thirty in the afternoon and it was eight before he began to talk.

By then, if I was anything to go by, he had lost all feeling from the waist down. He wore no gloves and his hands had turned blue-white, but he still held the gun ready, with his finger inside the trigger guard. His eyes still watched. His face, his whole body, were still stiff with near-unbearable tension.

He said suddenly, 'Arne Kristiansen told me that my father was arrested. He told me he was arrested because of you.'

His voice came out high and his breath condensed into a frosty plume.

Once started, he found it easier.

'He said . . . my father wanted us to go to Bergen . . . and on a boat to Stavanger . . . and fly . . .' He stopped.

'And you didn't go,' I said. 'Why didn't you go?'

The gun shook.

'They came in . . .' he said.

I waited.

He said, 'I was talking to him. Outside. About going away.' A pause. 'They came over the hill. On skis, with goggles.' Another pause. 'One of them told Arne to step away from me.' After a longer pause and with an even sharper burst of remembered terror he said, 'He had a knife.'

'Oh Mikkel,' I said.

He talked faster, tumbling it out.

'Arne said, "You can't. You can't. He wouldn't send you to kill his own son. Not Mikkel." He pushed me behind him. He said, "You're crazy. I talked to his father myself. He told me to come here to take Mikkel away." '

He stared across at me with stretched eyes, reliving it.

'They said . . . my father had changed his mind about Arne going. They said they were to take me themselves on a ship to Denmark and wait until my father sent money and instructions. Arne said it was not true. They said . . . it was true . . . and they said . . . Arne was going no further than right here . . . He didn't believe it . . . he said not even my father would do that. He watched only the one with the knife and the other one swung a ski stick and hit him on the head . . . He fell down in the snow . . . I tried to stop them . . . they just pushed me off . . . and they put him on the sleigh . . . they strapped him on . . . and pulled him up the path.'

The panic he had felt then came crowding back into his face. He said painfully, 'I remembered the gun in the cabin . . . I went inside and loaded it . . . and put on my skis and went after them . . . to stop them . . . but when I found them they were coming back . . . without the sleigh . . . and I thought . . . I thought . . . they were going to . . . they were going to . . .'

He took a deep shuddering breath. 'I fired the gun. The one with the knife . . . he fell down . . .'

'I fired again,' he said. 'But the other one was still on his skis . . . So I came back to the cabin because I thought he would come after me . . . I came back to reload the gun. But he didn't come . . . He didn't come . . .

'You came,' he said. 'I thought it was him.'

He stopped.

'Did you know the two men?' I asked. 'Had you ever seen them before?'

'No.'

'How long was it before I came?' I said.

'I don't know. A long time.'

'Hours?'

'I think so.'

I hadn't seen any of them on my way up.

'Killing is wrong,' he said jerkily.

'It depends.'

'No.'

'To defend your life, or someone else's life, it would be all right,' I said.

'I . . . I believe . . . I *know* it is wrong. And yet I . . . when I was so afraid . . .' His high voice cracked. 'I have done it. I despise killing and I've done it. And I would have killed you too. I know I would. If you hadn't jumped.'

'Never mind,' I said; but the horrors were still there in his eyes. Making it deliberately an emotion-reducing question I asked, 'Have you known Arne Kristiansen long?'

'What . . . ?' His own voice came down a bit. 'About three years, I suppose.'

'And how well do you know him?'

'Not very well. On the racecourse. That's all.'

'Has your father known him long?'

'I don't think so . . . The same as me. At the races.'

'Are they close friends?'

He said with sudden extreme bitterness, 'My father has no close friends.'

'Will you put the gun down now?' I said.

He looked at it.

'All right.'

He put it beside him on the floor. A relief not to be looking down those two round holes.

The lamp chose that moment to give notice it was running out of gas. Mikkel switched his gaze from me to the table, but the message of fading light didn't seem to pierce through the inner turmoil.

'The lamp is going out,' I said. 'Is there a spare gas cylinder?'

He slowly shook his head.

'Mikkel,' I said. 'It is freezing and it will soon be dark. If we are to survive the night we must keep warm.'

No response.

'Are you listening?'

'What?'

'You are going to have to face life as it is.'

'I . . . can't . . .'

'Are there any blankets?'

'There is one.'

I began to try to stand up and he reached immediately for the gun.

'Don't be silly,' I said. 'I won't hurt you. And you won't shoot me. So let's just both relax, huh?'

He said uncertainly. 'You had my father arrested.'

'Do you know why?'

'Not . . . not really.'

I told him about the oil transaction, playing down the disloyalty, to put it no higher, that Per Bjørn had shown to his country, but there was, it seemed, nothing basically wrong with Mikkel's brains. He was silent for some time after I'd finished and the muscles slowly relaxed limb by limb.

'Once he had been found out,' he said, 'he would lose his job. He would lose the respect of everyone. He wouldn't be able to live like that . . . not my father.'

His voice at last was sane and controlled; and almost too late. The lamp was going out.

'The blanket,' he said, 'is in the beds.'

He tried to stand up and found his legs were as numb and useless as mine, if not more so. It kicked him straight back to practical sense.

'I'm cold!'

'So am I.'

He looked across, seeing our predicament squarely for the first time.

'Stand up,' he said. 'Walk about.'

Easier said, but it had to be done.

'Can we light the stove?' I said. 'There are four more matches, the cardboard boxes, and the table and chairs, if we can break them up.'

We had both by then tottered to our feet. The lamp shone with one candle power, sadly.

'There is no axe,' Mikkel said.

The lamp went out.

'I'm sorry,' he said.

'Never mind.'

We jumped up and down in total darkness. Funny if it hadn't been urgent. Blood started circulating again, though, to the places where it was needed, and after half an hour or so we were both warm enough to give it a rest.

'I can find the blanket,' Mikkel said, and did so. 'Shall we share it?'

'We certainly shall.'

We both wore warm jackets and he, when he remembered where he'd put them, had a cap and mitts like my own. We laid the folded canvas beds on an insulating foundation of cardboard boxes, and wrapped ourselves from the waist down in one cocoon in the single blanket, sitting close together to share every scrap of warmth. It was too dark to see what he was thinking, but there were faint tremors still, occasionally, through his body.

'I took the rest of the bedding down to Berit's house yesterday,' he said. 'On the sleigh.'

'Pity.'

The word switched his thoughts. He said abruptly 'Do you think Arne is dead?'

'I don't know,' I said. But I did think so.

'What will happen to me, for killing that man?'

'Nothing. Just tell it as you told me. No one will blame you.'

'Are you sure?'

'Yes.'

'I am as bad as anyone else who kills,' he said, but this time there was adult acceptance and despair in his voice, not hysteria. I wondered if it were possible for a boy to age ten years in one night, because it would be better for him if he could.

'Tell me about Bob Sherman,' I said; and felt the jolt that went through him at the name.

'I . . . can't . . .'

'Mikkel . . . I know that Bob brought the stolen surveys from England to give to your father . . .'

'No,' he interrupted.

'What, then?'

'He had to deliver them to Arne. I didn't know they were for my father when I . . .' He stopped dead.

'When you what?'

'I mustn't tell you. I can't.'

In the darkness I said calmly, almost sleepily, 'Did Bob tell you he had brought a package?'

He said unwillingly, 'Yes.'

I yawned. 'When?'

'When I met him in Oslo. The night he came.'

I wondered if he felt in his turn the thud with which that news hit me.

'Where in Oslo?' I said casually.

'He was outside the Grand with his saddle and his overnight bag. I was walking home from a friend's house, and I stopped. He said he might go and catch the tram. I asked him if he would like some coffee first, so we walked along to our house. I carried his saddle.' He paused. 'I liked Bob. We were friends.'

'I know,' I said.

'My father was out. He usually is. Mother was watching television. Bob and I went into the kitchen, and I made the coffee. We ate some cake my mother had made.'

'What did you talk about?'

'At first about the horses he was riding the next day . . . Then he said he had brought a package from England, and he'd opened it, and it didn't contain what he'd been told. He said he had to give it to Arne Kristiansen at the races but he was going to ask for a bit more money before he handed it over.'

His body trembled against mine within the blanket.

'He was laughing about it, really. He said they'd told him

it was pornography, but it wasn't, and he didn't know what it was even though he'd seen it. Then he took the package out of his case and told me to look.'

He stopped.

'And,' I said, 'when you saw what was in the package, you knew what it was?'

'I'd seen papers like that before . . . I mean . . . I knew it was an oil survey. Yes.'

'Did you tell Bob what it was?'

'Yes. I did. We talked about it a bit.'

'And then?'

'It was late. Too late for the tram. Bob took a taxi out to Gunnar Holth's stable, and I went to bed.'

'What happened the next day?'

'I promised . . . I promised I wouldn't tell anybody. I didn't tell the police. I mustn't tell you. Especially not you. I know that.'

'All right,' I said.

Time passed. It was almost too cold to think.

'I told my father about Bob Sherman's package on the way to the races,' he said. 'He took me in the car. I only told him for something to say. Because I thought he might be interested. But he didn't say much. He never does. I never know what he's thinking.'

'Nor do I,' I said.

'I have heard people say he looks kindest when he is being most cruel. When I was small, I heard it first.'

'Is he cruel to you?'

'No. Just . . . cold. But he is my father.'

'Yes.'

'I think I want to tell you . . . but I can't.'

'All right.'

A long time passed. His breath and body movements betrayed his wakefulness and the churning thoughts in his mind.

'Mr Cleveland? Are you awake?'

'David,' I said.

'David . . . Do you think he meant those men to kill me?'

'No, I don't.'

'He told them where to come. He told me to come to Finse. He told Arne Kristiansen to come to Finse. And those men.'

'He did,' I said. 'But I should think they spoke the truth. I should think he meant them to take you out of the country, after they had dealt with Arne. I should think they were very clumsy to let you see them actually attack Arne, but then they have more strength than brains, those two. Arne is the only one who could go into court and give conclusive evidence against your father, and I do think that your father is ruthless enough to have him killed to prevent that.'

'Why . . . why do you think so?'

'Because he sent those two men after me, too.'

I told him about the boat in the fjord, the knife in Chelsea, the bomb in Erik's car.

'They're terrible men,' he said. 'They frightened me the instant I saw them.'

He relapsed into silence. I could almost feel him thinking, suffering, working it all out.

'David?'

'Yes?'

'It was my fault Bob died.'

'Certainly not.'

'But if I hadn't told my father that Bob knew he'd brought an oil survey . . .'

'Arne would have told him,' I said flatly. 'You can go on saying if for ever. If Bob hadn't opened the package. If your father hadn't been ruthless enough to get rid of him. But all these things happened. They all happened because your father is both greedy and proud, which is always a pretty deadly combination. But also he learned how to live a secret life when he was young. Against the Nazis, it was good. Everyone admired him. I should think he's never lost the feeling that anything anti-authority is daring and therefore all right. I should think he put the police into the place of the Nazis, as the enemy to be outwitted. He thinks like lightning, he gives away nothing under questioning, he coolly takes tremendous risks, he arranges without mercy for people to die. He's still acting the way he did when he was twenty. He always will.'

Time passed.

'David . . .'

'Yes?'

'I'll have to tell you,' he said.

I took a deep breath. It felt icy in my lungs.

'Go on,' I said.

He paused again. Then he said, 'I was talking to Bob at the races. He laughed and told me it was all fixed, Arne was going to drive him to the airport afterwards and pay him extra for the package.'

He stopped.

I waited.

His voice went on, hesitant but at last committed.

'By the end of the races it was dark. I went out to the car to wait for my father. He is often late because of being on the committee. I sat in the car and waited for him. I hadn't talked to him at all at the races. I usually don't see him much there. He's always busy.'

He stopped again. His breathing grew heavier, more disturbed.

'Most of the cars went. Then two people came past and in some passing headlights I saw they were Bob and Arne. I was going to call out to them . . . I wish I had . . . but I couldn't get the window down fast enough . . . and then they were over by Arne's car. They were talking face to face. I could only see them now and then, you see, when car lights pointed that way as people went home. But I saw another man walk up behind Bob and raise his arm. He held something shiny . . . Then he brought it down . . .'

He stopped. Gulped a bit. Went on. 'The next time I could see, there were only two people there. I thought . . . I couldn't *believe* . . . And then one of them turned and came towards our car. I was scared . . .'

He shuddered violently.

'But he just opened the boot and threw into it something which clinked, and then he got into the driving seat, and he was smiling.'

A long pause.

'Then he saw me sitting there, and he looked absolutely astonished. And he said . . . he said . . . "Mikkel! I'd forgotten you were at the races."'

His voice was full of pain.

'He'd forgotten me. Forgotten me.'

He was trying not to cry.

'My father,' he said. 'My father killed Bob Sherman.'

CHAPTER EIGHTEEN

We went down to Finse at first light, him sliding easily on his skis, me scrunching and slipping in my city shoes. If I looked anything like he did I had blue grey circles round my eyes, hollows at the corners of my mouth, and a certain overall air of extreme weariness.

He had said little more during the night. He had rolled his head on to my shoulder at one point and fallen exhaustedly asleep, and in the early morning, when he stirred, he had been calm and apparently untroubled, as if the final unburdening of the horror he'd lived with through eight long weeks had set him quietly free.

I left him with the warm comforting people of Finse, and went up the mountain again with several local men. This time I went on skis, shuffling along inexpertly up the slope. They waited for me, making jokes. They had cheerful faces, carefree smiles. And the sun came wanly through the clouds, the first time I'd seen it in Norway.

We reached the hut and went on past it, up beyond where the path petered out into a flat field of snow. Two of the men were pulling a sleigh, a lightweight affair sliding easily on ski-like runners; just like the one old Berit has, they said.

Brown eyes was lying face down in the snow.

Dead.

But he hadn't died from gunshot wounds: or not primarily. He'd died from exposure and cold.

The men from Finse looked in silence at the trail leading away behind his body. He'd been pulling himself along, crawling. The snow where he'd been was streaked black with his blood.

They wrapped him in canvas, put him on the sleigh, and turned to go to Finse.

'I'll go that way,' I said, pointing to where brown eyes had come from.

They nodded, consulted, and sent a man with me, as they didn't trust my rudimentary ability on skis.

We followed the blood-stained trail up a shallow slope and on to a sort of plateau whose far edge was a smooth horizon against a pale grey sky. The trail ended in a jumble of tracks which the man from Finse rapidly interpreted.

'This is where he was shot. See the blood. There was another man with him.' He pointed to a set of ski marks setting off at a tangent across virgin snow. 'That man is an expert cross country skier. He went fast. He left the other man lying wounded in the snow. He did not come back with help. If he had, he could have followed the trail of blood.'

Yellow eyes had just upped and left. But Knut would find him in the end.

'The two men came across to here skiing fast and easily,' my guide said, and pointed to tracks stretching away across the plateau.

'There are other tracks over there,' he said, turning to his right and stretching out a well gloved hand.

'Let's look,' I said.

We went over.

'Two men,' he said, 'Pulling a loaded sleigh.'

Although I expected it, it hit in my gut.

'They came that way,' I said, pointing back towards the hut.

He nodded. We went back along the trail until we found the marks of Mikkel's skis beside it.

'The boy came to here. Stopped. Then he turned and went back. You can see from his tracks that he was disturbed when he came. And panic stricken when he left. Look at the depth and the sharpness and the small steps.'

'We might find the cartridges,' I said.

He nodded. We looked for a while and found both of them, bright orange cylinders on the snow.

'And now...' I gestured ahead along the trail which Mikkel had been following: two men and a loaded sleigh.

The marks ran regularly across the plateau towards the horizon. We followed.

The horizon proved to be not the end of the world, but the brow of a hill. Down the other side the slope was steep, short, and sharp edged, and far beyond it, mile upon mile, lay a vista of snow-scattered peaks. We were standing at the top of the cliffs above the lake where Berit lived.

The marks of the two men on skis stopped at the brow of the hill, and turned back.

The sleigh marks ran on straight and true to the edge.

'I want to go down there,' I said, and unclipped my skis.

My guide didn't like it, but produced a rope from round his waist. He tied me to it, and paid it out foot by foot, standing four square and solid at the top of the slope.

I went down slowly in my borrowed boots, finding the snow surprisingly glassy and having to be careful not to slide. Having to concentrate, too, on not feeling giddy, and finding it as difficult as ever. When I stood at length on the edge I could see all the lake stretching away, with Berit's house a crimson blob far down to the left.

Beside my feet the marks of the runners looked shallow and crisp, speaking of speed. And they ran on without pity, pointing straight out into space.

The drop in front was six hundred feet, perpendicular. The ruffled green water lay secretively below. Nothing else. Nothing to see.

Arne, I thought. Flying through the air on a sleigh, down to his death.

Arne . . . who didn't look over his shoulder the one time the enemy was really there.

Arne, my treacherous friend.

You would have sworn that round the snowy cliffs you could hear crashing chords of Beethoven echoing in the wind.

KNOCK DOWN

INTRODUCTION

At Newmarket horse sales one October a friend told me that all bloodstock agents were crooks. I listened rather vaguely to the catalogue of accusations, learning about the price-fixing rings and the blackmailing extortions which drove the sale prices of thoroughbreds up and down artificially.

In January, casting about belatedly for the core of a novel I ought already to have started, I remembered my friend's cynical comments and sought her out, this time paying concentrated attention to the various scams she revealed.

Fortuitously I then heard of a small package tour being organized to fly British and Irish racehorse owners and bloodstock agents to the week-long bloodstock sales at Hialeah, Florida. Without hesitation I added my wife's and my name to the list, and we set out in a party of about twenty to spend glorious days by the sea in the sun, and fascinating warm evenings watching the glossy horses sold under bright lights.

We listened and asked questions, our eyebrows rising to the hairline as even the bloodstock agents themselves told us how to cheat the bloodstock breeders out of a fortune.

We returned to February snow and, very late but at last, I invented my ex-jockey honest bloodstock agent, Jonah Dereham, thrusting him into a series of violent confrontations with a racketeering pack determined to force him to be as corrupt as themselves. Good versus evil in pretty basic terms!

In the recognition that no individual life is without sadness and tribulations, I often give my chief characters experiences of shadows and regrets. I burdened Jonah Dereham with an alcoholic brother to whom he felt tied by an exasperated but immutable love, and I made this brother a working cog in the plot so that he was not there simply to embarrass.

I like self-reliant women who don't need to bang a feminist drum. I gave Jonah Dereham a silver-cool woman and waited to see, as I went along, how the relationship would work out. It's always more interesting, to me, not to know every single outcome of my stories too far in advance.

Of course my Newmarket sales friend had got it wrong, and of course she wildly exaggerated: not all bloodstock agents are crooks. The central message of *Knock Down*, however, is still valid and clear . . . *Caveat emptor*.

I

Mrs Kerry Sanders looked like no Angel of Death.

Mrs Kerry Sanders looked like a rich, cross, American lady opening a transparent umbrella against a spatter of cold rain.

'This,' she said in disbelief, 'is *Ascot* goddam *Sales*?'

She was small and exquisitely packaged in suede with mink trimmings. Her skin put peaches to rout and her scent easily prevailed over British October weather and a hundred nearby horses. With forty years behind her she wore assurance as naturally as diamonds; and she wore diamonds like crusty knuckle-dusters across the base of all her fingers.

'*Ascot?*' she said, her voice brimming with overtones of silk hats, champagne and Royal Lawns. 'This depressing dump?'

'I did try to warn you,' I said with mild apology.

She gave me a sharp, unfriendly glance. 'You didn't say it was like something out of Dickens.'

I looked across at the primitive sale ring: eight metres in diameter, open to the skies. A patch of rough field grass in the centre encircled by an asphalt path for the horses to walk on, and surrounding that, for the comfort of the customers, an elementary wooden shelter, backed and roofed with planks.

Plans for a bright new tomorrow were already past the drawing board stage, but on that day the future warm brick building with civilized armchairs was still a twinkle in the architect's eye. The only available seating was a six-inch-wide wooden shelf running round the inside wall of the shelter at hip height, upon which few people ever rested for long owing to the local numbness it induced.

Throughout the sale ring's wooden O the wind whistled with enthusiasm, but it was just possible when it was raining to find dry patches if you beat everyone else to them first.

'It used to be worse,' I said.

'Impossible.'

'There used to be no shelter at all.'

She diagnosed the amusement in my voice and if anything it made her more annoyed.

'It's all very well for you. You're used to a rough life.'

'Yes . . . Well,' I said. 'Do you want to see this horse?'

'Now that I'm here,' she said grudgingly.

To one side of the sale ring, and built to a specification as Upstairs as the wooden circle was Downstairs, was a magnificent turn-of-the-century stable yard, paved and tidy, with rows of neat-doored boxes round a spacious quadrangle. There was intricate stone carving on the arches into the yard, and charming little ventilation turrets along the roofs, and Mrs Kerry Sanders began to look more secure about the whole excursion.

The horses stabled in these prime quarters were in general those offered for sale last on the programme. Unfortunately the horse she had insisted on inspecting before I bought it for her came earlier and with a small sigh I wheeled her round in the opposite direction.

Thunder clouds immediately gathered again in the blue-green eyes, and two vertical lines appeared sharply between her eyebrows. Before her lay an expanse of scrubby wet grass with rows of functional black wooden stabling on the far side. The rain fell suddenly more heavily on the shiny umbrella, and the fine-grained leather of her boots was staining dark and muddy round the edges.

'It's too much,' she said.

I simply waited. She was there by her own choice, and I had used absolutely no pressure for or against.

'I guess I can see it in the ring,' she said, which was no way to buy a horse. 'How long before they sell it?'

'About an hour.'

'Then let's get out of this goddam rain.'

The alternative to the open air was the moderately new wooden building housing coffee urns at one end and a bar at the other. The Sanders nose wrinkled automatically at the press of damp humanity within, and I noticed, as one does when seeing through the eyes of visitors, that the board floor was scattered more liberally than usual with discarded plastic drinking cups and the wrappers from the sandwiches.

'Gin,' Kerry Sanders said belligerently without waiting to be asked.

I gave her a brief meant-to-be-encouraging smile and joined the scrum to the bar. Someone slopped beer down my sleeve and the man in front of me bought five assorted drinks and argued about his change: there had to be better ways, I thought resignedly, of passing Wednesday afternoons.

'Jonah,' said a voice in my ear. 'Not like you, chum, to chase the booze.'

I glanced back to where Kerry Sanders sat at a small table looking disgusted. The other eyes at my shoulder followed in her direction and the voice chuckled lewdly. 'Some lay,' he said.

'That chicken,' I said, 'is a customer.'

'Oh sure. Sure.' The hasty retreat from offence, the placatory grin, the old-pals slap on the shoulder, I disliked them all yet was aware they were only the desperate papering over no self-confidence. I had known him for years and we had jumped many a fence alongside: Jiminy Bell, one-time steeplechase jockey, currently drifting around horse places hoping for hand-outs. Where, but for the grace . . .

'Drink?' I suggested, and pitied the brightening eyes.

'Brandy,' he said. 'Large, if you could.'

I gave him a treble and a fiver. He took both with the usual mix of shame and bravado, consoling himself inwardly with the conviction that I could afford it.

'What do you know of the Ten Trees Stud?' he asked, which was much like asking what one knew of the Bank of England. 'I've been offered a job there.'

If it had been a good job, he wouldn't be asking my opinion. I said, 'What as?'

'Assistant.' He made a face over the brandy, not from the taste but from the realities of life. 'Assistant stud groom,' he said.

I paused. It wasn't much.

'Better than nothing, perhaps.'

'Do you think so?' he asked earnestly.

'It's what you are,' I said. 'Not what you do.'

He nodded gloomily, and I wondered if he were thinking as I was that it was really what you had *been* that mattered when you came face to face with the future. Without his ten years as a name in the sports pages he would have settled happily for what he now saw as disgrace.

Through a gap in the crowd I saw Kerry Sanders staring at me crossly and tapping her fingers on the table.

'See you,' I said to Jiminy Bell. 'Let me know how you get on.'

'Yeah . . .'

I elbowed back to the lady. Gin and jollying softened the sales' impact and eventually she recovered some of the fizz with which she had set out from London in my car. We had come to buy a steeplechaser as a gift for a young man, and she had made it delicately clear that it was not the young man himself that she was attached to, but his father. Pre-marital negotiations, I gathered, were in an advanced stage, but she had been reticent about names. She had been recommended to me, and me to her, by a mutual American acquaintance, a bloodstock agent called Pauli Teksa, and until two days earlier I had not known of her existence. Since then, she had filled my telephone.

'He will like it, don't you think?' she asked now for the seventh or eighth time, seeking admiration more than reassurance.

'It's a fantastic present,' I said obligingly, and wondered if the young man would accept it cynically or with joy. I hoped for her sake he would understand she wanted to please him more than bribe him, even if a bit of both.

'I think,' I said, 'that I ought to go over and take a quick look at the horse before it comes into the ring, just to make sure it hasn't bowed any tendons or grown any warts since I saw it last.'

She glanced out at the rain. 'I'll stay here.'

'Right.'

I squelched down to the drab old stables and found Box 126 with Lot 126 duly inside, shifting around on his straw and looking bored. Lot 126 was a five-year-old hurdler which someone with a macabre sense of humour had named Hearse Puller, and in a way one could see why. Glossy dark brown all over, he was slightly flashy looking, holding his head high as if preening. All he needed was a black plume on his head and he'd have been fine for Victorian trips to the cemetery.

Kerry Sanders had stipulated that her gift should be a young, good-looking past winner, with cast-iron future prospects. Also that in all its races it should never have fallen. Also that it should be of a calibre pleasing to the father even though it was to be given to the son. Also that it should be interesting, well bred, sensible, brave, bursting with health and keen to race: in short, the perfect chaser. Also that it should be bought by Friday which was the young man's birthday. Also it should cost no more than six or seven thousand dollars.

That had been the gist of her first call to me on Monday afternoon. She had conceived the idea of the gift at two o'clock, found my name by two-ten, and talked to me by two-twenty. She saw no reason why I should not put the same sort of hustle on and seemed delighted when I suggested Ascot Sales. Which was, of course, before she went there.

No one buys the perfect novice steeplechaser for seven thousand dollars. Most of my time since Monday had been taken both by persuading her to settle for a fifty-per-cent reduction on perfection and by searching through the Ascot catalogue for a cut-price paragon. I had come up finally with Hearse Puller, knowing that she would object to the name. It had no breeding to speak of but I had seen it race and knew it had guts, which was half the battle, and it was trained by a nervy trainer which meant it might do better somewhere more relaxed.

I felt the Hearse Puller legs and peered at the tonsils and went back and told Kerry Sanders that her money was on the way.

'You think we'll get him, then?' she asked.

'As long as no one else wants him very badly.'

'Do you think they will?'

'Can't tell,' I said, and wondered how many times every year I had this same conversation. Nothing warned me there was anything different this time.

The rain had slackened to drizzle by the time we went over to the ring but even so it was difficult to find room for Kerry Sanders in a dry spot. No one in the rain-coated assembly looked much except miserable. They stood with hunched shoulders, coat collars turned up, hands in pockets, the usual collection of bloodstock agents, race-horse trainers, breeders and hopeful would-be purchasers all out on the same trail of winners and loot.

Lot 122, a sad-looking chestnut, plodded round the asphalt path and failed to reach his reserve despite the auctioneer's cajoling. I told Kerry Sanders I would be back in a minute, and went to watch 126 being led round in the collecting ring as he waited his turn. He carried himself well enough but he looked a little too excited and I thought that the rain was probably hiding the fact that he was sweating.

'You interested in that black peacock?' said a voice at my shoulder, and there again was Jiminy Bell, following the direction of my eyes and giving me the benefit of the treble brandy at close quarters.

'Not specially,' I said, and knew he couldn't have read anything from my face. Nothing like bloodstock dealing for encouraging an expression to make poker players look indiscreet.

Hearse Puller pranced past and I switched my attention to 127 coming along next.

'Now that one,' Jiminy said approvingly. 'Bit of class there.'

I grunted noncommittally and turned towards him. He made way for me with a half-aggressive half-ingratiating smile, a short man with greying hair, deeply wrinkled skin, and teeth too good to be true. Four or five years out of the saddle had put weight on him like a padded coat and all his past pride in being able to do a job well had evaporated from his general carriage and the way he held his head. But feel sorry for him as I might, I had no intention of telling him in advance in which direction my interest lay: he was well into the stage of trotting off with the news to the vendor and asking a commission for bidding the price up high.

'I'm waiting for number one four two,' I said, and as soon as I walked off he started busily looking it up in the catalogue. When I glanced briefly back he was staring after me in amazement so I looked up 142 out of curiosity and found it was a crib-biting point-to-pointer still a maiden at ten.

Laughing inwardly I rejoined Kerry Sanders and watched the determined auctioneer wring twelve hundred pounds out of the UK Bloodstock Agency for the sinewy chestnut mare who was

Lot 125. As she was led out I felt Kerry Sanders stir beside me with her intentions showing to all and sundry like a flourish of trumpets. Inexperienced customers always did this if they came to the sales and it cost them a good deal of money.

Hearse Puller was led into the ring and the auctioneer checked his number against his notes.

'Bit on the leg,' a man behind us said disparagingly.

'Is that bad?' Kerry Sanders asked anxiously, overhearing.

'It means his legs are long in proportion to his body. It's not ideal, but some good chasers are like that.'

'Oh.'

Hearse Puller tossed his head and regarded the scene with eyes filled with alarm, a sign of waywardness which made me wonder if that were the basic reason for selling him.

Kerry Sanders' anxiety grew a little.

'Do you think he'll be able to manage him?'

'Who?'

'His new owner, of course. He looks damn wild.'

The auctioneer began his spiel, reeling off the gelding's origins and history. 'Who'll start me at a thousand? A thousand anywhere? Come along now, he'd look cheap at that wouldn't he? A thousand? Well, five hundred then. Someone start me at five hundred . . .'

I said to Kerry Sanders, 'Do you mean the young man is going to ride him himself? In races?'

'Yes.'

'You didn't tell me that.'

'Didn't I?' She knew she hadn't.

'Why didn't you, for heaven's sake?'

'Five hundred,' said the auctioneer. 'Thank you, sir. Five hundred I have. That's nowhere near his value. Come along now. Five hundred. Six. Thank you, sir. Six . . . Seven . . . Eight . . . against you, sir . . .'

'I just . . .' She hesitated, then said, 'What difference does it make?'

'Is he an amateur?'

She nodded. 'But he's got what it takes.'

Hearse Puller was no armchair ride and I would be doing my

job badly if I bought him for the sort of amateur who bumped around half fit. The customer's insistence on the horse never having fallen suddenly made a lot of sense.

'Twelve hundred. Fourteen. Against you at the back, sir. Fourteen. Come along now, you're losing him . . .'

'You'll have to tell me who it's for,' I said.

She shook her head.

'If you don't, I won't buy it for you,' I said, trying with a smile to take the discourtesy out of the words.

She stared at me. 'I can buy it myself.'

'Of course.'

The auctioneer was warming up. 'Eighteen . . . can I make it two thousand? Two thousand, thank you, sir. Selling all the time now. Two thousand . . . against you in front . . . Shall I say two thousand two? Two thousand one . . . thank you, sir. Two thousand one . . . Two . . . Three . . .'

'It will be too late in a minute,' I said.

She came to a decision. 'Nicol Brevett, then.'

'Jeez,' I said.

'Buy it then. Don't just stand there.'

'All done?' said the auctioneer. 'Selling at two thousand eight hundred. Selling once . . . all done then?'

I took a breath and waved my catalogue.

'Three thousand . . . New bidder. Thank you, sir . . . Against you in front. Can I make it three thousand two?'

As often happens when a fresh bidder comes in at the last moment the two contestants soon gave up, and the gavel came down at three thousand four.

'Sold to Jonah Dereham.'

Jiminy Bell was staring at me slit-eyed from the other side of the ring.

'What's that in dollars?' said my client.

'About seven thousand five hundred.'

We left the wooden shelter and she raised the umbrella again although the drizzle had all but ceased.

'More than I authorized you to spend,' she said, without great complaint. 'And your commission on top, I guess?'

'Five per cent,' I nodded.

'Ah well ... In the States you wouldn't buy a three-legged polo pony for that money.' She gave me a small smile as nicely judged as a tip and decided to walk on to wait in my car while I completed the paper work and arranged for the onward transport of Hearse Puller. He was to be stabled for the night in my own back yard and delivered to his new owner on the birthday morning.

Nicol Brevett . . . A surprise like a wasp at the honey, harmless unless you touched it on the stinging side.

He was a hard, forceful young man who put his riding cards on the table and dared the professionals to trump them. His obsessive will to win led him into ruthlessness, rudeness and rows. His temper flared like a flame thrower. No one could deny his talent, but where most of his colleagues won friends and races, Nicol Brevett just won races.

Hearse Puller was within his scope as a rider and if I were lucky they would have a good season together in novice chases: and I thought I would need to be lucky because of Brevett senior, whose weight could be felt all over the Turf.

My respect for Kerry Sanders rose several notches. Any woman who could interest Constantine Brevett to the point of matrimony had to be of a sophistication to put Fabergé eggs to shame, and I could well understand her coyness about naming him. If any announcements concerning him were to be made he would want to make them himself.

Constantine covered with velvet the granite core which showed in rocky outcrops in his son, and from brief racecourse meetings over the past few years I knew his social manners to be concentrated essence of old-boy network. The actions which spoke truer had repeatedly left a wake of smaller operatives who sadly wished they had never been flattered by his attention. I didn't know exactly what his business was, only that he dealt in property and thought in millions, and was now trying to build up the best collection of horses in the country. I had guessed it was being best that interested him more than the actual horses.

When I was ready to leave the sales the best thing of the day was due to come up in the ring, so it seemed that everyone was flocking in one direction to watch it while I went in the other towards the cars. I could see Kerry Sanders sitting waiting, her head turned towards me behind the rain-speckled glass. Two men were leaning on the car beside mine, cupping their hands over matches while they lit cigarettes.

When I passed them, one of them picked up some sort of bar from the bonnet of the car and hit me a crunching blow on the head.

Dazed and astonished I staggered and sagged and saw all those stars they print in comic strips. Vaguely I heard Kerry Sanders shouting and opening the door of my car, but when the world stopped whirling a little I saw that she was still sitting inside. Door shut, window open. Her expression as much outrage as fright.

One of the men clutched my right arm which probably stopped me falling flat on my face. The other calmly stood and watched. I leaned against the car next to mine and weakly tried to make sense of it.

'Muggers,' Kerry Sanders said scathingly. I thought she said 'buggers' with which I agreed, but finally understood what she meant.

'Four pounds,' I said. 'Only got four pounds.' It came out as a mumble. Indistinct.

'We don't want your money. We want your horse.'

Dead silence. They shouldn't have hit my head so hard if they wanted sense.

Kerry Sanders made things no clearer. 'I've already told you once,' she said icily, 'that I intend to keep him.'

'You told us, but we don't believe you.'

The one doing the talking was a large cheerful man with a bouncer's biceps and frizzy mouse-brown hair standing round his head like a halo.

'A fair profit, I offered you,' he said to Kerry. 'Can't say fairer than that, now can I, darlin'.'

'What the hell,' I said thickly, 'is going on?'

'See now,' he said, ignoring me. 'Three thousand six. Can't say fairer than that.'

Kerry Sanders said no.

Frizzy Hair turned his reasonable smile on me.

'Look now, lover boy, you and the lady is going to sell us the horse. Now we might as well do it civilized like. So give her some of your expensive advice and we'll be on our way.'

'Buy some other horse,' I said. Still a mumble.

'We haven't got all afternoon, lover boy. Three thousand six. Take it.'

'Or leave it,' I said automatically.

Kerry Sanders almost laughed.

Frizzy Hair dug into an inner pocket and produced wads of cash. Peeling a few notes away from one packet he threw the bulk of it through the car window onto Kerry Sanders' lap, followed by three closely taped packets which he didn't count. The lady promptly threw the whole lot out again and it lay there in the mud of the car park, lucre getting suitably filthy.

The haze in my head began to clear and my buckling knees to straighten. Immediately, sensing the change, Frizzy Hair shed the friendly persuader image in favour of extortionist, grade one.

'Let's forget the games,' he said. 'I want that horse and I'm going to get it. See?'

He unzipped the front of my rain-proof jacket.

I made a mild attempt at freeing myself from the other man's grasp, but my coordination was still shot to pieces. The net result was nothing except a fresh whirling sensation inside my skull, and I'd been knocked out often enough in the past to know that the time of profitable action was still a quarter of an hour ahead.

Under my jacket I wore a sweater, and under that a shirt. Frizzy Hair slid his hand up between these two layers until his fingers encountered the webbing strap I wore across my chest. He smiled with nasty satisfaction, yanked up the sweater, found the buckle on the strap, and undid it.

'Now you see, don't you, lover boy,' he said, 'how I'm going to get that horse?'

2

I sat in the driving seat of my car leaning my head against the window. Kerry Sanders sat beside me with the muddy packets of money on her expensive suede lap and unadulterated exasperation in her manner.

'Well, I couldn't just sit there and watch them putting you through a wringer,' she said crossly. 'Someone had to get you out of that fix, didn't they?'

I said nothing. She had stepped out of the car and picked up the money and told the thugs to leave me alone. She said they could have the goddam horse and much good might it do them. She had not tried screaming for help or running away or anything equally constructive, but had acted on the great modern dictum that you became less of a hospital case if you gave in to threats of violence right away.

'You looked as grey as death,' she said. 'What did you expect me to do? Sit and applaud?'

I didn't answer.

'What's the matter with your goddam arm, anyway?'

'It dislocates,' I said. 'The shoulder dislocates.'

'All the time?'

'Oh no. Not often. Only if it gets into one certain position. Then it falls apart, which is very boring. I wear the strap to prevent that happening.'

'It isn't dislocated now, is it?'

'No.' I smiled involuntarily. I tended not to be able to sit comfortably in cars whenever it went out.

'Thanks to you,' I added.

'As long as you realize.'

'Mm.'

They had taken the certificate of sale out of my pocket and had made Kerry Sanders write a receipt for the cash. Then they had simply walked away towards the centre of operations to claim their prize. Kerry Sanders had not felt like trying to stop them and I had still hardly been able to put one foot in front of the other with any certainty, and the one sure thing on that unsure afternoon was that Frizzy Hair and his pal would waste no time in driving off with Hearse Puller to destinations unknown. No one would question their right to the horse. Rapid post-sale sales were common.

'Why?' she said for the twentieth time. '*Why* did they want that goddam horse? Why *that* one?'

'I absolutely don't know.'

She sat fidgeting.

'You said you'd be able to drive by four.'

I glanced at the clock on the dashboard. Five past.

'Right.' I removed my head from the window and gave it a small tentative shake. Reasonable order seemed to have returned in that department so I started the engine and turned out towards London. She made a rapid assessment of my ability to drive and relaxed a shade after we had gone half a mile without hitting anything. At that point grievance took over from shock.

'I'm going to complain,' she said with vigour.

'Good idea. Who to?'

'Who to?' She sounded surprised. 'To the auctioneers, of course.'

'They'll commiserate and do nothing.'

'Of course they will. They'll have to.'

I knew they wouldn't. I said so.

She turned to look at me. 'The Jockey Club, then. The racing authorities.'

'They have no control . . . no jurisdiction . . . over the sales.'

'Who does, then?'

'No one.'

Her voice sharpened with frustration. 'We'll tell the police.'

'If you like.'

'The Ascot police?'

'All right.'

So I stopped at the police station and we told our story. Statements were taken and signed and no doubt filed as soon as we left, because as an overworked sergeant tiredly pointed out, we had not been robbed. A bang on the head, very nasty, very reprehensible, a lot of it about. But my wallet hadn't been stolen, had it? Not even my watch? And these rough customers had actually given Mrs Sanders a *profit* of two hundred pounds. Where was the crime in that, might one ask?

We drove away, me in resignation, Kerry Sanders in a boiling fury.

'I will not be pushed around,' she exploded. 'Someone ... *someone* has got to do something.'

'Mr Brevett?' I suggested.

She gave me one of her sharp glances and noticeably cooled her voice.

'I don't want him bothered with this.'

'No,' I said.

We drove ten miles in thoughtful silence. She said eventually, 'Can you find me another horse by Friday?'

'I could try.'

'Try, then.'

'If I succeed can you guarantee that no one else will knock me on the head and pinch it?'

'For a man who's supposed to be tough,' she said, 'you're soft.'

This dampening opinion led to a further five miles of silence. Then she said, 'You didn't know those two men, did you?'

'No.'

'But they knew you. They knew about your shoulder.'

'They did indeed.'

'You'd thought of that, had you?' She sounded disappointed.

'Mm,' I said.

I steered with care through the London traffic and stopped outside the Berkeley Hotel, where she was staying.

'Come in for a drink,' she said. 'You look as if you could use one.'

'Er...'

'Aw, c'mon,' she said. 'I won't eat you.'

I smiled. 'All right.'

Her suite looked out over Hyde Park with groups of riding

school ponies trotting in the Row and knots of household cavalry practising for state occasions. Late afternoon sunshine slanted into the lilac and blue sitting-room and made prisms of the ice-cubes in our glasses.

She protested over my choice.

'Are you sure you want Perrier?' she said.

'I like it.'

'When I said come up for a drink, I meant . . . a *drink*.'

'I'm thirsty,' I said reasonably. 'And a touch concussed. And I'm driving.'

'Oh.' Her manner changed subtly. 'I understand,' she said.

I sat down without being asked. It was all very well having had extensive experience of bangs on the head, but this had been the first for three years and the interval had not improved my speed of recovery.

She gave me a disillusioned glance and took off her beautiful, muddied coat. Underneath she wore the sort of simplicity only the rich could afford on the sort of shape that was beyond price. She enjoyed quietly my silent appreciation and took it naturally as the most commonplace courtesy.

'Now look,' she said. 'You haven't said a goddam thing about what happened this afternoon. Now what I'd like is for you to tell me just what you think those men were up to, back there.'

I drank the fizzy water and fractionally shook my head.

'I don't know.'

'But you must have ideas,' she protested.

'No . . .' I paused. 'Did you tell anyone you were going to Ascot Sales? Did you mention me? Did you mention Hearse Puller?'

'Hey, now,' she said, 'it was you they were after, not me.'

'How do we know?'

'Well . . . your shoulder.'

'Your horse.'

She moved restlessly across the room, threw the coat over a chair and came back. The slim boots had dirty water marks round the edges of the uppers which looked incongruous against the pale mauve carpet.

'I told maybe three people,' she said. 'Pauli Teksa was the first.'

I nodded. Pauli Teksa was the American who had given Kerry Sanders my name.

'Pauli said you were an honest bloodstock agent and therefore as rare as fine Sundays.'

'Thanks.'

'Then,' she said pensively, 'I told the guy who fixes my hair.'

'Who what?'

'Hairdresser,' she said. 'Right downstairs here in the hotel.'

'Oh.'

'And I had lunch with Madge yesterday . . . Lady Roscommon. Just a friend.'

She sat down suddenly opposite in an armchair with a blue and white chintz cover. A large gin and french had brought sharp colour to her cheeks and a lessening in her slightly dictatorial manner. I had the impression that for the first time she was considering me as a man instead of as an employee who had fallen down (more or less literally) on the job.

'Do you want to take your coat off?' she asked.

'I can't stay,' I said.

'Well then . . . Do you want more of that goddam water?'

'Please.'

She refilled my glass, brought it back, sat down.

'Don't you ever drink?' she said.

'Not often.'

'Alcoholic?' she said sympathetically.

I thought it odd of her to ask such a personal question, but I smiled, and said, 'No.'

She raised her eyebrows. 'Nearly all the non-drinkers I know are reformed alcoholics.'

'I admire them,' I said. 'But no. I was hooked on coke at six. Never graduated.'

'Oh.' She seemed to lose interest in me. She said, 'I am on the committee of a private hospital back home.'

'Which dries out drunks?'

She didn't care for the bluntness. 'We treat people with a problem. Yes.'

'Successfully?'

She sighed. 'Some.'

I stood up. 'You can't win them all.' I put the empty glass on a side-table and went ahead of her to the door.

'You'll let me know if you find another horse?' she said.

I nodded.

'And if you have any thoughts about those two men?'

'Yes.'

I drove slowly home and put the car in the garage in the stable yard. The three racehorses there moved around restlessly in their boxes, mutely complaining because I was two hours late with their evening feed. They were horses in transit, waiting to be shipped by air to foreign buyers; not my horses but very much my responsibility.

I talked to them and fondled their muzzles, and straightened their boxes and gave them food and water and rugs against the October night, and finally, tiredly, took my own throbbing head into the house.

There was no wife there waiting with a smiling face and a hot tempting dinner. There was, however, my brother.

His car was in the garage next to mine, and there were no lights anywhere in the house. I walked into the kitchen, flicked the switch, washed my hands under the hot tap in the sink, and wished with all my heart that I could off-load my drinking problem on to Kerry Sanders and her do-good hospital.

He was in the dark sitting-room, snoring. Light revealed him lying face down on the sofa with the empty Scotch bottle on the carpet near his dangling hand.

He didn't drink often. He tried very hard, and he was mostly the reason I stayed off it, because if I came home with alcohol on my breath he would smell it across the room, and it made him restless. It was no hardship for me, just a social nuisance, as Kerry Sanders was by no means alone in concluding that non-drinkers were ex-alcoholics. One had to drink to prove one wasn't, like natural bachelors making an effort with girls.

We were not twins, though much alike. He was a year older, an inch shorter, better looking and not so dark. People had mistaken us for each other continually when we had been young, but less so now at thirty-four and thirty-five.

I picked up the empty bottle and took it out to the dustbin. Then I cooked some scrambled eggs and sat down at the kitchen table to eat, and over coffee and aspirin and a sore head put up a reasonable fight against depression.

There was much to be thankful for. I owned outright the house and stable yard and ten acres of paddocks, and after two years' slog I was beginning to make it as an agent. On the debit side I had a busted marriage, a brother who lived off my earnings because he couldn't keep a job, and a feeling that Frizzy Hair was only the tip of an iceberg.

I fetched a pen and a sheet of paper and wrote three names.

Pauli Teksa.

Hairdresser.

Lady Roscommon (Madge).

None looked a winner in the villainy stakes.

For good measure I added Kerry Sanders, Nicol Brevett, Constantine Brevett and two smiley thugs. Shake that lot together and what did we get? A right little ambush by someone who knew my weakest spot.

I spent the evening trying by telephone to find a replacement for Hearse Puller. Not easy. Trainers with horses the owners might sell were not keen to lose them from their yards, and I could give no guarantee that Nicol Brevett would leave his horse with its present trainer. Bound by Kerry Sanders, I could not even mention his name.

I reread the Ascot Sale catalogue for the following day but there was still nothing suitable, and finally with a sigh offered my custom to a bloodstock dealer called Ronnie North, who said he knew of a possible horse which he could get if I would play ball.

'How much?' I said.

'Five hundred.'

He meant that he would sell me the horse for a price. I would then charge Kerry Sanders five hundred pounds more . . . and hand the five hundred over to North.

'Too much,' I said. 'If you get me a good one for two thousand I'll give you a hundred.'

'Nuts.'

'A hundred and fifty.' I knew he would probably acquire the horse for maybe fifteen hundred pounds, and sell it to me for double: he always considered he had wasted his time if he made less than one hundred per cent profit. Squeezing a large chunk more from my client was just icing on the cake.

'And,' I said, 'before we go any further, I want to know about it.'

'Do me a favour.'

He was afraid that if I knew who owned the horse I would go direct to the source, and cut him out altogether. I wouldn't have done that, but he would, and he judged me by himself.

I said, 'If you buy it and I don't like it, I won't take it.'

'It's what you want,' he said. 'You can trust me.'

I could perhaps trust his judgement of a horse, though that was absolutely all. If the horse hadn't been for Nicol Brevett I might have taken a chance and bought blind, but in this case I could not afford to.

'I have to OK it first.'

'Then no deal,' he said succinctly and disconnected.

I chewed the end of my pencil and thought about the bloodstock jungle which I had entered with such innocence two years earlier. It had been naïve to imagine that all it took to be a bloodstock agent was a thorough knowledge of horses, an intimate relationship with the stud book, hundreds of acquaintances in the racing industry and a reasonable head for business. Initial surprise at the fiddles I saw all around me had long since passed from revulsion to cynicism, and I had grown a thick skin of self-preservation. I thought that sometimes it was difficult to perceive the honest course, and more difficult still to stick to it, when what I saw as dishonesty was so much the general climate.

I understood, after two years, that dishonesty was much a matter of opinion. There were no absolutes. A deal I thought scandalous might seem eminently reasonable to others. Ronnie North saw nothing wrong at all in milking the market for every possible penny: and moreover he was likeable to meet.

The telephone rang. I picked up the receiver.

'Jonah?'

He was back, as I'd thought he might be.

'The horse is River God. You have it for three thousand five hundred with five hundred on top.'

'I'll call you back.'

I looked up the River God form and consulted a jockey who'd ridden it a few times, and finally dialled Ronnie North.

'All right,' I said. 'Subject to a vet's report, River God will do well.'

He said with elaborate resignation, 'I told you, you can trust me.'

'Yeah. I'll give you two thousand five hundred.'

'Three thousand,' he said. 'And that's rock bottom. With five hundred to come.'

'One fifty,' I said positively, and compromised at a hundred more.

River God, my jockey friend had said, belonged to a farmer in Devon who had bought it unbroken at three years old as a point-to-point prospect for his son. Between them they'd done a poor job of the breaking and now the son couldn't control the result. 'He's a ride for a pro,' said my informant, 'but he's quite fast and a natural jumper, and they haven't managed to cock that up.'

I stood up, stretched, and as it was by then half past ten, decided to tell Kerry Sanders in the morning. The room I used as an office, lined with book shelves and fitted cupboards, was half functional, half sitting-room, and mostly what I thought of as home. It had a lightish brown carpet, red woollen curtains and leather armchairs, and one big window which looked out to the stable yard. When I had tidied away the books and papers I'd been using I switched off the powerful desk lamp and stood by the window, looking out from darkness to moonlight.

Everything was quiet out there, the three lodgers patiently waiting for their aeroplane from Gatwick Airport five miles down the road. They should have been gone a week since and the overseas customers were sending irritable cables, but the shipping agents muttered on about unavoidable delays and kept saying the day after tomorrow.

'The day after tomorrow never comes,' I said, but they didn't think it funny.

I used the yard as a staging post and seldom kept horses there more than a night or two. They were a tie, because I looked after them myself, and I did that because until recently I had not been earning enough to think of employing anyone else.

In my first year in the business I had negotiated fifty sales, and in my second ninety-three, and during the past three months I had been almost constantly busy. Given a bit of luck, I thought, like, say, buying a Derby winner for five thousand as a yearling . . . just some such impossible bit of luck . . . I might yet achieve tax problems.

I left the office and went to the sitting-room. My brother Crispin was still where I'd left him, face down, snoring, spark out. I fetched a rug and draped it over him, knowing he wouldn't wake for hours, and that when he did he would be in his usual violent hangover temper, spewing out his bitter resentments like untreated effluent.

We had been orphaned when I was sixteen and he seventeen, first by a riding accident which killed our mother, and then three months later by a blood clot in Father. Abruptly, almost from one week to the next, our lives changed to the roots. We had been brought up in comfort in a house in the country, with horses to ride and a cook and gardener and stablemen to do the work. We went to expensive boarding schools and thought it natural, and holidayed on grouse moors in Scotland.

The glitter had by no means been founded on gold. Solicitors gravely told us that our parent had mortgaged all he possessed, had borrowed on his life assurance, had sold the family treasures and was only a Degas sketch away from bankruptcy. He had, it appeared, been living on the brink of disaster for several years, always finding a last minute goody to send to Sotheby's. When his debts had been paid and house, horses, cook, gardener, stablemen and all had vanished into limbo, Crispin and I, without close relatives, were left with no home to go to and precisely one hundred and forty-three pounds each.

The school had been understanding but not to the point of

keeping us without fees. We had finished the Easter term, but that was that.

It had affected Crispin more than me. He had been aiming for university and the law and could not bring himself to settle for the generously offered Articles in the grave solicitor's office. My more practical nature saved me from such torments. I faced prosaically the fact that from now on I would need to work to eat, totted up my assets which proved to be a thin body, good health and a certain facility on horseback, and got myself a job as a stable lad.

Crispin had been furious with me but I'd been happy. I was not academic. Stable life, after the confines of school, had been a marvellous freedom. I never regretted what I'd lost.

I left him snoring and went upstairs to bed, thinking about our different fates. Crispin had tried stockbroking and insurance and felt he had not been appreciated, and I, in becoming a jockey, had found total fulfilment. I always reckoned I'd had by far the best of it and didn't begrudge anything I could do to compensate.

My bedroom like the office looked out to the yard, and except when it was freezing I slept with the window open. At twelve-thirty I woke from the depths with the sudden instant awareness of the subconscious hitting the alarm switch.

I lay tinglingly awake, listening at full stretch, not knowing what I'd heard but sure that it was wrong.

Then unmistakably it came again. The scrape of a hoof on a hard surface. The clop of horse shoes where they had no business to be at that time of night.

I flung back the duvet and jumped to the window.

No movement down there in the moonlit yard. Just a yawning black oblong which should have been filled by a firmly closed stable door.

I cursed with a sinking heart. The most valuable of my lodgers, all seventy thousand pounds' worth, was out loose on the dangerous roads of Surrey.

3

He wasn't comprehensively insured, because his new owner had jibbed at the high premium. He wasn't finally paid for, because of a complicated currency transfer. I had had to guarantee the money to the vendor when I didn't actually have it, and if I didn't get that two-year-old back fast and unscratched the financial hot waters would close over my head. The foreign buyer was a ruthless man who would stop his cheque if the horse were damaged and my own insurers wouldn't pay up for anything less than death, and reluctantly at that.

Sweater, jeans, boots went on at high speed and I ran downstairs fumbling to do up the buckles of the strap which anchored my shoulder. In the sitting-room Crispin still snored. I shook him, calling his name. No response. The stupor persisted.

I stopped in the office to telephone the local police.

'If anyone reports a horse in their back garden, it's mine.'

'Very good,' said a voice. 'Saves time to know.'

Out in the yard there was no sound. The two-year-old had been already on the road when I woke, because it was metal on tarmac I'd heard, not the soft familiar scrunch on weedy gravel.

No sound on the road. It lay empty in the moonlight for as far as I could see.

He could be peacefully grazing the verge a few yards beyond my sight.

He could be halfway to the express line of the electric railway or on the dual carriageway to Brighton or on the main runway at the airport.

He could be crashing down rabbit holes in the local scrubby woodland.

I sweated in the cold night air. Seventy thousand bloody pounds I didn't have and couldn't raise.

Looking for a loose horse at night by car had high built-in

failure factors. One couldn't hear his movements and with his dark coat one could hit him as soon as see him. One could startle him into panic, into crashing through a fence, tearing himself on barbed wire, skidding to his knees, damaging beyond repair the slender bones and tendons of his legs.

I hurried back through the yard, picked up a bridle and a halter from the tackroom, and ran on out to the nearest paddock. There somewhere in the dim dappled light was the pensioned-off steeplechaser I used as a hack. Dozing on his feet and dreaming of long-past Gold Cups.

Climbing the rails I whistled to him in a trill through my teeth, the sound he responded to when he felt like it.

'Come on, boy,' I called. 'Come here you bugger, for God's sweet sake.' Come. Just come. But the field looked empty.

I whistled again, despairing.

He ambled over with all the urgency of a museum. Sniffed at my fingers. Resignedly allowed me to put on his bridle. Even stood moderately still when I led him to the gate and used it as usual as a mounting block. Jogging on his bare back, I trotted him through the yard, and at the gate let him choose his own direction.

Left lay the main roads and right the woods. He chose the right, but as I urged him on I wondered if he had gone that way because I subconsciously wanted it. Horses, highly telepathic, needed little steering.

If the two-year-old were in the woods he wasn't under the wheels of a twenty-ton lorry. If he were in the woods he could be calmly eating leaves from the branches and not sticking his feet down rabbit holes . . .

After half a mile, where the narrow road began to wind upward and the tangle of beech and bramble and evergreen grew thicker, I reined in my 'chaser, stood him still, and listened.

Nothing. Only the faint sound of moving air, hardly as much as a rustle. My mount waited, uninterested and unexcited. He would have known if the two-year-old had been near. He was telling me indirectly that he wasn't.

I went back, trotting him fast on the softer verge. Past the stable gate, where he wanted to turn in. Down the road to the village and across the moonlit green.

I tried to comfort myself with the thought that horses didn't usually go far when they got loose from their stable. Only as far as the nearest succulent grass. They wandered and stopped, wandered and stopped, and only if something frightened them would they decamp at a gallop. The trouble was they were so easily frightened.

There was grass enough on the village green, but no two-year-old. I stopped again on the far side, listening.

Nothing.

Worried and dry mouthed I went on towards the junction with the main road, where the village swept abruptly out into the three-lane double highway of the A23.

How could I, I thought, how could I have been so stupid as not to bolt the stable door. I couldn't remember not doing it, but then I couldn't remember doing it either. It was one of those routine actions one did automatically. I couldn't imagine not flicking the bolt when I left the box. I'd been doing it all my working life. I was not insured against my own negligence. How could I possibly ... how could I ever ... have been stupid enough not to bolt that door?

Even after midnight there was too much traffic on the Brighton road. Definitely not a place for horses.

I reined in again, and almost immediately my 'chaser lifted his head, pricked his ears, and whinnied. He twisted to the right, towards the oncoming headlights, and whinnied again. Somewhere out of sight he could hear or sense another horse, and not for the first time I envied that extra-human perception.

Hurrying, I set off southwards along the green edge, hoping against hope that it was the right horse ahead and not a lay-by full of gypsy ponies.

In the distance there was suddenly a horrific screech of tyres, some wildly scything headlights, a sickening bang and a crash of breaking glass.

My mount let out a whinny that was more a shriek. His rider felt sick.

Oh God, I thought. Oh dear God.

I slowed to a walk and found I was trembling. There were shouts ahead and cars pulling up, and I rubbed my hand over my face and wished I didn't have to face the next bit. Not the next hour, the next day or the next year.

Then, unbelievably, a shape detached itself from the jumble of light and dark ahead. A shape moving very fast, straight towards me, and *clattering*.

Hooves drummed on the hard surface with the abandon of hysteria. The two-year-old raced past at a forty-mile-an-hour full-stretched gallop, going as if the Triple Crown depended on it.

Swamped with relief that at least he was still undamaged, and blotting out fears for the car which had crashed, I swung my 'chaser round and set off in pursuit.

It was an unequal contest: an ageing jumper against a hot-blooded sprinter. But my anxiety was spur enough for my mount. He was infected by it and aroused, and achieved a pace that was madness on that sort of surface.

The two-year-old, sensing us behind him, could have taken up the challenge and raced harder, but in fact he seemed to be reassured, not galvanized by the approach of another horse, and although he showed no sign of stopping he allowed me gradually to move alongside.

I came up on his outside, with him on my left. He had worn no headcollar in the stable and although I had brought a halter it would have taken a circus stunt man to put it on at such a gallop, let alone an unfit ex-jockey with three fused vertebrae and a shoulder which came apart with one good tug.

We were nearly back to the fork in the village. Straight ahead lay a major roundabout with crossing traffic, and the thought of causing a second accident was too appalling. Whatever the risk to the two-year-old, he had simply got to be directed into the village.

I squeezed my 'chaser to the left until my leg was brushing the younger horse's straining side, and I kicked my toe gently into his ribs. I did it three or four times to give him the message, and then when we came to the fork kicked him most insistently and pulled my own mount quite sharply onto him, leaning to the left.

The two-year-old veered into the fork without losing his balance and as positively as if he had been ridden. He fled ahead again into the village, no doubt because once off the main road I had instinctively slowed down. One couldn't take the narrow bends flat out.

The two-year-old discovered it the hard way. He skidded round the corner to the green, fought to keep his feet under him, struck sparks from his scrabbling shoes, tripped over the six-inch-high edge of the turf, and fell sprawling in a flurry of legs. Dismounting and grabbing the 'chaser's reins I ran towards the prostrate heap. My knees felt wobbly. He couldn't, I prayed, have torn a tendon here on the soft green grass, with so much agonizing danger all behind him.

He couldn't.

He hadn't. He was winded. He lay for a while with his sides heaving, and then he stood up.

I had put the halter on him while he was down, and now led him and the 'chaser, one in each hand, along the lane to the yard. Both of them steamed with sweat and blew down their nostrils; and the hack, having been bridled, dropped foamy saliva from his mouth; but neither of them walked lame.

The moonlight was calming, quiet and cool. In the yard I hitched the 'chaser to a railing and led the two-year-old back to his box, and realized there for the first time that he was no longer wearing his rug. Somewhere on his escapade he had rid himself of it. I fetched another and buckled it on. By rights I should have walked him round for another half hour to cool him down, but I hadn't time. I went out, shut his door, and slammed home the bolt, and simply could not understand how I could have left it undone.

I backed the car out of the garage and drove through the village and down the main road. There was a fair crowd now at the scene of the crash, and people waving torches to direct the traffic. When I pulled on to the grass and stopped one of the self-elected traffic directors told me to drive on, there were enough onlookers already. I told him I lived nearby and perhaps could help, and left him to move along the next fellow.

Across in the north-bound lane also the traffic was on the move, as the wreckage was all on the near side. With something like dread I crossed over and joined the group at the heart of things. Car headlights threw them into sharp relief, bright on one side, dark on the other. All men, all on their feet. And one girl.

It was her car that was most smashed. One side of it seemed to have hit the metal post of the advance signpost to the village and the backside of it had been rammed by a dark green Rover which stood askew across the roadway spilling water from its dented radiator and frosty fragments from its windscreen.

The owner of the Rover was stamping about in loquacious fury, shouting about women drivers and that it was not his fault.

The girl stood looking at the orange remains of an MGB GT which had buried itself nose first into the ditch. She wore a long dress of a soft floaty material, white with a delicate black pattern and silver threads glittering in the lights. She had silver shoes and silver-blonde hair which hung straight to her shoulders, and she was bleeding.

At first I was surprised that she was standing there alone, that the masculine onlookers were not wrapping her in rugs, binding up her wounds and generally behaving protectively, but when I spoke to her I saw why. She was in icy command of herself, as cool and silver as the moonlight. Despite the oozing cut on her forehead and the smears she had made trying to wipe it, despite the much heavier stain on her right arm and the scarlet splashes down the front of the pretty dress, she somehow repelled help. And she was not as young as she looked at first sight.

'She cut right across me,' the Rover driver was shouting. 'Swerved right across me. I didn't have a chance. She went to sleep. That's what she did. And now she gives us all this crap about a horse. I ask you. A horse! Swerved to avoid a horse. She went to sleep. She dreamed the horse. The silly *bitch*.'

Shock took people like that sometimes, and to be fair he had had a bad fright.

I said to the girl, 'There was a horse.'

She looked at me without eagerness.

'Of course there was,' she said.

'Yes . . . He got loose from my stable and strayed up here on to the road.'

I was immediately the focus of a hedge of accusing eyes and also the new target for the Rover driver's ire. He had really been quite restrained with the girl. He knew a lot of words one seldom heard even on a racecourse.

In a gap in the tirade the girl spoke. She had one hand pressed against her abdomen and a strained look on her face.

'I need,' she said distinctly, 'to go to the bathroom.'

'I'll take you to my house,' I said. 'It's not far.'

The Rover driver was against it. She should stay until the police arrived, which would be at any second, he said. But some of the men showed that they understood what such an occasion could do to the viscera and silently parted to let her go with me across to my car.

'If the police want her,' I said, 'tell them she's at Jonah Dereham's house. First turn left, through the village, a house and stable yard out on the far side, on the right.'

They nodded. When I looked back I could see most of them returning to their own cars and driving away, and only one or two staying to support the Rover man.

She said nothing on the short journey. There was sweat on her face as well as blood. I drew up outside the kitchen and led her inside without delay.

'The cloakroom is there,' I said, showing her the door.

She nodded and went inside. White walls, bright unshaded light bulb, gumboots, waterproofs, two framed racing photographs and an ancient shotgun. I left her to this uncosy decor and went outside again to where my 'chaser still patiently stood hitched to the railing.

I patted him and told him he was a great fellow. Fetched him a couple of apples from the tackroom and led him back to his paddock. He hadn't galloped so fast or felt such excitement since the day they cheered him home up the hill at Cheltenham. He snorted with what was easy to read as pride when I released him and trotted away on springy ankles like a yearling.

She was coming out of the cloakroom when I returned. She had washed the streaked blood off her face and was dabbing the still unclotted cut on her forehead with a towel. I invited her with a gesture back to the kitchen and she came with the same marked and unusual composure.

'What you can give me now,' she said, 'is a large drink.'

'Er . . . How about some hot strong tea?'

She stared. 'No. Brandy.'

'I haven't any.'

She gestured impatiently. 'Whisky, then. Gin. Anything will do.'

'I'm afraid,' I said apologetically, 'that I haven't anything at all.'

'Do you mean,' she said in disbelief, 'that you have no alcohol of any sort in this house?'

'I'm afraid not.'

'Oh my God,' she said blankly. She sat down suddenly on the kitchen chair as if her knees had given way.

I said, 'Tea is honestly better when you're injured. I'll make you some.'

I went over to the kettle and picked it up to fill it.

'You bloody fool,' she said. Her voice was a mixture of scorn, anger, and, surprisingly, despair.

'But . . .'

'But nothing,' she said. 'You let your stupid horse out and it nearly kills me and now you can't even save me with a bloody drink.'

'Save you?' I echoed.

She gave me a cutting glance. Same mix: scorn, anger, despair. She explained the despair.

'Look . . . I've been to a party. I was driving myself home. Now thanks to you and your stupid horse there's been an accident and even though it wasn't my fault the police will be along with their little breath tests.'

I looked at her.

'I'm not drunk,' she said unnecessarily. 'Nowhere near it. But

I'd be over the eighty milligrammes. Even eight-one is enough. And I can't afford to lose my driving licence.'

My horse had got her into the mess. I suppose I should do my best to get her out.

'All right,' I said. 'I'll fix it.'

'Wake a neighbour,' she said. 'But do it quick, or the police will be here.'

I shook my head. I went out to the dustbin and retrieved the empty Scotch bottle.

'No time for neighbours,' I said. 'And it would look too deliberate.' I fetched a glass and gave it to her. Then I held the empty bottle under the tap, splashed in a thimbleful of water, swilled the water around and finally dripped it into the glass.

'Do you think,' she said ominously, 'that this is going to fool anybody?'

'Don't see why not.'

I put the empty bottle on the kitchen table and returned to the kettle. 'And we'd better get your cuts seen to.'

She blotted her forehead again and looked indifferently at the crimson state of her right forearm. 'I suppose so,' she said.

While the kettle boiled I telephoned my own doctor and explained the situation.

'Take her to the Casualty Department at the Hospital,' he said. 'That's what they're there for.'

'She's pretty,' I said. 'And you'd make a better job of it.'

'Dammit, Jonah, it's half past one,' he said, but he agreed to come.

The tea was made and brewing by the time the police arrived with their little breath tests. They accepted mugs with sugar and milk and sniffed sourly into the whisky bottle and the glass in the girl's hand. Didn't she know she shouldn't have a drink before she had blown into the breathalyser? She shook her head tiredly and indicated that she hadn't given it a thought.

Tests within fifteen minutes of alcohol intake were not acceptable as evidence. They filled in the time by taking down her view of the facts.

'Name, miss?'

'Sophie Randolph.'
'Married?'
'No.'
'Age?'
'Thirty-two.' No feminine hesitation. Just a fact.
'Address?'
'Primrose Court, Scilly Isles Drive, Esher, Surrey.'
'Occupation?'
'Air traffic controller.'

The policeman's pen remained stationary in the air for five seconds before he wrote it down. I looked at the girl; at Sophie Randolph, unmarried, thirty-two, air traffic controller, a woman accustomed to working on equal terms among males, and I remembered her instinctive reaction to the men at the scene of the crash: even in a crisis she repelled protective cosseting because in everyday life she could not afford it.

She gave them a straightforward statement. She had been to dinner with friends near Brighton. She left at twelve-fifteen. At about twelve-fifty she was driving in good visibility at forty-five miles an hour, listening to all-night radio. A horse suddenly emerged into the road from the central area of bushes. She braked hard but had no chance to stop. She steered sharply to the left to avoid the horse. She had passed the Rover a mile or so back and did not realize he was still so close behind her. The Rover struck the back of her car, slewing it round. Her car then bounced off a signpost at the side of the road, and slid to a stop in the ditch. She had been shaken. She had been wearing a seat belt. She had been slightly cut by broken glass.

One of the policemen asked what she had had to drink during the evening. In the same calm factual voice she itemized sherry before dinner, wine with.

Eventually they got her to blow into the bag. She did so without anxiety.

The policeman who took the bag from her gave the crystals a sharp scrutiny and raised his eyebrows.

'Well, miss,' he said. 'Unofficially I can tell you that if you hadn't drunk that whisky you'd have been on the right side. It isn't much over, even now.'

'I'm not really surprised,' she said, and that at least was true.

'You'd be amazed the number of people who try to drink before we test them.'

'Do they really?' She sounded tired, and as if evasive tactics had never come into her orbit. The police packed up their notes and their bottle kit, gave me a lecture about letting animals get loose, and in their own good time went away.

Sophie Randolph gave me the beginnings of a smile.

'Thanks,' she said.

4

She slept in my bed and I slept in Crispin's, and Crispin slept on, unknowing, on the sofa.

She had been stitched up neatly by the doctor but had been more concerned that he should take care of her dress. She had insisted that he unpick the seam of her sleeve rather than rip the material to get to her wound, and I had smiled at the meticulous way he had snipped through the tiny threads to please her.

'My arm will mend itself,' she explained. 'But the dress won't, and it was expensive.'

The cut, once revealed, had been jagged and deep, with fragments of glass embedded. She watched with interest while he anaesthetized it locally and worked on the repairs, and by the end I was wondering just what it would take to smash up such practised self-command.

The morning found her pale and shaky but still basically unruffled. I had been going to tell her to stay in bed but when I came in at eight-thirty after feeding and mucking out the lodgers she was already down in the kitchen. Sitting at the table, wearing my dressing-gown and slippers, smoking a cigarette and reading the newspaper. There were dark smudges round her eyes and most of the thirty-two years were showing in her skin. I thought that very probably her bandaged arm was hurting.

She looked up calmly when I came in.

'Hullo,' I said. 'Like some coffee?'

'Very much.'

I made it in the filter pot. 'I was going to bring it to you upstairs,' I said.

'I didn't sleep too well.'

'Not madly surprising.'

'I heard you out in the yard. Saw you from the window, and thought I might as well come down.'

'How about some toast?' I asked.

She said yes to the toast and yes also to three strips of crispy bacon to go with it. While I cooked she looked round the workmanlike kitchen and finally asked the hovering question. 'Are you married?'

'Divorced.'

'Some years ago, I would guess.'

I grinned. 'Quite right.' Married, repented, divorced, and in no hurry to make another mistake.

'Can you lend me any clothes I won't look ridiculous in?'

'Oh . . . a jersey. Jeans. Would that do?'

'Lovely with silver shoes,' she said.

I sat down beside her to drink my coffee. She had a face more pleasant than positively beautiful, a matter of colouring and expression more than bone structure. Her eyebrows and eyelashes were brownish blonde, eyes hazel, mouth softly pink without lipstick.

Her composure, I began to understand, was not aggressive. It was just that she gave no one any chance to patronize or diminish her because she was female. Understandable if some men didn't like it. But her colleagues, I thought, must find it restful.

'I'm very sorry,' I said, 'about my horse.'

'So you damn well ought to be.' But there was none of the rancour she would have been entitled to.

'What can I do to make amends?'

'Are you offering a chauffeur service?'

'By all means,' I said.

She munched the toast and bacon. 'Well . . . I'll need to see about getting my car towed away. What's left of it. Then I'd be grateful if you could drive me to Gatwick Airport.'

'Do you work there, then?' I asked, surprised.

'No. At Heathrow. But I can hire a car at Gatwick. Special discount . . . goes with the job.'

She was using her right hand to cut the toast with, and I saw her wince.

'Do you have to work today?' I asked.

'Nothing wrong with my voice,' she said. 'But probably not. I'm on stand-by from four this afternoon for twelve hours. That means I just have to be home in my flat, ready to take over at an hour's notice in case anyone is ill or doesn't turn up.'

'And what are the chances?'

'Of working? Not high. Most stand-bys are just a bore.'

She drank her coffee left handed.

'And you?' she asked. 'What do you do?'

'I'm a bloodstock agent.'

She wrinkled her forehead. 'I have an aunt who says all bloodstock agents are crooks.'

I smiled. 'The big firms wouldn't thank her for that.'

'Do you work for a firm?'

I shook my head. 'On my own.'

She finished the toast and fished a packet of cigarettes out of my dressing-gown pocket.

'At least you smoke,' she said, flicking my lighter. 'I found these in your bedroom . . . I hope you don't mind.'

'Take what you like,' I said.

She looked at me levelly and with a glint of amusement.

'I'll give you something instead. That man in the Rover, do you remember him?'

'Who could fail to!'

'He was doing about forty until I tried to pass him. When I was level with him he speeded up.'

'One of those.'

She nodded. 'One of those. So I put my foot down and passed him and he didn't like it. He kept weaving around close behind me and flashing his headlights and generally behaving like an idiot. If he hadn't been distracting me I might have seen your horse a fraction sooner. The crash was just as much his fault as your horse's.'

'Well,' I said. 'Thank you too.'

We smiled at each other, and all the possibilities suddenly rose up like question marks, there in the kitchen over the crumbs of toast.

Into this subtle moment Crispin barged with the sensitivity of a tank. The kitchen door crashed open and in he came, crumpled, unshaven, ill and swearing.

'Where the bloody hell have you hidden the whisky?'

Sophie looked at him with predictable calm. Crispin didn't seem to notice she was there.

'Jonah, you vicious sod, I'll cut your bloody throat if you don't give it back at bloody once.' It was his tragedy that he was more than half serious.

'You finished it last night,' I said. 'The empty bottle's in the dustbin.'

'I did no such bloody thing. If you've poured it down the drain I'll bloody strangle you.'

'You poured it down your throat,' I said. 'And you'd better have some coffee.'

'Stuff your effing coffee.' He strode furiously round the kitchen, wrenching open cupboards and peering inside. 'Where is it?' he said. 'Where have you put it, you stinking little stable boy?'

He picked up a bag of sugar and threw it on the floor. The paper burst and the crystals scattered in a frosty swathe. He pulled several tins out to look behind them, dropping them instead of putting them back.

'Jonah, I'll kill you,' he said.

I heated him some coffee and put the mug on the table. A packet of rice and another of cornflakes joined the mess on the floor.

He gave up the search with a furious slam of a cupboard door, sat down at the table and stretched for his coffee. His hand was shaking as if he were ninety.

He seemed to see Sophie for the first time. His gaze started at her waist and slowly travelled up to her face.

'Who the bloody hell are you?'

'Sophie Randolph,' she said politely.

He squinted at her. 'Jonah's bloody popsy.'

He swung round to me, a movement which upset his semicircular canals and brought on an obvious wave of nausea. I hoped urgently he was not going to vomit, as on other vile occasions in the past.

'You lecherous bastard,' he said. 'All you had to do was ask me to go out. I'd have gone out. You didn't have to get me drunk.'

The easy tears began to roll down his cheeks. And after the

self pity, the promises, I thought. Always the same pattern.

'You got yourself drunk,' I said.

'You shouldn't have given me the Scotch,' he said. 'It was your bloody fault.'

'You know damn well I never gave you any Scotch.'

'You just put it here on the table and left it here for me to find. If that's not giving it to me, then what is?'

'You'd convince yourself it grew on a tree in the garden. You went out and bought it.'

'I tell you I didn't,' he said indignantly. 'I just found it on the table.'

He managed to get the mug to his mouth without spilling the contents.

I considered him. If by some extraordinary chance he was telling the truth, someone wished him very ill. But as far as I knew he had no active enemies, just bored acquaintances who tended to cross the road at his approach and disappear into convenient doorways. On balance I thought it more likely he had bought the bottle somewhere and was trying to shift the blame. The days when I could effortlessly believe what he said were ten years back.

'As God's my judge, Jonah, it was here on the table.' A couple more tears oozed out. 'You never believe a bloody word I say.'

He drank half the coffee.

'I'd never buy whisky,' he said. 'Sour bloody stuff.'

Once the craving took him he would drink whatever he could get hold of. I'd known him pass out on crème de menthe.

He worked on the grudge that I didn't believe him until he was back to full-scale anger. With a sudden half-coordinated swing he hurled his mug of coffee across the room where it shattered against the wall. Brown rivulets trickled downwards on the floor.

He stood up, upsetting his chair, his head lowered aggressively.

'Give me some bloody money.'

'Look . . . Go to bed and sleep it off.'

'You stupid sod. I need it. You and your goody-goody airs. You've no bloody idea. You don't begin to understand. You've pinched my whisky. Just give me some bloody money and go stuff yourself.'

Sophie Randolph cleared her throat.

Crispin swung violently around to her to forestall any adverse suggestion she might make, and that time the sudden movement took his nausea out of control. At least he had enough self-respect left not to sick up in her face: he bolted for the back door and we could hear his troubles out in the yard, which was quite bad enough.

'He's my brother,' I said.

'Yes.'

She seemed to need no further explanation. She looked around at the debris. 'Will he clear that up?'

'No chance,' I said, smiling. 'I'll do it later, when he's asleep. If I do it too soon it enrages him . . . he would just make a worse mess.'

She shook her head in disapproval.

'He isn't like this all the time,' I said. 'He goes weeks sometimes without a drink.'

Crispin came back looking greener than ever.

'Money,' he said aggressively.

I stood up, went along to the office, and returned with five pounds. Crispin snatched it out of my hands.

'The pub isn't open yet,' I observed.

'Bugger you.' Crispin's gaze swung round to include Sophie. 'Bugger you both.'

He lurched out of the door and through the window we watched him walk a slightly pompous path to the gate, trying to behave like a country gent and forgetting that he still wore yesterday's clothes and yesterday's beard.

'Why did you give him the money?'

'To save him stealing it.'

'But . . .' She stopped doubtfully.

I explained. 'When the craving's on him, he'll do literally anything to get alcohol. It's kinder to let him have it with some shred of dignity. He'll be drunk all today and tonight but maybe by tomorrow it will be over.'

'But the pub . . .'

'They'll let him in,' I said. 'They understand. They'll sell him a bottle and send him home again, when he shows signs of passing out.'

Although to my mind she would have been better off in bed, Sophie insisted that she should be out seeing to her car. She compromised finally to the extent of letting me ring the local garage, where I was known, and arranging the salvage. Then, dressed in jeans and sweater two sizes too big, she spent most of the morning sitting in the squashy leather armchair in the office, listening to me doing business on the telephone.

Kerry Sanders was pleased about River God and didn't quibble about the price.

'That's more like it,' she said. 'I never did go for that goddam name Hearse Puller.'

'Well . . . I can have him fetched from Devon any time, so where and when would you like him delivered?'

'I'm visiting with the family this weekend.' Even now, I noticed, she avoided using their names. 'I'll be going down there for lunch and I'd like the horse van to arrive at around four-thirty.'

'Certainly,' I said. 'What address?'

'Don't you have it?'

I said I could find it, no doubt.

She came across with the information reluctantly, as if imparting a secret. A village in Gloucestershire, as open as the day.

'OK. Four-thirty on the dot,' I said.

'Will you be there yourself?'

'No. I don't usually.'

'Oh.' She sounded disappointed. 'Well . . . could you make it?'

'You wouldn't need me.'

'I'd sure like it,' she said, her voice hovering uncertainly between cajolery and demand, and I realized that for all her assurance she was still unsure about this gift.

'You mean,' I said, 'to perform introductions?'

'Well. I guess so.'

Nicol Brevett, this is River God. River God, meet Nicol Brevett. Howdy partner, shake a hoof.

'All right,' I said. 'I'll arrive with the horse.'

'Thanks.' Again the mixture in her voice. Partly she definitely thought I ought to jump to it when asked, and partly she was genuinely relieved I had agreed. I thought she was crazy to marry into a family which made her nervous, and I wondered why they had that effect on her.

'Have you heard any more about those two men?' she asked.

'No.' Apart from a sore spot when I brushed my hair, I had forgotten them. Too much seemed to have happened since.

'I'd like you to find out why they took that horse.'

'I'd like to know, sure,' I said. 'But as to finding out . . . If you care enough, how about hiring the Radnor Halley Agency? They'd do it.'

'Private detectives?'

'Specialists in racing,' I said.

'Yes, well. But . . . I don't know . . .'

It came back every time to the way she reacted to the Brevetts.

'I'll do my best,' I said, and she was pleased, but I had no confidence at all.

I spoke next to a transport firm in Devon, arranging that they should pick up River God early the following morning, and meet me at three o'clock beyond Stroud. What was the ultimate destination, they asked, and with sudden caution I didn't give it. Ten miles beyond our rendezvous, I said, and I would show them the way. I put the receiver down feeling slightly foolish, but the loss of Hearse Puller had been no joke.

I telephoned to the Devon farmer and asked him to send a man with River God to look after him, and also to produce him well groomed with his feet and shoes in good condition. The farmer said he hadn't the time to be bothered, and I said that if the horse looked too rough he'd get him straight back. He grunted, groused, agreed, and hung up.

'You sounded very tough on him,' Sophie said with a smile.

'Horses straight from small farms sometimes look as if they've been pulling a plough . . .'

She lit a cigarette, the bandaged arm moving stiffly.

'I've got some codeine,' I said.

She twisted her mouth. 'Then I'd like some.'

I fetched the pain killers and a glass of water.

'Are you everyone's nurse?' she said.

'Mostly my own.'

While I had been telephoning, she had taken note of the racing photographs on the walls.

'Those are of you, aren't they?' she asked.

'Most of them.'

'I've heard of you,' she said. 'I don't go racing myself, but my aunt has a stud farm, and I suppose I see your name in newspapers and on television.'

'Not any more. It's nearly three years since I stopped.'

'Do you regret it?'

'Stopping?' I shrugged. 'Everyone has to, sometime.' Especially when on the receiving end of six months in a spinal brace and severe warnings from gents in white coats.

She asked if I would drive her along to where she had crashed so that she could see the place in daylight.

'Sure,' I agreed. 'And I want to look for the rug my horse got rid of on his travels, though it's bound to be torn. Pity he lost it, really, as it's a light fawn ... much easier to see in the dark than his own bay coat.'

She stubbed out her cigarette but before we could move the telephone rang.

'Hi, Jonah,' said a cheerful American voice. 'How did the sale go?'

'Which one?' I asked.

'Well ... I guess the one for Kerry. You know. Kerry Sanders.'

'Oh sure,' I agreed. 'Only I've bought two for her. Didn't she tell you?'

'Uh uh. Only that you were off to Ascot for some nag with a God awful name.'

Pauli Teksa. I pictured him at the other end of the line, a short, solidly built man in his early forties, bursting with physical and mental energy and unashamedly out to make money. I had met him only a few times and thought his most outstanding quality was the speed with which he reached decisions. After a session with him one felt as if one had been carried along irresistibly by a strong tide, and it was only afterwards that one wondered if any of his instant assessments ever turned out to be wrong.

He was over in England for the Newmarket Yearling Sales, a bloodstock agent on a large scale in the States keeping tabs on the worldwide scene.

We had had a drink together in a group of others at Newmarket the previous week, and it was because of that and other equally casual meetings that he had, I supposed, given my name to Kerry Sanders.

I told him what had become of Hearse Puller. Out of the corner of my eye I could see Sophie listening with her mouth open in incredulity. Pauli Teksa's astonishment was tempered by greater cynicism about the world we both moved in, but even he was outraged at the use of force.

'Pressure,' he said vigorously. 'Even unfair pressure. Sure. But *violence* . . .'

'I'm surprised she didn't tell you.'

'I've been out of town since Tuesday. Just got back from Ireland. Guess she couldn't reach me.'

'Anyway,' I said. 'No great harm done. She made a profit on Hearse Puller and I bought her another horse instead.'

'Yeah, but you sure ought to raise a hell of a ruckus over what went on back there at Ascot.'

'I'll leave it to Mrs Sanders.'

'It sure makes me feel bad that it was I who got you into this mess.'

'Never mind,' I said.

'But I'm glad you managed to do a deal for her in the end.' He paused, his voice heavy with meaning.

I smiled wryly at the telephone. 'You're saying you want a cut of the commission?'

'Jonah, fella,' his voice sounded hurt, 'did I ask?'

'Il earn,' I said. 'I learn.'

'Two per cent,' he said. 'A gesture. Nothing more. Two per cent, Jonah. OK?'

'OK,' I said, sighing. The two per cent, which sounded so little, was in fact two fifths of my fee. I should have charged Kerry Sanders more than five per cent, I thought. Silly me. Except that five per cent was fair.

It was no good refusing Pauli. The remaining three per cent was better than nothing, even with a bang on the head thrown in, and there was goodwill involved. Pauli on my side was a good future prospect. Pauli against, a lousy one.

By the time I put the receiver down Sophie had shut her mouth and regained her calm. She raised her eyebrows.

'Hey ho for a quiet life in the country.'

'Quiet is internal,' I said.

Up on the main road the orange MG dangled like a crumpled toy at the rear of the breakdown truck. Sophie watched with regret as it was towed away, and picked up a bent silver hub cap which fell off in the first few feet.

'I liked that car,' she said.

The Rover had already gone. All that remained after distance swallowed the breakdown truck were some black brake marks on the road and a pathetic heap of swept up glass.

Sophie threw the hub cap into the ditch, shrugged off her regrets, and said we would now look for my rug.

We found it not very far away and across on the far side of the road, a damp, haphazard heap half hidden by bushes. I picked it up expecting a complete ruin, as horses mostly rid themselves of their rugs by standing on one edge and becoming so frightened by the unexpected restraint that they tear the cloth apart in a frenzy to get free. Horses standing quietly in stables almost never shed their rugs, but horses loose among bushes could do it easily.

'What's the matter?' she said.

I looked up. 'There's nothing wrong with it.'

'Well, good.'

'Yes,' I said doubtfully. Because I didn't see how any horse could get out of his rug by undoing the three fastening buckles, one across the chest, the others under the stomach; and on this rug, which was totally undamaged, the buckles were quite definitely undone.

5

Sophie was adamant about returning home, the steel in her character showing little spikes when I tried to persuade her to give my number to the people who might call her out on stand-by. She unbent to the extent of grilled chicken for lunch in the still untidy kitchen, and at Gatwick Airport she even allowed me to pay the deposit for her hired car, though this was entirely because she had set out to the dinner party without cheque book or identification and felt less than impressive in my clothes. I said I liked pale blue socks with silver sandals. She said I was a bloody fool. I wished very much that she wasn't going.

Crispin's return from the pub coincided with mine from Gatwick. He was maudlin, bleary eyed, expansive, waving his arms around in large gestures and clutching a full bottle of gin. According to him he didn't know how I put up with him, I was the salt of the earth, the salt of the effing earth, he didn't care who knew it.

'Sure,' I said.

He belched. I wondered if one struck a match whether gin fumes would ignite like gas.

He focused on the remains of chicken and said he wanted some.

'You won't eat it,' I said.

'I will.' He squinted at me. 'You'll cook for a bloody popsy but not for your own brother.'

I put another piece in the griller. It smelled good, looked good, and he didn't eat it. He sat at the table, picked it up in his fingers and took a couple of small bites before pushing the plate away.

'It's tough,' he said.

He lit a cigar. It took six matches, a lot of squinting and a variety of oaths.

We'd been through so many cures. Six weeks in a private

nursing home drying out with a psychiatrist listening daily to his woes had resulted in precisely one month's sobriety. Then, having been scooped by the police from a Park Lane gutter, he woke in a public ward and didn't like it. I told him I wasn't riding races just to keep him in trick cyclists. He said I didn't care about him. The whole hopeless circus had been going on for years.

Sophie telephoned at nine o'clock that evening. Her voice sounded so immediately familiar that it was incredible to think I had known her for less than twenty-four hours.

'... Just to thank you for everything ...'

'For crashing your car?'

'You know what I mean,' she said.

'How's the arm?'

'Oh, much better. Look ... I don't have a lot of time. I have to go to work after all ... rather a nuisance but it can't be helped.'

'Say you don't feel up to it.'

She paused. 'No. It wouldn't really be true. I slept for hours when I got home and honestly I feel fine now.'

I didn't argue. I already knew it was impossible to persuade her against her will.

She said, 'How are your knight-in-shining-armour instincts?'

'Rusty.'

'I could provide brasso.'

I smiled. 'What do you want done?'

'Yes. Mm. Well, when it comes to the point, I don't know that I've got any right to ask.'

'Will you marry me?' I said.

'*What* did you say?'

'Er ...' I said. 'Never mind. What was it you wanted done?'

'Yes,' she said.

'Yes what?'

'Yes, I will. Marry you.'

I stared across the office, seeing nothing. I hadn't meant to ask her. Or had I? Anyway, not so soon. I swallowed. Cleared my throat.

'Then ... you've a right to ask anything.'

'Good,' she said crisply. 'Button your ears back.'

'They're buttoned.'

'My aunt . . . the one who has the stud farm . . .'

'Yes,' I said.

'I've been talking to her on the telephone. She's in a grade-one tizzy.'

'What about?'

'To be honest, I don't exactly understand. But she lives near Cirencester and I know you are going over that way tomorrow with Mrs Sanders' horse . . . and . . . well . . . I suppose I sort of vaguely offered your help. Anyway, if you've got time to call on her, she'd be grateful.'

'All right,' I said. 'What's her name?'

'Mrs Antonia Huntercombe. Paley Stud. Her village is Paley, too. Near Cirencester.'

'Right.' I wrote it down. 'Are you working tomorrow evening?'

'No. Saturday morning.'

'Then . . . I could come to your place . . . on my way home . . . to tell you how I got on with her.'

'Yes.' Her voice was tentative, almost embarrassed. 'I live . . .'

'I know where you live,' I said. 'Somewhere at the end of the five-furlong straight of Sandown Racecourse.'

She laughed. 'If I lean out, I can see the stands from the bathroom window.'

'I'll be there.'

'I've got to go now, or I'll be late.' She paused, then she said doubtfully, 'Did you mean it?'

'Yes,' I said. 'I think so. Did you?'

'No,' she said. 'It's silly.'

Friday morning saw the long delayed departure of the seventy-thousand-pound two-year-old, who seemed to have suffered no harm from his nocturnal junket. I knew, as I thankfully dispatched him with his two slightly less valuable fellows, that I had been luckier than I deserved, and I still sweated at the thought of that headlong gallop down the main road.

Crispin, that Friday morning, lay in the customary coma on his bed. I rang the doctor, who said he would look in on his rounds.

'How's the girl I stitched?' he asked.

'Gone home. Gone to work.'

'A lot of starch in that one.'

'Yes.'

I thought about her every ten minutes or so. A cool girl I had kissed once, on the cheek in the afternoon, standing beside a hired car in Gatwick Airport. She had done nothing in return but smile. One couldn't call it love .Recognition, perhaps.

Mid-morning I set off for Gloucestershire and without much trouble found the aunt's stud farm at Paley. As a business breeding venture it had all the first-sight marks of imminent skids: weeds in the gravel, an unmended fence, tiles off the stable roof and paint too old to keep out the rain.

The house itself was a pleasant Cotswold stone affair with too much creeper on the walls. I knocked on the front door, which was open, and was told by a rich voice to come in. Dogs greeted me in the hall, a whippet, a labrador, two bassets and a dachshund, all displaying curiosity tempered by good manners. I let them sniff and lick, and they'd know me next time, I thought.

'Come in, come in,' called the voice.

I went further, to the door of a long sitting-room where much-used antique furniture stood on elderly Persian rugs. Padded and pelmeted curtains and silk lampshades and Staffordshire china dogs all spoke of enough money somewhere in the past, but the holes in the flowery chintz sofa covers were truer of the present.

Antonia Huntercombe sat in an armchair fondling yet another dog. A Yorkshire terrier, a walking hearthrug. She was a woman of about sixty with strong facial bones and an air of first-class stoicism in the face of titanic submersion.

'Are you Jonah Dereham?'

'Mrs Huntercombe?'

She nodded. 'Come in and sit down.'

At closer quarters the voice was fruity in the lower notes and punctiliously articulated. She did not seem over friendly considering that I was supposed to be there to offer help.

'Excuse me not getting up,' she said. 'Little Dougal here is not very well, and I don't want to disturb him.'

She stroked the hearthrug soothingly. One couldn't see which end of it was which.

'Sophie asked me to call,' I said.

'Can't see what good you can do,' she said forbiddingly. 'And besides, you're one of *them*.'

'One of who?'

'Bloodstock agents.'

'Oh,' I said. Several shades of light began to dawn.

She nodded grimly. 'I told Sophie it was no good asking you for help, but she insisted that I should at least tell you my complaints. She's a very forceful girl, Sophie.'

'She is indeed.'

Antonia Huntercombe looked at me sharply. 'She seems to think well of you. She telephoned to find out how I was, but she talked mostly of you.'

'Did she?'

She nodded. 'Sophie needs a man. But not a crook.'

I thought privately that few young women needed a man less than Sophie but quarrelled only with the second half of the pronouncement.

'I'm not a crook.'

'Hmph.'

I said, 'I looked you up in the books, before I came. You've got one good stallion, Barroboy, but he's getting old now, and one young one, Bunjie, who might be better if he were keener on his job. You have eight brood mares, the best being Winedark who came third in the Oaks. She was bred last year to a top sire, Winterfriend, and you sent the resulting filly as a yearling to Newmarket Sales last week. She fetched only eighteen hundred guineas because of a heart murmur, which means that you lost a lot of money on her, as the stud fee was five thousand in the first place and then there is all her keep and care and overheads . . .'

'It was a lie,' she said fiercely.

'What was?'

'That the filly had a heart murmur. She didn't. Her heart is as sound as a bell.'

'But I was there at the sales,' I said. 'I remember hearing that the Winterfriend filly would never race and might be doubtful even as a brood mare. That's why no one bid for her.'

'That's why, right enough.' Her voice was bitter. 'But it wasn't true.'

'You'd better tell me who spread such a rumour,' I said. 'Who and why.'

'Who is easy. All you crooked sharks calling yourself bloodstock agents. Bloodsucking agents more like. As for *why* . . . need you ask? Because I won't give you kick-backs.'

She was referring to the practice which had grown up among some agents of going to a breeder before a sale and saying, in effect: 'I'll bid your horse up to a good price if you give me a share of what you get.' Far more intimidating was the follow-up: 'And if you don't agree to what I suggest I'll make sure no one bids for your horse and if you sell it at all it will be at a loss.' Dozens of small breeders were coughing up the kick-backs just to keep themselves in business and Mrs Antonia Huntercombe's difficulties were what happened if they didn't.

I knew all about it. I knew that the big, reputable firms never asked for kick-backs at all, and that individual agents varied from nil to nearly extortionate.

'I was offered eight thousand for the filly,' Mrs Huntercombe said bitterly. 'I was to give back half of anything she made over that price.' She glared at me. 'I refused to agree. Why should I? She cost eight thousand to produce. They wanted half of any profit I made. And for doing what? Nothing at all except bidding in a sale ring. No work, no worry, no thought and care. It's downright wicked to come and demand half of my profit.'

'Who was it?'

'I'm not going to tell you. You're one of them, and I don't trust you.'

'So you sent her to the sales to take her chance.'

'She should have made at least ten thousand. At least.' She glared at me. 'Don't you agree?'

'Twelve or fourteen, I would have thought.'

'Of course she should.'

'Didn't you put a reserve on her?' I asked.

'Reserves are a racket in themselves,' she said furiously. 'But no, I didn't. There was no reason why she shouldn't make her price. Her breeding, her looks . . . you couldn't fault her.'

'And you didn't go with her to Newmarket?'

'It's so far. And there's too much to do here. I sent a groom with her. I couldn't believe . . . I simply couldn't believe it when she went for eighteen hundred. I didn't hear that story about a heart murmur until two days afterwards when the man who bought her rang up to ask for the vet's report.'

I thought about the general lack of prosperity about the place.

'You needed her to make a good profit?' I suggested.

'Of course I did. She was the best foal I've had for years.'

'But not the first request for a kick-back?'

'The worst,' she said. 'I've told them all . . . I always tell them . . . they've no right to what they do nothing to earn . . . but this time . . . it was *wicked*.'

I agreed with her. I said, 'And for some time your yearlings have not been fetching good prices?'

'For two years,' she said fiercely. 'You're all in it. You know I won't give kick-backs so you won't bid for my horses.'

She was wrong about us all being in it. I had bought several bargains at various sales when half my rivals had turned their backs. Bargains for me and my clients, disasters for the people who'd bred them. And it was always the small breeder, the honest or naïve breeder who lost, because the big firms could look after themselves and others were crooks too and had some scandalous tricks of their own.

The kick-back system probably stemmed from the Irish 'luck penny': if you bought a horse from an Irishman he gave you back a penny of your money for luck. A penny! What a laugh.

There was no harm in a breeder giving an agent a thank-you present for getting him a good price for his horse. The harm came when the agent demanded it first. The crime came when he demanded it with threats and carried them out when he was refused.

Rumours rocketed round sale rings with the speed of light. I had heard the Winterfriend filly had a heart murmur ten minutes before she was sold, and I had believed it like everyone else.

I had often been told that the kick-back lark was on the increase. Some breeders made the best of it and some positively welcomed it, because it more or less guaranteed a good price for their horses. Only the Mrs Huntercombes who wouldn't play ball were coming to grief.

'Well?' she said belligerently. 'Sophie said to ask your advice. So what is it?'

I was too much of a realist for Aunt Antonia. I knew she wouldn't like what I would say, but I said it all the same.

'You've three choices. The first is to pay the kick-backs. You'd be better off in the end.'

'I won't.' She narrowed her eyes in anger. 'That's exactly what I would have expected from one of you.'

'The second,' I said, 'is to sell your stud, raise a mortgage on the house and live on an annuity.'

The anger grew. 'And just how do I get a fair price for my stallions and mares? And as for a mortgage . . . I already have one.' From the way she said it I guessed it was the largest she could get.

'Third,' I said, 'you could go every time to the sales when you sell a horse. Put a sensible reserve on it and get a friend to help with starting the bidding. Take a vet with you bristling with certificates. Tell the agents from the big firms, and as many other people as you can reach, whatever they may hear to the contrary, your horse is in good health, and offer to repay instantly if it is found to be not.'

She stared at me. 'I haven't the strength. It would be exhausting.'

'You sell only six or seven a year.'

'I am too old. I have high blood pressure and my ankles swell up.'

It was the first really human thing she'd said. I smiled at her. She did not smile back.

'It's the best I can do,' I said, standing up.

'Don't shut the front door when you go out,' she said. 'Or I'll have to get up to open it for the dogs.'

It was barely five miles from Paley to where I had arranged to meet the horsebox bringing River God from Devon. I had expected to reach the rendezvous first, but from some distance away I could see a blue box already parked in the designated place.

I had chosen one of those useful half-moons carved by road-straightening programmes where the loop of old country road remained as a leafy lay-by. There was one other car there, an old green Zodiac station wagon, which hadn't been cleaned for weeks. I passed it and the horse box, and stopped in front, getting out to go back to talk to the driver.

Talking to the driver had to be postponed, as he was otherwise engaged. I found him standing with his back to that side of the box which faced away from the gaze of passing motorists on the main road. He was standing with his back to the box because he could retreat no further. Before him, adopting classic threatening poses, were two men.

I knew them well enough. I had met them at Ascot.

Frizzy Hair and his mate.

They hadn't expected to see me either and it gave me at least an equal chance. I picked up the nearest weapon to hand, which was a nice solid piece of branch fallen from one of the road-lining trees, and positively raced to the attack. If I'd stopped to think I might not have done it, but fury is a great disregarder of caution.

My face must have been an accurate mirror of my feelings. Frizzy Hair for one indecisive moment looked mesmerized, horrified, paralysed by the spectacle of a normally moderate man rushing at him murderously, and because of it he moved far too slowly. I cracked the branch down on him with a ferocity that frightened me as much as him.

He screeched and clutched at the upper reaches of his left arm, and his mate made an equally comprehensive assessment of my general intentions and bolted towards the green wagon.

Frizzy Hair followed him, flinging nothing into the battle but one parting verbal shot.

'It won't help you.'

I ran after him, still holding the stick. He was going like a quarter horse and the mate was already in the driving seat with the motor turning over.

Frizzy Hair gave me a sick look over his shoulder, scrambled into the passenger seat and slammed the door. Short of being dragged along the highway I could see no way of stopping them: but I could and did take a quick look at the mud-coated number plate as they shot away, and before I could forget it I fished out pen and paper and wrote it down.

I went much more slowly back to the driver, who was staring at me much as if I were a little green man from outer space.

''Struth,' he said. 'I thought you was going to kill 'em.'

Hell hath no fury like the vanquished getting his own back.

I said 'What did they want?'

'Blimey ...' He pulled out a crumpled handkerchief and wiped his face. 'Didn't you even know?'

'Only in general,' I said. 'What in particular?'

'Eh?' He seemed dazed.

'What did they want?'

'Got a fag?'

I gave him one and lit for us both. He sucked in the smoke as if it were oxygen to the drowning.

'I s'pose you are . . . Jonah Dereham?' he said.

'Who else?'

'Yeah . . . I thought you were smaller, like.'

Five feet nine inches. Eleven stone. Couldn't be more average. 'A lot of jump jockeys are taller,' I said.

He began to look less stirred up. He ran his tongue round his teeth and seemed to feel a fresh flow of saliva to a dry mouth.

'What did they want?' I asked for the third time.

'That one you hit . . . with all that fluffy sort of hair . . . it was him did the talking.'

'What did he say?'

'Rum sort of bloke. All smiley. Came up to me cab as nice as you please asking for the loan of a spanner for 'is brokendown car.' He stopped to look at the empty road along which the brokendown car had vanished at high speed.

'Yeah . . . Well, see, I reached back to the tool kit and asked what size. Come and look see, he said. So I jumped down from me cab. And then, see, he sort of grabbed me and shoved me back against the side of the box. And he never let off smiling.

Creepy bastard. So then he says, look mate, there's someone as wants this horse more than you do.'

'I suppose he didn't say who?'

'Eh? No. He just says there's someone as wants him more than you do, so I says it isn't mine in the first place and he says not to make jokes . . . and him laughing his bleeding head off all the time.'

'What else did he say?'

'Nothing else. 'Struth, he didn't have time. Well, he did say as how I'd better let him take the horse peaceful like if I didn't want me ribs kicked in . . . well, I ask you . . . who would?'

Who indeed? 'So then what?'

'That's when you came belting into them like they'd raped your sister.'

'They didn't say just how they proposed to take the horse?'

He stared. 'No. I didn't ask. I s'pose they meant to drive off with the whole bleeding lot.' The idea offended him. 'Bleeding bastards,' he said.

'Did they offer to pay for it?'

''Struth, you don't half have some funny ideas.'

I wondered if they would have done, if I'd given them time. I wondered if I would have found the box driver clutching the cash plus another two hundred profit, and no River God in sight.

I sighed and stubbed out my cigarette.

'Let's look at the cargo,' I said, and climbed aboard the box.

The farmer had done a smartening up job along the lines of paint over rust. The feet had been seen to: the shoes were patently new, and the newly trimmed hooves had been darkened with oil. The mane and tail had been brushed out, and the coat was clean. On the other hand there was a lot too much hair everywhere which spoke of little or no regular grooming; too much mane growing between the ears, too many whiskers around the muzzle, hairs too long on the chest, hairs sticking out everywhere instead of lying down neat and flat. The whole mess was shrouded by a tatty rug with two holes in it; and there was no attendant in sight.

'I asked the farmer to send a groom,' I said.

'Yeah. He said he didn't have nobody to spare. If you ask me he isn't fit to keep a pit pony, much less a racehorse. When I got there, you'd hardly credit it, there was this poor bleeding animal standing in the yard tied up to the outside of the stable door, and there was this big bleeding pool of water all round him on the ground. Shivering, he was. I reckon they just hosed him down to get all the muck off. The farmer said he was sweating, that was why his coat looked damp. I ask you, who did he think he was kidding. I made him give me the rug to put on the poor bleeder. He didn't want me to take it in case I didn't bring it back.'

'OK,' I said. 'Let's get him out.'

He was surprised. 'What, out here on the road?'

'That's right,' I agreed.

'But he's warm enough now. He's dried off, like, on the journey up.'

'All the same . . .' I said, and helped the box driver, who said his name was Clem, unload the River God. *Deus ex machina*, I thought irrelevantly, and nothing much about this one either was divine.

I removed the rug, folded it, and returned it to the box. Then with Clem holding the horse's farm-stained headcollar I went along to my car and took off my jacket, and in shirt sleeves collected from the boot my bag of gear.

'What are you going to do?' Clem asked.

'Tidy him up.'

'But I had to meet you at three . . . you were early but it's a quarter past already.'

'I left time enough,' I said. 'We're not due until four-thirty.'

'Did you reckon he'd look this rough, then?'

'Thought he might.'

Once I was committed to turning up with the horse I was also committed to defend what he looked like. I took out hand clippers, two pairs of scissors, a heavy steel comb and some wax tapers, and set to work.

Clem held the horse's head and watched while with comb in one hand and lighted taper in the other I worked on the rough coat, singeing off all the too-long, sticking out hair which in a good stable would have been removed by daily brushing. The tiny candle flame was too small to disturb the horse, who felt no fear or pain, and he looked a lot less like a throwback to a carthorse when I'd finished. Next I clipped out the mane between his ears and over his withers, then snipped off the worst of the whiskers round his muzzle, and with a large pair of scissors finally straightened the bottom of his tail.

''Struth,' Clem said. 'He looks a different horse.'

I shook my head. Nothing but care, good food and brushing could bring a shine to that coat. He looked like a poor boy after a haircut, tidy but still poor.

Before we loaded him up again I wound neat dark blue bandages round his forelegs and buckled on the clean rug I'd brought from my own yard. Eliza Doolittle off to the ball, I thought, but it was the best I could do.

6

Kerry Sanders looked from Nicol to Constantine in carefully camouflaged anxiety while they inspected her gift. One of Brevett's own men was showing him off, trotting him now and then or making him stand with his legs arranged as for a photograph.

River God could move, I'd give him that. A good strong walk and a straight collected trot. Nothing to be ashamed of in that department.

Constantine was saying comfortingly, 'My dear girl, I realize you got him at very short notice. I'm sure he'll make up into a very good performer one of these days. Look at those legs . . . the bone is there.'

'I hope he'll win for Nicol,' she said.

'Of course he will. He's a very lucky boy to be given such a generous present.'

The lucky boy himself drew me aside and said abrasively, 'Couldn't you have found me something better?'

I had ridden against him often enough in races, at the end of my career and the beginning of his, and he knew me as well and as little as any jockey in the changing room.

'She gave me two days . . . and its form isn't bad.'

'Would you have ridden it?'

'Definitely. And if it turns out no good, I'll sell it for you later.'

He sucked his teeth.

'It did quite well in a bad stable,' I said. 'It should improve a mile in yours.'

'D'you think so?'

'Give it a try.'

He smiled sourly. 'And don't look a gift horse in the teeth?'

'She wanted to please you,' I said.

'Huh. Buy me, more like.'

'Happy birthday,' I said.

He turned to watch Kerry Sanders talking to his father, the neat, small, feminine figure overshadowed by the large, protecting, paternal male. As before, the Sanders wrappings were as uncluttered as gold bricks and the slanting autumn sunlight drew fire from the diamond knuckledusters.

'At least she's not after his money,' Nicol said. 'I had her checked out. She's way ahead.'

For an also-ran, Constantine was not doing so badly. Clem's horsebox stood on a clear quarter acre of front drive with Clem himself fidgeting around for a signal that he could set off home. There were buildings along two sides of the mini parade ground, a modern garage and stable block at one end set at right angles to a much older, slightly austere stone house. Not quite a mansion, but more than enough for two.

The outside surface was being cleaned, with nearly one third showing warm cream instead of forbidding grey. One could see that it would look a good deal more welcoming when it was finished, but the effect meanwhile was undignified piebald. One should not, I reflected, ever make the mistake of thinking one would catch its master at such public disadvantage.

Nicol strode over to the man leading River God and the man nodded and took the horse away to the stables.

Kerry Sanders looked a fraction disappointed until Nicol rejoined her and said, 'Thought I'd just try it. Can't wait, you see.'

River God came back with saddle and bridle, and Nicol swung easily onto his back. He trotted him a little round the gravel and then took him through a gate into a railed field alongside and quickened the pace to a working canter. Constantine Brevett watched with heavy good humour, Kerry Sanders with hope, Clem with impatience and I with relief. Whatever I thought of his financial methods, Ronnie North had delivered the goods.

Nicol came back, handed the reins to the stableman, and strode over and kissed Kerry Sanders with enthusiasm on the cheek.

'He's great,' he said. His eyes shone. 'Absolutely great.'

Her face filled with joy enough to melt the hardest case. Nicol took note of it, and as she and his father turned away to return to the house he gave me a twisted smile and said, 'See? I'm not always a bastard.'

'And besides,' I said, 'the horse is better than he looks.'

'Cynical sod. It's got a mouth like the back end of a rhino.'

'A ride for a pro, I was told.'

'The first nice thing you've ever said to me.' He laughed. 'Come on in and have a drink.'

'Just a sec . . .' I turned away to go over to Clem to give him a fiver and send him off home and found Nicol following me to double the ante. Clem took both notes with cheerfulness, hopped up into the cab and rolled away to the gate.

Champagne stood ready in tulip-shaped glasses in the sitting-room to which Nicol led the way, the last rays of sun making the bubbles glisten like silver in liquid gold. Constantine handed us a glass each and we drank rather pompously to Nicol's health. He gave me a private, irreverent grin and greatly to my surprise I began to like him.

We sat in cloud nine armchairs and Constantine fussed over Kerry Sanders. She glowed with happiness, the peach bloom cheeks as fresh as a child's. It was extraordinary, I thought, how clearly and quickly the mental state of a woman showed in her skin.

'You almost didn't get a horse at all,' she told Nicol. 'The most infuriating thing happened to the first one Jonah bought.'

They listened to the saga in bewilderment, and I added to it by saying that the same two thugs had tried a repeat with River God.

Constantine took up a heavily authoritarian stance which went well with his smooth silver hair and thick black spectacle frames, and assured Kerry that he would see they got their just deserts. As it was fairly likely I had broken Frizzy Hair's arm I thought he had probably got his already, but I had no quarrel with any plans Constantine might have for finding out what was going on. He had the weight to lean heavily in places where I had none.

'What do you think, Jonah?' Nicol asked.

'Well . . . I can't believe either Hearse Puller or River God would themselves be the cause of so much action. They came from widely different places, so it can't be anyone close to them resenting them being sold. It seems even crazier when you think that we'll find out who bought Hearse Puller as soon as he's entered in a race. Even if he's changed hands more than once we should be able to trace him back.'

Constantine shook his head heavily and spoke from personal knowledge. 'Easy enough to cover up a sale if you know how.'

'Maybe someone simply wanted to stop Kerry giving me a horse,' Nicol said.

'But why?' Kerry asked. 'Why should they?'

No one knew. 'Who did you tell about River God?' I asked her.

'After last time? You must be crazy. At least when you got another horse I had the sense not to shout it around.'

'You didn't tell Lady Roscommon or your hairdresser or Pauli Teksa? None of the same people as last time?'

'I sure did not. I didn't see Madge or the hairdresser guy, and Pauli was out of town.'

'Someone knows,' Nicol said. 'So who did you tell, Jonah?'

'No one. I didn't tell the man I bought it from who it was for, and I didn't tell the transport firm where they were taking it.'

'Someone knew,' Nicol said again, flatly.

'Do you have any particularly bad friends?' I asked him.

'The professional jockeys all hate my guts.'

'And the amateurs?'

He grinned. 'Them too, I dare say.'

Constantine said, 'However jealous the other riders might be of Nicol's success I cannot see any single one of them going around buying up or stealing horses simply to prevent Nicol riding winners.'

'They'd have a job,' Nicol said.

Constantine's voice was resonant and deep and filled the room to overflowing. Nicol had the same basic equipment but not the obvious appreciation of his own power, so that in him the voice was quieter, more natural, not an announcement of status.

'What about Wilton Young?' he said.

Constantine was ready to believe anything of Wilton Young.

Constantine saw only one threat to his bid to dominate British racing, and that was a bullet-headed Yorkshireman with no social graces, a huge mail-order business and the luck of the devil with horses. Wilton Young trampled all over people's finer feelings without noticing them and judged a man solely on his ability to make brass. He and Constantine were notably alike in ruthlessness and it was no doubt immaterial to their flattened victims that one steamroller was smoothly oiled while the other was roughly clanking.

'Of course,' Constantine said, his face filling with anger. 'Wilton Young.'

'The two men didn't have Yorkshire accents,' I said.

'What's that got to do with it?' Constantine demanded.

'Wilton Young makes a point of having Yorkshiremen working for him. He looks down on everyone else.'

'Arrogant little pipsqueak,' Constantine said.

'I can't honestly see him taking such trouble to stop Mrs Sanders giving Nicol a horse for his birthday.'

'Can't you?' Constantine looked down his nose as if he could believe half a dozen more improbable things before breakfast. 'He'd do anything he could think of to irritate me, however petty.'

'But how could he have known I was buying the horse for Nicol?'

He took barely three seconds to come up with an answer. 'He saw you at the sales with Kerry, and he has seen her at the races with me.'

'He wasn't at the sales,' I said.

He shrugged impatiently. 'All you mean is that you didn't see him.'

I doubted if it were possible to be in so small a place as Ascot Sales' paddock and not know whether Wilton Young was there or not. He had a voice as loud as Constantine's and a good deal more piercing, and he was not a man who liked to be overlooked.

'Anyway,' Nicol said, 'I'll bet his bloodstock agent was there. That carrot-headed little Yorkshireman who buys his horses.'

I nodded. 'So was your own chap, Vic Vincent.'

Constantine had nothing but praise for Vic Vincent.

'He's bought me some great yearlings this time. Two he bought at Newmarket last week . . . classic colts, both of them. Wilton Young will have nothing to touch them.'

He went on at some length about the dozen or so youngsters which according to him were about to sweep the two-year-old board, patting himself on the back for having bought them. Vic Vincent was a great judge of a yearling. Vic Vincent was a great fellow altogether.

Vic Vincent was a great fellow to his clients, and that was about where it ended. I listened to Constantine singing his praises and drank my champagne and wondered if Vic Vincent thought me enough of a threat to his Brevett monopoly to whip away any horse I bought for the family. On balance I doubted it. Vic Vincent looked on me as Wilton Young looked on non Yorkshiremen: not worth bothering about.

I finished the champagne and found Kerry Sanders watching me. For signs of alcoholism, I supposed. I smiled at her and she smiled a little primly back.

'Kerry my dear, you couldn't do better, another time, than to consult Vic Vincent . . .'

'Yes, Constantine,' she said.

From Gloucester to Esher I thought about Frizzy Hair a little and Sophie Randolph a lot. She opened her door with the composure all in place and greeted me with a duplicate of the Gatwick kiss, cheek to cheek, a deal too chaste.

'You found me, then,' she said.

'How long have you lived here?'

'Just over a year.'

'So you weren't here when I used to race next door.'

'No,' she said. 'Come in.'

She looked different. She was wearing another long dress, not white and black and silver this time, but a glowing mixture of greens and blues. The cut on her forehead had crusted over and her system had recovered from the state of shock. Her hair looked a warmer gold, her eyes a deeper brown, and only the inner self reliance hadn't changed a lot.

'How's your arm?' I asked.

'Much better. It itches.'

'Already? You heal fast.'

She shut the door behind me. The small lobby was an offshoot of the sitting-room which opened straight ahead, warm, colourful and full of charming things.

'It's pretty,' I said, and meant it.

'Don't sound so surprised.'

'It's just . . . I thought perhaps your room might be more bare. A lot of smooth empty surfaces, and space.'

'I may be smooth but I'm not empty.'

'I grovel,' I said.

'Quite right.'

There were no aeroplanes on her walls, but she wore a little gold one on a chain round her neck. Her fingers strayed to it over and over again during the evening, an unconscious gesture from which she seemed to gain confidence and strength.

A bottle of white wine and two glasses stood ready on a small silver tray.

She gestured towards them noncommittally and said, 'Would you like some? Or don't you ever?'

'When Crispin is drunk,' I said, 'I drink.'

'Well, hallelujah.' She seemed relieved. 'In that case, take your jacket off, sit on the sofa, and tell me how you got on with my aunt.'

She made no mention at all of my invitation to marry. Maybe she had decided to treat it as a joke, and yesterday's joke at that. Maybe she was right.

'Your aunt,' I said, 'wouldn't take my advice if I showed her the way to Heaven.'

'Why not?' She handed me a glass and sat down comfortably opposite in an armchair.

I explained why not, and she was instantly angry on her aunt's behalf.

'She was swindled.'

'I'm afraid so.'

'Something must be done.'

I sipped the wine. Light, dry, unexpectedly flowery, and definitely not supermarket plonk.

'The trouble is,' I said, 'that the kick-back system is not illegal. Far from it. To many it is a perfectly sensible business method and anyone who doesn't take advantage of it is a fool.'

'But to demand half her profit . . .'

'The argument goes that an agent promised a large kick-back will raise the auction price much higher than it might have gone, so the breeder positively benefits. Some breeders don't just put up with having to pay the kick-backs, they offer to do so. In those cases everyone is happy.'

'Except the person who buys the horse,' she said severely. 'He comes off badly. Why do the buyers stand for it?'

'Ah,' I said. 'What clients don't know would sink a battleship.'

She looked disapproving. 'I don't like the sound of your profession.' She added, in the understatement of the year, 'It isn't straightforward.'

'What sort of agent you are depends on how you see things,' I said. 'Honesty is your own view from the hill.'

'That's immoral.'

I shook my head. 'Universal.'

'You're saying that honesty in the bloodstock business is only a matter of opinion.'

'And in every business, every country, every era, since the world began.'

'Jonah, you talk nonsense.'

'How about marriage?'

'What are the kick-backs?'

'Oh God,' I said. 'You learn fast.'

She laughed and stood up. 'I'm a lousy cook but if you stay I'll give you a delicious dinner.'

I stayed. The dinner came out of frozen packs and would have pleased Lucullus; lobster in sauce on shells and duck with almonds and honey. The freezer was the largest item in the small white kitchen. She stocked it up every six months, she said, and did practically no shopping in between.

Afterwards, over coffee, I told her about Frizzy Hair turning up to take River God. It did nothing much to improve her view of my job. I told her about the flourishing feud between Constantine Brevett and Wilton Young, and also about Vic Vincent, the blue-eyed boy who could do no wrong.

'Constantine thinks the yearlings he's bought must be good because they were expensive.'

'It sounds reasonable.'

'It isn't.'

'Why not?'

'Year after year top prices get paid for the prize flops.'

'But why?'

'Because,' I said, 'yearlings haven't been raced yet, and no one knows whether they will actually be any good. They make their price on their breeding.' And that too could be rigged, though I didn't think I had better tell her.

'This Vic Vincent . . . he's been paying high prices for good breeding?'

'High prices for moderate breeding. Vic Vincent is costing Constantine a packet. He's the biggest kick-back merchant of the lot, and getting greedier every minute.'

She looked more disgusted than horrified. 'My aunt was right about you all being crooks.'

'Your aunt wouldn't tell me who demanded half her profits . . . if you ring her again, ask her if she's ever heard of Vic Vincent, and see what she says.'

'Why not right now?'

She dialled her aunt's number, and asked, and listened. Antonia Huntercombe spoke with such vehemence that I could hear her from the other side of the room, and her words were earthy Anglo-Saxon. Sophie made a face at me and nearly burst out laughing.

'All right,' she said, putting down the receiver. 'It was Vic Vincent. That's one of life's little mysteries cleared up. Now what about the rest?'

'Let's forget them.'

'Let's absolutely not. You can't just forget two fights in three days.'

'Not to mention a loose horse.'

She stared. 'Not the one . . .'

'Well,' I said. 'I might have believed that I hadn't shut a stable door properly for the first time in eighteen years, but not that a horse could get out of his rug by undoing the buckles.'

'You said . . . he was darker without his rug.'

'Yes.'

'You mean . . . someone took off his rug and shooed him out in front of my car . . . just to cause a crash?'

'To injure the horse,' I said. 'Or even to kill it. I'd have been in very great trouble if you hadn't reacted so quickly and missed him.'

'Because you would have been sued for your horse causing an accident?'

'No. The law is the other way round, if anything. Loose animals are no one's fault, like fallen trees. No . . . The way the insurance on that horse was fixed, I could have lost seventy thousand pounds if he'd been damaged but not dead. And that,' I added fervently, 'is a position I am never going to be in again.'

'Have you *got* seventy thousand pounds?'

'Along with six castles in Spain.'

'But . . .' She wrinkled her forehead. 'Letting that horse loose means that whoever it is is attacking you personally. Not Kerry Sanders or the Brevetts . . . but you.'

'Mm.'

'But why?'

'I don't know.'

'You must have some idea.'

I shook my head. 'As far as I know I've done no one any harm. I've thought about little else for two days but I can't think of anyone with a big enough grudge to go to all this trouble.'

'What about small grudges?'

'Dozens of them, I dare say. They flourish like weeds.'

She looked disapproving.

'You get them everywhere,' I said mildly. 'In every working community. Schools, offices, convents, horse shows . . . all seething with little grudges.'

'Not in control towers.'

'Oh yeah?'

'You're a cynic.'

'A realist. How about marriage?'

She shook her head with a smile that took the suggestion

still as a joke, and her hand strayed for the twentieth time to the little gold aeroplane on its slender chain.

'Tell me about him,' I said.

Her eyes opened wide with shock. 'How did you . . . ?'

'The aeroplane. You wear it for someone else.'

She looked down at her hand and realized how often she held it in just that position, touching the talisman.

'I . . . He's dead.'

She stood up abruptly and carried the coffee pot out to the kitchen. I stood also. She came back immediately with the calm friendly face, no grief showing and no encouragement either. She gestured to me to sit down again and we took our former places, me on the sofa, her in an adjacent armchair. There was a lot of space beside me on the sofa, but no way of getting her to sit there before she was ready.

'We lived together,' she said. 'For nearly four years. We never bothered to marry. It didn't seem to matter. At the beginning we never expected it to last . . . and it just grew more and more solid. I suppose we might have taken out a licence in the end . . .'

Her eyes looked back into the past.

'He was a pilot. A first officer on Jumbos, always on long trips to Australia . . . We were used to being apart.'

Still no emotion in her voice. 'He didn't die in an aeroplane.' She paused. 'Eighteen months ago yesterday he died in a hospital in Karachi. He had a two-day rest stop there and developed an acute virus infection. . . . It didn't respond to antibiotics.'

I looked at her in silence.

'I was mad to say I would marry you,' she said. A smile twitched the corners of her eyes. 'It was just . . . a rather nice bit of nonsense.'

'A nonsense a day is good for the digestion.'

'Then you certainly will never get ulcers.'

We looked at each other. A moment like that in the kitchen, but with this time no Crispin to interrupt.

'Would you consider,' I said, 'coming to sit on the sofa?'

'Sit on it. Not lie on it.'

Her meaning was plain.

'All right.'

She moved to the sofa without fuss.

'I'll say one thing for you,' she said. 'When you make a contract, you keep it.'

'How do you know?'

'Too proud not to.'

'Beast.'

She laughed. She put her head on my shoulder and her mouth eventually on mine, but it was more a matter of warmth than of kindling passions. I could feel the withdrawal lying in wait only a fraction below the surface, a tenseness in the muscles warning me how easily I could go too far.

'Stop worrying,' I said. 'A contract's a contract, like you said.'

'Is this enough for you?'

'Yes.'

She relaxed a good deal. 'Most men nowadays think dinner leads straight to bed.'

Most men, I reflected, had exactly the right idea. I put my arm round her and shoved the most basic of urges back into its cave. I had won a lot of waiting races in my time. Patience was an old friend.

She lifted her head off my chest and rubbed her cheek.

'Something's scratching me.'

I explained about the dislocating shoulder, and the strap I wore to keep it anchored in place. She traced the line of webbing across my chest and rubbed her fingers on the scratching buckle.

'How does it work?'

'A small strap round my arm is linked to the one round my chest. It stops me lifting my arm up.'

'Do you wear it always?'

I nodded. 'Mm.'

'Even in bed?'

'Not this one. A softer one.'

'Isn't it a nuisance?'

'I'm so used to it I never notice.'

She looked up at my face. 'Couldn't you get it fixed? Isn't there an operation?'

'I'm allergic to scalpels.'

'Reasonable.'

She stretched for a cigarette and I lit it, and we sat side by side talking about her job, and mine, her childhood and mine, her tastes in books and places and people, and mine.

Exploration, not conflagration.

When the time was right I kissed her again. And went home.

7

I spent most of the next week in Newmarket, staying with a trainer friend for the sales and the races.

Crispin, sober and depressed, had sworn to stay off drink in my absence and find a job, and as usual I had assured him he had the will power to do both. Experience always proved me wrong, but to him the fiction was a prop.

Sophie had worked awkward hours all weekend and Monday but said she would come down to my house for lunch the next Sunday, if I would like. I could bear it, I said.

The whole mob was at Newmarket. All the bloodstock agents, big and small. All the trainers with runners, all the jockeys with mounts, all the owners with hopes. All the clients with their cheque books ready. All the breeders with their year's work at stake. All the bookies looking for mugs. All the Press looking for exclusives.

I had commissions for eleven yearlings if I could find good ones at the right price, and in most cases my clients' money was already in my bank. I should have been feeling quietly pleased with the way business was expanding but found instead a compulsive tendency to look over my shoulder for Frizzy Hair.

The fact that nothing else had happened over the weekend had not persuaded me that nothing would. The attacks still seemed senseless to me, but someone somewhere must have seen a point to them, and the point was in all likelihood still there.

Crispin had sworn on everything sacred from the Bible to his 2nd XV rugger cap that he had found the bottle of whisky standing ready and uncapped on the kitchen table, and had smelled it as soon as he went through the door. At the tenth vehement repetition, I believed him.

Someone knew about my shoulder. Knew about my brother. Knew I kept horses in transit in my yard. Knew I was buying a horse for Kerry Sanders to give to Nicol Brevett. Someone knew a damn sight too much.

The Newmarket sale ring would have suited Kerry Sanders: a large, enclosed amphitheatre, warm, well lit and endowed with tip-up armchairs. At ground level round the outside, under the higher rows of seating, were small offices rented by various bloodstock agents. Each of the large firms had its own office, and also a few individuals like Vic Vincent. One had to do a good deal of business to make the expense worth it, though the convenience was enormous. I would have arrived, I thought, when I had my own little office at every major sale ring. As it was I did my paperwork as usual in the margins of the catalogue and conducted meetings in the bar.

I turned up on the first day, Tuesday, before the first horse was sold, because often there were bargains to be had before the crowds came, and was buttonholed just inside the gate by Ronnie North.

'I got your cheque for River God,' he said. 'Now tell me, wasn't that just what you wanted?'

'You should have seen it.'

He looked pained. 'I saw it race last spring.'

'I shouldn't think it had been groomed since.'

'You can't have everything for that money.'

He was a small whippet of a man, as quick on his feet as in his deals. He never looked anyone in the face for long. His eyes were busy as usual, looking over my shoulder to see who was arriving, who going and what chance of the quick buck he might be missing.

'Did he like it?' he asked.

'Who?'

'Nicol Brevett.'

Something in my stillness drew his attention. The wandering eyes snapped back to my face and he took rapid stock of his indiscretion.

I said, 'Did you know it was for Nicol before you sold it to me?'

'No,' he said, but his fractional hesitation meant 'yes'.

'Who told you?'

'Common knowledge,' he said.

'No, it wasn't. How did you know?'

'Can't remember.' He showed signs of having urgent business elsewhere and edged three steps sideways.

'You just lost a client,' I said.

He stopped. 'Honest, Jonah, I can't tell you. Leave it at that, there's a pal. More than my life's worth to say more, and if you want to do me a favour you'll forget I mentioned...'

'A favour for a favour,' I said.

'What?'

'Start the bidding for number four.'

'You want to buy it?'

'Yes,' I said.

He looked at me doubtfully. No one who wanted to buy liked to show eagerness by making the first bid, but on the other hand no astute bloodstock dealer ever told another which horse he was after. I produced all the earnest naïvety I could muster and he smirked a little and agreed to bid. When he had darted off I slowly followed, and saw him from across the paddock talking excitedly to Vic Vincent.

Together they turned the first few pages of the catalogue and read the small print. Vic Vincent shook his head. Ronnie North talked quickly, but Vic Vincent shook his head even harder.

I shrugged. All I'd proved was that Ronnie North wouldn't do me a favour without clearing it with Vic Vincent. It didn't follow that it was Vic Vincent who had told him that River God was for Nicol Brevett.

The first few horses were being led up from the stables to the collecting rings, and I leaned on the rails and took a close look at number four. A chestnut colt grown out of proportion with a rear end too tall for its front. Time would probably right that but would do little to improve the narrow head. Its breeding was fairly good, its full sister had won a decent race, and it was being offered for sale by Mrs Antonia Huntercombe of Paley Stud.

'Morning, Jonah,' said a voice half behind me.

I turned. Jiminy Bell, half ingratiating, half aggressive, as at Ascot. A great one for arriving unheard at one's elbow. He looked pinched with cold in the brisk wind because his overcoat was too thin for the job.

'Hullo,' I said. 'Care to earn a tenner?'

'You're on.' No hesitation at all.

'Start the bidding on number four.'

'What?' His mouth stayed open with surprise.

'Go up to two thousand.'

'But you never . . . you never . . .'

'Just this once,' I said.

He gulped, nodded, and presently disappeared. He was less obvious than Ronnie North, but in a remarkably short time he too fetched up beside Vic Vincent, and he too got the emphatic shake of the head.

I sighed. Sophie's Aunt Antonia was about to make another loss. For Sophie's sake I had tried to ensure her a good price, but if Vic Vincent had put the evil eye on the colt I was going to get it for almost nothing. I thought on the whole that I had better not buy it. I wouldn't be able to explain it to either Sophie or her aunt.

Very much to my surprise I found Vic himself drifting round to my side. He rested his elbows on the rails beside me, and nodded a greeting.

'Jonah.'

'Vic.'

We exchanged minimal smiles that were more a social convention than an expression of friendship. Yet I could have liked him, and once had, and still would have done had he not twice pinched my clients by telling them lies.

It was so easy to believe Vic Vincent. He had a large, weather-beaten face with a comfortable double chin and a full mouth which smiled easily and turned up at the corners even in repose. A lock of reddish brown hair growing forward over his forehead gave him a boyish quality although he must have been forty, and even his twinkling blue eyes looked sincere.

The bonhomie was barely skin deep. When I protested about my lost clients he had laughed and told me that all was fair in love, war and bloodstock, and if I didn't like the heat to get out of the kitchen but he would stoke up the fire as much as he liked.

He turned up his sheepskin coat collar round his ears and banged one thickly gloved hand against the other.

'Parky this morning.'

'Yes.'

'I heard you had a spot of bother at Ascot,' he said.

'That's right.'

'Constantine Brevett told me.'

'I see.'

'Yeah.' He paused. 'If Mrs Sanders wants any more horses, you'd better let me get them.'

'Did Constantine say so?'

'He did.'

He watched the first horses walk round the ring. Number four looked reasonable from behind but scratchy in front.

'I bought a colt just like that, once,' Vic observed. 'I thought his shoulders would develop. They never did. Always a risk when they grow unevenly.'

'I suppose so,' I said. Poor Antonia.

He stayed a few more seconds, but he had delivered his two messages as succinctly as if he'd said straight out 'Don't step on my toes, and don't buy that colt.' He gave me the sort of reinforcing nod that the boss gives the cowed and ambled bulkily away.

The loudspeakers coughed and cleared their throats and said good morning everyone the sale is about to begin.

I went inside. Apart from four or five earnestly suited auctioneers in their spacious rostrum the place was deserted. Electric lights augmenting the daylight shone brightly on tiers of empty seats, and the sand on the circular track where the merchandise would walk was raked fine and flat. The auctioneers looked hopefully towards the door from the collecting ring and Lot 1 made its apologetic appearance attended by a few worried-looking people who were apparently its vendors.

There was no bid. No one there bidding. Lot 1 made its way through the far door and the worried people went after it.

There was no bid for Lot 2 and ditto for Lot 3. British auctioneers tended to arrange their catalogues so that the potential money-makers came up in mid-session, and small studs like Antonia's got the cold outer edges.

Lot 4 looked better under bright lights. All horses always did, like jewellery, which was why auctioneers and jewellers spent happily on electricity.

The auctioneer dutifully started his sale while clearly expecting nothing to come of it. He stretched the price up to one thousand without one genuine bid, at which point I rather undecidedly waved my catalogue. Antonia would be livid if I got it for a thousand.

'Thank you sir,' he said sounding surprised, and picked 'Eleven hundred' expertly out of the totally empty ranks of seats facing him.

Glory be, I thought. The aunt had had the sense to slap on a reserve. I made it twelve, the auctioneer said thirteen, and between us we limped up to his own bid of nineteen.

'You're losing him,' said the auctioneer warningly.

Three or four people came in from the outside and stood near me on the edge of the track where Lot 4 plodded patiently round and round. Everyone outside could hear on the loudspeakers how the sale was going, and some had come in to see.

I wondered how high Antonia had made the reserve. Two thousand was all I would give for that colt. If she wanted more she could have him back.

I nodded to the auctioneer. He fractionally relaxed, said smoothly, 'Two thousand . . . Selling all the time now . . .' His gaze went past me to the people who had just come in. 'Shall I say two thousand one . . .?'

No one said two thousand one. He made a few more efforts to no avail and Jonah Dereham got the colt.

I turned round. Behind me stood Vic Vincent, looking like thunder.

'Jonah,' he said. 'I want to talk to you.'

'Sure, Vic, how about coffee?'

He brushed the suggestion aside. He took me strongly by the arm in a mock-friendly gesture and practically propelled me out of the door.

'Now look,' he said.

'What's the matter?'

'I told you that colt was no good.'

'I'm grateful for your interest.'

He glared at me. 'How much is Mrs Huntercombe giving you?'

'It's cold out here,' I said.

He looked near to fury.

'She's giving you nothing,' he said.

'I haven't asked her to.'

'That's the point, you stupid sod. We must all stick together. We must all let the breeders know that we all stick together. Do you understand what I'm saying? We can't have you working for less than the rest of us. It's not fair on us. You'll make more money yourself too if we all stick together. It makes sense. Do you follow me?'

'Yes,' I said. All too well.

'Mrs Huntercombe and people like her must be made to understand that unless they reward us properly we are not interested in buying their horses.'

'I follow you,' I said.

'Good. So you'll go along with us in future.' A positive statement, not a question.

'No,' I said.

There may be quicker ways of stirring up hornets, but I doubt it. The rage flowed out of him like a tangible force. He was so near to explosive physical assault that his arms jerked and his weight shifted to his toes. Only the gathering sales crowd stopped him lashing out. He flicked glances left and right, saw people watching, took an almighty and visible grip on his feelings and put the frustrated violence into words.

'If you don't join us we'll ruin you.'

There was no mistaking the viciousness in that voice, and the threat was no idle boast. People found it easy to believe Vic Vincent. The two clients I had already lost to him had believed I cheated them because Vic Vincent had told them so. He could stop the sale of a good filly just by saying she had a heart murmur. He could no doubt smash my growing business with a rumour just as simple and just as false. A bloodstock agent was only as secure as his clients' faith.

I could think of no adequate answer. I said, 'You used not to be like this,' which was true enough but got me nowhere.

'I'm telling you,' he said. 'You play ball or we'll get you out.'

He turned on his heel and walked jerkily away, the anger spilling out of the hunched shoulders and rigid legs. Ronnie North and Jiminy Bell circled round him like anxious satellites and I could hear his voice telling them, low, vigorous and sharp.

Within an hour most of the bloodstock agents knew of the row and during the day I found out who my friends were. The bunch I had said I wouldn't join drew their skirts away and spoke about me among themselves while looking at me out of the corners of their eyes. The chaps in the big firms treated me exactly as usual, and even one or two with approval, as officially they frowned on exorbitant kick-backs.

The uncommitted in the no-man's-land between were the most informative.

I had coffee and a sandwich with one of them, a man who had been in the game longer but was in much my position, more or less established and just beginning to prosper. He was distinctly worried and cheered up not at all when I confirmed what Vic had threatened.

'They've approached me as well,' he said. 'They didn't say what would happen if I didn't join them. Not like with you. They just said I would be better off if I did.'

'So you would.'

'Yes ... but ... I don't know what to do.' He put down his sandwich half finished. 'They're getting so much worse.'

I said I'd noticed it.

'There used to be just a few of them,' he said. 'When I started, only a few. But lately they're getting so powerful.'

'And so greedy,' I said.

'That's it,' he said in eager agreement. 'I don't mind a little extra on the side. Who does? It's just that ... they've started pushing so hard. I don't know what to do ... I don't like their methods and I can't afford ...' He stopped, looked depressed, and went on slowly, 'I suppose I could just not bid when the word goes round. There wouldn't be much harm in that.'

The make-the-best-of-it syndrome. The buttress of every tyrant in history. He took his worries away and later I saw him smiling uneasily with Vic.

During the day I bought one more yearling, bidding against one of the big firms and securing it for a fair price. However extensively Vic's tentacles might stretch they had not reached every breeder in the country, or at any rate not yet. Neither he nor his friends showed any interest in my second purchase.

Towards the end of the day one of my regular clients arrived with a flashy girl in one hand and a cigar in the other. Eddy Ingram, member of the well-heeled unemployed.

'Staying for the week,' he said cheerfully, waving the cigar in a large gesture. 'How about you joining me and Marji for dinner tomorrow night?'

'I'd like to.'

'Great, great.' He beamed at me, beamed at Marji. An overgrown school-boy with a nature as generous as his inheritance. I thought him a fool and liked him a lot. 'Have you found me a couple of good 'uns, then?' he asked.

'There's one tomorrow . . .'

'You buy it. Tell me after.' He beamed again. 'This lad,' he said to Marji, 'he's bought me four horses and they've all shown a profit. Can't complain about that, can you?'

Marji smiled sweetly and said 'Yes Eddy' which was a fair measure of her brain-power.

'Don't forget now. Dinner tomorrow.' He told me where and when, and I said I would see him at the races or the sales before that, if not both.

He beamed and led Marji away to the bar and I wished there were more like him.

In the morning I bought him a well-bred filly for eleven thousand pounds, outbidding one of Vic Vincent's cronies. As none of his bunch looked upset, I guessed that one or all of them jointly would be collecting a kick-back from the breeder. Even though they hadn't bought the horse they would collect just for raising the price.

By mid-morning the crowd had swelled tremendously and

almost every seat in the amphitheatre was taken. Two highly bred colts, due to come up towards noon, were bringing in the punters on their way to the races and the town's wives with their shopping baskets and the semi-drunks from the bars. None had the slightest intention of buying, but there was an irresistible fascination in seeing huge sums being spent. I watched the two star attractions stalk grandly round the collecting ring and then with the tide moved inside for the actual sale. No seats vacant near the door. I leaned against one of the dividing partitions and found myself next to Pauli Teksa. Short, tough, American. Wearing a wide-shouldered light blue overcoat.

'Hi,' he said. 'How're you doing?'

'Fine. And you?'

'Grand . . . I hear Nicol Brevett liked his horse. Kerry called me.'

'Did she tell you we nearly lost that one too?'

'She sure did. That's some mystery you've got there.'

His attention however was not on Kerry or me or the problem of our disappearing purchases, but on the sale in hand. Heavy scribblings and calculations surrounded the high-bred colts in his catalogue, and it looked as though one American agent at least was about to try for a slice of British bloodstock.

The double doors from the collecting ring opened and the first of the colts was led in. The crowd stirred expectantly. The auctioneers put their best man forward. Pauli Teksa cleared his throat.

I glanced at his face. Nothing relaxed about it. Strong features, hard muscles beneath the skin, a face of resolution and decision, not of kindness and compassion. He had crinkly black hair receding at the temples and smoky grey eyes which could move faster than thought.

'The first of two colts by Transporter.' The auctioneer trotted through his spiel. '. . . Offered for sale by the Baylight Stud . . . Someone start me at ten thousand.'

Someone started him at five. When the price rose to ten, Pauli Teksa started bidding. I owed him something, I thought, for giving me Kerry Sanders' commission, however oddly it had turned out.

'I wouldn't buy that colt if I were you,' I said.

'Why not?' He raised the price another two thousand with his eyebrows.

'Because of its colour.'

'Nothing wrong with its colour. Perfectly good chestnut.' Another two thousand.

I said, 'Transporter has sired about three hundred horses and that's the only chestnut. All the rest are dark bay or light brown.'

'So?' Another two thousand.

'So I wouldn't bet on the paternity.'

Pauli stopped bidding abruptly and turned towards me with an intent, concentrated expression.

'You sure do your homework.'

I watched the chestnut colt going round the sand track while the price rose to forty thousand.

'I've seen a lot of Transporter's progeny,' I said. 'And they don't look like that.'

The auctioneer looked over to Pauli inquiringly. 'Against you, sir.'

Pauli shook his head, and the bidding went on without him.

'This guy from New Zealand,' he said. 'When he was over Statesside, he asked me to buy him a Transporter colt at Newmarket if one came up, and ship it out to him so he could mix the blood line with his stock.'

I smiled and shook my head.

'How much do you want?' Pauli said.

'What do you mean?'

'For the information.'

'Well... nothing.'

Pauli looked at me straightly. 'You're a goddam fool,' he said.

'There's things besides money,' I said mildly.

'No wonder these other guys are against you!'

'What have you heard?' I asked curiously.

'Why don't you go along with them?'

'I don't like what they're doing.'

He gave me an old-man-of-the-world look and told me I'd get hurt if I didn't go along with the crowd. I said I would chance it. I was a triple goddam fool, he said.

The chestnut colt made fifty-six thousand pounds. The second potential star seller came into the ring looking as a Transporter should, dark bay with a slightly narrow neck and sharp pelvic bones high on the rump.

'What about this one?' Pauli demanded.

'The real McCoy.'

'You slay me.'

He bid for it but dropped out at his authorized limit of fifty thousand. I reflected upon how terribly easy it was to influence a sale. Pauli had believed me on two counts, first against the chestnut and then for the bay, and had acted unhesitatingly on what I'd said. Just so had others with Vic Vincent. Who could blame anyone at all for heeding off-putting advice when so much money was at risk.

At fifty-two thousand all the big firms had dropped out and the bidding had resolved itself into a straight contest between Vic Vincent and the carrot-headed Yorkshireman, Fynedale, who bought for Wilton Young. Constantine Brevett, I suddenly saw, had brought his smooth silver hair and dark-framed spectacles into the arena and was standing at Vic's shoulder talking urgently into his ear.

Wilton Young's man was nodding away as if he had the whole mint to call on. Constantine was looking both piqued and determined. Yearlings who cost more than sixty thousand were not a great financial proposition, even with the stud potential from Transporter, and I guessed that against anyone but Wilton Young he would have dropped out long ago.

At seventy thousand he began to scowl. At seventy-five he shook his head angrily and stalked out of the sale ring. The carrot-headed Fynedale winked at Vic Vincent.

Pauli Teksa said, 'Say, that was some figure.'

'Too much,' I agreed.

'I guess pride comes expensive.'

It did, I thought. All sorts of pride came expensive, in one way or another.

He suggested a drink and with the sale's main excitement over we joined the general exodus barwards.

'Seriously, Jonah,' Pauli said, glass in hand and strong features full of friendly conviction. 'There's no place any more for the individualist in the game. You either have to join a big firm or else come to an agreement with the small men like yourself and act together as a body. You can't buck the system . . . not if you're out for profits.'

'Pauli, stop trying,' I said.

'I don't want to see you in big trouble, fellah.'

'Nothing will happen,' I said, but he shook his head, and said he was afraid for me, he surely was. I was too honest for my own good.

8

Constantine, Kerry and Nicol were all at the track that afternoon, to see Constantine's colt start favourite for the big race. Constantine was in such a bad mood that they would have had more fun in a dentist's waiting-room, and soon after they arrived Nicol detached himself from the general gloom and joined me with a grimace.

'That bloody Wilton Young . . .'

We strolled over to see the runners for the apprentice race walk round the parade ring.

'Tell your father to console himself with the thought that Wilton Young has probably poured his money down the drain.'

'Do you think so?'

'How many horses earn anything like seventy-five thousand?'

'He's convinced it'll win the Arc de Triomphe.'

'More likely a consolation race at Redcar.'

Nicol laughed. 'That'll cheer him up.'

I asked him how River God was doing and he said he was eating well and already looking better. He asked if I had found out why Frizzy Hair had wanted his horses and I said I hadn't. We spent two or three chunks of the afternoon together, cementing an unexpected friendship.

Vic Vincent took a note of it and disliked what he seemed to see as a threat to his Brevett monopoly. Even Nicol noticed the blast of ill will coming my way.

'What have you done to upset Vic?' he asked.

'Nothing.'

'You must have done *something*.'

I shook my head. 'It's what I won't do,' I said, 'and don't ask what it is, because I can't tell you.'

He sniffed. 'Professional secret?'

'Sort of.'

He gave me the flashing sideways grin. 'Like when you knew I was lying my head off to keep a race on an objection, and you didn't split?'

'Well...'

'Yeah,' he said. 'I remember, even if you don't. You finished fourth. You listened to me giving my owner a right lot of codswollop and you never said a word.'

'You'd won the race.'

'Yeah ... and they'd have taken it off me if you'd given me away.'

'It was a long time ago.'

'All of three years.' He grinned. 'The leopard still has the same claws.'

'Spots.'

'Claws.' The grin came and went. 'You were a ferocious bastard to ride against.'

'No.'

'Oh sure. Milk and honey on the ground and a bloody nuisance as an opponent.' He paused. 'I'll tell you ... I learned something from you. I learned not to go around squealing when things weren't fair. ... I learned to shrug off small injustices and get on with the next thing and put my energies in the future instead of rabbiting about the past. I learned not to mind too much when things went against me. And I reckon I owe you a lot for that.'

'You just paid it,' I said.

I leaned later alone against the rails of the balcony on the Members' roof and looked down to where Vic Vincent was moving desultorily from group to group. Talking, smiling, taking notes, nodding, patting people on the back. He looked pleasant, knowledgeable and useful. He looked boyish, harmless and trustworthy. He wore a heavy tweed suit and a slightly dandified dark red shirt with a white collar and tie, and no hat on the reddish-brown hair.

I wondered why he had recently grown so aggressively rapacious. He had been successful for a long time and as one of the top one-man bands he must have been handling about two million pounds' worth of business every year. At a flat five per cent that meant a hundred thousand stayed with him, and even after heavy expenses and taxes he must have been well off.

He worked hard. He was always there, standing in the bitter winds round the winter sale rings, totting up, evaluating, advising, buying, laying out his judgement for hire. He was working even harder now that he was going around intimidating breeders in far-flung little studs. Something had recently stoked up his appetite for money to within a millimetre of open crime.

I wondered what.

Pauli Teksa rapturized about Newmarket and compared it favourably with every American track from Saratoga to Gulf Stream Park. When pinned down by my scepticism he said he guessed he liked Newmarket because it was so *small*. And *quaint*. And so goddam *British*. The stands at Newmarket were fairly new and comfortable; but I reflected wryly that small, quaint and British usually meant hopelessly inadequate seating, five deep in the bars and not enough shelter from the rain.

He liked the Heath, he said. He liked to see horses running on grass. He liked the long straight course. He liked right-handed races. He'd always liked Newmarket, it was so quaint.

'You've been here before?' I asked.

'Sure. Four years ago. Just for a look-see.'

We watched an untidy little jockey squeeze home after five furlongs by a shorter margin than he ought, and on the way down from the stands found ourselves alongside Constantine and Kerry.

She introduced the two men to each other, the big silver-haired man of property and the short wide-shouldered American. Neither took to the other on sight. They exchanged social politenesses, Constantine with more velvet than Pauli, but in less than two minutes they were nodding and moving apart.

'That guy sure thinks a lot of himself,' Pauli said.

Wilton Young arrived in a helicopter a quarter of an hour before the big race. Wilton Young had his own pilot and his own Bell

Ranger, which was one up on the Brevett Rolls, and he made a point of arriving everywhere as noticeably as possible. If Constantine thought a lot of himself, Wilton Young outstripped him easily.

He came bouncing through the gate from the air strip straight across the paddock and into the parade ring, where his fourth best three-year-old was on display for the contest.

The loud Yorkshire voice cut through the moist October air like a timber saw, the words from a distance indistinct but the overall sound level too fierce to be missed.

Constantine stood at the other end of the parade ring towering protectively over the little knot of Kerry, his trainer and his jockey, and trying to look unaware that his whole scene had just been stolen by the poison ivy from the skies.

Nicol said in my ear 'All we want now is for Wilton Young's horse to beat Father's,' and inevitably it did. By two lengths. Easing up.

'He'll have apoplexy,' Nicol said.

Constantine, however, had beautiful manners even in defeat and consoled his trainer in the unsaddling enclosure without appearing to notice the ill-bred glee going on six feet away, in the number one slot.

'It always happens,' Nicol said. 'The one you least want to win is the one which does.'

I smiled. 'The one you choose not to ride . . .'

'They make you look a bloody fool.'

'Over and over.'

At the end of the afternoon I drove from the racecourse, which lay a mile out on the London road, down into the town again, taking the right-hand turn to the sale paddocks. Nicol came with me, as Constantine was returning with Kerry to his hotel to lick his wounds in private, and we went round the stables looking at the dozen or so yearlings I had noted as possibles. He said he was interested in learning how to buy his own horses so that he wouldn't have to rely on an agent all his life.

'More like you, I'd be out of business,' I said.

There was a filly by On Safari that I liked the look of, a big, deep-chested brown mare with a kind eye. She had speed in her pedigree and her dam had produced three two-year-old winners already, and I thought that if she didn't fetch an astronomical amount she would do very nicely for Eddy Ingram.

She was due to come up about an hour after the evening session started, and I filled in the time by buying two moderate colts for a thousand each for a trainer in Cheshire.

With Nicol still in tow I went outside to watch the On Safari filly walk round the collecting ring. She walked as well as she looked and I feared that Eddy Ingram's limit of fifteen thousand might not be enough.

Jiminy Bell did his appearing act, sliding with a wiggle into the space between Nicol and myself as we stood by the rail.

'Got a note for you,' he said.

He thrust a folded piece of paper into my hand and vanished again even before I could offer him a drink, which was as unlikely as a gatecrasher leaving before the food.

I unfolded the paper.

'What's the matter?' Nicol said.

'Nothing.'

I put the paper into my jacket pocket and tried to take the grimness out of my face. The message was written in capital letters and allowed for no mistakes.

DON'T BID FOR 182.

'Jonah . . . you're as tense as a high wire.'

I looked at Nicol vaguely. He said again, 'For God's sake, what's the matter?'

I loosened a few muscles and said flippantly, 'If you've got to go, you've got to go.'

'Go where?'

'I expect I'll find out.'

'I don't understand you.'

'Never mind,' I said. 'Let's go and see this filly sold.'

We went into the big circular building and sat in the section of seats nearest the door, the section crowded as usual with breeders, agents and an all-sorts mixture of racing people. Ronnie North was in the row behind us. He leaned forward and spoke into the space between our heads.

'The word is that the On Safari filly is likely to be sterile.

Some infection or other ... No good as a breeding prospect, they say. Such a pity.'

Nicol looked startled and disappointed on my behalf. He asked Ronnie one or two questions but Ronnie shook his head sadly and said he didn't know details, only that he'd heard it on the best authority.

'She wouldn't be worth so much in that case,' Nicol said, turning back to me.

'Not if it's true.'

'But... don't you think it is?'

'I don't know.'

Lot 180 was being sold. There was so little time. 'Got some business,' I said to Nicol. 'See you later.'

I scudded to the telephone. The On Safari filly came from an Irish stud I'd scarcely heard of, and it took two precious minutes for the Irish service to find me the number. Could they ring it at once, I asked.

'Half an hour's delay.'

'If it isn't at once it will be too late.'

'Hold on...'

There were clicks and distant voices and then suddenly, clearly, a very Irish voice saying 'Hello?'

I asked if the On Safari filly had ever had an infection or an assessment of fertility.

'Well now,' said the voice, deliberating slowly. 'I wouldn't know about that now. I wouldn't know anything about the horses, do you see, because I'm just here minding the children until Mr and Mrs O'Kearey get home on the train from Dublin... they'll be home in an hour, so they will. They'll be able to answer your question in an hour.'

When I got back the filly was already being led round and the bidding, such as it was, had started. The seat beside Nicol had been taken. I stood in the chute through which the horses were led into the ring and listened to the auctioneer assuring everyone that she had a clean bill of health.

A man beside me shook his head dubiously. I glanced at him. A senior partner from one of the big firms. He stared morosely at the filly and made no move to buy her.

A couple of people in the crowd had taken the price up to six thousand five hundred, and there she stuck. The last bidder began to look intensely worried and obviously didn't want her. I guessed he was acting for the breeder and would have to buy the filly back if she didn't fetch a better price.

'Six thousand five . . . any advance on six thousand five? She's on the market . . .' He looked round the ranks of bloodstock agents and took note of the shuttered impassive faces. 'Six thousand five once then. Six thousand five twice . . . All done?' He raised his gavel and I lifted my hand.

'Six thousand six.'

The last bidder's face relaxed in pure relief. Several heads turned in my general direction, looking to see who had bid, and the senior partner beside me stirred and said out of the corner of his mouth, 'They say she's sterile.'

'Thank you,' I said.

No one else made a move. The auctioneer tried harder for another hit but without result, and knocked her down with a shake of the head.

'Jonah Dereham,' he announced, writing it down.

A ripple like a shudder went through the small group round Vic Vincent. I didn't wait to hear what they had to say but beat it hastily down to the stables to see about transport. On the way back an hour and a strong cup of coffee later I came face to face with Eddy Ingram who said loudly and without a smile that he had been looking for me.

'If you've bought that On Safari filly for me,' he said positively, 'you can forget it.'

The bright lights around the collecting ring shone on a face from which most of the good nature had evaporated. The delectable Marji registered scorn.

'She's bound to be fast, with that breeding,' I said.

'I've been told she's infected and sterile.' He was angry about it. Not the usual beaming Eddy at all. 'You're not spending my money on rubbish like that.'

'I haven't bought you a dud yet, Eddy,' I said. 'If you don't want this filly, well, fair enough, I'll find someone who does. But she's a bargain at that price and I'd have liked you to benefit.'

'But she's sterile. And you knew it before you bid for her. You weren't acting in my best interests.'

'Ah,' I said. 'Now there's a nice phrase. Not acting in your best interests. Who said that?'

His eyes flickered. 'I don't see . . .'

'I do,' I said drily.

'Anyway . . .' He shrugged off his doubts. 'Anyway, I'll take the one you bought for me this morning, but I don't want you to get me any more.'

Someone had been very quickly persuasive, but then Eddy was gullible and a fool. I wondered whether all my clients would desert with such speed.

Eddy came out with the clincher which had alienated him fastest. 'You didn't think I would find out she was sterile. You thought you'd collect your five per cent from me for buying her even though you knew she was probably useless.'

'How do you know she's sterile?' I asked.

'Vic says so.'

'And is Vic going to buy your horses in future?'

He nodded.

'Good luck to you, Eddy,' I said.

He still hovered indecisively. 'You haven't denied it.'

'I did not buy that filly just to get five per cent.'

He began to look unhappy. 'Vic said you'd deny it and I'd be a fool to believe you . . .'

'Vic's a persuasive fellow,' I said.

'But you've bought me four good ones . . .'

'You sort it out, Eddy. Think it over and let me know.'

I walked away and left him.

An hour later I again telephoned to Ireland.

'Is she *what?*'

I took my eardrum away from the receiver and winced.

'Of course she's not sterile.' The Irish voice yelled out as if crossing the Irish Sea without benefit of wires. 'She's never had a day's illness since she was foaled. Where the devil did you hear that?'

'At the sales.'

'What?' Alarm joined the indignation. 'How much did she make?'

I told him. I removed the receiver a good ten inches and still had no difficulty in hearing. Vic Vincent's victims all seemed to be endowed with good lungs.

'I told a neighbour of mine to bid up to ten thousand and I'd be sure to pay him back if he had to buy her.'

'His nerve broke at six thousand five,' I said.

'I'll murder him.' He sounded as if he meant to. 'I told that Vic Vincent fellow I didn't need his help, I'd get my own bidding done thank you very much, and now look. Now look.' He gurgled.

'What did Vic offer?' I asked.

'He said he'd raise the filly to ten thousand, and if it made more than that he wanted half. *Half!* I ask you. I offered him one fifth and that's a bloody liberty, even that much. He said half or nothing so I said nothing and go to hell.'

'Will you do what he wants next time?'

'Next time!' The idea of a next and a next and a next time slowly sank in. 'Well . . .' Some of the fire went out. There was a long pause and when he finally spoke it was clear he had thought of the advantages of Vic's help and realized what refusing him might cost. 'Well now,' he said. 'Perhaps I will.'

When next I saw Eddy Ingram he was beaming away at Vic, and Marji likewise. All three of them in a little huddle, as thick as thieves.

I reflected uncharitably that I was in no way bound to tell Eddy there was nothing wrong with the filly. If she turned out to be the best brood mare of the century it would serve him damn well right.

Towards the end of the evening, after Nicol had left to have dinner, my arm was grabbed by a man who said fiercely, 'I want to talk to you,' and such was the readiness of my flight reflexes that I nearly hit and ran before I realized that his grievance was not with me. He was, he said, the breeder of the Transporter colt which Wilton Young's agent Fynedale had bought for seventy-five thousand pounds. He nearly spat the words out and did not look as one should if one's produce were among the top prices in the sales.

He insisted that he should buy me a drink and that I should listen to him.

'All right,' I said.

We stood in a corner of the bar drinking brandy and ginger ale while the bitterness poured out of him like acid.

'I heard Vic Vincent's out to get you. That's why I'm telling you this. He came down to my place last week and bought my colt for thirty thousand.'

'Oh did he,' I said.

Private sales before the auctions were not supposed to take place. Every horse in the catalogue had to appear in the sale ring unless excused by a vet's certificate, because otherwise, as the auctioneers complained with some reason, the buyers and sellers would just use their catalogue as a free information and advertising medium, and not send their horses to the auction at all. The auctioneers produced the catalogue and set up the sales, and wanted their ten per cents for their trouble. At one or two sales the catalogue had not been produced until the very last minute because of the number of private bargains which had been struck at other times before the auction.

Late catalogues made my job a lot more difficult. On the other hand I knew that some breeders were avoiding paying the auctioneers' commission by selling privately for a good sum and then doing everything they could to keep the auction price at rock bottom. One couldn't blame the auctioneers for fighting back.

'Vic gave me a double promise,' said the breeder, his lips tight with fury. 'He said they wouldn't bid the price up to thirty thousand if nobody else was trying to buy.'

'So that you wouldn't have to pay the full commission to the auctioneers?'

He stared. 'Nothing wrong in that, is there? Business is business.'

'Go on,' I said.

'He said that if the price went up to fifty thousand he would give me half of everything over thirty.'

He drank, nearly choking himself. I watched.

'And then . . . then . . .' He spluttered, hardly able to get the words out. 'Do you know what he has the gall to say? He says our agreement only went as far as fifty thousand. Everything over that, he takes it *all*.'

I admired the beauty of it in an odd sort of way.

'Was the agreement in writing?' I asked.

'Yes,' he said furiously.

'Unfortunate.'

'*Unfortunate!* Is that all you have to say?'

I sighed. 'Why didn't you let the colt take its chance at the sale instead of selling to Vic first?'

'Because he didn't think it would make as much as thirty at auction, but he had a client who would give that much, and he said I might as well benefit.'

'Have you ever dealt with Vic before?' I asked curiously.

'Not directly. No. And to be honest, I was flattered when he came to my place specially . . . *Flattered!*'

He crashed his empty glass with a bang onto one of the small tables scattered in the bar. A man sitting at the table looked up and waved a beckoning arm.

'Join the club,' he said.

I knew him slightly; a small-scale trainer from one of the northern counties who came down south occasionally to buy new horses for his owners. He knew as much about horses as any agent, and I reckoned his owners had been lucky he could buy for them himself as it saved them having to pay an agent's commission.

He was lightly smashed, if not drunk.

'That bastard,' he said. 'Vic Vincent. Join the anti-Vic Vincent club.'

The breeder, hardly attending, said, 'What are you talking about?'

'Can you beat it?' the trainer asked of the world in general. 'I've bought horses for an owner of mine for years. Damn good horses. Then what happens? He meets Vic Vincent and Vic persuades him to let him buy him a horse. So he buys it. And then what happens? Then I buy him a horse, like I've always done. And then what happens? Vic Vincent complains to my owner, saying I shouldn't buy the horses because it does him, Vic Vincent, out of the fair commission he would be getting if he bought them. Can you believe it? So I complain to my owner about him buying horses through Vic Vincent because I like to train horses I choose, not horses Vic Vincent chooses, and then what do you think happens?'

He threw his arms wide theatrically and waited for his cue.

'What happens?' I supplied obligingly.

'Then my owner says I'm not being fair to Vic Vincent and he takes his horses away from me and sends them to another trainer that Vic Vincent picked out for him and now between them they're rooking my owner right and left, but he doesn't even realize, because he thinks horses must be twice as good if they cost twice as much.'

The breeder listened in silence because he was deep anyway in his own grudges; and I listened in silence because I believed every incredible word of it. People who bought racehorses could be more easily conned than any old lady parting with her savings to a kind young man on the doorstep. People who bought racehorses were buying dreams and would follow anyone who said he knew the way to the end of the rainbow. A few had found the crock of gold there, and the rest never gave up looking. Someone ought to start a Society for the Protection of Gullible Owners, I thought smiling, with Constantine and Wilton Young as its first cases.

The breeder and the trainer bought large refills and sat down to compare wounds. I left them to their sorrows, went back to the ring, and bid unsuccessfully for a well-grown colt who went to Vic Vincent for nearly double my authorized limit.

The under bidder was Jiminy Bell. I saw Vic giving him a tenner afterwards and patting him on the back. Some other Gullible Owner would be paying Vic. It was enough to make you laugh.

* * *

Vic was not laughing, however, in the car park.

I was fishing out my keys to unlock the car door when someone shone a torch straight at my face.

'Turn that bloody thing off,' I said.

The light went out. When the dazzle cleared from my eyes there were six or seven men standing round me in a ring at a distance of six feet.

I looked at them one by one. Vic Vincent and the carrot-headed Yorkshireman Fynedale, Ronnie North and Jiminy Bell. Three others I met every day at the sales.

All deadly serious.

'What have we here?' I said. 'A lynch mob?'

No one thought it funny. Not even me.

9

Vic said, 'You're going to have to be told, Jonah.'

'Told what?'

There were people within shouting distance, going to their cars. I thought maybe I would shout, but not perhaps just yet.

The seven men took a small step forwards almost as if moved by a signal. I stood with my back against my car and thought I was getting tired of being attacked in car parks. Have to travel more by train.

'You're going to do what we tell you, whether you like it or not.'

'No,' I said. 'I am not.'

They took another step and stood in a solid wall, shoulder to shoulder. If I reached out I could touch them.

'You'll fall over yourselves in a minute,' I said.

They didn't like me trying to make a joke of them. The anger Vic had throttled earlier rose up again in his face and none of his clients would have recognized their friendly neighbourhood bloodsucker. A vein in his forehead swelled and throbbed.

The Yorkshireman Fynedale put his shoulder in front of Vic's as if to hold him back.

'You're more trouble than you're worth,' he told me, 'and you might as well get this straight. You're not to bid when we say not. Right?'

Vic elbowed him back. Vic didn't like his lieutenant usurping the role of number one thug.

'If we get rough, you've asked for it,' he said.

'Get,' I said, 'what do you call that bang on the head at Ascot? A friendly pat?'

He snapped out, 'That wasn't us,' and instantly regretted it. His face closed like a slammed door.

I glanced round the ring of faces. Some of them didn't know

what had happened at Ascot. But Vic did. Fynedale did. Ronnie North and Jiminy Bell did . . .

'Who was it?'

'Never you mind. You just reckon you've had a taster. And you bloody will do what you're told.'

They all looked so furiously intent that I wanted to laugh: but when they suddenly wheeled away and went off to their own cars I found I didn't want to laugh after all. I stood where they'd left me and breathed in deep lungfuls of winter night. However ludicrous I might think it that some perfectly ordinary citizens should threaten to beat me up if I didn't join their strong-arm union, their collective menace had been real enough.

All I suddenly wanted was a cigarette.

There were few cars left in the park, but the one next to mine turned out to be Pauli Teksa's.

'Jonah?' he said, peering at me through the dim lighting.

'Hullo.'

'You're just standing there smoking?'

'Yeah.'

'Want to come to my place for a bite to eat?'

By tacit consent my dinner date with Eddy and Marji had lapsed, but my hosts for the week were not expecting me back. If I wanted to eat at all it might as well be in company.

'Couldn't think of anything better,' I said.

He was staying in a pub outside Newmarket which put on late dinners especially for people after the sales. The cosy bar and dining-room were full of familiar faces and the general conversation was predictable.

He moved his strong, stocky body through the crowd with ease, and there was some quality about him which parted the crush like Moses and the Red Sea. I watched him being served at the bar at once where others had waited longer and saw that the others acknowledged rather than resented his priority. I wondered what it must be like to be Pauli, generating such natural and unconscious power.

We ate smoked salmon and then roast pheasant, and drank

Chateau Haut Badon 1970, which was my choice, not his, as he said Americans knew goddam all about French wines and he was no exception. He preferred Bourbon, he said.

'All these guys here,' he said over coffee, waving a hand at the other crowded tables. 'They kinda like you.'

'You imagine it.'

'Nope.' He gave me a cigar from a crocodile case with gold mountings. A Havana. He inhaled the smoke deeply, and sighed, and said the only good thing ever to come out of Cuba was its cigars and life in the States was hardly worth living now they were banned. He had stocked up in England, he said. He was going to smuggle a hundred or so through in his baggage.

'You looked a bit shook up back there in the car park,' he said.

'Did I?'

'Those guys I saw standing round you when I came out of the gate. They friends of yours?'

'Business acquaintances.'

He smiled sympathetically. 'Ganging up on you, eh? Well I sure did warn you.'

'You sure did,' I said, smiling back.

He looked at me assessingly. 'They don't seem to have made it stick.'

'No.'

'You want to take care, fellah,' he said earnestly. 'Remember you got bashed at Ascot.'

'Tonight's lot said they didn't do that.'

He was surprised. 'They said . . . ?'

I nodded. 'They clammed up as soon as they'd said it. It might be true in a way, because the two men who took Hearse Puller and tried to get River God aren't regulars on the racing scene. I'd never seen them before. But at a guess . . . tonight's crowd supplied the basic information.'

'How do you mean?'

'Between them they knew everything the two strangers knew.'

'What sort of things?'

His strong face was intent, receptive, helpful. I told him about the two-year-old getting loose on the main road, and about Crispin's whisky.

He was astounded. I said, 'Of the people there tonight, Jiminy Bell knew about my dicey arm as he'd seen the strap often enough in the changing room, when we were both jockeys. Ronnie North knew I'd bought River God, because he'd sold it to me. Vic Vincent knew I kept horses in transit in my yard. Any of them could have known I have an alcoholic brother, it's no secret. All of them were at Ascot the day I bought Hearse Puller. It's quite clear they could have supplied the info if they'd wanted to. The trouble is that I simply don't see the point.'

He carefully edged half an inch of ash off the end of his cigar and took his time over replying.

'I'll tell you what they might have been after,' he said.

'What?'

'To soften you up.'

'What?' I laughed. 'You can't be serious.'

He shrugged. 'It's possible. They rough you up a little. Nothing you'd make too much of a fuss of. Kick you around a bit. Then they give out with the threats . . . Join us or else.'

I shook my head. 'It can't be that simple.'

'Why not?'

'Because I'm not that much of a threat to them. Why should they go to all that trouble?'

He leaned back in his chair, smiling gently through the Cuban smoke. 'Don't you know the classic law of the invader, fellah? Single out the strongest guy around and smash him. Then all the weaker crowd come to heel like lambs.'

'Vic has invaded like the Mongol hordes,' I agreed, 'but I'm by no means the strongest guy around.'

'You sell yourself short, fellah.'

'Don't be a nut.'

He shook his head. 'I back my own judgement. Make my decisions. Buy my horses. Quick. Snap.' He snapped his fingers. 'And I don't get things wrong.'

The circus left Newmarket after the races on Saturday.

By that time relations between Vic and myself were if possible worse. He had instructed me not to bid on five occasions: three of those yearlings I hadn't wanted anyway, and the other two I bought. The mood of the mob had hardened to the point where I was careful to keep out of lonely car parks.

By Saturday Vic had warned Constantine that I was not a good companion for Nicol. Constantine had warned Nicol, and Nicol, grinning over a sandwich, had warned me.

Wilton Young had become the owner of three more yearlings at near record prices and Fynedale was smirking from ear to ear.

Constantine had pretended not to be mortified, and had cheered up considerably when his horse beat Wilton Young's in the Cesarewitch.

Eddy Ingram asked to have the On Safari filly after all as he had discovered on his own account that she was undamaged, but I had already passed her on to another client and felt regrettably unsympathetic when I told him so.

On the business side I had had quite a good week in spite of all Vic's threats, but I drove away down the A11 to London with a deep sigh of relief.

The relief lasted until I turned down towards the village at home.

The village was in a turmoil with all the people out of the houses, and the street blocked with cars, bicycles, prams and kids. The time was ten past eight. The cause of the upheaval was a bright glow in the night sky with leaping flames and flying sparks, and I knew at once and without hope that the place on fire was mine.

It was impossible to drive there. I left my car and went forward on foot, competing it seemed to me with every man, woman and wheelchair in the parish. The nearer I got the more I had to push, and it was a six-deep seething mass which was being held back by a portable barrier placed across the gateway. I squeezed round one end of it to get into the yard and was roughly told to get out by a busy fireman.

'It's my bloody house,' I snapped. 'I've just got home.'

'Oh.' He paused fractionally. 'The wind's against us, I'm afraid. We're doing our best.'

I looked around me and took stock.

The stables were alight and gone. Bright orange from end to end. Flames shot up high from what had been the roof, roaring and crackling like thunder and lightning shaken together in some demoniacal cocktail. The heat was incredible. Smoke swirled everywhere, stinging the eyes. It was like being on the wrong side of a giant bonfire, and I could see what he had meant by the wind. It was blowing showers of bright splintery sparks like rain onto the still black bulk of the house.

Half the firemen were trying to damp down the stables. The rest, back to back and cramped for room, were focusing on what might still be saved. Silver jets of water swept the tiles and the back face of the house and poured through my bedroom window, which was broken.

There were two fire engines, both of them through the other side of the yard, out in the paddock. I wondered stupidly what they were doing there, and then realized they were pumping water directly from the brook, which ran along one side. Not a very big brook, I thought uneasily. The long, narrow yard itself was a sea of puddles and hoses and men in black helmets doing a difficult job efficiently, part-time firemen who'd left their Saturday night beer in the local and come out enthusiastically to try to save my house. It was crazy to think of their beer at a time like that, but I did.

The fireman I'd spoken to before said sympathetically that I'd had a hell of a homecoming. He said that there was never much hope for places like stables and farms, once they caught fire, not if there was any hay or straw stored there. Burned like tinder, he said.

'We sent for another appliance,' he said. 'It ought to have been here by now.' He had almost to shout for me to hear.

'The road's blocked right back into the village,' I said.

He looked resigned, which was not what I felt.

'Sorry about your car,' he shouted.

'What car?'

He swept an arm round to the garage at the end of the stable block and pointed. The remains of Crispin's car were burning in there like a skeleton.

I caught the fireman by the arm.

'Where's my brother?' I shouted. 'He's here . . . Where is he?'

He shook his head. 'The place was empty. We checked. The fire hadn't got such a hold when we came and there was no danger inside the house then.'

'He might be asleep.'

'No one could have slept through this lot, mate,' he shouted, and looking and listening to the disaster, one could see his point.

'I'll have to make sure.'

'Come back,' he yelled. 'You can't go in there now. You'll suffocate.'

He fielded me forcibly on my way to the kitchen door. I said we must find my brother.

He began to tell me again that he wasn't there.

'He might be dead drunk.' It was no time to save Crispin's face. 'Unconscious.' And he might have walked down to the pub and be sitting there obliviously over his sixth double gin; but I couldn't waste time finding out.

'Oh.' The fireman pulled me through the scrum of men and hoses to the nearest fire engine and thrust a breathing pack into my arms.

'Put it on,' he said. 'The lights will be shot to hell by now and you can find him quicker than I can, if he's there.' He gave me a helmet and gloves and we ran over to the house, with me struggling to fasten everything on.

The house was unbelievably full of smoke, dark, pungent, hot and oily. The only light was from the flames outside, which meant that all the far rooms were filled with black fog. It stung in my eyes worse than ever and made them water. I straightened the breathing mask over them and tried to see where I was going.

'Where would he be?' yelled the fireman.

'Maybe the sitting-room. This way.'

We blundered down the passage and into the pitch black room. Impossible to see. I felt all over the sofa, the armchairs, and the floor around, which was where he usually passed out.

No Crispin.

'No good.'

We went upstairs. Everything was very hot indeed up there and the smoke was, if anything, denser. Patches of woodwork round the doors were charred, as if they had already burnt, but there were no actual flames.

I couldn't find him anywhere in his bedroom, which was dark, or in mine, which glowed vividly orange through the smoke and was as drenching as a tropical rainstorm from the water pouring through the window.

'He isn't here,' shouted the fireman.

'Bathroom . . . ' I said.

'Hurry. The roof's smouldering.'

The bathroom door was shut but not locked. I opened it, took one step, and tripped over Crispin's feet.

The air in there was clearer. The fireman pushed past me, threw Crispin over his shoulder as if he were a child, and went out of the house faster than I could with no burden.

He laid Crispin on a patch of wet grass because there was nowhere else to put him. I pulled off the breathing mask and looked down at him anxiously.

'Is he alive?'

'Don't know. Put your mask on him.'

He started at once giving Crispin artificial respiration by the method of pulling his arms backwards over his head, while I clipped on the mask and checked the air flow.

Without pausing the fireman glanced up at the staring crowd at the gate and at the rows of faces looking over the hedge for as far down the road as the flames lit them, and I could read his mind as if he'd spoken. The third appliance, an ambulance, doctor, police . . . no other vehicle was going to reach us until the village went home.

The roof down the half of the stables nearest us fell in with a roar and a sudden out-gushing of sizzling heat. The fireman raised his eyes from his exertions on Crispin and said encouragingly, 'Now if the rest of that roof falls in quickly, the house has more of a chance.'

I looked up. The incendiary shower of sparks had diminished, but the house looked more than ever as if it would burst all over into flames in explosive spontaneous combustion. Despite all their efforts the eaves at the far end were blackly burning.

Crispin showed not the slightest sign of life, but when I felt for his pulse, it was there. Faint and slow, but there.

I nodded to the fireman in relief, and he stopped the respiration. He watched Crispin's chest. There was no perceptible movement. The fireman slid his hand inside Crispin's clothes, to feel his ribs. Nothing. He shook his head, and went back to pumping.

'I can do that,' I said.

'Right.'

I took his place and he went back to help with the fire, and the hot, roaring, smoky nightmare seemed to go on and on and on.

Crispin lived and they more or less saved the house.

At some point that I wasn't quite clear about the police arrived, and soon afterwards an ambulance took my still unconscious brother away to a more thorough decoking.

The first thing the firemen told the police was that it looked like arson, and the first thing the police asked me was had I started it.

'I wasn't even here.'

'Have you got any money troubles?'

I looked at them incredulously. Standing there in all that shambles with thick, hot smoke still pouring off the damp and blackening embers they were stolidly conducting inquiries.

'Is that all the help you can give?' I said, but their manner said plainly enough that they weren't there to give help.

It seemed the final unreality on that disjointed night that they should believe I had brought such destruction on myself.

By dawn one of the fire engines had gone but the other was still there, because, the firemen told me, with old houses you never knew. Sometimes a beam would smoulder for hours, then burst into flames and start the whole thing over again.

They yawned and rolled up hoses, and smoked cigarettes which they stubbed out carefully in little flat tins. Relays of tea in thermos flasks came up from the village and a few cautious jokes grew like flowers on the ruins.

At nine I went down to the pub to borrow the telephone and caught sight of myself in a mirror. Face streaked with black, eyes red with smoke and as weary as sin.

I told Sophie not to come, there wouldn't be any lunch. She would come anyway, she said, and I hadn't the stamina to argue.

The pub gave me a bath and breakfast. My clothes smelled horrible when I put them on again, but nothing to the house and yard when I got back. Wet burnt wood, wet burnt straw, stale smoke. The smell was acrid and depressing, but the departing firemen said nothing could be done, things always smelled like that after blazes.

Sophie came, and she was not wearing the gold aeroplane.

She wrinkled her nose at the terrible mess and silently put her arm through mine and kissed me. I felt more comforted than I had since childhood.

'What's left?' she said.

'Some wet furniture and a tin of peanuts.'

'Let's start with those.'

We went through the house room by room. Watery ash and stale smoke everywhere. My bedroom had a jagged black corner open to the sky where the roof had burned right through, and everything in there was past tense. I supposed it was lucky I had had some of my clothes with me in Newmarket.

There was an empty gin bottle in Crispin's room, and another in the bathroom.

In the office the ash covered everything in a thick, gritty film. The walls were darkened by smoke and streaked with water and my rows of precious, expensive and practically irreplaceable form books and stud records would never be the same again.

'What are you going to do?' Sophie said, standing on the filthy kitchen floor and running one finger through the dust on the table.

'Emigrate,' I said.

'Seriously?'

'No . . . Seriously, the pub opens in five minutes and we might as well get drunk.'

10

We rolled home happily at two o'clock and found the police there. Two of them, one a constable, one with the shoulder badges of Chief Inspector.

'Enjoying yourself, Mr Dereham?' the Chief Inspector said sarcastically. 'Celebrating on the insurance money, are you?'

It seemed, however, that this opening was more a matter of habit than threat, because they had not after all come to accuse, but to ask and inform.

'Chilly out here, sir,' the Chief Inspector said, looking up pointedly at the dull wintery sky.

'Chilly indoors now too,' I said. 'The central heating oil tank was in the stables.'

'Ah,' he said. 'Yes, exactly.'

He chose all the same to go indoors, so I took them into the office and fetched a duster for the chairs. The duster merely smeared the dirt. I had to fetch others for them to spread out and sit on.

'Tell us about your enemies, Mr Dereham,' said the Chief Inspector.

'What enemies?'

'Exactly, sir. What enemies do you have?'

'I didn't know I had any who would set fire to my stable.'

'You may not have known it before, sir, but you know it now.'

I silently nodded.

'Give us a name, sir.'

'I don't think I can. But it isn't the first thing that's happened.' I told them about Hearse Puller, and about my loose two-year-old, and he asked immediately why I hadn't reported these things to the police.

'I did report the Ascot incident,' I said, thanking Kerry's indignation. 'And as for the horse . . . some of your men came here after the accident, but I didn't think then that the horse had deliberately been let loose, I thought I'd just been careless.'

As they had thought the same thing they could hardly quarrel with that. The Chief Inspector also knew perfectly well that they wouldn't have called out the reserves if I'd turned up with the unbuckled rug.

'Well, sir,' he said. 'It seems you were lucky this time. We have a witness. A fourteen-year-old boy who'd been up in the woods at the end of your lane. He was going home. He says he saw what he saw from the lane, but I reckon he'd come here to help himself to what was lying around loose. He says he knew you were away in Newmarket. Anyway, he said he saw a man go into the store-room in the stable block and he heard him making metallic noises in there, and thought it odd that whoever it was had not switched the lights on. He seems to know his way round your stables pretty well. He saw the man strike a match and bend down. Then the man came out of the stable and hurried away along the lane to the village. The boy didn't try to intercept him, but went to the store-room and switched on the light.'

The Chief Inspector paused, with a fine sense of theatre. His riveted audience waited impatiently for him to get on with it.

'He took one look and retreated without delay. He says the pipe from the oil storage tank at the back of the stove was broken and the oil was coming out onto the floor. Standing in the pool of oil was a cardboard box, and on that there was a large firework. A golden shower, he says. He observed that the touch paper was red and smoking. He did not advance into the store-room, he says, because in his opinion anyone who had done so would have needed his brains examined, that is if his brains hadn't been burning with the rest of him.'

Sophie laughed at this verbatim bit of reporting. The Chief Inspector permitted himself the smallest of smiles.

'Anyway, sir, it seems he then made best speed down the village to tell his mum to call the Fire Brigade, which, once he had convinced her, she did. When the firemen arrived here the oil tank had exploded and the stables, being built internally largely of wood, were hopelessly alight. The firemen say that if they had arrived much later they could not have saved the house.'

He smiled lopsidedly. 'They usually ruin what they only just save.'

'The house is fine,' I said.

'Good. Now what young Kenneth saw is not evidence that you didn't set the whole thing up yourself. People often arrange to have fires start while they themselves have an unbreakable alibi.'

Sophie started to protest. The Chief Inspector gave her an amused glance, and she stopped abruptly.

'All right, miss. This time it's different. This time we know a bit more. Young Kenneth gave us a description of the man he saw.'

'But it was dark,' I said.

'Something about the man was very distinctive. Apart from that, we found the car he came in. After everyone had gone home last night there were two cars left in the village street. One was yours. One was a Zodiac station wagon, and the man Kenneth had seen here was reported as having been observed trying to start it, failing to do so, kicking its wheels in disgust, and walking towards the main road, presumably to thumb a lift. Upon examining the station wagon we found two things. One was that the starter motor had jammed and that was why it would not start. The other was that the number plates did not coincide with the number written on the licence. We checked the licence. The car belongs to a Mr Leonard Williamson who says a young fellow took it away from him. He was asked if he knew the young fellow's name and eventually he said he did. The young fellow was a Mr Frederick Smith. We went to the home of Mr Frederick Smith and invited him to come down here and help with our inquiries.'

'Or in other words,' I said smiling, 'Leonard Williamson shopped Fred Smith who is now swearing blue murder in one of your cells.'

The Chief Inspector said primly, 'We would like you to come and see if you know him.'

* * *

It was Frizzy Hair.

He looked hard, arrogant and unrepentant. The taunting smile he gave his victims had become a taunting sneer for his captors, and the way he sprawled on a chair with his legs spread wide was a statement of defiance.

You could see at once why young Kenneth had been able to describe him. On his left arm from biceps to knuckles he wore a large white plaster cast.

He stared boldly at me without recognition.

'Hello, lover boy,' I said.

The Chief Inspector looked at me sharply.

'So you do know him.'

'Yes. He attacked me at Ascot.'

'I never.'

'Mrs Kerry Sanders saw you.'

He blinked. Remembered. Narrowed his eyes with a snap and gave me a look that would have done credit to a crocodile.

'You broke my bleeding elbow.'

'I never,' I said.

'I hear your stable burnt,' he said viciously. 'Pity you weren't in it.'

The Chief Inspector drew me back to his office.

'He's got form as long as your arm,' he said cheerfully. 'Well known on his own patch, is Fred Smith.'

'Someone's paying him,' I said.

'Oh yes. But we've no chance of him telling us who it is. He's hard as nails. The Fred Smiths of this world never grass.' He sounded as if he admired him for it. 'He'll do his time, but he'll tell us nothing.'

Sophie came with me to see Crispin, who was sick and sorry for himself in the local hospital. His skin was pallid and sweaty, he coughed with a hand pressed to his chest, and his eyes showed that the gin level had ebbed as far as maximum agony. Like an axe chopping his brain, he'd once described it.

The first thing he said when he saw us was, 'Give me a bloody drink. They won't give me a bloody drink.'

I produced a small bottle of orange juice. He stared at it balefully.

'You know what I bloody mean.'

'Yes,' I said. 'Vitamin C. Marvellous for hangovers.' I poured the orange juice into a glass and gave it to him. A nurse watched approvingly from across the room. Crispin sniffed it crossly, tasted it, and drank the lot. He lay back against his pillows and closed the swimmy eyes.

'Bloody orange juice,' he said.

He lay for a minute or two as if asleep, but then with his eyes still shut said, 'I hear you saved my bloody life.'

'Not exactly.'

'Near enough . . . Don't expect me to be grateful.'

'No.'

Another long pause. 'Come and fetch me tomorrow morning,' he said. 'About noon, they said.'

'All right.'

'As for now, you can bugger off.'

Sophie walked away with me down the ward with her disgust escaping like steam.

'Why on earth do you put up with him?'

'He's my brother.'

'You could kick him out.'

'Would you?'

She didn't answer. When it came to the point, one couldn't.

I thought of him lying there in his acute self-made misery, a lonely, defeated man in a private hell. He'd had girlfriends once but not any more. There was no one except me between him and the gutter, and I knew he relied on me as if I'd been a solid wall.

'Isn't there any cure?' Sophie said.

'Oh yes. One certain cure. The only one.'

'What is it?'

'Wanting to be cured.'

She looked at me dubiously. 'Does that make sense?'

'He would automatically be cured if his urge to be cured was stronger than his urge to drink.'

'But sometimes it is,' she said. 'You said he sometimes doesn't drink for weeks.'

I shook my head. 'He always means to drink again. He just postpones it, like a child saving its sweets.'

We collected my car and drove off towards the ill-smelling cinders.

'I thought it was a disease,' she said.

'An addiction. Like football.'

'You've been at the nonsense again.'

'Under the influence of football,' I said, 'you can tear railway carriages apart and stampede people to death.'

'More people die of alcohol,' she protested.

'I expect you're right.'

'You're having me on.'

I grinned.

'I thought there was a drug that could cure it,' she said.

'You mean antabuse?'

'What's that?'

'Some stuff which makes alcohol taste disgusting. Sure, it works. But you've got to want to stop drinking in the first place, otherwise you don't take it.'

'Crispin won't?'

I nodded. 'You're so right. Crispin won't.'

'How about Alcoholics Anonymous?' she asked.

'Same thing,' I said. 'If you want to stop drinking, they're marvellous. If you don't, you keep away from them.'

'I never thought about it like that.'

'Lucky old you.'

'Pig.'

We went a mile or so in companionable silence.

'All the same,' she said, 'I've always been told it was an illness. That you couldn't help it. That one drink sets off a sort of chain reaction.'

'It isn't the one drink. It's the wanting to drink. Alcoholism is in the mind.'

'And in the legs.'

I laughed. 'OK, it invades the body. In fact the bodies of

ultra-persistent alcoholics become so adjusted chemically to the irrigation that a sudden cut-off in the supply can cause epileptic fits.'

'Not . . . in Crispin?'

'No. Not so bad. But when he says he needs a bloody drink . . . he needs it.'

Which was why the drink I'd given him had been only half orange juice and the other half gin.

We stood in the yard for a while with the last of daylight fading over the cooling embers of the stables.

'What are you thinking?' Sophie said.

'Oh . . . That I'd like to break Fred Smith's other elbow. Also his knees, toes, ankles and neck.'

'In that order,' she said, nodding.

I laughed, but the inner anger remained. This time the assault had been too much. This had gone beyond a skirmish to a major act of war. If Pauli Teksa were by any chance right and Vic or someone besides him were trying to frighten me off the scene they were having the opposite effect. Far from persuading me to go along with Vic's schemes they had killed the tolerance with which I had always regarded them. In my own way I could be as bloodyminded as frizzy Fred Smith. Vic was going to wish he had left me alone.

I turned away from the ruins. I would rebuild what had been lost. Soon, and better, I thought.

'Where are you planning to sleep?' Sophie asked.

I looked at her in the dusk. Smooth silver hair. Calm sky-reflecting eyes. Nothing but friendly interest.

Where I was planning to sleep was going to need more welcome than that.

'Could I borrow your sofa?' I said.

A pause.

'It's not long enough,' she said.

Another pause. I looked at her and waited.

A smile crept in around her eyes.

'Oh, all right. You gave me your bed . . . I'll give you mine.'

'With you in it?'

'I don't suppose you burned your bedroom just to get there?' she asked.

'I wish I could say yes.'

'You look smug enough as it is,' she said.

We drove sedately to Esher, she in her car, me in mine. We ate a sedate dinner out of her freezer, and watched a sedate old movie on her box.

She was also in a way sedate in bed. The inner composure persisted. She seemed to raise a mental eyebrow in amusement at the antics humans got up to. She was quiet, and passive.

On the other hand she left me in no doubt that I gave her pleasure; and what I gave, I got.

It was an intense, gentle love making. A matter of small movements, not gymnastics. Of exquisite lingering sensations. And done, on her part also, without reservation.

She lay afterwards with her head on my shoulder.

She said, 'I can't stay here till morning.'

'Why not?'

'Have to be at Heathrow on duty by six o'clock.'

'Fine time to say so.'

I could feel her smile. 'Better than ten minutes ago.'

I laughed in my nose. 'The off-put of the century.'

She rubbed her hand lazily over my chest. 'I'll think of this when I'm up in the tower.'

'You'll knit the approaches.'

'No.' She kissed my skin. 'I'm on departures. I tell them when to take off.'

'When?'

'And where. But not what.'

I smiled. Shut my eyes in the warm dark.

'You don't take your strap off even for love making,' she said, running her fingers along inside the soft crepe bandage I slept in.

'Especially,' I said. 'Very high risk activity for dislocating shoulders.'

'You speak from experience?'
'You might say so.'
'Serve you right.'
We slid slowly, contentedly, to sleep.

11

At Ascot Sales on Wednesday Vic and his pals closed their ranks when they saw me coming, and moved in my direction in a body.

I met them halfway. Like something out of High Noon, I thought frivolously. All we lacked were the Sheriff's badge and the guns.

'I warned you,' Vic said.

They all stared at me. I looked at them one by one. Vic all open aggression, the rest in various shades from satisfied spite to a trace of uneasiness.

'People who play with fire get burnt,' I said.

Vic said, 'We didn't do it.'

'Quite right. Fred Smith did. And he's not telling who paid him. But you and I know, don't we Vic?'

He looked extraordinarily startled. '*You* know?' he exclaimed. 'You couldn't.' He considered it and shook his head. 'You don't.'

'But *you* know,' I said slowly. 'And if it isn't you . . . who is it?'

Vic gave a fair imitation of a clam.

'You just do as we tell you and nothing else will happen,' he said.

'You've got your psychology all wrong,' I said. 'You bash me, I'll bash back.'

Jiminy Bell said to Vic 'I told you so.'

Vic gave him a reptilian glance. Jiminy was a great one for losing friends and not influencing people.

Ronnie North stood on one side of their battalion commander and the carrot-headed Fynedale on the other. Neither of them looked either impressed or worried about my vaguely stated intentions.

'How about a truce?' I suggested. 'You leave me entirely alone, and I'll leave you.'

Six upper lips curled in unison.

'You can't do a damn thing,' Vic said.

I bought four horses for various clients uninfected by Vic, and went home. Crispin, morosely sober, had spent the day watching a demolition gang shift the burnt rubble of the stables into lorries. The stale smell persisted, and the air was full of dust and fine ash, but the hard concrete foundations had been cleared and cleaned in some places and looked like the first outlines of the future.

He was sitting in the office drinking fizzy lemonade in front of a television programme for children. Two days had seen rapid action by the electricity people, who had insulated all burnt-through wires and restored the current, and by the Post Office, who had reconnected me with the outer world. With help from the village I had cleaned up the office and the kitchen and borrowed dry beds, and even if the house was partly roofed by tarpaulin and as sodden as an Irish bog, it was still where I lived.

'About twenty people telephoned,' Crispin said. 'I've had a bloody awful day answering the damn thing.'

'Did you take messages?'

'Couldn't be bothered. Told them to ring again this evening.'

'Have you eaten anything?'

'Someone brought you an apple pie from the village,' he said. 'I ate that.'

I sat down at the desk to make a start on the ever-present paperwork.

'Get me some lemonade?' I asked.

'Get it yourself.'

I didn't, and presently with an ostentatious sigh he went out to the kitchen and fetched some. The thin, synthetic fizz at least took away the taste of brick dust and cinders, though as usual I wished someone would invent a soft drink with a flavour of dry white wine. A great pity all soft drinks were sweet.

During the evening apart from answering the postponed inquiries and finalizing various sales I made three more personal calls.

One was to the breeder of the Transporter colt which Vic had bought for thirty thousand and let go to Wilton Young for seventy-five.

One was to Nicol Brevett. And one to Wilton Young himself.

As a result of these the breeder met Nicol the next day in Gloucester, and on the Friday morning I drove them both to see the mail order tycoon in Yorkshire.

The row between Wilton Young and his carrot-headed agent at Doncaster races that Saturday could be heard from Glasgow to The Wash. Along with everyone else I listened avidly and with more than general satisfaction.

Wilton Young had not wanted to believe he had been made a fool of. What man would? I was wrong, he said. His agent Fynedale would never conspire with Vic Vincent to drive the price of a colt up by thousands so that he, Wilton Young, would shell out, while they, the manipulators, split the lolly between them.

I hadn't said much at the interview. I'd left it all to the breeder. The furious indignation he'd been exploding with at Newmarket had deepened into a bitter consuming resentment, and he had pounced like a starving cat on the opportunity of doing Vic a lot of no good.

Nicol himself had been astounded and angry on his father's behalf and had sat next to me all the way to Yorkshire saying he couldn't believe it at regular intervals. I was sure Nicol's surprise was genuine but I privately doubted whether Constantine's would be. Nicol's father was quite subtle enough to make Wilton Young pay and pay and pay for the privilege of outbidding a Brevett. That was, of course, if his pride would allow so private a victory, and on that point I was in a fog.

Wilton Young and Fynedale stood on the grass in front of the weighing room shouting at each other as if oblivious of the fascinated audience of five thousand. Wilton Young attacked like a tough little terrier and Fynedale's temper burned as flaming bright as his hair. One or two Stewards hovered on the perimeter looking nervous about the outcome and the jockeys on their way out to the first race went past with smiles like water-melon slices.

'... Bare-faced bloody fraud,' Wilton Young was shouting, the Yorkshire accent thick and blunt. 'I tell thee straight, no one makes a bloody monkey out of me and gets away with it. You don't buy no more horses for me, I tell thee straight. And I want back from you every penny you've swindled out of me these past two years.'

'You've no bloody chance,' scoffed Fynedale, driving nails into his own coffin with the recklessness of all hotheads. 'You paid a fair price for those horses and if you don't like it you can bloody lump it.'

'A fair price to you and that damned Vic Vincent is every penny you can screw out of people who trust you. All right, I've been a right bloody fool, but that's all finished, I tell you straight.' He stabbed the air with his forefinger, emphasizing every angry word. 'I'll sue you for that money, see if I don't.'

'Don't bother. Tha'll not win.'

'Enough mud'll stick on you to save any other mugs wasting their brass. I tell thee straight, mister, by the time I've finished every single person in this country is going to know they pay through the bloody nose for every horse you buy them.'

'I'll bloody sue you for libel,' Fynedale yelled.

'And it'll be bloody worth it.'

'I'll take you for millions,' Fynedale screamed, almost jumping up and down with fury.

'You do already.'

The row hotted up in noise level and degenerated to straight abuse, and when the race began the unprintable insults rose in volume above the commentary. Along with many others I was chuckling so much I couldn't hold my race glasses still enough to watch the distant runners. Nicol, standing beside me, had tears running down his cheeks.

'Oh my God,' he said, gasping for breath. 'What is a fat-arsed hyena-faced blood-sucking son of a sodding bitch?'

'A mongrel,' I said.

'Oh don't. It hurts.' He pressed a hand to his heaving ribs. 'It's too much.'

Even after the main row was over little eddies of it persisted all afternoon, both Wilton Young and Fynedale separately being anxious to air their grievances loudly to all who would listen. Wilton Young's forefinger stabbed the air as if he were poking holes in it and Fynedale's voice took on a defensive whine. I kept away from them for most of the time but before the end they both came looking for me.

Wilton Young said, 'Like a bloody piece of quick-silver, you are. I keep seeing you in the distance and then when I go that way you've disappeared.'

'Sorry,' I said.

'You were right and I was wrong. There you are then.' He made a large gesture of magnanimity, letting me know how generous he thought himself to be making such an admission. 'The little tyke was swindling me. Like you said. All legal-like, mind. I've been told this afternoon I won't have a chance of getting anything back.'

'No,' I said.

'Cut your losses, that's what I always say. Any line in my mail order business that's not pulling its weight, I scrap it. Same with employees, see?'

'I see.'

'You don't approve. I can see it in your face. You're soft, lad, you'll never get anywhere.'

'Depends where you want to go,' I said.

He stared, then laughed. 'Right, then. You go to the sales next week and buy me a horse. Any horse you think is good. Then we'll see.'

'Good for what?'

'A fair return for outlay.'

'In cash terms?'

'Naturally in cash terms. What else is there?'

If he didn't know, I couldn't tell him.

'I wasn't born in Yorkshire,' I said.

'What the hell has that got to do with it?'

'You only employ Yorkshiremen.'

'And look where it bloody got me. No, lad, you buy me a good horse and I'll overlook you being born in the wrong place.'

Nicol drifted near and Wilton Young gave him a stare suitable for the son of his dearest enemy, even if the two of them had the common bond of victims.

'Another thing you can do for me,' Wilton Young said to me,

stabbing the inoffensive air. 'Find me a way of taking that effing Fynedale for every penny he screwed out of me. I tell thee straight, I'll not rest till I'm satisfied.'

I hesitated, but I'd already gone a long way down the road. I said slowly, 'I do know . . .'

He seized on it. 'What? What do you know?'

'Well . . .' I said. 'You remember those three horses you sent out to race in South Africa?'

'Damned waste of good money. They had useful form here, but they never did any good in Durban. The climate was all wrong. And of course they couldn't come back because of the quarantine laws.'

'One died soon after it arrived in South Africa,' I said. 'And the other two never saw a racecourse.'

He was surprised. 'How the hell do you know?'

'They went by sea,' I said.

'They didn't then,' he interrupted positively. 'They went by air. Had a bad flight, by all accounts.'

'They went by sea,' I said. 'I sent two horses out there, and they went on the same boat. I sent a groom with mine, and quantities of food. Your three travelled alone for three weeks with no one to look after them. They were shipped with a total of half a ton of hay, and not even good hay at that. No oats, bran, or horse cubes. Just a starvation ration of poor hay, and no one to see that they even got that. The man I sent looked after them as best he could and gave them enough of my food to keep them alive, but when they reached Durban they were in such a poor state that they were almost not allowed into the country.'

He listened in disbelief. 'I sent them by air,' he repeated.

'You thought you did. I read in the *Sporting Life* that they'd flown out to Durban. But when my man came back, he told me what had really happened.'

'But I paid for air . . . I paid more than four thousand quid.'

'And who did you pay?'

'By God.' He looked murderous. 'I'll screw him to the wall, I tell thee straight.'

'Get a lawyer to do it,' I said. 'I'll tell him which ship it was, and give him the name and address of the groom I sent.'

'By God, I will,' he said. He turned on his heel and hurried off as if going to do it there and then.

Nicol said, 'When you start a fire you do it properly.'

'They shouldn't have burned my stable.'

'No,' he said. 'That was a bad mistake.'

Fynedale's anger was in a different category altogether. He caught me fiercely by the arm outside the weighing room and his face made me determine to stay in well-lit, populated places.

'I'll kill you,' he said.

'You could have had a truce,' I said.

'Vic will kill you.'

It sounded ridiculous. Fynedale might do at a pinch, but Vic wasn't the killing sort.

'Don't be silly,' I said. 'You two can't even light your own fires. And Fred Smith won't kill me for you, he's in clink.'

'Someone else will.'

'Jiminy Bell?' I suggested. 'Ronnie North? You're all good at using threats but you need a Fred Smith to carry them out. And Fred Smiths don't grow on trees.'

'We keep telling you,' he said fiercely. 'We didn't pay Fred Smith. We didn't tell him to burn your yard. We didn't.'

'Who did?'

'Vic did. No . . . Vic didn't.'

'Sort it out.'

'Vic reported that you wouldn't play ball. He said you needed a bloody good lesson.'

'Reported to who?'

'How do I know?'

'You ought to find out. Look where he's got you. Out of a cushy job with Wilton Young and into a nasty prosecution for fraud. You're a bloody fool to let someone you don't know get you into such a mess.'

'*You* got me into the mess,' he yelled.

'You bash me, I bash back.'

The message at last got through, and the result on him was the same as it had been on me. Aggression created counter-aggression. The way full-scale wars started. He expressed no sorrow.

Made no apologies. No offer of amends. Instead he said again and with increased intention, 'I'll kill you.'

Nicol said, 'What are you going to do next?'

'Pork pie and a bottle of coke.'

'No, you ass. I mean . . . about Vic.'

'Stoke up his kitchen fire.' Nicol looked mystified. I said, 'He told me once if I didn't like the heat . . .'

'To stay out of the kitchen.'

'Right.'

The cold, dank winter afternoon seeped under my anorak and my feet were freezing. Nicol's face looked pale blue. A little kitchen heat would have come as no harm.

'How?'

'Not sure yet.'

It had been comparatively easy to break up the entente between Wilton Young and Fynedale, for the two hot-headed Yorkshire tempers had needed only a small detonation to set them off. Detaching Constantine from Vic might take longer. Constantine was not as bluntly honest as Wilton Young, and in his case face-saving might have priority.

'There's also someone else,' I said.

'Who?'

'Don't know. Someone helping Vic. Someone who engaged Fred Smith to do the dirty work. I don't know who . . . but I won't stop until I find out.'

Nicol looked at me speculatively. 'If he could see the look on your face he'd be busy covering his tracks.'

The trouble was, his tracks were far too well covered already. To find him, I'd have to persuade him to make fresh ones. We went into the snack bar for the warmth as much as the food and watched the fifth race on closed-circuit television.

Nicol said, 'Do you know of any other fiddles Vic and Fynedale have got up to?'

I smiled. 'One or two.'

'What?'

'Well . . . there's the insurance premium fiddle.'

'What's that?'

'I shouldn't be telling you.'

'Things have changed. You don't owe them a scrap of loyalty any more.'

I wryly agreed. 'Well . . . Say you sell a horse to an overseas customer. You tell him you can arrange insurance for the journey if he sends the premiums. So he sends the premiums, and you pocket them.'

'Just like that?'

'Just like that.'

'But what happens if the horse dies on the way? Surely you have to pay up out of your own money?'

I shook my head. 'You say you were very sorry you couldn't arrange the insurance in time, and you send the premiums back.'

'By God.'

'By the time you've finished you should be more clued up than your father,' I said with amusement.

'I should damn well hope so. Vic's been taking him for one almighty ride.'

'*Caveat emptor*,' I said.

'What does that mean?'

'Buyer beware.'

'I know one buyer who'll beware for the rest of his life, and that's me.'

The next week at the Newmarket Mixed Sales I bought a two-year-old colt for Wilton Young.

He was there himself.

'Why that one?' he demanded. 'I've looked him up. He's run in three races and never been nearer than sixth.'

'He'll win next year as a three-year-old.'

'How do you know?'

'Scorchmark's progeny need time to grow. It's no good being impatient if they don't win at two. He's being sold by an impatient owner and he's been trained by a two-year-old specialist. They both wanted quick results, and Singeling wasn't bred for that. Next summer he'll win.'

'He didn't cost very much,' he said disparagingly.

'All the better. One good prize and he'll be making you that profit.'

He grunted. 'All right. I said buy me a horse, and you've bought it. I won't go back on my word. But I don't think that Singeling is any bloody good.'

Owing to the natural loudness of his voice this opinion was easily overheard, and a little while later he sold Singeling himself to someone who disagreed with him.

With typical bluntness he told me about it. 'He offered me a good bit more than you paid. So I took it. I didn't reckon he'd be much good, that Singeling. Now, what do you have to say to that?'

'Nothing,' I said mildly. 'You asked me to buy you a horse which would give you a good return in cash terms. Well . . . it has.'

He stared. He slapped his thigh. He laughed. Then a new thought struck him and he looked suddenly suspicious. 'Did you find another buyer and send him to offer me a profit?'

'No,' I said, and reflected that at least he seemed to be learning.

'I'll tell you something,' he said grudgingly. 'This chap I sold it to . . . when we'd shaken hands on it and it was too late for me to back out, he said . . . I tell thee straight . . . he said any horse Jonah Dereham picked as a good prospect was good enough for him.'

'Flattering,' I said.

'Ay.' He pursed his mouth and screwed up his eyes. 'Maybe I was too hasty, getting rid of that Singeling. I reckon you'd better buy me another one, and I'll keep it, even if it's got three legs and a squint.'

'You positively ask to be cheated,' I said.

'You won't cheat me.'

'How do you know?'

He looked nonplussed. Waved his arm about. 'Everybody knows,' he said.

Vic was not his confident, cheerful self. He spent a great deal of his time drawing people into corners and talking to them vehemently, and in due course I learned that he was saying I was so desperate for clients I was telling outright lies about sincere men like Fynedale, and that I had a fixed obsession that he, Vic Vincent, had set fire to my stables, which was mad as well as wicked because the police had arrested the man who had really done it. I supposed the extent to which people believed his version was a matter of habit: his devotees never doubted him, or if they did they kept it to themselves.

Vic and Pauli Teksa stood alone together on the far side of the collecting ring, with Vic's tongue working overtime. Pauli shook his head. Vic spoke faster than ever. Pauli shook his head again.

Vic looked around him as if to make sure he was not being overheard, then advanced his head to within three inches of Pauli's, his red-brown forward-growing hair almost mingling with Pauli's crinkly black.

Pauli listened for quite a while. Then he drew back and stood with his head on one side, considering, while Vic talked some more. Then slowly again he shook his head.

Vic was not pleased. The two men began to walk towards the sale building: or rather Pauli began to walk and Vic, unsuccessfully trying to stop him, had either to let him go or go with him. He went, still talking, persuading, protesting.

I was standing between them and the sale building. They saw me from four paces away, and stopped. Vic looked as lividly angry as I'd ever seen him, Pauli as expressionless as a concrete block.

Vic gave Pauli a final furious look and strode away.

Pauli said, 'I plan to go home tomorrow.'

There were some big American sales the next week. I said, 'You've been here a month, I suppose . . .'

'Nearer five weeks.'

'Has it been a successful trip?'

He smiled ruefully. 'Not very.'

We went together for a cup of coffee, but he seemed preoccupied.

'I'd sure like to have bought a colt by Transporter,' he said.

'There'll be another crop next year.'

'Yeah . . .'

He said nothing more about me going along with the crowd, with conforming unless I got hurt. What he did say, though, with his mind clearly on his recent encounter, was, 'You don't want to stir up that Vic Vincent more than you can help.'

I smiled.

He looked at the smile and read it right. He shook his head.

'He's an angry man, and angry men are dangerous.'

'That makes two of us,' I said.

He soberly consulted his stock of inner wisdom and came up with a cliché. 'It's easier to start something than to stop it.'

12

Wilton Young came to the following Doncaster Sales not to buy but to see some of his horses-in-training sold. Cutting his losses, he said. Weeding out all those who'd eaten more during the just-ended flat season than they'd earned. He slapped me jovially on the back and told me straight that slow horses ate as much as fast, and he, Wilton Young, was no meal ticket for flops.

'Profit, lad,' he boomed. 'That's what it's all about. Brass, lad. Brass.'

I bought one of his cast-offs, a three-year-old colt with little form and a reputation for kicking visitors out of his box. I got him cheap for a Sussex farmer who couldn't afford more.

His ex-owner said disparagingly, 'What did you buy that for? It's no bloody good. If that's what you buy, what the hell will you buy for me?'

I explained about the poorish farmer. 'He'll geld it and hack it about the farm. Teach it to jump. Make it a four-year-old novice hurdler by April.'

'Huh.'

Second-rate jumpers were of less account than marbles to self-made tycoons with cheque books open for Derby prospects. I realized that whatever his fury against Fynedale he was still expecting to pay large sums for his horses. Perhaps he needed to. Perhaps he felt a reflected glory in their expense. Perhaps he wanted to prove to the world how much brass he'd made. Conspicuous consumption, no less.

Which meant that to please him best I would have to buy an obviously good horse at a shade above what I thought it worth. Given a bargain like Singeling he had rid himself of it within an hour, and for all his twinge of regret afterwards he would be likely to do the same again. Accordingly I picked out the pride of the sale, a two-year-old with near-classic expectations, and asked if he would like it.

'Ay,' he said. 'If it's the best, I would.'

'It'll fetch at least twenty thousand,' I said. 'How far do you want me to go?'

'It's your job. You do it.'

I got it for twenty-six, and he was delighted.

Fynedale was not.

From across the ring his eyes looked like stark black holes in his chalk-white face. The carrot hair on top flamed like a burning bush. The hate vibrated in him so visibly that if I could have seen his aura it would have been bright red.

Constantine had brought Kerry to the Friday sales, although the chief purpose of their journey to Yorkshire was to see Nicol try out River God in Saturday's novice chase.

Constantine was saying authoritatively to whomever would listen that keeping a large string of horses in training was becoming impossibly expensive these days, and that he thought it a prudent time to retrench. Only fools, he intimated, were still ready to buy at the inflated prices of recent months.

I saw Vic Vincent go across to greet them when they came. Amicable handshakes. Smiles with teeth. A good deal of window dressing to establish that whatever some people might think of their agents, Constantine was satisfied with his.

Nicol came and leaned beside me on the rail of the collecting ring.

'I told him,' he said. 'I said Vic had been rooking him of thousands. Vic and Fynedale, pushing up the prices and splitting the proceeds.'

'What happened?'

He looked puzzled. 'Nothing. He didn't say much at all. I got the impression . . . I know it's silly . . . but I got the impression he already knew.'

'He's nobody's fool,' I said.

'No . . . but if he knew, why did he let Vic get away with it?'

'Ask him.'

'I did. He simply didn't answer. I said I supposed he would ditch him now and he said I supposed wrong. Vic could pick horses better than any other single agent, he said, and he had no intention of cutting himself off from his advice.'

We watched the merchandise walk round the collecting ring. Nothing in the current bunch looked worth the outlay.

Nicol said gloomily, 'They think I'm a traitor for listening to you at all. You're absolutely *persona non grata* with my parent.'

Predictable. If Constantine wasn't going to admit he'd been swindled, he wouldn't exactly fall on the neck of the person who'd publicly pointed it out.

'Is he really cutting down on his string?' I asked.

'Heaven knows. He's not noticeably short of the next quid, though some big deal or other fell through the other day, which irritated him more than somewhat.' He gave me a quick sideways sardonic glance. 'My new step-mama will be able to maintain us in the style to which we are accustomed.'

'Why don't you turn professional?' I asked with mild reproof. 'You're good enough.'

I had, it seemed, touched him on a jumpy nerve. He said angrily, 'Are you trying to tell me I should earn my own living?'

'Not really my business.'

'Then keep your trap shut.'

He shifted abruptly off the rail and walked away. I didn't watch him go. A minutel ater he came back.

'You sod,' he said.

'I try.'

'You bloody well succeed.'

He hunched his shoulders inside his sheepskin coat. 'Professional jockeys aren't allowed to own horses in training,' he said.

'Nothing to stop them running in your father's name.'

'Shut up,' he said. 'Just shut up.'

I shut.

I came face to face with Vic by accident, he coming out of the sale building, I going in. He was moderately triumphant.

'You've got nowhere,' he said.

'Because you'll soon find another stooge to replace Fynedale?'

His mouth compressed. 'I'm admitting nothing.'

'How wise.'

He gave me a furious look and stalked away. He'd said nothing this time about me toeing the line or else. Perhaps because with Fynedale out of action there was no effective line to toe. Perhaps the or else campaign was temporarily in abeyance. Nothing in his manner persuaded me it was over for ever.

Having Wilton Young for a client positively galvanized my business. During that one Friday I received as many inquiries and definite commissions as in any past whole month, mostly from Northern trainers with bustling would-be owners who like Wilton Young had made their own brass.

As one trainer for whom I'd ridden in the past put it, 'They know eff-all about horses but the money's burning their fingers. All they want is to be sure they're getting the best possible. That they're not being done. Get me ten good two-year-olds and I'll see you right.'

Both Vic and Fynedale noticed the constant stream of new clients and the swelling of my order book: they would have to have been blind not to. The effect on them was the reverse of joyful. Vic's face grew redder and Fynedale's whiter and as time wore on neither of them was capable of ordinary social conversation.

Finally it worried me. All very well prospering in front of their eyes, but when success could breed envy even in friends, in enemies it could raise spite of Himalayan proportions. Several of my new customers had transferred from Fynedale and one or two from Vic, and if I'd wanted a perfect revenge, I'd got it: but revenge was a tree with sour fruit.

Between Vic and Fynedale themselves things were no better. Under Constantine's faithful umbrella Vic had disowned his former lieutenant and had been heard to say that if he had realized what Fynedale was up to he would of course have had nothing to do with it. Antonia Huntercombe and the breeder of the Transporter colt would have been interested.

Probably the fact that Fynedale had two directions for hatred exhausted him to immobility. He stood about looking dazed, in a trance, as if Vic's perfidy had stunned him. He shouldn't have been so surprised, I thought. Vic always lied easily. Always had. And had always had the gift of the good liar, that people believed him.

On the Saturday afternoon River God won the novice chase by a short head thanks entirely to Nicol's riding. I watched the triumphant unsaddling party afterwards and noted that Vic was there too, oozing bonhomie in Nicol's direction and being very man-of-the-world with Constantine. His big, boyish face was back to its good-natured looking normal, the manner easy again, and confident. Kerry Sanders patted his arm and Constantine's heavy black spectacles turned repeatedly in his direction.

All sweetness and light, I thought uncharitably. Vic would always bounce back like a rubber ball.

From habit I went to watch the next race from the jockeys' box, and Nicol climbed the steps to my side.

'Well done,' I said.

'Thanks.'

The runners came out into the course and jauntily ambled down in front of the stands. Eight or nine, some of them horses I'd once ridden. I felt the usual tug of regret, of nostalgia. I wouldn't entirely get over it, I thought, until there was a completely new generation of horses. While my old partners were still running, I wanted to be on them.

Nicol said with surprised discovery, 'You wish you were still riding!'

I mentally shook myself. It was no good looking back. 'It's finished,' I said.

'No more crashing falls. No more booing crowds. No more bloody-minded trainers telling you you rode a stinking race and engaging a different jockey next time.'

'That's right.'

He smiled his quick smile. 'Who'd wish it on a dog?'

The runners assembled, the tapes flew up, the race went away. They were experienced hurdlers, crafty and fast, flicking over the low obstacles without altering their stride. Even though I dealt mostly with young stock for the Flat, I still liked watching jumpers best.

'If I suggested to Father I would be a pro, he'd have a fit.'

'Particularly,' I said, 'if you mentioned me in connection.'

'God, yes.'

The runners went down the far side and we lifted race-glasses to watch.

'Vic looks happy today,' I said.

Nicol snorted. 'Father told him to go to the States after Christmas and buy Kerry some colt called Phoenix Fledgling.'

'With her money?'

'Why?'

'He was saying yesterday he was cutting down. So today he has a hundred thousand quid lying about loose?'

'So much?' He was surprised.

'It could be even more.'

'Would Father know?' Nicol asked doubtfully.

'Vic would,' I said.

Nicol shook his head. 'I don't know what they're up to. Thick as thieves again today.'

The runners turned into the straight. Positions changed. The favourite came through and won smoothly, the jockey collected, expert, and totally professional.

Nicol turned to me abruptly.

'If I could ride like *that*, I'd take out a licence.'

'You can.'

He stared. Shook his head.

'You do,' I said.

Crispin had been sober since the fire. Sober and depressed.

'My life's a mess,' he said.

As usual during these periods he sat every night in my office while I got through the paperwork and did the inevitable telephoning.

'I'm going to get a job.'

We both knew that he wouldn't. Those he wanted, he couldn't keep. Those he could keep, he despised.

'You can have one here,' I said. 'At this rate, I'll have to get help with the paperwork. I can't cope with it all.'

'I'm not a bloody typist,' he said scornfully.

'You can't type.'

'We all know I'm absolutely useless. No need to rub it in.'

'You can keep the accounts, though. You know all about figures.'

He thought it over. Unreliable he might be, but not untrained. If he wanted to he could take over the financial half of the office load and do it well.

'I'll see,' he said.

Outside in the yard the demolition work was nearly finished. Plans for the new stables lay on my desk, drawn up at high speed by a local architect from the scribbled dimensions I'd given him. Depending on the time it took the Council to pass them, I'd be open for business again by the summer.

The rebuilding of the roof of the house was due to be started the following week. Rewiring from stem to stern had to be done after that, and there were several fallen ceilings to be replastered. Despite day and night oil heaters astronomicalizing my fuel bills in every room, the damp and the damp smell persisted. Repainting lay a long way ahead. It would take almost a year, I reckoned, to restore in full what had been done to intimidate me.

Vic had not seen the damage he'd caused and maybe he could put it comfortably out of his mind, but I came home to it night after night. He might forget, but he had made sure that I didn't.

Sophie had had two weeks of night shift, telling departing freight flights where to get off.

'What are you doing tomorrow?' she asked on the telephone.

'Day or night?'

'Day.'

'Damn.'

She laughed. 'What's wrong with the day?'

'Apart from anything else . . . I have to go to Ascot Sales.'

'Oh.' A pause. 'Couldn't I come with you?'

'If you don't mind me working.'

'I'd love it. See all the little crooks doing the dirty. And Vic Vincent . . . will I see him?'

'I'm not taking you,' I said.

'I won't bite him.'

'Can't risk it.'

'I promise.'

When I picked her up at nine she was still yawning from five hours' sleep and a system geared to waking at noon. She opened her door in jeans, sweater, toast and honey.

'Come in.' She gave me a slightly sticky, sweet-tasting kiss. 'Coffee?'

She poured two cups in her tiny kitchen. Bright sunshine sliced through the window, giving a misleading report of the freezing day outside, where the north-west wind was doing its Arctic damnedest.

'You'll need warm boots,' I said. 'And sixteen layers of insulation. Also a nose muff or two and some frostbite cream.'

'Think I'll stay at home and curl up with a good television programme.'

When wrapped up she looked ready for Outer or even Inner Mongolia and complained that the padding made her fat.

'Ever seen a thin Eskimo?'

She tucked the silver hair away inside a fur-lined hood. 'So everyone has problems.'

I drove to the Ascot sale ring. Sophie's reaction, although forewarned, was very much like Kerry's.

'*Ascot*,' she said.

'At least today it isn't raining.'

She huddled inside the fat-making layers. 'Thank God you insisted on the igloo bit.'

I took her down to the stables where there were several horses I wanted to look at, the underfoot conditions that day rock hard, not oozing with mud. She dutifully stuck her head inside each box to look at the inmates, though her claim to know less about horses than quantum mechanics was quickly substantiated.

'Do they see two views at once, with their eyes on opposite sides of their head like that?'

'Their brains sort it out,' I said.

'Very confusing.'

'Most animals look sideways. And birds. And fish.'

'And snakes in the grass,' she said.

Some of the horses had attendants with them. Some didn't.

Some had attendants who had vanished temporarily to the refreshment room. Everywhere lay the general clutter of stables in the morning: buckets, muck sacks, brushes, bandages, haynets and halters, mostly in little clumps either outside or inside each box door. Most of the early lot numbers had stayed overnight.

I asked for three or four horses to be led out of their boxes by their attendants to get an idea of how they moved. They trotted obligingly along and back a wider piece of ground, the attendant running alongside holding them by the head on a short rope. I watched them from behind and from dead ahead.

'What do you look for?' Sophie said.

'Partly whether they dish their feet out sideways.'

'Is that good?'

I shook my head, smiling. 'The fastest ones generally don't do it.'

We went up to the O-shaped sale ring, where the wind whistled through with enthusiasm and the meagre crowd of participants stamped their feet and tucked their hands under their armpits. Ronnie North was there, breathing out clouds of steam and wiping a running nose; and Vic was there, dandified in a belted white shiny jacket with a blue shirt underneath.

While he was deep in conversation with a client I pointed him out to Sophie.

'But he looks *nice*,' she objected.

'Of course he does. Hundreds of people love him.'

She grinned. 'Such sarcasm.'

I bought two three-year-old fillies for a client in Italy and Vic watched broodingly from directly opposite.

Sophie said, 'When he looks at you like that ... he doesn't look nice at all.'

I took her to warm up over some coffee. It occurred to me uneasily and belatedly that maybe I had not been clever to bring her to Ascot. It had seemed to me that Vic was as much interested in Sophie herself as in what I was buying, and I wondered if he were already thinking of ways to get at me through her.

'What's the matter?' Sophie said. 'You've gone very quiet.'

'Have a doughnut?'

'Yes please.'

We munched and drank, and I checked ahead through the catalogue, making memory-jogging notes about the horses we had seen in their boxes.

'Does it go on like this all day?' Sophie asked.

'A bit boring for you, I'm afraid.'

'No . . . Is this what you do, day after day?'

'On sales days, yes. Other days I fix up deals privately, or go to the races, or see to things like transport and insurance. Since last week I've barely had time to cough.' I told her about Wilton Young and the consequently mushrooming business.

'Are there a lot of horses for sale?' she said doubtfully. 'I wouldn't have thought there were enough for so many people all to be involved in buying and selling.'

'Well . . . In Britain alone there are at present about seventeen thousand thoroughbred broodmares. A mare can theoretically have a foal every year, but some years they're barren and some foals die. I suppose there must be about nine thousand new foals or yearlings on the market every season. Then there are about twenty thousand horses in training for flat races, and heaven knows how many jumpers, but more than on the Flat. Horses which belong to the same people from birth to death are exceptions. Most of them change hands at least twice.'

'With a commission for the agent every time?' Her expression held no approval.

I smiled, 'Stockbrokers work for commission. Are they more respectable?'

'Yes.'

'Why?'

'I don't know. Don't confuse me.'

I said, 'France, Italy and especially America are all at it in the bloodstock business hammer and tongs. There are about thirteen hundred stud farms in the British Isles and thousands more round the world.'

'All churning out horses . . . and only so that people can gamble.'

I smiled at her still disapproving expression. 'Everyone needs some sort of fantasy on their bread.'

She opened her mouth and shut it, and shook her head. 'I can never decide whether you are very wise or an absolute fool.'

'Both.'

'Impossible.'

'Dead easy, I'm afraid. Most people are.'

We went back to the ring and watched Vic and Ronnie North beat up the price of a weedy four-year-old hurdler to twice the figure his form suggested. Vic would no doubt be collecting a sizeable kick-back from the seller along with the commission from his client, and Ronnie North looked expansively pleased both with his status as underbidder for this one horse and with life in general.

Fynedale's successor, it seemed to me, had been elected.

Fynedale himself, I noticed, had arrived in the ring in time to see what was happening. He seemed to be in much the same state as before, white-faced, semi-dazed and radiating unfocused hatred.

Sophie said, 'He looks like gelignite on the boil.'

'With luck he'll explode all over Vic.'

'You're pretty heartless . . . he looks ill.'

'Buzz off and mother him then,' I said.

'No thanks.'

We looked at some more horses and I bought another; we had some more coffee and the wind blew even colder. Sophie, however, seemed content.

'Nose needs powdering,' she said at one point. 'Where will I meet you?'

I consulted the catalogue. 'I'd better look at eighty-seven and ninety-two, in their boxes.'

'OK. I'll find you.'

I looked at eighty-seven and decided against it. Not much bone and too much white around the eye. There was no one with him. I left his box, bolted both halves of the door and went along to ninety-two. There I opened the top half of the door and looked inside. No attendant there either, just patient Lot 92 turning an incurious gaze. I opened the bottom half of the door and went in, letting them swing shut behind me. Lot 92 was securely tied by a headcollar to a ring in the wall, but it was too cold for open doors.

The horse was a five-year-old hurdler being sold for a quick profit while he still showed promise of being useful at six. I patted his brown flank, ran my hand down his legs, and took a good close look at his teeth.

When the door opened and closed I paid no especial attention to whatever had come in. It should have been an attendant for the horse or another like me inspecting the goods at close quarters.

It wasn't.

No instinct made me look up as I let go of the hurdler's mouth, stroked his nose and stood back for a final appraisal.

I saw only a flash in the air. Felt the thud in my chest. And knew, falling, that the white face of Fynedale was coming forward to finish the job.

13

He had thrown at me like a lance the most lethal of all stable equipment. A pitchfork.

The force behind his arm knocked me off my feet. I lay on my side on the straw with the two sharp prongs embedded and the long wooden handle stretched out in front.

He could see that in spite of a deadly accurate throw and all the hate that went into it he still hadn't killed me. The glimpse I got of his distorted face convinced me that he intended to put that right.

I knew the pitchfork had gone in, but not how far. I couldn't feel much. I jerked it out and rolled over and lay on it face down, burying it under me in the straw. He fell on me, pulling, clutching, dragging, trying to get at it, and I simply lay on it like a log, not knowing what else to do.

The door opened again and light poured in from outside. Then a voice shouting. A girl's voice.

'Help . . . Someone help . . .'

I knew dimly from under the flurry of Fynedale's exertions that it was Sophie. The troops she mobilized came cautiously to the rescue. 'I say . . .' said a well-bred voice plaintively, and Fynedale took no notice.

'Here. What's going on?'

The voice this time was tough and the owner tougher. Hands began to pull Fynedale off me and then others to help him, and when I took my nose out of the straw I could see three men trying to hold on to Fynedale while Fynedale threw them off like pieces of hay.

He crashed out through the door with my rescuers in pursuit, and when I got from my knees to my feet the only audience was Sophie.

'Thank you,' I said with feeling.

'Are you all right?'

'Yes . . . I think so.'

I bent down and picked up the pitchfork.

'What's that?'

'He threw it at me,' I said.

She looked at the stiletto prongs and shuddered. 'Good job he missed.'

'Mm.' I inspected the two small tears in the front of my anorak. Then I slowly unzipped it and put a hand inside, exploring.

'He did miss, didn't he?' said Sophie, suddenly anxious.

'Direct hit. Don't know why I'm not dead.'

I said it lightly and she didn't believe me, but it was the truth. I could feel the soreness of a tear in my skin and the warm stickiness of blood, but the prongs had not gone through to heart or lungs, and the force with which they'd landed had been enough to get them there.

I smiled idiotically.

'What is it?' Sophie asked.

'Thank the Lord for a dislocating shoulder . . . The pitchfork hit the strap.'

Unfortunately for Fynedale two policemen in a patrol car had come to the sales on some unrelated errand, but when they saw three men chasing another they caught the fugitive out of habit. Sophie and I arrived to find Fynedale sitting in the police car with one policeman while the other listened to the three chasers saying that if Jonah Dereham wasn't a hospital case it was because they had saved him.

I didn't argue with that.

Sophie with unshaken composure told them about the pitchfork, and the policeman, having taken a quick look inside my anorak, told me to go and find a doctor and then come along to the local station to make a statement. I reckoned it would be the same nick I'd been to with Kerry: there would be a certain amount of doubtful eyebrow-raising over a man who got himself attacked twice in the same small sales' paddock within six weeks.

At the nearest doctor's surgery the damage resolved itself into one long slit over a rib. The doctor, a girl of less than thirty, swabbed away prosaically and said that ten days earlier she'd been called to attend a farm worker who'd driven a pitchfork right through his own foot. Boot and all, she added.

I laughed. She said she hadn't meant to be funny. She had nice legs but no sense of humour. My own amusement rather died when she pointed out the state of the buckle on my strap, which she'd taken off to get at the cut. The buckle was bent. The mark of the prong showed clearly.

'One prong hit the buckle. The other went into you but slid along against a rib. I'd say you were exceptionally lucky.'

I said soberly, 'I'd say so too.'

She stuck on some plaster, gave me a couple of anti-infection injections, and refused my offer of a fee.

'On the National Health,' she said sternly, as if offering to pay were immoral. She handed me the strap. 'Why don't you get that shoulder repaired?'

'Can't spare the time . . . and I'm allergic to hospitals.'

She gave my bare chest and arms a quick glance. 'You've been in a few. Several of your bones have been fractured.'

'Quite so,' I agreed.

She allowed herself a sudden small smile. 'I recognize you now. I've seen you on television. I backed your horse once in the Grand National when I was a student. I won six pounds and spent it on a book on blood diseases.'

'Glad to have been of service,' I said.

'I shouldn't wear that strap for a week or so,' she said. 'Otherwise it will rub that wound and prevent it healing.'

'All right.'

I thanked her for her skill, dressed, collected Sophie from the waiting-room, and drifted along to the police station. Once again Sophie was offered a chair to sit on. She showed signs of exasperated patience and asked if I would be long.

'Take my car,' I said contritely. 'Do some shopping. Go for a walk to Windsor Park.'

She considered it and brightened. 'I'll come back in an hour.'

The police wanted a statement from me but I asked if I could first speak to Fynedale.

'Speak to him? Well . . . there's no law against it. He hasn't been charged yet.' They shook their heads dubiously. 'He's in a violent state, though. Are you sure you want to?'

'Certain.'

They shrugged. 'This way, then.'

Fynedale was in a small, bare interview room, not sitting beside the table on one of the two plain wooden chairs, but standing in the centre of the largest available clear space. He vibrated still as if strung as tight as piano wire and a muscle jumped spasmodically under his left eye.

The room, brown paint to waist height, cream above, had no windows and was lit by electric light. An impassive young policeman sat in a chair just inside the door. I asked him and the others to leave me and Fynedale to talk alone. Fynedale said loudly 'I've nothing to bloody say to you.'

The policemen thought I was being foolish, but eventually they shrugged and went away.

'Sit down,' I said, taking one of the chairs by the table and gesturing to the other.

'No.'

'All right, don't.' I pulled out cigarettes and lit one. Whatever was said about cancer of the lungs, I thought, there were times worth the risk. I drew the smoke down and was grateful for its comfort.

Fynedale began pacing around in jerky little strides.

'I *told* you I'd kill you,' he said.

'Your good luck that you didn't.'

He stopped dead. 'What did you say?'

'If you had, you'd have spent ten years inside.'

'Bloody worth it.' He went back to pacing.

'I see Vic's got another partner,' I said.

He picked up a chair and threw it viciously against the wall. The door opened immediately and the young policeman stepped hurriedly in.

'Please wait,' I said. 'We've hardly started.'

He looked indecisively at Fynedale, the fallen chair, and me sitting calmly smoking, and decided that perhaps after all it would be safe to leave. The door closed quietly behind him.

'Vic's done the dirty on you, I reckon,' I said.

He circled behind me. The hairs on my neck bristled. I took another lungful of smoke and didn't look round.

'Getting you into trouble and then ditching you.'

'It was you got me into trouble.' The voice was a growl in the throat.

I knew that any tenseness in my body would react on him and screw him up even tighter, but it took a fair amount of concentration to relax every muscle with him out of sight behind my head. I tried to make my voice slow, thoughtful, persuasive, but my mouth was as dry as a Sunday in Salt Lake City.

'Vic started it,' I said. 'Vic and you. Now it's Vic and Ronnie North. You and I . . . we've both come off worst with Vic . . .'

He reappeared jerkily into my field of vision. The carrot hair looked bright orange under the electric bulb. His eyes alternately shone with manic fire when the light caught them and receded into secretive shadows when he bent his head. Sophie's remarks about gelignite on the boil came back to me; and his instability had if anything increased.

'Cigarette?' I suggested.

'Get stuffed.'

It was better when I could see him.

I said 'What have you told the police?'

'Nothing. Bloody nothing.'

'Did they get you to make a statement?'

'That they bloody did not.'

'Good,' I said. 'That simplifies things.'

'What the hell are you on about?'

I watched the violence and agitation in every physical movement. It was as if his muscles and nerves were acting in spasms, as if some central disorganization were plucking wires.

I said, 'What is upsetting you most?'

'Most?' he yelled. 'Most? The fact that you're bloody walking in here as cool as bloody cucumbers, that's what. I tried to kill you. *Kill you.*'

He stopped as if he couldn't explain what he meant, but he'd got his message across to me loud and clear. He had taken himself beyond the edge of sense in his compulsion to do me harm, and there I was, proving that it had all been for nothing. I guessed that he badly needed not to have failed entirely. I took off my jacket and explained about the strap and buckle saving my life. I undid my shirt, showed him the plaster, and told him what lay underneath.

'It hurts,' I said truthfully.

He stopped pacing and peered closely at my face. 'Does it?'

'Yes.'

He put out his hand and touched me. I winced.

He stood back, bent and picked up the chair he'd thrown, set it on its feet on the far side of the table, and sat down opposite me. He stretched for the packet of cigarettes and lighter which I'd left lying, and lit one with hands still shaking with tension.

I left my shirt undone and falling open. He sat smoking jerkily, his eyes flicking every few seconds to the strip of plaster. It seemed to satisfy him. To reassure. Finally to soothe. He smoked the whole cigarette through without speaking, but the jerky movements gradually quietened, and by the time he threw the stub on the floor and twisted his foot on it the worst of the jangle had disappeared.

'I'll make a bargain with you,' I said.

'What bargain?'

'I'll say the pitchfork was an accident.'

'You know bloody well it wasn't.'

'I know. You know. The police know. But there were no witnesses ... If I swear it was an accident there would be no question of you being even charged with attempted murder, let alone tried and convicted.'

He thought it over. There were a lot of little twitches in the muscles of his face, and the skin stretched gauntly over the cheekbones.

'You don't actually want to do time, do you?' I asked.

'No.'

'Suppose we could get you off all the hooks ... Assault, fraud, the lot.'

'You couldn't.'

'I could keep you out of jail, that's for sure.'

A long pause. Then he said, 'A bargain. That means you want something in return.'

'Mm.'

'What, then?'

I ran my tongue round my teeth and took my time over replying.

'I want . . .' I said slowly, 'I want you to talk about the way you and Vic tried to make me join your ring.'

He was surprised. 'Is that all?'

'It'll do for a start.'

'But you know. You know what Vic said to you.'

'I don't know what he said to *you.*'

He shrugged in bewilderment. 'He just said if you wouldn't go along with us, we'd break you.'

'Look,' I said, 'the price of your freedom is every word, every scrap of conversation that you can remember. Especially everything about that ally of Vic's who got my stable burned.'

'I told you . . . I don't know.'

'If you want to get out of here, you're going to have to do better than that.'

He stared across the table. I saw his understanding of my offer deepen. He looked briefly round the bleak, crowding walls of the little interview room and shivered. The last vestiges of the exalted murderous state evaporated. He looked smaller and colder and no danger to anybody.

'All right,' he said. 'I reckon I don't owe Vic any more. I'll not go to jail just to save his bloody skin. I'll tell you what I can.'

It took three more cigarettes and a lot of pauses, but he did his best.

'I reckon it started about six weeks ago. I mean, for some time before that Vic had said a few things about you being the biggest danger on the horizon, you were pretty good as an agent and dead honest, and he thought you might drain off some of the business which he'd otherwise corner.'

'Room for us all,' I murmured.

'Not what Vic thought. Anyway, about six weeks ago he said it was time to bust you once and for all.' He thought for a while, sucking deep on his cigarette. 'See, Vic and I and some of the others had this thing going . . .'

'The kick-backs systems,' I said.

'Ay. All right, so goody-goody sods like you can look down their noses and sniff, but it's not illegal and it does a lot of people a lot of bloody good.'

'Some people.'

'All right, so the client pays over the odds, so what? Anyway, as Vic always says, the higher the prices the more commission the auctioneers get and the better they like it, so they're just as bad, running things up as far as they bloody can.'

They also had a duty to the seller, I thought, but it wasn't the time to argue.

'Well, there we were, running this little ring and doing better and better out of it and then one day . . . I suppose it was just before the first yearling sales at Newmarket . . .' He paused, looking back in his mind. His voice died away.

'What happened?' I prompted.

'Vic was sort of . . . I don't know . . . excited and scared . . . both at once.'

'Vic was scared?' I said sceptically.

'Ay, he was. Sort of. Sort of excited, though. Like someone had put him up to something he wanted to do but knew he shouldn't.'

'Like stealing apples?'

He brushed off the childish parallel. 'These were no apples. Vic said we'd make so much money that what had gone before was only peanuts. He said there was a deal we could do with a breeder that had a colt by Transporter that was a perfect peach . . .'

'Was it Vic's own idea?' I asked.

'I thought so . . . I don't know . . . Anyway, it worked a dream. He gave me five thousand quid just for bidding, and he made twenty out of it himself.'

'By my reckoning he made thirty.'

'Oh no . . .' He stopped, surprised, then went on more slowly. 'No . . . I remember him saying . . . ten thousand pounds went to the bloke who wrote the agreement that Vic got the breeder to sign. I said I thought it was a lot, but Vic says you have to pay for expert advice.'

'Does he often pay for expert advice?'

He nodded. 'All the time.'

'Cheerfully?'

'What? Of course.'

'He isn't being blackmailed?'

He looked scornful. 'I'll say not. You can't see any piddling little blackmailer putting one over on Vic.'

'No . . . but what it amounts to is that Vic is collecting huge kick-backs from breeders and other vendors, and out of that he is paying his own kick-backs to someone else for expert advice.'

He frowned. 'I suppose you could say so.'

'But you don't know who?'

'No.'

'How long would you say he had been receiving this advice?'

'How the hell do I know? A year. Two. About that.'

'So what was different about the last six weeks?'

'You were. All of a sudden Vic says it's time to get rid of you. Either that or make you back down and take your cut with the rest of us. We all thought you'd come in with us with a bit of pressure. Well, see, it didn't make sense you holding out. Only do yourself a lot of harm. Jiminy Bell, he says now he told us you'd never agree, but he bloody didn't. That little sod, he said then that you were pretty soft really. A soft touch, he always said. Always good for a sob-story. So now he says he told us you were a tough nut, the squirmy little liar.'

'Does Vic see this friend of his every day?'

'Couldn't say.'

'Well . . . think.'

He thought. 'I'd say that most days he either sees him or talks on the phone. See, Vic always get things done quickly, like pinching that horse you bought at Ascot . . .'

'How was that done?'

He blinked. Shifted uneasily on his chair. I shoved the cigarettes across and tried to look as if the whole question was quite impersonal.

'Er . . .' he said. 'Vic said you were buying a horse for Mrs Sanders and he couldn't have that, she was marrying Constantine Brevett and he was Vic's exclusive territory.'

'When did he say that?'

'At the sales the day you bought Hearse Puller.'

'Had he already fixed up with Fred Smith?'

He hesitated. 'He knew Fred Smith was going to take away whatever horse you bought. Yes.'

'Did Vic himself fix it with Fred Smith?'

'See, I don't really know. Vic said he didn't, but I don't know, he'd say his grandmother was a pigmy if it suited him.'

'Ronnie North,' I said slowly. 'Did he know Fred Smith?'

Fynedale's face twisted into the sardonic sneer. 'Old mates, weren't they?'

'Were they?'

'Well . . . Ronnie, he came from Stepney way, same as Fred Smith. Ronnie started in the horse coping business in the old days when they sold horses on market days in all the big towns. He started as a boy, helping his dad. Bloody lot of gypsies if you ask me. Up to every damn trick in the book, is Ronnie. But bright, see? Got brains, Ronnie has.'

'Ronnie sold me the next horse I bought for Kerry Sanders.'

'Ay. Him and Vic, laughing themselves sick about it, they were. Then Ronnie afterwards said you needed a bloody lesson, busting Fred Smith's arm.'

'Did you yourself ever meet Fred Smith?'

'I saw him, like. Saw him at Ascot, with Ronnie. Ronnie pointed you out to him. We all did, see?'

'I see.'

'Then, well, with River God it was dead easy, wasn't it? Ronnie found which transport firm you'd engaged and got them to tell him their instructions, and he just sent Fred Smith to pick you off on the lay-by.'

'Ronnie sent him?'

'Ronnie . . . or Vic.' He shrugged. 'One of them.'

'Not Vic's unknown friend?'

'Might have been, I suppose.' He didn't think it made much

difference. 'We weren't going to steal River God, see? Fred Smith had the money for it. He was going to make you take it, like at Ascot.'

'And River God was going back to Ronnie North?'

'Ay.'

'Then why did he agree to sell it to me in the first place?'

He said with exaggerated patience as if telling to a dim child, 'See, he wasn't going to, first off. Then he rings Vic and says you're looking for another horse instead of Hearse Puller. Then Vic rings back and says sell you River God and it'll be a good opportunity of bashing you up a bit more.'

'Did you actually hear either of these calls?'

'Eh?' He shook his head. 'I don't live in Vic's pocket, do I? No, Vic told me.'

I thought for a while. 'All right,' I said, 'which of you thought of burning my yard?'

He shifted his chair abruptly so that he was no longer facing me, but spoke to the bare walls.

'See . . . Vic said . . . a real smash, and you'd cave in. See . . . he saw you talking to that Transporter breeder . . . and that trainer whose owner he'd swiped . . . in the bar, see?'

'Yes.'

'Ay. Well then, Vic says this time no messing, you've got to be put right out of action, because this expert friend of his has thought up a fiddle to make the Transporter colt look like hayseeds, only he wouldn't tell Vic what it was while you were still around at the sales. Vic said this expert was afraid you would make a public fuss which would mean everyone would be a lot more careful about buying horses in future and that was the last thing they wanted. So Vic said you either had to join in or be got rid of and you'd made it crystal clear you wouldn't join in, so it was your own bloody fault you got your yard burned.'

I grunted: 'And what happened afterwards?'

'Well, there you bloody were at the sales as if nothing had happened. The whole thing had been a flop and Fred Smith was in jail and Vic was furious because he couldn't start the new fiddle. He said he'd just have to go on with the kick-backs and anyway we'd been doing pretty well out of those for two years so it didn't seem too bad.'

He swung round again, his face full of renewed anger.

'And then you had to bugger the whole thing up by ratting to Wilton Young.'

'Calm down,' I said flatly. 'Did you expect me to go on meekly taking whatever you cared to dish out?'

He looked indecisive. 'Don't know.'

You know now, I thought.

'Are Vic and his expert friend still planning this new big fiddle for some time in the future?'

'Ay. They are. Today ... Today?' He seemed suddenly astounded that it was only that morning that he had gone to Ascot Sales.

'Today ... I could have killed Vic ... I told him I could kill him ... and kill you too ... and he said ... why didn't I just kill you, then he could get on with the fiddle ... and he was bloody laughing ... but I reckon now he meant to egg me on.'

'I expect he did,' I said.

'Ay. He'd be rid of you and me too. He'd have the whole bloody field to himself.'

He leaned his elbows on the table and picked up my lighter and fidgeted with it.

'Here,' he said. 'I'll tell you something. You can put Vic in the same boat as you did me.'

'Do you mean ... had up for fraud?'

'Ay ... Makes shipping horses by sea instead of air look like kids' stuff.'

'Tell me, then.'

He looked up. 'You meant it straight, didn't you, about getting me out of here?'

'I did.'

He sighed. 'Reckon I can trust you. And that's a bloody laugh, for a start.'

He threw down the lighter and leaned back.

'Right, then,' he said. 'Vic swindled the High Power Insurance Company out of a hundred and fifteen thousand quid.'

14

'Are you sure?' I said.
'Positive.'
'Can you prove it?'
'I reckon *you* could, if you wanted to.'
'How did he do it?'
'See . . . it was about three years ago . . . he shipped a four-year-old stallion out to Japan. Polyprint, it was called.'
I said, 'I remember that. It died on the way.'
'Ay. It did. And Vic had insured it for a hundred and fifteen thousand for the journey, with himself to collect if anything happened to the horse.'
'Nothing especially unusual in that.'
'No. And he insured it a week before it was due to go. That is what made the insurance firm pay up. Because a week before the horse set off, Vic couldn't have known it was going to die, because a vet had been over it from nose to arse and given it the OK, and it was the High Power Company's own vet, which strung them up proper.'
'I can't remember what it died of . . .'
'Tetanus,' he said. 'Three days by air to Japan. They took it out of Gatwick looking as right as rain . . . it walked up the ramp into the aircraft as quiet as you please. By the time they got to the Middle East it was sweating something chronic. Next stop, they got it out and walked it around, but it was staggering a bit. Next stop they had a local vet waiting. Tetanus, he said. So they cabled the insurance company and they wanted to send their own man out to take a look. See, there was a lot of brass involved. Anyway he never went because the horse died while he was still in England getting cholera jabs or something. So Vic claims the money, and the High Power has to pay up.'
'Did Vic travel with the horse himself?'

'No. He was right here in England.'

'So . . . where was the fraud?'

'Ah . . . See, the horse that set off for Japan and died of tetanus, that horse wasn't Polyprint.'

He lit a cigarette, absorbed in his story.

'It was a horse called Nestegg.'

I stared at him. 'Nestegg is standing at stud in Ireland.'

'Ay,' he said. 'And that's Polyprint.'

The gaunt face twisted into the ghost of a smile. 'See, Vic bought Nestegg because he had a client who wanted it. Nestegg was six and had won a few long-distance races, and this client had a small stud and wanted a stallion that wouldn't cost too much. Well, Vic bought Nestegg for ten thousand and was going to pass him on for fifteen, and then this client just dropped down dead one afternoon and the widow said nothing doing she didn't want to know. Vic wasn't much worried because Nestegg wasn't bad, really.'

He took a few deep puffs, sorting things out.

'One evening I was at Vic's place near Epsom and we looked round the yard, like one does. He shows me Polyprint, who's due to set off to Japan the next day. Big bay horse. Full of himself. Then, three boxes along, there was Nestegg. Another bay, much the same. We went in and looked at him and he was standing there all hunched up and sweating. Vic looked him over and said he would go out and see him again later, and if he was no better he would get the vet in the morning. Then we went into Vic's house for a drink, and then I went home.'

He looked at me broodingly.

'So the next day off goes this horse to Japan and dies of tetanus two days later. Next time I saw Vic he sort of winks at me and gives me a thousand quid in readies, and I laughed and took it. Then later he sold this bay which he still had, which was supposed to be Nestegg but was really Polyprint, he sold him to a stud in Ireland for seventeen thousand. He wouldn't have made a penny if he'd sent Polyprint off to Japan and got a vet to try to save Nestegg. Just by swapping those two horses when he had the chance, he made himself a proper packet.'

'And it gave him a taste for more easy money in large amounts?'

'Ay... It was after that that he latched on to the kick-backs in a big way. He asked me to help... Tell you the truth, I was glad to.'

'And he found this expert,' I said.

'Ay...' He hesitated. 'It was maybe the other way round. Vic more or less said this chap had come to him and suggested more ways Vic could make money.'

'He hadn't done so badly on his own,' I observed.

'Well... Polyprint was a one-off, see. You couldn't work that again. He only did it because he realized Nestegg had tetanus and would die pretty quickly if he wasn't treated and even maybe if he was. See, tetanus isn't that common. You couldn't have two die of it on journeys when they were heavily insured, even if you could infect them on purpose, which you can't. Vic walked that horse around all night to keep it moving and fed it a bucketful of tranquillizers so that it looked all right when it was loaded on to the plane at Gatwick. But to get another one to die on a journey you'd have to fix some sort of accident. The insurance people would be dead suspicious, and even if they paid up they might afterwards refuse to insure you altogether and you couldn't risk that. But the thing about this expert chap was that nearly everything he suggested was legal. Vic said it was like property development and land speculation. You could make a great deal of money without breaking the law if you knew how to set about it.'

The police were understandably sour about my assertion that I had fallen on the pitchfork by accident and that Fynedale was as innocent of assault as a bunch of violets. They argued and I insisted, and half an hour later Fynedale stood outside on the pavement shivering in the wind.

'Thanks,' he said briefly. He looked shrunken and depressed.

He huddled inside his jacket, turned on his heel, and walked away up the street to the railway station. The carrot hair was a receding orange blob against the dead copper leaves of a beech hedge.

Sophie was waiting by the kerb, sitting in the driving seat of my car. I opened the passenger side door and slid in beside her.

'Will you drive?' I said.

'If you like.'

I nodded.

'You look bushed,' she said. She started the engine, shifted the gears, and edged out into the road.

'Couldn't beat Muhammad Ali right now.'

She smiled. 'How did it go?'

'Like a torrent, once he'd started.'

'What did you learn?'

I thought, trying to put everything into its right order. Sophie drove carefully, flicking glances across, waiting for an answer.

I said, 'Vic swindled an insurance company very neatly, about three years ago. Some time after that someone who Fynedale calls an expert sought Vic out and suggested a sort of alliance, in which Vic would extort money in various more or less legal ways and pay a proportion of it to the expert. I imagine this expert guessed Vic had swindled the insurance and was therefore a good prospect for a whole career of legal robbery.'

'There's no such thing as legal robbery.'

I smiled. 'How about wealth taxes?'

'That's different.'

'Taking by law is legal robbery.'

'Ah well . . . go on about Vic.'

'Vic and the expert started redistributing wealth in no uncertain terms, chiefly into their own pockets but with enough pickings to entice six or seven other agents into the ring.'

'Fynedale?' Sophie said.

'Yes. Especially Fynedale, as he knew about the original insurance swindle. It just seems to have been my bad luck that I started being an agent at about the time Vic and the expert were warming things up. Pauli Teksa had a theory that Vic and his friends wanted me out of the way because I was a threat to their monopoly, and from what Fynedale says I should think he might have been right, though I thought it was nonsense when he suggested it.'

I yawned. Sophie drove smoothly, as controlled at the wheel

as everywhere else. She had taken off the fur-lined hood, and the silver blonde hair fell gently to her shoulders. Her profile was calm, efficient, content. I thought that probably I did love her, and would for a long time. I also guessed that however often I might ask her to marry me, in the end she would not. The longer and better I knew her, the more I realized that she was by nature truly solitary. Lovers she might take, but a bustling family life would be alien and disruptive. I understood why her four years with the pilot had been a success: it was because of his continual long absences, not in spite of them. I understood her lack of even the memory of inconsolable grief. His death had merely left her where she basically liked to be, which was alone.

'Go on about Vic,' she said.

'Oh . . . well . . . They started this campaign of harassment. Compulsory purchase of Hearse Puller at Ascot. Sending Fred Smith down to my place to do what harm he could, which turned out to be giving Crispin whisky and letting loose that road-hogging two-year-old. Arranging for me to buy and lose River God. When all that, and a few bits of intimidation from Vic himself, failed to work, they reckoned that burning my stable would do the trick.'

'Their mistake.'

'Yeah . . . well . . . they did it.' I yawned again. 'Fred Smith, now. Vic and the expert needed some muscle. Ronnie North knew Fred Smith. Vic must have asked Ronnie if he knew anyone suitable and Ronnie suggested Fred Smith.'

'Bingo.'

'Mm . . . You know something odd?'

'What?'

'The insurance company that Vic swindled was the one Crispin used to work for.'

Sophie made us tea in her flat. We sat side by side on the sofa, bodies casually touching in intimate friendship, sipping the hot reviving liquid.

'I ought to sleep a bit,' she said. 'I'm on duty at eight.'

I looked at my watch. Four-thirty, and darkening already towards the winter night. It had seemed a long day.

'Shall I go?'

She smiled. 'Depends how sore you are.'

'Sex is a great anaesthetic.'

'Nuts.'

We went to bed and put it fairly gently to the test, and certainly what I felt most was not the stab along my rib.

The pattern as before: sweet, intense, lingering, a vibration of subtle pleasure from head to foot. She breathed softly and slowly and smiled with her eyes, as close as my soul and as private as her own.

Eventually she said sleepily, 'Do you always give girls what suits them best?'

I yawned contentedly. 'What suits them best is best for me.'

'The voice of experience ...' She smiled drowsily, drifting away.

We woke to the clatter of her alarm less than two hours later.

She stretched out a hand to shut it off, then rolled her head over on the pillow for a kiss.

'Better than sleeping pills,' she said. 'I feel as if I'd slept all night.'

She made coffee and rapid bacon and eggs, because to her it seemed time for breakfast, and in an organized hurry she offered her cheek in goodbye on the pavement and drove away to work.

I watched her rear lights out of sight. I remembered I had read somewhere that air traffic controllers had the highest divorce rates on earth.

Wilton Young came to Cheltenham races the following day in spite of the basic contempt he held for steeplechasing because of its endemic shortage of brass. He came because the rival tycoon who was sponsoring the day's big race had asked him, and the first person he saw at the pre-lunch reception was me.

'What are you doing here?' he said bluntly.

'I was invited.'

'Oh.'

He didn't quite ask why, so I told him. 'I rode a few winners for our host.'

He cast his mind back and gave a sudden remembering nod. 'Ay. So you did.'

A waiter offered a silver tray with glasses of champagne. Wilton Young took one, tasted it with a grimace, and said he would tell me straight he would sooner have had a pint of bitter.

'I'm afraid I may have some disappointing news for you,' I said.

He looked immediately belligerent. 'Exactly what?'

'About Fynedale.'

'Him!' His eyes narrowed. 'Any bad news about him is good news.'

I said, 'The man I sent to South Africa says he can't swear the extra horses he looked after on the way were yours.'

'You seemed sure enough that he would.'

'He says he had the impression they were yours, but he couldn't be sure.'

'That'll not stand up in court.'

'No.'

He grunted. 'I'll not sue, then. I'll not throw good brass after bad. Suing's a mug's game where there's any doubt.'

His plain honesty rebuked me for the lie I'd told him. My man had been absolutely positive about the horses' ownership: he'd seen the papers. I reckoned my promise to get Fynedale off was fully discharged and from there on he would have to take his chances.

'What's past is past,' Wilton Young said. 'Cut your losses. Eh, lad?'

'I guess so,' I said.

'Take my word for it. Now, look here. I've a mind to buy an American horse. Tough, that's what they are. Tough as if they came from Yorkshire.' He wasn't joking. 'There's one particular one I want you to go and buy for me. He comes up for sale soon after Christmas.'

I stared at him, already guessing.

'Phoenix Fledgeling. A two-year-old. Ever heard of it?'

'Did you know,' I said, 'that Constantine Brevett is after it too?'

He chuckled loudly. 'Why the hell do you think I want it? Put his bloody superior nose out of joint. Eh, lad?'

The bloody superior nose chose that precise moment to arrive at the reception, closely accompanied by the firm mouth, smooth grey hair, thick black spectacle frames and general air of having come straight from some high up chairmanship in the City.

As his height and booming voice instantly dominated the assembly, I reflected that the advantage always seemed to go to the one who arrived later: maybe if Constantine and Wilton Young both realized it they would try so hard to arrive after each other that neither would appear at all, which might be a good idea all round. Constantine's gaze swept authoritatively over the guests and stopped abruptly on Wilton Young and me. He frowned very slightly. His mouth marginally compressed. He gave us five seconds' uninterrupted attention, and then looked away.

'Has it ever occurred to you,' I said slowly, 'that it might just be *your* nose that *he's* putting out of joint?'

'Don't be daft.'

'How many times have you had to out-bid him to get a horse?'

He chuckled. 'Can't remember. I've beaten him more times than he's sold office blocks.'

'He's cost you a great deal of money.'

The chuckle died. 'That was bloody Fynedale and Vic Vincent.'

'But . . . what if Constantine approved . . . or even planned it?'

'You're chasing the wrong rabbit, I tell thee straight.'

I chewed my lower lip. 'As long as you're happy.'

'Ay.'

Nicol won the amateurs' race by some startlingly aggressive tactics that wrung obscenities from his opponents and some sharp-eyed looks from the Stewards. He joined me afterwards with defiance flying like banners.

'How about that, then?' he said, attacking first.

'If you were a pro on the Flat you'd have been suspended.'

'That's right.'

'A proper sportsman,' I said drily.

'I'm not in it for the sport.'

'What then?'

'Winning.'

'Just like Wilton Young,' I said.

'What do you mean?'

'Neither of you cares what winning costs.'

He glared. 'It cost you enough in your time in smashed up bones.'

'Well . . . maybe everyone pays in the way that matters to them least.'

'I don't give a damn what the others think of me.'

'That's what I mean.'

We stood in silence, watching horses go by. All my life I'd stood and watched horses go by. There were a lot worse ways of living.

'When you grow up,' I said, 'you'll be a bloody good jockey.'

'You absolute sod.' The fury of all his twenty-two pampered years bunched into fists. Then with the speed of all his mercurial changes he gave me instead the brief, flashing, sardonic smile. 'OK. OK. *OK*. I just aged five years.'

He turned on his heel and strode away, and although I didn't know it until afterwards, he walked straight into the Clerk of the Course's office and filled out an application form for a licence.

Vic didn't come to Cheltenham races. I had business with him, however, so after a certain amount of private homework I drove to his place near Epsom early on the following morning.

He lived as he dressed, a mixture of distinguished traditional and flashy modern. The house, down a short well-kept drive off a country by-road on the outskirts of Oxshott Woods, had at heart the classically simple lines of early Victorian stone. Stuck on the back was an Edwardian outcrop of kitchens and bathrooms and to one side sprawled an extensive new single-storey wing which proved to embrace a swimming pool, a garden room, and a suite for guests.

Vic was in his stable, a brick-built quadrangle standing apart from the house. He came out of its archway, saw me standing by my car and walked across with no welcome written plain on his large unsmiling face.

'What the hell do you want?' he said.

'To talk to you.'

The cold sky was thick with clouds and the first heavy drops spoke of downpours to come. Vic looked irritated and said he had nothing to say.

'I have,' I said.

It began to rain in earnest. Vic turned on his heel and hurried away towards the house, and I followed him closely. He was even more irritated to find me going in with him through his own door.

'I've nothing to say,' he repeated.

'You'll listen, then.'

We stood in a wide passage running between the old part of the house and the new, with central heating rushing out past us into the chilly air of Surrey. Vic tightened his mouth, shut the outer door, and jerked his head for me to follow.

Money had nowhere been spared. Large expanses of pale blue carpeting stretched to the horizon. Huge, plushy sofas stood around. Green plants the size of saplings sprouted from Greek-looking pots. He probably had a moon bath, I thought, with gold taps: and a water bed for sleep.

I remembered the holes in Antonia Huntercombe's ancient chintz. Vic's legal robbery had gone a long way too far.

He took me to the room at the far end of the hallway, his equivalent of my office. From there the one window looked out to the pool, with the guest rooms to the left, and the garden room to the right. His rows of record books were much like mine, but there ended the resemblance between the two rooms. His had bright new paint, pale blue carpet, three or four Florentine mirrors, Bang and Olufsen stereo and a well-stocked bar.

'Right,' Vic said. 'Get it over. I've no time to waste.'

'Ever heard of a horse called Polyprint?' I said.

He froze. For countable seconds not a muscle twitched. Then he blinked.

'Of course.'

'Died of tetanus.'

'Yes.'

'Ever heard of Nestegg?'

If I'd run him through with a knitting needle he would have been no more surprised. The stab went through him visibly. He didn't answer.

'When Nestegg was foaled,' I said conversationally, 'there was some doubt as to his paternity. One of two stallions could have covered the dam. So the breeder had Nestegg's blood typed.'

Vic gave a great imitation of Lot's wife.

'Nestegg's blood was found to be compatible with one of the stallions, but not with the other. Records were kept. Those records still exist.'

No sign.

'A full brother of Polyprint is now in training in Newmarket.'

Nothing.

I said, 'I have arranged a blood test for the horse now known as Nestegg. You and I both know that his blood type will be entirely different from that recorded for Nestegg as a foal. I have also arranged a blood test for Polyprint's full brother. And his blood type will be entirely compatible with the one found in the supposed Nestegg.'

'You *bugger*.' The words exploded from him, all the more forceful for his unnatural immobility.

'On the other hand,' I said, 'the tests have not yet been made, and in certain circumstances I would cancel them.'

His breath came back. He moved. 'What circumstances?' he said.

'I want an introduction.'

'A what?'

'To a friend of yours. The friend who drew up the agreement that the breeder of the Transporter colt signed. The friend who decided to burn my stable.'

Vic moved restlessly.

'Impossible.'

I said without heat, 'It's either that or I write to the High Power Insurance people.'

He fidgeted tensely with some pens lying on his desk.

'What would you do if you met . . . this friend?'

'Negotiate for permanent peace.'

He picked up a calendar, looked at it unseeingly, and put it down.

'Today's Saturday,' I said. 'The blood tests are scheduled for Monday morning. If I meet your friend today or tomorrow, I'll call them off.'

He was more furious than frightened, but he knew as well as I did that those blood tests would be his first step to the dock. What I didn't know was whether Vic, like Fred Smith, would swallow the medicine with, so to speak, his mouth shut.

Vic said forcefully, 'You'd always have that threat over me. It's bloody blackmail.'

'Sort of,' I agreed.

Ripples of resentment screwed up his face. I watched him searching for a way out.

'Face to face with your friend,' I said. 'Five minutes will do. That's not much when you think what you stand to lose if I don't get it.' I gestured round his bright room and out to the luxurious pool. 'Built on Polyprint's insurance, no doubt.'

He banged his fist down on the desk, making the pens rattle.

'Bloody Fynedale told you,' he shouted. 'It must have been. I'll murder the little rat.'

I didn't exactly deny it, but instead I said matter-of-factly, 'One calculation you left out . . . my brother Crispin worked for High Power.'

15

Crispin stood in the yard at home looking miserable and broody. I stopped the car on my return from Vic's and climbed out to meet him.

'What's the matter?' I said.

'Oh . . .' He swung an arm wide in inner frustration, indicating the flattened stable area and the new scaffolding climbing up to the burnt part of the roof.

'All this . . . If I hadn't been drunk it wouldn't have happened.'

I looked at him. 'Don't worry about it.'

'But I do. If I'd been around . . . if there had been lights on in the house . . . that man wouldn't have set fire . . .'

'You don't know that he wouldn't,' I said.

'Stands to reason.'

'No. Come on in, it's cold out here.'

We went into the kitchen and I made coffee. Crispin's mood of self-abasement flickered on fitfully while he watched me put the water and coffee grounds into the percolator.

'It would have been better if you had let me die.'

'It was a good job you passed out in the bathroom,' I said. 'It was the only room which had natural ventilation through an airbrick.'

He wasn't cheered. 'Better if I'd snuffed it.'

'Want some toast?'

'Stop bloody talking about food. I'm saying you should have let me die.'

'I know you are. It's damn silly. I don't want you dead. I want you alive and well and living in Surrey.'

'You don't take me seriously.' His voice was full of injured complaint.

I thought of all the other conversations we'd had along those lines. I ought to have let him drown in the bath, the time he went to sleep there. I ought to have let him drive into a tree, the time I'd taken his car keys away. I ought to have let him fall off the Brighton cliffs, the time he tottered dizzily to the edge.

Blaming me for not letting him die was his way of laying all his troubles at my door. It was my fault he was alive, his mind went, so it was my fault if he took refuge in drink. He would work up his resentment against me as a justification for self-pity.

I sighed inwardly and made the toast. Either that day or the next he would be afloat again on gin.

There was no word from Vic. I spent all day working in the office and watching racing on television, with Crispin doing his best to put his mind to my accounts.

'When you worked for High Power,' I said, 'did you have anything to do with a claim for a horse called Polyprint?'

He sniffed. 'You know damn well I was in Pensions, not Claims.'

'Just thought you might have heard...'

'No.'

We drank coke and fizzy lemonade and coffee, and I grilled some lamb chops for supper, and still Vic didn't telephone.

Same thing the next morning. Too much silence. I bit my nails and wondered what to do if my lever didn't work: if Vic wouldn't tell and the friend wouldn't save him. The blood typing tests could go ahead and chop Vic into little pieces, but the friend would be free and undiscovered and could recruit another lieutenant and start all over again, like cancer.

I wandered round the place where the stable had been, desultorily kicking at loose stones.

A car turned into the yard, one I didn't know, and from it stepped a total stranger. Tall, young, blond. Surely this couldn't be Vic's friend, I thought: and it wasn't. There were two other people in the car with him, and from the back of it stepped Sophie.

'Hi...' She grinned at my face. 'Who were you expecting? The bailiffs?'

She introduced the friends, Peter and Sue. They were all on their way to lunch with Sue's parents, but if I liked she could stop off with me and they would pick her up on their way back.

I liked. The friends waved and went, and Sophie tucked her arm through mine.

'How about marriage?' I said.

'No.'

'Why not?'

'Because you like oysters and I don't.'

I smiled and steered her into the house. It was as good an answer as any.

Crispin was highly restless and not in the least pleased to see her.

'I'll go for a walk,' he said. 'I can see I'm not wanted.'

'You'll stay right where you are and pour us some cokes,' I said firmly. We looked at each other, both knowing that if he went for a walk it would lead to the pub.

'All right,' he said abruptly. 'You bloody bully.'

I cooked the lunch: steaks and grilled tomatoes. Crispin said that Sophie ought to do it and Sophie said you should never interfere in someone else's kitchen. They looked at each other with unfriendly eyes as if each wishing that the other wasn't there. Not the most relaxed of Sunday lunch parties, I thought: and Vic telephoned with the coffee.

'My friend will meet you,' he said. 'For five minutes only. Like you said.'

'Where?' I asked.

'Here. At my house. Six o'clock.'

'I'll be there,' I said.

His voice held a mixture of instructions and anxiety. 'You'll cancel those blood tests?'

'Yeah,' I said. 'After the meeting, I will.'

I went back to the kitchen. Sophie was smoking and Crispin glowered at his coffee as if it were an enemy. When we were alone he often stacked the plates in the dishwasher but I knew he wouldn't do it while she was there. He took it for granted that if there was a woman in the room she would do the household chores, even if she were a guest. Sophie saw no reason to do jobs she disliked, and her host's jobs at that, simply because she was female. I watched the two of them with a sad sort of amusement, my liability of a brother and the girl who wouldn't be my wife.

During the afternoon Peter and Sue rang to say they were staying overnight with Sue's parents and consequently couldn't take Sophie home. Would I mind frightfully driving her home myself.

I explained to Sophie that I had an appointment near Epsom.

'That's all right,' she said. 'I'll wait in the car while you do your business, and we can go on to my place after.'

A flicker of caution made me uneasy. 'I'm going to see Vic Vincent,' I said.

'Is he likely to be as lethal as Fynedale?'

I smiled. 'No.'

'And don't forget it was a good job I was with you at Ascot.'

'I haven't.'

'Well, then.'

So I took her.

Crispin followed us out to the car. 'I suppose you won't be back till bloody morning,' he said.

'Whether I am or not, you'll be all right.'

He looked at me in desperation. 'You know I bloody won't.'

'You can be if you want to,' I said persuasively.

'Sod you, Jonah.'

He stood and watched us as I started the car and drove away. As usual he had made me feel a grinding guilt at leaving him to struggle alone. As usual I told myself that if he were ever to beat the drink he would have to stay off it when I wasn't there. I simply couldn't be beside him every minute of his life.

We drove towards Epsom. We were early, by design. Vic had said six o'clock, but I thought that a preliminary scout around might be prudent. The friend, whoever he was, had already sent a load of trouble my way, and I had a minimum of faith that all would henceforth be caviar and handshakes.

I drove fifty yards past the entrance to Vic's drive, and pulled up on the grass verge with Sophie's door pressed close against the hedge. I switched off the lights and turned to her.

'When I go, lock my door behind me,' I said. 'And don't get out of the car.'

'Jonah . . . You really do think Vic might be lethal.'

'Not Vic. But he might have someone else with him . . . I don't know. Anyway, I'll be much happier if I'm sure you're sitting here snug and safe.'

'But . . .'

'No buts.' I kissed her lightly. 'I'll be back in half an hour or so. If I'm not here by six-thirty, drive on into Epsom and raise a posse.'

'I don't like it.'

'Put the rug round you, or you'll get cold.'

I slid out of the car and watched her lock the door. Waved. Smiled as if I were going to the circus. Went away.

The night was not pitch dark. Few nights are. My eyes adjusted to the dimness and I went quietly through the gateway and up alongside the drive, walking on the grass. I had worn for the occasion a black sweater and dark trousers, black rubber-soled shoes. I pulled a pair of gloves from my pocket and put them on. I had dark brown hair, which helped, and apart from the pale blob of my face I must have looked much at one with the shadows.

There were two cars outside the front of Vic's house, both of them unfamiliar. A Ford Cortina and a Jaguar XJ 12.

I drifted round the house towards the pool, hoping and guessing that Vic used his office, as I did, as the natural place to take his friends. Most of the house was in darkness. Vic's window shone with light. Round one, I thought.

Carefully I skirted the pool and approached under the protection of the dark overhang of the roof over the guest suite keeping tight against the wall. Faint light from the sky raised a sheen on the unruffled pool water. There was no wind, no sound except from an occasional car on the road. I edged with caution closer.

Vic's window was hung with thick fawn-coloured crusty net in clustered folds. I found that one could see a certain amount when trying to look through it straight ahead, but that slanting vision was impossible. It also seemed possible that as the curtaining was not opaque, anyone inside could see through it to someone moving about outside. Inconvenient for peeping Toms.

I crawled the last bit, feeling a fool. The window stretched down to within eighteen inches of the paving stone. By the time I reached the wall I was flat on my stomach.

Vic was walking around the room, talking. I risked raising my eyes over the level of the sill, but to little purpose. All I could clearly see was a bit of the table which stood near the window and a distant piece of Florentine mirror. I shifted sideways a little and looked again. A sliver of bookcase and a chair leg. Another shift. More bookcase, and a quick impression of Vic moving.

His voice came through the glass whenever he walked near the window. I put my head down and listened to unconnected snatches.

'... Polyprint and Nestegg ... bloody dynamite ...'

'... what does it matter how he found out? How did you find out in the first place ...'

'... beating him up wouldn't have worked either. I told you ... burning his place hurt him more ...'

'... you can't put pressure on a wife and children if he hasn't got any ...'

'... brother ... no good ... just a lush ...'

I shifted along on my stomach and looked again. Another uninformative slice of furnishings.

I couldn't see who Vic was talking to nor hear the replies. The answering voice came to me only as a low rumble, like a bass drum played quietly. I realized in the end that its owner was sitting against the window wall but so far to the left that unless he moved I was not going to be able to see him from where I was. Never mind, I thought. I would see him face to face soon enough. Meanwhile I might as well learn as much as I could. There might be a gem for the bargaining session ahead.

'... can't see any other way out ...' Vic said.

The reply rumbled briefly.

Vic came suddenly close to the window. I buried my face and stretched my ears.

'Look,' he said. 'I more or less promised him you would meet him.'

Rumble rumble, seemingly displeased.

'Well I'm damn well not going inside just to save him from knowing who you are.'

Rumble rumble.

'Damn right I'll tell him.'

Rumble rumble rumble.

Vic hadn't been exactly frank, I thought. He hadn't told his rumble-voiced friend that I was due there at six o'clock. Vic was going to hand the friend to me on a plate whether the friend liked it or not. I smiled in the dark. Round two.

'I don't give a damn about your reputation,' Vic said. 'What's so bloody marvellous about your reputation?'

A long rumble. Infuriating not to be able to hear.

Vic's voice in reply sounded for the first time as if he were stifling doubts.

'Of course I agree that business is founded on trust...'

Rumble rumble.

'Well, it's too bad because I'm not bloody going to jail to save your reputation, and that's flat.'

Rumble.

Vic moved across the window from right to left, but I could still hear him clearly.

'Where are you going?' His voice suddenly rose sharply into anxiety. 'What are you doing? No ... No ... My God ... Wait ...' His voice went higher and louder. 'Wait ...'

The last time, he screamed it. 'Wait ...'

There was a sort of cough somewhere inside the room and something heavy fell agrinst the window. I raised my head and froze in absolute horror.

Vic was leaning back against the glass. The net curtain all around him was bright scarlet.

While I watched he twisted on his feet and gripped hold of the curtain for support. On the front of his lilac shirt there was an irregular scarlet star.

He didn't speak. His grip slackened on the curtains. I saw his eyes for a second as he fell.

They were dead.

Without conscious thought I got to my feet and sprinted

round to the front of the house. It's easy enough looking back to say that it was a mad thing to do. At the time all I thought was that Vic's murdering friend would get clean away without me seeing who he was. All I thought was that I'd set Vic up to flush out the friend, and if I didn't see who it was he would have died for nothing. The one thing I didn't think was that if the friend saw *me*, he would simply shoot me too.

Everything happened too fast for working out probabilities.

By the time I had skirted the pool and the garden room the engine of one of the cars in the drive was urgently revving. Not the big Jaguar. The Cortina. It reversed fiercely in an arc to point its nose to the drive.

I ran. I came up to it from behind on its left side. Inside the car the dark bulk of the driver was shifting the gears from reverse to forward. I put my hand on the handle of the rear door, wanting to open it, to make him turn his head, see who he was, to stop him, fight him, take his gun away, hand him over to justice . . . heaven knows.

The Cortina spurted forward as if flagged off the grid and pulled my arm right out of its socket.

16

I knelt on the ground in the familiar bloody agony and thought that a dislocated shoulder was among the ultimates.

What was more, there were footsteps coming up the drive towards me.

Scrunch scrunch scrunch.

Inexorable.

All the things have to be faced. I supported my left elbow in my right hand and waited, because in any case I could barely move, let alone run away.

A figure materialized from the darkness. Advanced to within six feet. Stopped.

A voice said, 'Have you been run over?'

I nearly smiled. 'I thought I told you to stay in the car.'

'You sound funny,' Sophie said.

'Hilarious.'

She took two paces forwards, stretching out her hands.

'Don't touch me,' I said hastily.

'What's the matter?'

I told her.

'Oh God,' she said.

'And you can put it back.'

'What?'

'Put my shoulder back.'

'But . . .' She sounded bewildered. 'I can't.'

'Not here. In the house.'

She had no idea how to help me up. Not like jump jockeys' wives, I thought briefly, for whom smashed up husbands were all in the day's work. I made it to my feet with the loss of no more than a pint of sweat. Various adjectives occurred to me. Like excruciating.

One foot gingerly in front of the other took us to the door that

Vic's friend had left open, the door to the hallway and the office. Light spilled out of it. I wondered if there was a telephone anywhere except in the office

We went very slowly indoors with me hunched like Notre Dame.

'Jonah!' Sophie said.

'What?'

'I didn't realize . . . you look . . . you look . . .'

'Yeah,' I said. 'I need you to put it back.'

'We must get a doctor.'

'No . . . the police. Vic Vincent's been shot.'

'*Shot.*' She followed my gaze to Vic's office and went along there to take a look. She returned several shades paler, which made two of us.

'It's . . . awful.'

'See if you can find another telephone.'

She switched on several lights. There was another telephone on a table flanked by a sofa and a potted palm.

'Call the police,' I said.

She dialled three nines. Told them a man had been killed. They would come at once, they said. She put the receiver down and turned towards me purposefully.

'I'm going to dial again for an ambulance.'

'No. You do it. It has to be done now. At once.'

'Jonah . . . don't be stupid. How can I? You need professional help. A doctor.'

'I need a doctor like yesterday's news. Look . . . doctors don't put shoulders back. By the time they arrive all the muscles have gone into spasms, so they can't. They send you to hospital in bloody jerking ambulances. The hospitals sit you around for hours in casualty departments. Then they send you for X-rays. Then they trundle you to an operating theatre and by then they have to give you a general anaesthetic. It takes about four hours at the best of times. Sunday evenings are not the best of times. If you won't do it . . . I . . . I . . .' I stopped. The prospect of those long hours ahead was enough to scare the saints.

'I can't,' she said.

'I'll tell you how . . .'

She was appalled. 'You must have a doctor.'

I muttered under my breath.

'What did you say?' she demanded.

'I said . . . God give me a woman of strength.'

She said in a low voice, 'That's unfair.'

I went slowly past her through the hall into the open-plan dining-room and sat gingerly on one of the hard straight-backed chairs. What I felt was beyond a joke.

I shut my eyes and thought about Vic's friend. Thought about the glimpse of him I'd had in the split second before he blasted off and took my comfort with him. There had been a seepage of light from the house's open door. Enough to show me the shape of a head.

There had been little time for certainty. Only for impression. The impression remained in my mind indelibly.

Sophie said, 'Jonah . . .'

I opened my eyes. She was standing in front of me, huge eyed and trembling.

I'd wanted to know what could break up her colossal composure. Now I knew. One man shot to death and another demanding an unimaginable service.

'What do I do?' she said.

I swallowed. 'It will take ten minutes.'

She was shocked. Apprehension made her eyes even bigger.

'If you mean it . . .' I said.

'I do.'

'First instruction . . . smile.'

'But . . .'

'Six deep breaths and a big smile.'

'Oh Jonah.' She sounded despairing.

'Look,' I said. 'I don't want you messing about with my precious body unless you go back to being your normal confident, relaxed, efficient, hard-hearted self.'

She stared. 'I thought you were past talking. You're a fraud.'

'That's better.'

She took me literally. Six deep breaths and a smile. Not a big smile, but something.

'OK,' I said. 'Put your left hand under my elbow and hold my wrist with your right.'

I shifted an inch or two back on the seat until the base of my spine was firmly against the chair back. She very tentatively stepped close in front of me and put her hands where I'd said. For all her efforts I could see she still did not believe she could help.

'Look ... Do it slowly. You can't wrench it back. When you get my arm in the right position, the top of the bone will slide back into the socket ... Do you understand?'

'I think so.'

'Right ... there are three stages. First, straighten my arm out, slightly to the side. Then keep my wrist out and pull my elbow across my chest ... it will look awkward ... but it works. If you pull hard enough the top of the bone will come in line with the socket and start to slide into it. When it does that, fold my wrist up and over towards my right shoulder ... and my arm will go back where it ought to be.'

She was in no way reassured.

'Sophie ...'

'Yes?'

I hesitated. 'If you do it, you'll save me hours of pain.'

'Yes.'

'But ...' I stopped.

'You're trying to say,' she said, 'that I'm going to hurt you even worse, and I mustn't let it stop me.'

'Attagirl.'

'All right.'

She began. Straightened my arm out, slowly and carefully. I could feel her surprise at the physical effort it demanded of her: an arm was a good deal heavier than most people realized and she had the whole weight of it in her hands.

It took five minutes.

'Is that right?' she said.

'Mm.'

'Now do I pull your elbow across?'

'Mm.'

Always the worst part. When she'd gone only a short way I could feel her trembling. Her fingers under my elbow shook with irresolution.

I said, 'If you . . . drop my elbow . . . now . . . I'll scream.'

'Oh . . .' She sounded shattered but her grip tightened blessedly. We proceeded, with no sound but heavy breathing on both sides. There was always a point at which progress seemed to end and yet the arm was still out. Always a point of despair.

We reached it.

'It's no good,' she said. 'It isn't working.'

'Go on.'

'I can't do it.'

'Another . . . half inch.'

'Oh, no . . .' But she screwed herself up and went on trying.

The jolt and the audible scrunch when the bone started to go over the edge of the socket astounded her.

'Now . . .' I said. 'Wrist up and over . . . not too fast.'

Two more horrible crunches, the sweetest sounds on earth. Hell went back into its box. I stood up. Smiled like the sun coming out.

'That's it,' I said. 'Thank you very much.'

She was bewildered. 'Do you mean . . . the pain goes away . . . just like that.'

'Just like that.'

She looked at the transformation she'd wrought in me. Her eyes filled with tears. I put my right arm round her and held her close.

'Why don't you get the bloody thing fixed?' she said.

'You won't catch me having any more orthopaedic operations if I don't absolutely have to.'

She sniffed the tears away. 'You're a coward.'

'All the way.'

I walked with her to Vic's office. We stood in the doorway, looking in. He lay by the window, face down, the back of his purple shirt a glistening crimson obscenity.

Whatever he had done to me, I had done worse to him. Because of the pressure I'd put on him, he was dead. I supposed I would never outlive a grinding sense of responsibility and regret.

'I half saw who killed him,' I said.

'Half?'

'Enough.'

The indelible impression made sense. The pattern had become plain.

We turned away.

There was a sound of a car drawing up outside, doors slamming, two or three pairs of heavy feet.

'The police,' Sophie said in relief.

I nodded. 'Keep it simple, though. If they start on Vic's and my disagreements we'll be here all night.'

'You're immoral.'

'No . . . lazy.'

'I've noticed.'

The police were their usual abrasive selves, saving their store of sympathy for worthier causes like old ladies and lost kids. They looked into the office, telephoned for reinforcements and invited us in a fairly hectoring manner to explain what we were doing there. I stifled an irritated impulse to point out that if we'd chosen we could have gone quietly away and left someone else to find Vic dead. Virtue's own reward was seldom worth it.

Both then and later, when the higher ranks arrived, we gave minimum information and kept quiet in between. In essence I said, 'There were no lights on in the front of the house when I arrived. I know the house slightly. I walked round to the side to see if Vic was in his office. I had a tentative arrangement to see him for five or six minutes at six o'clock. I was driving Miss Randolph home to Esher and called in at Vic's on the way, parking outside on the road and walking up the drive. I saw him in his office. I saw him fall against the window, and then collapse. I hurried round to the front to try to get into the house to help him. A light-coloured Ford Cortina was starting up. It shot away in a hurry but I caught a glimpse of the driver. I recognized the driver.'

They listened to my identification impassively, neither pleased nor sceptical. Did I see a gun, they asked. There was no gun in Vic's office.

'No,' I said. 'Nothing but the driver's head.'

They grunted and turned to Sophie.

'Jonah left me in his car,' she said. 'Then this other car came crashing out of the drive at a reckless speed. I decided to see if everything was all right. I walked up here and found Jonah in front of the house. The house door was open, so we went inside. We found Mr Vincent lying in his office. We telephoned immediately to you.'

We sat for nearly three hours in Vic's beautiful dining-room while the end of his life was dissected by the prosaic professionals for whom murder was all in the day's work. They switched on every light and brought more of their own, and the glare further dehumanized their host.

Maybe it was necessary for them to think of him as a thing, not a person. I still couldn't.

I was finally allowed to take Sophie home. I parked outside and we went up to her flat, subdued and depressed. She made coffee, which we drank in the kitchen.

'Hungry?' she said. 'There's some cheese, I think.'

We ate chunks of cheese in our fingers, absent-mindedly.

'What are you going to do?' she said.

'Wait for them to catch him, I suppose.'

'He won't run . . . he doesn't know you saw him.'

'No.'

She said anxiously, 'He doesn't . . . does he?'

'If he'd seen me he'd have come back and shot us both.'

'You think the nicest thoughts.'

The evening had left smudgy circles round her eyes. She looked more than tired: over-stretched, over-strained. I yawned and said I ought to be going home, and she couldn't disguise her flooding relief.

I smiled. 'You'll be all right alone?'

'Oh yes.' Absolute certainty in her voice. Solitude offered her refuge, healing, and rest. I didn't. I had brought her a car crash, a man with a pitchfork, a bone-setting and a murder. I'd offered an alcoholic brother, a half-burnt home and a snap engagement. None of it designed for the wellbeing of someone who needed the order and peace of an ivory control tower.

She came with me down to the car.

'You'll come again?' she said.

'When you're ready.'

'A dose of Dereham every week . . .'

'Would be enough to frighten any woman?'

'Well, no.' She smiled. 'It might be bad for the nerves, but at least I'd know I was alive.'

I laughed and gave her an undemanding brotherly kiss. 'It would suit me fine.'

'Really?'

'And truly.'

'I don't ask for that,' she said.

'Then you damn well should.'

She grinned. I slid into the driving seat. Her eyes looked calmer in her exhausted face.

'Sleep well,' I said. 'I'll call you tomorrow.'

It seemed a long way home. My shoulder ached: a faint echo, but persistent. I thought with longing of a stiff brandy and stifled a sigh at the less reviving prospect of coke.

When I got back the house was dark.

No lights, no Crispin.

Hell, I thought. He had no car any more; no transport but his feet. The one place his feet could be trusted to take him was straight to the source of gin.

I parked outside the kitchen as usual, opened the unlocked back door, went in, switched on the lights, and shouted through the house.

'Crispin?' No answer. 'Crispin.'

Total silence.

Swearing under my breath I went along to the office, intending to telephone the pub to ask what state he was in. If he were too far gone, I'd drive up and fetch him. I had picked up the receiver and begun to dial when I heard the door behind me squeak on its hinges.

So he hadn't gone after all. I turned with the beginnings of a congratulatory smile.

It wasn't Crispin who had come in. I looked at the heavy pistol with its elongated silencer, and like Vic the urgent words which shaped in my mind were no and my God and wait.

17

'Put the telephone down,' he said.

I looked at the receiver in my hand. I'd dialled only half the number. Pity. I did as he said.

'I saw you at Vic's,' I said. 'I told the police.'

The gun merely wavered a fraction. The round black hole still faced my heart. I'd seen what it had made of Vic, and I had no illusions.

'I guessed you were there,' he said.

'How?'

'A car parked by the hedge ... Saw it when I left. About twelve miles on I realized it was yours. I went back ... the place was crawling with police.'

My tongue felt huge and sluggish. I looked at the gun and could think of nothing useful to say.

'You and Vic,' he said. 'You thought you had me in a corner. Too bad. Your mistake.'

I swallowed with difficulty. 'I saw you,' I repeated, 'and the police know.'

'Maybe. But they'll have trouble making it stick when you're not alive to give evidence.'

I looked desperately around for a way of diverting him. For a weapon to attack him with.

He smiled faintly. 'It's no good, Jonah. It's the end of the road.'

He straightened his arm to the firing position adopted by people who knew what they were about.

'You won't feel much,' he said.

The door behind him swung on its hinges while he was already beginning to squeeze the trigger. The sudden shift of my attention from sick fascination at the round hole from which death was coming to a point behind his back was just enough to jerk his hand.

Enough was enough.

The flame spat out and the bullet missed me.

Crispin stood in the doorway looking with horror at the scene. In one hand he waved a heavy green bottle of gin.

'The old heave-ho,' he said distinctly.

He wasn't drunk, I thought incredulously. He was telling me to go right back to a rugger tackle we'd perfected in boyhood. Instinctively, faster than thought, I feinted at our visitor's knees.

The gun came round and down towards me and Crispin hit him hard on the head with the gin bottle.

The pistol swung away from me and fired, and I snapped up and lifted the only heavy object within reach, which was my typewriter. I crashed it down with all my strength in the wake of the gin bottle, and the visitor sprawled on the floor with blood gushing from his scalp and the typewriter ribbon rolling across his unconscious face and away to the wall.

'You old crazy loon,' I said breathlessly, turning to Crispin. 'You old blessed ...'

My voice died away. Crispin half sat, half lay on the floor with his hand pressed to his side.

'Crispin!'

'I'm ... not ... drunk,' he said.

'Of course not.'

'I think ... he shot me.'

Speechlessly I knelt beside him.

He said, 'Was he the one ... who burnt the yard?'

'Yes.'

'Hope ... you killed him.'

His body sagged. I caught him. Eased him down to the floor and with one hand grabbed a cushion for his head. His pressing fingers relaxed and fell away, and there on the waistband of his trousers was the spreading patch of blood.

'I'm ... floating,' he said. He smiled. 'It's better ... than ... being drunk.'

'I'll get a doctor,' I said.

'No . . . Jonah . . . Don't leave me . . . you sod.'

I didn't leave him. Three minutes later, without speaking again, he left me.

I closed his eyes gently and got stiffly to my feet, trying to fold numbness around me like a coat.

The pistol lay where it had fallen. I pushed it carefully with my toe until it was completely out of sight under the low-slung armchair. I didn't want the visitor waking to grab it again.

The visitor hadn't moved. I sat on the edge of my desk and looked down at the two of them, the unconscious and the dead.

Time enough, I thought, to call in those more or less constant companions, the busy and probing police. A quarter of an hour sooner or later, what did it matter. There was nothing any more to be gained. Too much had been irrevocably lost.

I didn't care how much damage I'd done with the typewriter. The head I'd busted with it looked more bloody than dented, but I felt a strong aversion to exploring. In all my life I had never wanted to kill anyone; had never thought I could come within a mile of it. I had not even intended to kill with the typewriter, but only to stun. I sat quietly on the desk and shook with fury inside, and wished I could have that blow back again, so that I could make it heavier, avenging and fatal.

Whatever my brother had been, he had been my brother. No one had the right to kill him. I think at that moment I felt as primitive as the Sicilians.

From greed the visitor had set out to destroy me. Not because I'd done him any harm. Simply because I stood in his plundering way. He'd sent me a message: join or be flattened, an ultimatum as old as tyranny.

My own fault, as they had tirelessly pointed out, if the answer I'd chosen was flatten and be damned.

Kerry Sanders had been only a convenient door. Had she not thought of her equine birthday present, another way would have been found. The intention was the activating force. The means were accidental.

I remembered what Pauli Teksa had said at dinner that

evening at Newmarket. I remembered his exact words. The classic law of the invader was to single out the strongest guy around and smash him, so that the weaker crowd would come to heel like lambs.

At various times I had thought of the man who lay on my carpet as 'someone', as the expert, as Vic's friend, as the driver, and as the visitor; Pauli's word – the invader – suited him best.

He had invaded the bloodstock game with gangster ethics. Invaded Vic's life and business as a dangerous ally. Invaded mine as a destroyer.

The fact that I did not feel that I filled the role he'd cast me in had not mattered. It was the invader's view which had mattered. My bad luck that he'd seen me as the strongest guy around.

There was no way of winning against a determined invader. If you gave in at once, you lost. If you fought to the death you still lost, even if you won. The price of victory was sore.

Pauli Teksa had said, just before he went back to America, that it was easier to start things than to stop them. He had been warning me that if I lashed back at Vic I could find myself in even more trouble than before.

He had been right.

But he had been speaking also of himself.

Pauli Teksa, the invader, lay face down on my carpet, my broken typewriter beside his bloody head.

The stocky, tough, wide-shouldered body looked a solid hunk of bull muscle. The crinkly black hair was matted and running with red. I could see half of his face; the strong distinctive profile with the firm mouth now slackly open, the swift eye shut.

His hands lay loosely on the floor, one each side of his head. He wore two thick gold rings. A gold and platinum wrist-watch. Heavy gold cufflinks. The tip of the gold mountain he had siphoned off through Vic.

I thought it likely that his British venture had been an extension of activities at home. The super-aggressive kick-back operation had been too polished to be a trial run. Maybe he had set up Vic-equivalents in other countries. Maybe Vics in South America and Italy and Japan were rooking the local Constantines and Wilton Youngs for him and driving the Antonia Huntercombes to despair.

Vic and Fynedale had been amateurs, compared with him. Fynedale working himself into a white murdering manic state. Vic nearing apoplexy with easy rage. Pauli stayed cool and used his eyes and made his snap decisions, and when he saw the need to kill he did it without histrionics. An unfortunate necessity, best done quickly.

He had even with macabre kindness told me I wouldn't feel much, and I believed him. I'd heard shot people say all they had felt was a sort of thud, and hadn't realized they were wounded until afterwards. If you were shot through the heart there was no afterwards, and that was that.

He had himself urged me several times to throw in my lot with Vic, and to go along with the crowd. He'd warned me of the dangers of holding out. He'd given me the advice as a friend, and behind the smile there had been an enemy as cold as bureaucracy.

I realized slowly that perhaps at one point he had in fact done his best to stop what he'd started. He had said no to some demand of Vic's, and he had gone home to America. But by then it was too late because in burning my stable he had switched me from tolerance to retaliation. Bash me, I bash back. The way wars started, big and small.

On the floor, Pauli stirred.

Not dead.

Across the room the gin bottle lay where Crispin had dropped it. I shoved myself off the desk and went over to pick it up. If Pauli were to return to consciousness, groggy or not, I'd trust him as far as I could throw the Empire State Building. A reinforcing clunk with green glass would be merely prudent.

I looked closer at the bottle. It was full. In addition the seal was unbroken.

I returned to the desk and set the bottle on it, and looked down with impossible grief at my brother. I knew that I had needed him as much as he needed me. He was at the roots of my life.

Pauli stirred again. The urge to finish off what I'd started was almost overwhelming. No one would know. No one could tell whether he'd been hit twice or three times. Killing someone who was trying to kill you was justifiable in law, and who was to guess that I'd killed him ten minutes later.

The moment passed. I felt cold suddenly, and old and lonely and as tired as dust. I stretched out a hand to the telephone, to call the cops.

It rang before I touched it. I picked up the receiver and said dully, 'Hello?'

'Mr Crispin Dereham?' A man's voice, educated.

'I'm his brother,' I said.

'Could I speak to him?'

'I'm afraid . . .' I said, 'he's . . . unavailable.'

'Oh dear.' The voice sounded warmly sympathetic. 'Well . . . this is Alcoholics Anonymous. Your brother telephoned us earlier this evening asking for help, and we promised to ring him back again for another chat . . .'

He went on talking for some time, but I didn't hear a word he said.

Dick Francis

Driving Force £4.99

'A thundering good read' DAILY MAIL

Jockey Freddie Croft thought he'd left the perils behind him when he retired from the jump game. These days he was happy to transport horses from their stables to the races. Until one of his drivers picked up an unlicensed passenger. And brought him back dead.

The corpse on the doorstep was Freddie's unwelcome introduction to the shadowy, big-money conspiracy which muscled into his business and started to threaten his life. But Freddie was a fighter, and winning was in his blood . . .

First identify the danger. Then beat them out of sight . . .

'I enjoyed this book hugely' JULIE BURCHILL, SUNDAY TIMES

'Galloping heroics . . . the old master still engages all your interest' MAIL ON SUNDAY

All Pan books are available at your local bookshop or newsagent, or can be ordered direct from the publisher. Indicate the number of copies required and fill in the form below.

Send to: Pan C. S. Dept
Macmillan Distribution Ltd
Houndmills Basingstoke RG21 2XS
or phone: 0256 29242, quoting title, author and Credit Card number.

Please enclose a remittance* to the value of the cover price plus: £1.00 for the first book plus 50p per copy for each additional book ordered.

*Payment may be made in sterling by UK personal cheque, postal order, sterling draft or international money order, made payable to Pan Books Ltd.

Alternatively by Barclaycard/Access/Amex/Diners

Card No. | | | | | | | | | | | | | | | | |

Expiry Date | | | | | | |

____

Signature:

Applicable only in the UK and BFPO addresses

While every effort is made to keep prices low, it is sometimes necessary to increase prices at short notice. Pan Books reserve the right to show on covers and charge new retail prices which may differ from those advertised in the text or elsewhere.

NAME AND ADDRESS IN BLOCK LETTERS PLEASE:

....

Name ______________________________

Address ______________________________

____

____

____

6/92